I0527832

ANIMAS WITHIN

Casey Jo Jukes

ISBN 10: 0615803008
ISBN-13: 978-0615803005

DEDICATION

IN LOVING MEMORY OF MY MOTHER,
CHARLOTTE. HER BEAUTIFUL AND GENEROUS
SPIRIT WILL NEVER BE FORGOTTEN.
WITH LOVE ALWAYS!

ACKNOWLEDGMENTS

I am extremely grateful to my friend, Michelle, who struggled through my first "rough" draft, and diligently corrected the multitude of grammatical errors. She also provided an excellent sounding board to ensure many of my conceptual ideas came through within the writing. In addition, Emily (who I truly respect) put in a great deal of effort to help edit this novel. Her opinions and feedback were invaluable in improving the quality of this work. Finally, I am full of gratitude to Linda, who provided the final editing, especially in terms of polishing, timing, and honing of this story. I am truly thankful to each and all for your wonderful contributions and insights.

I give a special thanks to Greg and his son, Eric, who provided support and assistance with the cover design. I also extend my gratitude to my many friends and relatives who read and provided their heartfelt feedback, which helped me to make instrumental changes throughout the process. Finally, I am very thankful for my husband and family for their continual and consistent support along the way; I love you!

DISCLAIMER

PROLOGUE

"Ecstatic, simply heavenly!" Ally reflected. She was brimming with unbridled joy and contentment. It was difficult to believe how euphoric and exhilarated she felt after being plagued with unwavering morning sickness until last week. Her morning sickness had indelibly marred the first few months and caused her to believe that her whole pregnancy would be spent in abject misery; then abruptly the tide shifted, bringing this blissful release. The day was surreal because she felt absolutely fantastic, and everything around her was so vibrantly beautiful.

Along with Ally's well-being, the dismal weather had evolved over the prior week to its present magnificence. The sky had emerged from its dark and gloomy casing to unveil this vivid, intense blue expanse. The trees and under-growth were dazzling green as dew gently clung to the wild flowers and grasses which carpeted the forest floor. The few remaining patches of snow glistened in the sunlight, giving the morning a crisp freshness as a slight breeze whispered through the high tree branches above. The savory smell of pines, wildflowers, and new growth filled the air, each sweet scent vying for her attention. Absorbed in the scenery, Ally tenderly cradled her swollen stomach, expectantly feeling for the baby and then shivering excitedly as she detected the slight movements within her womb.

Ally was elated that David suggested this spontaneous trip because it was exactly what they both needed! Even though they hadn't traveled far from their home in Cedarwood, it felt like they were a world away. This past winter had been so stressful; David was trying to get a managerial position at the boulevard store for the grocery chain where he worked. Whereas Ally, besides dealing with her morning sickness, was fed up with her job. The tension of putting up with customer complaints and the grueling routine of her work with a credit card company was becoming unbearable. No, she wasn't going to spoil her current mood by thinking about work. She consciously lets her mind drift back to the present; this idyllic drive, feeling the tension and pressure slide away again in a huge wave.

As they slowly transcended the muddy, unpaved road, David rounded the curve of the hillside, and a panoramic view came into sharper focus; the perimeter of pines framing a large honey-gold meadow spattered with an abundant array of wild flowers. David pulled over and stopped their SUV to study the topography map. Ally tried to imprint the image of this meadow into her memory, for it was so picturesque.

"I thought so!" David exclaimed as he pointed to some wooden structures and buildings beyond the tree line. "This is the site of the old Animas Mine."

"Yes, I see the buildings over there. Interesting, Animas. There's a river called 'Rio De Las Animas Perdidas,' in Colorado, translated it means: the river of lost souls. They shortened the name to the Animas River. I wonder if that's where the miners got the name for this mine."

"I'm not sure where the name came from," David continued on enthusiastically. "It was a small mining operation which closed in the 1940's. See that triangular edifice which resembles some sort of hoist? That's the partial remains of a headframe, and below it should be a vertical shaft entrance into some underground mine workings. See those huge rock piles which form ridges off to the right?" David pointed off in the distance; "...those rock piles are called tailings, which are waste deposits left from the mine."

"How do you know about all this stuff?" Ally inquired.

"Just read up about it, that's all. I'd like to explore the area, but it's still too wet out here." David said wistfully.

"We can come back during the summer. I love it out here, it's so peaceful and beautiful." Ally responded.

"And it's close to home," David paused..."I need another minute to study the map and make sure I know the way to the reservoir," David said as he picked up and examined the map again.

Yes, Ally deliberated, she did enjoy the seasonal climate changes more in Northern California than in Colorado where she had been raised. The weather in the California Mountains is milder and more predictable, not so windy. As they always say in Denver, "If you don't like the weather, wait five minutes."

David proceeded to drive slowly forward, eyeing the map. He was probably looking for a route marker. Ally used this time to leisurely scan the meadow, taking stock of the wide variety of wild flowers. She caught a glimpse of a youngster playing off in the distance of this vast meadow. The sight of this beautiful golden-haired girl captivated Ally as she watched the little one run with the familiar abandonment of early childhood. The small girl was completely absorbed in her surroundings and failed to even glance in the direction of their oncoming vehicle. Ally softly rubbed her stomach again, and contemplated what their own child would look like, be like. Would their baby have the same blond hair as her own when she was younger, or would their infant have David's dark hair and serious eyes?

Ally abruptly broke away from her silent musings, now uncomfortably aware of her surroundings. Alert to the complete isolation of this back-country, Ally visually searched the area for the rest of the little girl's family but saw no one. Odd, there weren't any homes or ranches in the immediate area. The child couldn't be alone; she wasn't more than six or seven years old! A hawk startled by their approaching vehicle and flew skyward, momentarily drawing Ally's attention away from the young girl.

She turned back towards the child, but the girl had simply disappeared. Ally continued to search the meadow, but she couldn't see the young child anywhere. She shrugged off the moment and reasoned, the family must be picnicking in the nearby woods.

"David," Ally started to say as she turned towards him. She was about to ask if he had noticed a family or any other people in the area, but David was busy. He had now stopped the SUV again, in the middle of the roadway, and was intently studying the topography map.

"Yes, yes. This clearing must be Horseshoe Bend, and if we continue on this trail another mile or so, we'll be at the reservoir," he said abstractly. "Ally, please tell me what the next survey post reads. It must be marked on this map somewhere?"

Ally squinted her eyes to make out the numbers on the small marker. "24," she reported as he continued to scrutinize the map. David placed the map on the dashboard and set their Ford Explorer in motion. Ally took her last glance at the meadow and noted the new growth on the trees; it was still early March, not even officially springtime yet.

Throughout the remainder of the weekend, Ally kept thinking about that golden-haired girl, she had seen at Horseshoe Bend. The child's image continued to flicker in her mind as an incessant nagging concern. Again, Ally questioned why she had not checked into the identity of this girl or reassured herself of the child's safety. Then, she chastised herself for this continued reflection as she recalled her conversation with David, earlier today.

When she had told David about seeing the child at Horseshoe Bend, he basically asked how she could get so "hung-up on inconsequential things because a kid that age, would not be alone in that area. There had been no reports of a lost or missing girl. He asserted that she had been right in the first place, and the family of the kid must have been somewhere nearby. He reminded her that the matter was not significant enough to mention during their outing and now, she was building up the incident in her mind. "Damn!" Sometimes David's pragmatism was so irritating; it drove her crazy, but she also had to admit that he was absolutely right in his assessment of the situation. 'So forget about it.' Tomorrow is Monday. Ally was already dreading her job, as she prepared for the week ahead.

CHAPTER 1

"I'm so tired of being pregnant!" Ally lamented, as she slowly lowered herself onto one of the hard, straight-back chairs; then with the abrupt shifting of her body weight, plopped into a sitting position. The protracted process of seating herself was preposterous; alternatively, Ally knew that if she remained on her feet for too long, she would collapse in a massive heap. Mercy, she still had sixteen weeks to go in her pregnancy, so she'd just have to adapt. On the bright side, the unrelenting fatigue had dissipated, leaving her energy level considerably more normal.

The break-room was empty and dead silent, which seemed aberrant in comparison to the endless noisy clatter of the office cubicles. Ally shielded her eyes from the blinding intensity of the sunlight streaming through the shade-less horizontal window. Hesitant to get back up again, she clumsily shifted her chair away from the bright glare and then tried to stretch out her aching back in an unsuccessful attempt to gain a comfortable position.

The local newspaper was spread haphazardly over the wood-veneer table; checking the date: May 7, 1998...yes, it's today's edition. She quickly scanned the local news for any interesting articles. The headline news story was about a local man, Kyle James, who'd shot his entire family, and then turned the gun on himself. No survivors. ...It seemed inconceivable that this tragedy could happen here in Calaveras County. Quit being biased, Ally conceded; family violence isn't exclusive to the big cities; the same problems do exist in suburbia, too.

Ally recalled that Patricia from accounting was having a tough time coming to terms with this tragedy for it hit too close to home. Patricia had known this man, Kyle James, because his children had played on the same soccer team as her own. Their daughters had even baked and decorated cookies for the team at Patricia's house. Her words echoed in Ally's mind,   "Kyle seemed so normal, just a regular family man; the family and especially Kyle seemed so perfect." Ally cynically wondered if any family was that perfect. She honestly doubted that their family situation could have gone from perfection to this devastation overnight. No one knows what goes on behind closed doors.

In related news, there had been several deaths of children due to child abuse over the past several months in their neighboring city, Acacia. Ally's hand instinctively moved to protectively shelter her stomach as burning tears clouded her vision. Why would a person, much less a parent, actually hurt a small child? These people must be demented and unstable! How could they even live with themselves afterwards? No, she did not want to understand how anyone could commit such a vicious act. Raw anger surged as Ally threw down the newspaper section she was reading. She glared at it as if the paper was to blame for her current emotions.

"Boy am I getting hormonal, I shouldn't let myself get carried away like that!" Ally chided herself as she took several deep breaths to regain her composure. An overwhelming sadness and sense of helplessness prevailed over her anger as Ally wondered, "Was there any way to prevent such tragedies from happening? She picked up the newspaper again, hoping to find answers -some insightful reason why these tragedies could have happened. Anything to ease her troubled thoughts.

Ally reluctantly read yet another related article regarding the names and circumstances of each death due to child abuse within Calaveras County. Wait...-a six-year-old girl, Shilo Wilson's, dead body was discovered at Horseshoe Bend by the authorities about nine years ago. A massive search was conducted for this child after she was reported as missing, by her mother. Later, the mother, Tammy Lee, was arrested in connection to this murder.

"Horseshoe Bend?" Ally tensely sat up straight as the goose bumps rose on the back of her neck. She'd seen a beautiful golden-haired child there alone in the meadow, two months ago. Could she have seen a ghost? "Don't be an idiot!" She always did have an active imagination, but to think she saw a ghost, now that was ludicrous. Yet, Ally couldn't shake off the image of that young child as she returned to her desk.

"I sure, hope this one is good, I'm so hungry," Ally said to David as she cut up the vegetables for a casserole.

"What, the 'Cassero' Queen making a lousy casserole?" David said jokingly as he came up behind, wrapping his arms around her, and kissed her cheek.

"All I want to do is eat; I'm never really full! I hope I don't put on fifty pounds by the end of this pregnancy. But it's an improvement from last month; at least, I'm not nauseous when I cook." Ally commented half-plaintively, "David, could you please grab the salad and dressing from the fridge?"

"You look great; I don't know what you're worried about. You're eating a healthy diet."

"Hey, come here quick, I'm sure junior's dancing a jig," Ally yelped. David came quickly around the counter and placed his hand on her stomach. Smiling, he was still astonished when he felt the baby move.

"I think this little one is going to be an athlete! Sometimes the baby feels like a little linebacker in there," she asserted. Ally and David had agreed to leave the sex of the baby a mystery. David had told her that he didn't have a preference in either having a boy or a girl, as long as the baby was healthy. However, she secretly thought he wanted a son first.

Ally was preoccupied during dinner because she kept thinking of the young girl that she'd seen in Horseshoe Bend. Since reading the newspaper earlier today, she had thought of little else. "Shilo Wilson? No...She couldn't have seen a ghost." There must be a rational explanation for that child being out there alone; yet she vacillated, the area is so remote, why would a parent just let their child run unattended?

Ally idly tried to make conversation with David to get her mind off that child, only her comments seemed stilted, even though David didn't seem to notice. Finally, Ally couldn't stifle her concerns any longer; she began tentatively, "David, remember our trip to the reservoir in March and we stopped at Horseshoe Bend to read the map?"

"Yeah," he nodded.

"Well, when we stopped, you remember, I told you about briefly seeing a little girl playing in the meadow. At first, I didn't think much about it, but then I became alarmed because I didn't see anyone else around. When I looked back again, she was gone. I figured she must have had family nearby. Later, I talked to you about my concerns regarding this child, and that I was upset about not making sure she was okay."

"Okay, what about it?" questioned David. He could vaguely recall her mentioning a kid at the time.

"I keep thinking about this small child, and that she shouldn't have been out there, alone. We would have seen other people or at least the vehicle they were driving, wouldn't we?" Ally nervously asked, her words rushed.

"I don't remember if I saw any other cars or not," David shrugged his shoulders, looking perplexed.

"Well, I was reading the newspaper today, and I ran across an article about child deaths within the county. A girl was murdered nine years ago; the police found the body at Horseshoe Bend. The child - I saw at Horseshoe Bend in March was there one minute, and then, she was suddenly gone. "Ally suggested, but left unspoken that what she saw was supernatural. David stared blankly at her, making Ally feel stupid as she realized how ridiculous this conversation sounded.

"So what are you saying Ally? Do you think you saw a ghost?" David responded incredulously.

"God, I don't know? I just can't get that little girl out of my mind!" Ally said, shaking her head,   "I really don't know what I saw. It was really strange!"

"Well, I don't really know what to tell you," he responded derisively. "I'm not an authority on spooks."

"So, there is something you're not an expert on!" She knew he'd already dismissed the conversation. Ally was angry with herself for the absurdity of this conversation and miffed at David for taking her concerns so lightly.

"Oh forget it," Ally said, blaming her hormones for her sudden moodiness.

11

Ally was more disturbed by these unrelenting mental images than she cared to admit. Why was she having these obsessive thoughts, this protective swelling towards that unknown child? It wasn't rational or natural! ...Maybe her maternal instincts and typical motherly fears were just kicked into high gear, fueled by her hormone levels. This bizarre obsession was probably a hormonal side-effect, related to the upcoming birth of their child. Ally discovered, at least in her case, that motherhood generates frequent, subtle, and mostly unjustified fears. ...She had been a nervous wreck since she found out she was pregnant, worried that something could harm the baby. She agonized about effects of any food she ate or the effects any medication might have on her baby despite the doctor's reassurances. These strange reflections about this youngster, Ally summarized, seemed to be an externalization of this maternal instinct and common fears related to her hormone levels. She took solace in this explanation.

"Oh God, I miss Jennie," Ally uttered as she restlessly laid in bed that evening, her mind still fixated on the small child in Horseshoe Bend. Jennie had been her friend and confidante; they used to start talking in the middle of the afternoon and finish in the wee morning hours, when neither of them could hold their eyelids open any longer. Her conversations with Jennie used to span from the mere trivial to philosophical theories, and beyond or so they would say. Their shared joke at the end of a long discussion would be to turn to each other and say "and beyond."... Jennie would've understood her nagging concerns regarding that little girl and would've provided some precious insights. But Ally couldn't talk to Jennie because her friend was killed in a car crash two years ago.

Ally wished there was someone else she could talk to about this. She had many acquaintances but no close friendships in California. No one that she'd feel comfortable talking to about these bizarre circumstances and the possible implications of this sighting. What could Ally possibly say that would make cogent sense? And David, well, she should have known better than to discuss it with him! She couldn't talk about any spiritual or metaphysical topics with David, without him getting so uptight. It had progressively gotten worse since his mother died fifteen months ago. He had not allowed himself to think about what happens after death, let alone grieve, Eventually, Ally drifted into a disturbed sleep.

"Oh Lord," Ally muttered as she awakened. Her body drenched in cold sweat; she had an unfathomable chill deep within her bones as the tears slid silently down her face. Stemming the flow of her tears, she reflected on the dream which had caused this distress. All Ally could remember now was that the golden-haired girl was dead, wrapped in an old, stained rug, lying on a barren, dirt covered floor. In a dungeon-like room, the only dim light came from the dingy window above. The dust was swarming through filtered light, giving the room a smoking haze. Ally had seen a menacing orb, obscure and pulsating; she sensed the cold and hostile energy of it, surrounding the child like a living entity. This visual had a terrifying, tangible quality that left her deeply disturbed, and shaken to the core, as if she had born witness to this vile scene.

This vision did not feel like a typical dream or even a nightmare, nor was it as easy to shrug off. Ally turned over, attempting to go back to sleep but she knew it was useless. She quietly crept out of their room, careful not to wake David. She picked out a book, and settled onto the sofa, nestling her stomach.

Ally tried to focus on the words in the book, but her mind kept drifting back to that innocent child. "The sweet girl within her dream was dead so could she be Shilo Wilson? Oh hell, what's this all about?"...It must be hormonal; she'd heard hormones could play havoc with a woman's system. If not, then she must be delusional, for these persistent thoughts and images certainly weren't normal. ... No, she wasn't crazy, she was just overly emotional right now, that's all.

Ally spent the rest of the night in mindless turmoil as unfocused thoughts crowded her overtaxed mind. The chill and dim-gray light heralded that the morning had arrived. Due to her lack of sleep, this pre-dawn hue was truly an unwelcome sight. She grudgingly headed into the kitchen to start coffee.

Ally couldn't wait to climb into bed; she was exhausted from her lack of sleep last night. And her day had been hectic, made even more challenging because she couldn't concentrate due to her shifting focus. Why couldn't her thoughts be diverted from that child? It was incomprehensible. Ally's eyes shut almost before her head hit the pillow. Before daybreak, Ally opened her eyes again, suddenly alert. Something seemed amiss. The room was bathed in quiet stillness. She could see the outline of her bedroom furniture within the darkness. She turned. David was sleeping peacefully, his back turned towards her.

What awoke her? ...Then Ally looked up and saw her: the golden-haired cherub looming above the bed, watching her! The beautiful girl was wearing a white dress over a light blue tee-shirt top. The pupils of her eyes were very large in the light blue irises of her eyes. She looked so solid and real that Ally felt she could reach out and touch her flesh. (Ally impulsively reached forward to touch her arm, but unconsciously retracted) This sweet child's expression looked so incredibly sad, various emotions seemed to flicker across her candid face: anger, defiance, opposition; then, a wounded expression crossed the girl's face. Her lips parted as if to speak but no words followed. She reached out her arm and her hand motioned for Ally to come.

Ally shrank against the bed trying to put distance between her and this apparition. Her eyes clamped shut, she brought her hands up and tightly clenched them to her face. "NO!" Ally felt as if the word had been shouted from the tight muscles of her throat, but then realized that the word came out in a volume-less whisper. Several moments passed; she pulled her hands back through her hair and opened her eyes. The vision had disappeared; it was gone.

Was she disappointed? Ally was bewildered. She'd been irresistibly drawn to this little angel, believing that the child needed her help and protection. Was she losing touch with reality? Ally looked around the darkened room, seeing the solidness of the furniture, the outline of the lamp, and the subdued outlines of the pictures on the walls. She was looking for evidence of this being a dream, but all seemed evident of her wakeful state.

"Dream?" she whispered, it had been so real. "Oh great, now I'm hallucinating," she continued to whisper for the sound of her voice brought comfort in the quiet room.

Was she becoming psychic or psychotic? Ally clearly couldn't differentiate between what was real and what wasn't anymore. Her reaction; that's what scared her more than the vision itself. Even if Shilo wasn't a ghost, she was being haunted, just the same. Ally had to take concrete action before she lost her connection with reality but how do you verify the supernatural?

"What to do? What to do?" She quietly muttered, "That's it!" Ally decided to go to the historical library during her lunch, since the library was only open weekdays. She'd find out all she could about the death of Shilo Wilson.

Ally entered the historical library on Monday and approached the librarian. Her plan was to search through the back issues of the local newspaper, The "*Lake View Mountaineer*," spanning the year in which Shilo had died.   It wasn't the best plan of attack, but she couldn't think of another one.

"Excuse me, could I please get the microfilm of the "*Lake View Mountaineer*" newspaper for January and February of 1989?"

"Could I help you find something in particular?" The Librarian asked, glancing at Ally as she placed a book on the shelf.

Ally stared at her foolishly. ..."I'm just doing some general research," came her faltering response.

"Well, what is your research pertaining to?" Questioned the Librarian.

"Could I please -just get the Microfilm for January and February of 1989?" Ally repeated tersely, feeling very uncomfortable.

The librarian eyed her curiously and retrieved the films; she then showed Ally how to operate the machine.

Ally managed to scan through the months of January, February, and March of 1989 without finding any articles related to Shilo Wilson before returning to work. She returned to the library two more times during the week, until she found what she was looking for. September 28, 1989: The article recounted that a six-year old child, Shilo Wilson, had vanished on her way to school. The authorities were conducting a massive search to find the missing youth.

A photo of Shilo Wilson accompanied the article. She was a slight child with dark brown, curly hair and a medium dark complexion. The child sparkled with a huge grin. Shilo appeared to be of African/Caucasian dissent. This was not the girl she saw at Horseshoe Bend or in any of her subsequent dreams.

"Oh God," I really am losing it!" Ally let out a large sigh, running her fingers through her hair and stared at the photo of Shilo Wilson. However, with her interest piqued and solidified, Ally researched the rest of the articles relating to Shilo. Maybe they could shed some light onto her nightmares but she couldn't see how.

In the subsequent weeks following the initial article, there were newspaper accounts of efforts made to find Shilo Wilson: On October 2, 1989, the still-missing child, Shilo Wilson, would be seven years old this date, since Shilo was born on October 2, 1982. Authorities still have no leads. On October 16, 1989, the local police discover the remains of Shilo Wilson in the remote region of Horseshoe Bend. On October 18, 1989, evidence found on the scene along with discrepancies in Tammy Lee's account of the circumstances lead to the mother's arrest in connection with the murder of her daughter. On October 21, 1989, Tammy Lee found dead in her jail cell. She committed suicide.

Ally (without a reason for doing so) recorded all the dates of the newspaper articles before she returned the microfilm. It seemed morbid, but somehow she needed to bring closure to all of this. She couldn't shake the wave of depression that these articles had engendered as she walked out into the bright sunshine, and heat of late May.

Ally left work early; planning to arrive home before David. She needed professional help, she thought. These delusions aren't normal. Picking up and looking through the yellow pages for the listings of mental health services, she dialed a facility but quickly lost her nerve and hung up before anyone answered the line. Ally continued to stare at the phone. Should she call?

What could she possibly tell a doctor that would make any sense? She saw a child for less than a minute, several months ago, and now she can't think of anything else. Why was she having all these weird dreams? Did she really see a child that day or was it all in her imagination? Now, she was really making herself crazy. The ringer of the phone let out a blaring whine. Startled, Ally lurched backwards; her heart-rate surged, and then adjusted back to normal as she grabbed the phone.

"Hello?' Oh, hi Mom!" Ally said in an artificially exuberant and breathless manner. "Yes, we're doing fine. I'm just a bit exhausted from being very pregnant, and entering the summer season. How about you? Tell my brother I love him, and ask him to give me a call when he's on his next semester break from school. Hey Mom, I need to let you go. Just feel like I need to lay down and rest. Yes, I love you, too."

Ally hung up the phone; just hearing her mother's voice had brought some measure of comfort and relief. "Did Mom sense that something was wrong?" Her mother always had an uncanny ability to call when she was troubled about something, or when Ally needed her the most. She should've discussed these visions or whatever they were, with her Mom. But she didn't know what was happening to her and she was afraid of what the answers might be. No, she didn't want to deal with this problem and hoped it would simply go away. Her mother would want to confront and fix the problem. Sometimes, she still felt like such a child around her mother.

17

Besides, Ally still speculated that there could be a supernatural component to these visions. Her mother was very religious; would she consider anything supernatural inherently evil or indicative of demonic possession? Ally couldn't bear a hell and damnation speech. Her mother had been upset when she stopped attending church. She was spiritual but not religious; she didn't feel the need to be "saved."

Ally needed to do something to keep her mind busy. "No,' she adverted, 'I need to rest, I'm so tired!" This was a deep, draining tiredness. She was afraid even sleep wouldn't erase it, her body felt like it weighed a ton! She trudged into the bedroom, pulled down the spread, and after slipping off her shoes, laid down.

She fell asleep thinking of all the people who had killed, been killed, or persecuted throughout the centuries, simply due to their religious convictions. Wars fought over differing spiritual ideologies. This seemed completely amoral and sacrilege to her. How can a person believe in a perfect, omniscient being and kill in his name? It was illogical and senseless. She turned over, willing her mind to go blank, and finally drifted off to sleep.

Ally serenely sits alone on a downy blanket under a massive oak tree with a picnic basket close at hand. She idly sips at her glass of sweet tea as she delightfully absorbs the idyllic landscape, before her. The ethereal sunlight plays warmly and blesses the countryside below with a golden hue. Emerald green grass grows long and wild, next to a gently flowing brook -the light glitters like stars off the rippling water. Ally can hear birds chirping softly in the distance. Upon hearing a rustling sound, Ally turns and tenderly gazes at the enchanted child. The golden-haired angel giggles and skips down to the water's edge. Ally happily watches the child as she seats herself next to the brook. The little girl starts to delicately braid long blades of grass together and then instead, begins to float single blades of grass down the stream as she sings loudly in her youthful voice: Row, row, row your boat, gently down the stream...Merrily, merrily, life is but a dream....

"Ally," David calls out, "are you home?" Ally woke abruptly from her nap as David entered the bedroom. Ally sat up in bed, rubbing her eyes.

"Sorry Ally, I didn't mean to wake you," David apologized.

"It's okay, I was just taking little nap."

"Ally, are you okay?...I noticed that you haven't been sleeping throughout the night," David asked with concern.

"I've been having a hard time sleeping, it's probably just related to the pregnancy."

David hesitated and then said, "I noticed that the phone book was opened to mental health services...Is there something wrong?"

"Don't worry about it, David. I've not been able to sleep too well. I'm a bit tense and irritable. I was going to call and ask if it was normal. It might be hormonal due to the pregnancy. Then I figured I was making too much out of it. I didn't call; I'll talk to the doctor at my appointment next week."

"If you're sure you're okay."

"Really, I'm fine," Ally responded. "I'm just going to bed early tonight."

Screaming and drenched in sweat, Ally woke from her ghastly nightmare, trembling violently with tears streaming down her face. David rocked her in his arms as he tried to console her.

"Ally, Ally, it's okay, it's okay...It's just a dream, sweetheart." David reassured.

"The baby...our baby...dead!" Ally wailed brokenly through the hacking sobs.

"It was a nightmare Ally, that's all. You and the baby are safe," David said calmly. ...Ally continued to weep uncontrollably and David asked, "Would it help to tell me about it?"

Ally remained silent for several minutes before she started speaking: "I took our baby for a walk in the stroller. ...We were at the park. A mountain lion lunged down from a high tree branch - knocking over the stroller, and the baby fell out onto the hard ground. The mountain lion pounced on top of the baby. I grabbed a stick and repeatedly struck, trying to beat off the animal, but it was slashing and clawing. (Ally sobbed). Our tiny baby was covered with bloody red gashes - had deep, open wounds all over the stomach and across the neck. ...Our child was lying in a pool of blood. Finally, the cat backed away from the baby, glaring and growling at me, ready to spring. I fell on top of the baby before it leapt on top of me, tearing at my back and head."

"It's over Ally, it was just a horrible nightmare." David held her until her sobs subsided. "Would you like a glass of water or better yet, a hot chocolate?" Ally nodded and David went to the kitchen.

Ally now hated to go to sleep! Too often, she had vivid, horrid nightmares, which involved harm or danger coming to her baby. Many nights she awoke in tears, shaken to the core. Could these nightmares signify impending danger? She couldn't shake off this persistent anxiety, this looming dread that her baby was somehow at risk. This same question kept resurfacing in her mind: Did she have this vision as an omen to alert her to a pending disaster?

"Damn, it's hot!" Ally was extremely pregnant - her back ached, her legs hurt, the heat was unbearable, and she was eager for her maternity leave to begin in a couple of weeks. It was only July 7th, her baby wasn't due until the end of August.

She entered the post office, grateful for the air-conditioned environment. She checked her watch because she still had three more errands before she had to return to work from lunch. The line at the counter was probably about ten minutes long. She hoped she could remain standing that long because she had to get this package mailed off.

Ally waited for her turn at the counter, killing time by reading the various posted bulletins. ... "It can't be!" Her throat tightened, her breathing became shallow, and she was lightheaded. On the far wall, there was a missing-child flyer -on it: the child she'd seen at Horseshoe Bend, and so many times since, in her dreams and visions. Ally left her position in line and quickly walked over to the public announcement board to get a closer look. She still couldn't believe her eyes, but there could be no mistake. ...This was the child!

The child's name was Bree Jamison; last seen, March 7, 1993, and she had been seven years old at the time of her disappearance. Ally tried to reconcile her visions with the reality of the picture in front of her. She tried to control her erratic breathing, which was coming out in short strangled gasps, as if an immense force engulfed her.

She tore the flyer off the board, knocking over her package and the contents of her purse all over the faded linoleum floor. She stooped over and urgently grabbed at the scattered contents of her purse, shoving them haphazardly back into her bag before racing out the door, unaware of the attention she had generated. Other post office patrons regarded her with a mixture of expressions from curious glances to overt concern; many eyes followed her rapid departure.

"God, help me, what should I do?" Ally didn't have any answers as she got into her car. She was still shaking uncontrollably as she tried to collect her rioting thoughts. An elderly woman approached her car and asked if she needed help. Ally opened the window, aware of the intense heat, and shook her head in the negative. "No, no, I'm fine, I'll-I'll be all right." She started the engine and headed back to work.

Ally couldn't focus on her job because her mind fixated on Bree Jamison. She tried to clear her head, but it was useless. After an hour, she reported to her supervisor, Joan that she was sick, and needed to leave.

"Are you sure you're doing okay?" Joan asked, noting the gray pallor of her face.

"I'm just tired, being this far along, I haven't been sleeping so well." Ally responded, making a light excuse.

"Well, you go home and take care of yourself. Perhaps you could start your maternity leave early?" Joan replied.

"Thank you Joan, I'll see you in the morning," Ally responded. Ally suspected that there was a lot Joan wasn't saying. It had to be evident that she'd been so preoccupied and tense, and thus it was impacting her work performance.

When David returned home after work, she told him that she was not feeling well. "Are you okay? The baby?" he asked quickly.

"I'm fine, I just need to rest." Ally lied. She needed to figure out what to do, given the unusual set of circumstances.

The next day brought no new answers but at least Ally was calmer. She wished that she could view this situation objectively, without any emotion. The flyer contained contact information for the Calaveras County Sheriff's office. What would she say to a sheriff's deputy? Tell him she saw the ghost of Bree Jamison in Horseshoe Bend! Imagine the reaction she would get if she weren't hauled off to the loony bin first. Maybe given time, the answers would become apparent. Then, she'd do what needed to be done.

CHAPTER 2

It was August already, and Ally could go into labor at any moment. She should have been exultant as she prepared for the arrival of her first child, but she wasn't. Ally knew exactly what was causing her to be so morose; it had been weeks since she first saw the missing child bulletin involving Bree, but still, she hadn't done anything about it. She retrieved and then carefully reviewed the information on the flyer: Bree Jamison was born on February 9, 1986; the child had just turned seven at the time of her disappearance. She had been missing since March 7, 1993. No information was given regarding the suspected abductor. Any new information could be phoned into the National Hotline for Missing Children. Ally didn't believe she would be free from this guilt or anxiety unless she took some form of action regarding Bree Jamison.

Rubbing her weary eyes, Ally couldn't dispel the sleepiness because she was still plagued with recurrent dreams and nightmares. Some were focused on the disappearance of Shilo Wilson; others on the death of Bree Jamison; but most often, the nightmares were centered on her baby being in peril. Were these night terrors due to guilt because she was procrastinating and had yet to resolve the situation with Bree? Alternatively was this experience a warning that something terrible was going to happen to the baby? Ally tried to dismiss this unbearable thought, but it continued to resound like a well-worn refrain. She rubbed her stomach for reassurance, feeling movement; her little one was very active right now. ...This tension couldn't be good for the babe.

It was silly, but Ally felt that she was being neglectful. It was a betrayal of her child to have so much of her concentration and attention directed towards Bree. However, this young girl innately trusted and relied on Ally's support because Bree needed to be found, and her family needed to know what happened to her. Ally couldn't even imagine the agony of having your child missing. The parents of Bree Jamison must be devastated.

It was ironic that she had not given the parents or their loss much attention. Initially, Ally's psychic experience had been unreal to her and then she'd been too self-absorbed; concerned with her own reactions and emotions to consider anyone else's. The questions resumed in a steady procession. The parents -what were they like? Were they good parents? Was either parent involved? Had they done anything to contribute to the disappearance of their daughter? Is it natural in such circumstances to ponder the guilt or innocence of the parents?   Is the mother so devastated with grief that she cannot function on a daily basis? Does she often cry out in frustration and desperation? Does she walk around in a shadow, grieving as she searches the face of each child she encounters?   Bree's mother would need to have answers. 'Not knowing' would be pure hell. Ally knew she couldn't live like that! ...No one could.

After this silent reflection, Ally's determination jelled and she had to act, to do something to find Bree. Her dilemma was what to do. She assumed that no law enforcement agency would take her seriously because she had no concrete proof or evidence. Would they even dispatch an officer to investigate the area? She'd have to take a ride to Horseshoe Bend; a quest to see if the atmosphere would generate any new information or impressions. Ally grabbed her car keys. Then, she remembered just how far along she was, and just how remote the Horseshoe Bend region was.

Ally would have to wait until David got home and pray for the right words to convince him that she wasn't crazy or irrational. She dreaded telling David about this situation, envisioning his condescending reaction to what she had to say. She doubted her ability to convince David of the cogent reality of her psychic experience because he was a true skeptic and an atheist to boot. She had frequently observed his disdain of all matters which weren't scientifically evident or couldn't be supported logically, such as his reaction when she initially tried to discuss Bree's manifestation. Although she couldn't really blame him, it had taken her time to accept her insights as genuine.

When David arrived home, Ally slowly outlined her experiences involving Bree Jamison. She started with the sighting of the little girl and the subsequent newspaper article which indicated that a child was found dead in Horseshoe Bend. Ally continued by telling David about the recurrent visions and dreams, which caused her to research the death of Shilo Wilson, and finally her unexpected discovery of the missing child flyer picturing Bree Jamison. Ally held out the flyer to show him.

"David at first, these visions, the obsessive thoughts, my irritability, didn't seem to have a rational basis; I believed that I might be mentally unstable and doubted my own sanity. But after seeing this flyer, it's evident that I've had some sort of psychic experience. I saw this little girl repeatedly in my visions for weeks before I inadvertently discovered this bulletin. I can't go to the police or call the hotline without any solid information. Could you take me to Horseshoe Bend to have a look around?"

David stared with dumbfounded expression, Ally amusedly said, "Well now, you look like you've seen a ghost!"

"You-you want to go to Horseshoe Bend, now?" David stammered, and Ally slowly nodded. "Well, I don't know what you think you'll find there. This kid has been missing since, what 1993-that's over five years ago. "

"To tell you the truth," Ally responded. "I don't have any clue as to what I may be looking for. Maybe something unusual, atypical, or suspicious, anything concrete for law enforcement to check into."

Ally looked at David, but he remained silent. She trivialized, "Do you think that there may be something to this or do you just consider me flaky?" What was David thinking? She knew David couldn't entirely accept her psychic insight. However, now, what was he thinking about her? Did she want to know?

David shrugged his shoulders and conceded, "You obviously believe there is something to all this. Might as well enjoy the ride. We had better get up there before it gets dark." His response was guarded, probably the best that she could've expected given the circumstances.

During the drive, David tried to think of something to say to her, but he was at a loss for words. Lately Ally seemed preoccupied; and when approached she was so edgy and irritable, unlike her usual self. David knew she hadn't been sleeping very well, but she'd simply blamed it on her pregnancy. David worried that she might have trouble caring for the baby. Ally had always been so ultra-sensitive, temperamental, almost to the point of being flighty. But she'd always been practical, until now. He knew that she honestly believed in this psychic business. How could he prove to her that it wasn't real, that it was all in her imagination? Maybe when they found nothing sinister at Horseshoe Bend, he could slowly dispel her beliefs by pointing out the flaws in her reasoning and put an end to this nonsense.

They arrived at six-fifteen in the evening; there were a couple of hours left of daylight. Ally glanced at David, "What do you think we should do now?"

David was silent for a long period of time, "Where was it exactly that you saw this kid?"

"About a hundred feet, northeast of that survey post, over there," Ally responded.

He couldn't believe he was doing this. They drove slowly along the meadow; David stopped the Explorer near the survey post. Ally walked through the meadow. She could hear the birds' overhead, but otherwise there was complete silence, and not even a breeze disturbed the quietude.

Ally searched for over thirty minutes and discovered nothing extraordinary in the meadow. She seriously started to question what she was doing. What had she expected to find here? Her eyes scanned the area. She looked beyond the meadow and into the tree line; eyeing the old dilapidated wooden sheds and other structures of the Animas Mine.

Ally called out to David, "I'd like to look around that mine over there."

"Okay, I'd like to see that site, myself." David said as he started towards her.

26

There were several outer buildings surrounding the headframe. Rusted barbed wire fenced the area but had been trotted down and laid flush with the ground in several spots. Ally spied a wooden shed that stood in the shelter of several old pines; she walked the perimeter towards the shed. Ally had a peculiar sensation as she approached the shed; as if she were being watched. Shaking off her uneasiness, Ally instinctively reasoned that exploring any ghost town or ruin would likely be unsettling, but just contemplating the history of this place itself was disturbing.

The shed was old; the wooden slats were broken in places, leaving gaping holes in the exterior walls. The birds or other animals must use these buildings for shelter. She looked around for any evidence of wildlife, but all was still. What had drawn her attention to this building was that it looked vaguely familiar; as though she had seen this place before. As Ally drew nearer, her sense of déjà-vu intensified.

The single window stood at least six feet off the ground; it was long and rectangular. Even if Ally was able to reach the window ledge to look through it somehow, she doubted that she would have been able to see much. The window was weathered and covered in dust.

Ally slowly approached the shed, stepping over the barbed wire in a low spot. She tried to look into the shed through the gaping slats of wood, but the wild shrubs that surrounded the shed made it impossible to get close enough.

David had caught up with her. He went straight over to the door of the shed and opened it. Why hadn't she thought of trying the door? Was this private property? Hopefully not. Ally's unease was steadily increasing as they entered the shed. It was difficult to see anything due to the darkness within. Luckily, she had grabbed the flashlight before leaving the car.

The interior dimensions of the shed were about twelve feet square. A workbench spanned the rear interior wall. The long horizontal window was centered on the left sidewall. Little light filtered through the window, leaving the interior of the shed in shadowed darkness. Rusted metal objects lay haphazardly on the ground and in dark recesses within the shed. They must be parts or tools, and an old rusted linked chain was piled in the corner.

Ally visually scanned the dark expanse of the shed but she did not see anything out of the ordinary. She crossed the span of the shed. Then starting at the rear, near the workbench; she slowly started walking backwards, drawing the flashlight back and forth the width of the shed. She had gotten about a third way through the interior of the shed when she noticed a small colored object on the dirt floor. She bent down to get a closer look; it was a dirty pink pom-pom that was made into a little rabbit with felt ears sticking up. One of the little plastic bubble eyes was missing. Ally flinched. No-even though the presence of this tiny rabbit didn't 'feel right' in a mining shed, it definitely wasn't sufficient enough to contact the police. It may not have even belonged to Bree. It could be coincidental; other children may have ventured into this shed at some point, but she didn't notice any other objects of a child-like nature.

"Hey David, look at this," Ally called to David, who was absorbed in inspecting some of the metal objects within the shed.

"Yes?" David questioned as he moved towards her.

"This bunny is the sort of thing that is sewn onto a little girl's shirt, maybe part of a child's slipper, or something like that. It certainly looks out of place here! In a mining shed?" Ally said as if to convince David of its' importance.   David reached a hand towards the bunny.

"No. Don't touch it!" Ally instructed. "It may be evidence or something." David grimaced and thought, Ally was going to make this insignificant object into insurmountable proof that the kid had been in this shed, adding additional layers to her current flight of fancy.

"Really? That rascally wabbit there?" David scoffed, putting his hands in the air and backing away. "How much longer do you think you'll be?"

"Just a little bit longer," Ally replied absently, oblivious to his sarcasm.

Ally and David finished their inspection of the shed without finding anything else out of the norm. Ally stretched as she stepped out of the shed into the light of the setting sun. She turned to David, "It will be dark in about half an hour. Do you think we can come back here on Saturday?"

David looked irritated but acquiesced to her request, "Yes, we'll come back."

David didn't know how he was going to handle this situation with Ally. He wanted to be supportive, but he also didn't want to indulge this whim. He acknowledged that Ally could be obstinate at times; it was going to be difficult to persuade Ally that this psychic mumbo-jumbo was all part of her imagination.

Ally was extremely tired when she retired to bed. She awoke with a jerk, then sat up and stared straight ahead.

"Another dream, Ally?" David asked solicitously, he'd been lying in bed, awake, unable to sleep.

"Yes, it was strange and rather child-like, but not frightening;" Ally responded.

"Okay give, what happened in your dream?"

"I was out at that mine, looking around. I was hot and tired, so I found a boulder to sit and rest on. As I'm sitting there, a glittery, pastel-colored mist shrouds the landscape, and I cannot see anything until two black paws cross and expand outward. A beautiful head of a red fox rises, and moves forward until its whole body is standing fully upright, on its hind legs in the middle of this haze. The eyes of this red fox are extremely intelligent, gentle, and ageless, and he's magnificently dressed in a top hat and cape, like a magician. The fox steps to the side as if conducting a show, and arches his front leg downward, saying, "now you see her." Bree appears, looking vibrantly animate. Then, the fox sweeps his front paw in an upward wave and says, "Now you don't." A plastic doll in a flowered dress is standing there instead, in the spot where Bree had stood a moment earlier." Ally finished with a yawn.

"That sounds like a regular dream to me," David cajoled.

"I guess so. I'm going back to sleep now," Ally murmured as she turned over onto her side.

Early Saturday morning, David and Ally started out towards Horseshoe Bend. Ally had packed a cooler with soft drinks, juice, grapes, and sandwiches for their lunch. They would have a picnic by the river. Driving along, she felt the heat of the sun beating through the windshield. God, it's going to be another hot day! It wasn't fun being pregnant during the summer. Ally prayed that she would have the baby soon.

"Maybe these rough roads will help induce my labor," she said wistfully to David, eyeing the rugged dirt-trail that they were traveling on.

"I hope you don't go into labor out here," David looked squeamish. "Well at least, we're not too far from civilization."

"What, you're not up to the delivery?" Ally asked innocently. He shot her 'the look," and she chuckled. Ally needed to stop teasing him because he looked so relaxed out here. She didn't want him to start getting all worried and uptight again.

Arriving at Horseshoe Bend, Ally and David started their quest at the abandoned mine buildings. Ally gingerly watched her step, while walking over the uneven ground, stopping frequently to rest. She looked over at David, he was really enjoying this outing for he was enthusiastically studying all the buildings and remnants of the mine. It was strange that he'd taken such an avid interest in the history of the area.

Ally eyed the dilapidated headframe, and prudently choose to stay away from it. The possible hazards of exploring the headframe were too great, she decided, rubbing her large belly. If needed, David could check out this area. They continued to scour the various buildings and grounds for over an hour. Ally concluded that if this place held any secrets, it seemed devoid of any clues. This search was futile; they might as well head for home.

The heat and the physical exertion had taken their toll, as Ally made her way towards the shade of a big pine, sitting on an adjacent tree stump. She could hear the gentle lapping sound of the nearby river, and yearned to sit next to it. Ally visually combed the area to find David, smiling when she saw him. His dark, curly hair was unruly in the breeze, he looked so young and carefree out here, like a young boy. Ally rubbed her stomach, imagining a smaller, younger version of David, a son, who looked just like him. David must have seen something of interest because he headed off in an eastward direction.

Enjoying her respite, Ally listened to the distant sound of the flowing river. She watched the erratic flight of a bird overhead, looking in the upper branches of the trees for signs of its nest. She then heard a small animal scurrying through the brush near the mountains of rock. Ally quickly recalled that David said these enormous rock piles were called tailings, which were waste deposits left from the mining operation. Curious, Ally hurried towards the sound, hoping to catch a glimpse of her visitor. Breathing heavily, she carefully made her way around the mountain of granite stones, spotting the frantic flight of a lizard, which was uprooted by the noise. The sunlight glistened off some odd, small white stones which were nestled between low-lying shrubs and the tailings pile. "Quartz-crystal?" She wondered, walking over to take a closer look.

Ally leaned down to inspect the stones, and gasped, as she fell back into a seated position. Goosebumps rose on her heated flesh, sending chills throughout her body. Ally pushed backwards with the heels of her hands, trying to distance herself from this discovery. Covering her eyes, she drew her hands backwards towards her scalp as if to erase the image before her. She took a deep breath and held it, attempting to regain control.

"David," Ally's voice was shrill. She heard David's quick approach.

"Are you hurt? What, did you fall? What in the hell are you doing in all these dammed rocks!" David urgently questioned.

"Ahh," Ally opening her mouth to speak but the words refused to come. She swallowed with difficulty, and attempted to speak again.

David was next to Ally on the ground, pulling her towards him. Ally braced both hands against her thighs, her eyes downcast, as she pointed forward in the direction of her discovery.

"Over there," Ally managed a hoarse whisper. David, half-standing, turned in the direction she'd indicated, and spotted the bones of a small hand sticking out from beneath the tailings pile Stunned, he paused momentarily.

"We need to contact the police, now," came David's monotone command.

"Really?" Ally clipped facetiously.

"I'll go back to the car to get something to mark the location," David affirmed. "Will you be okay?"

"Yeah," Ally faltered, uneasy about being left alone. "David, please hurry!" Ally wrapped her arms tightly across her chest, refusing to look into the direction of the bones. David please, please hurry, Ally pleaded repeatedly. Now intensely apprehensive, she had to get out of this place!

"I'm back," David beckoned, returning promptly with a wooden pine branch, pen, tape, and a few paper plates. With his pocketknife, he cut slits into the paper plate and placed it over the narrow end of the branch. He stuck the branch into the pile of rocks, incongruously marking the location as you would a camping site.

"Let's go." David reached down to help her up. David made and attached a few more directional markers as they left the mining camp in silence.

Twenty minutes later, they arrived at the county cafe with an attached convenience store. David went to call the police while she sat down in a booth. When the waitress came over, Ally ordered two ice teas.

"I ordered you an ice tea." Ally said as David walked up to the table.

He nodded, "a sheriff's deputy should be here in ten, fifteen minutes. I told him that we'd gone to Horseshoe Bend for a picnic, and found human bones. Asked him to meet us here, and then, I'd lead him to the location." He glanced quickly in her direction, "is that okay?'

"Yes," she nodded.

"You should stay here and relax. I should only be gone about an hour," he reassured.

"Yes and thank you, this heat is killing me. I'm exhausted," Ally conceded. She had reached her limit, and did not know if she was physically capable of continuing on.

She knew however, that her "condition" was a shallow excuse for not returning to Horseshoe Bend. Ally didn't want to go back! The vision in which she was with Bree as the little angel floated the grass blades down the stream had been overwhelmingly sweet and wonderful. She wanted to picture Bree as that lovely golden-haired child. Ally didn't want to desecrate this tender image by viewing her skeletal remains. It was so surreal! Ally knew Bree was dead. But emotionally, she just couldn't wrap her mind around it. Besides, David might revolt, taking them both home before the Deputy arrived if she insisted on returning. She sympathized; he was concerned about her and must be utterly bewildered by the circumstances.

Deputy Neal Bryant arrived, and introductions were made, "Hi, I'm Alyssa Sullivan and this is my husband, David...." Ally liked Deputy Bryant right away. He looked to be in his late fifties with gray hair, a mustache, and a solid build. He had an air of quiet, reassuring strength. The Deputy asked some demographic information, along with some basic questions, while taking notes.

"Are you okay?" Deputy Bryant inquired, making a quick appraisal. "It doesn't look like you have long to go."

"About two more weeks or less, if I'm lucky," Ally said eyeing her stomach. "I'm feeling fine, but I think I'll let you and my husband return to Horseshoe Bend if that's all right?"

"Of course," he nodded understandably. Deputy Bryant and David headed out.

A man cruised his Porsche through traffic, noting the look of envy from the men and the covetous gleam in women's eyes. How abruptly the bitches adverted their eyes when he caught their stare. He had what they called "the full package." Now, be a good boy, he reminded himself. He was in-route to pick up Jill at the airport.

Fuck, he would be stuck, catering to Jill's immense ego for the next few days. Didn't it get old for her, as well? What the fuck! She'd be gone by Tuesday on another assignment, and everything would return to normal. He maneuvered onto the freeway entrance.

He scanned the radio channels, stopping briefly before proceeding to the next channel. Listening to a news station, he briefly lost control of his Porsche and swerved onto the shoulder. He shifted into neutral as the newscast continued. The broadcaster recapped that skeletal remains were discovered in an isolated region, Horseshoe Bend, near the old Animas Mine workings. As yet, no cause of death had been determined. The station would update as further details were made available.

The carcass had been uprooted. It should still be entombed where he dumped it: next to the tailings pile before causing the barrage of falling rocks to submerge the body. He had taken meticulous care to make sure nothing had looked anomalous. Yet his discard had been found! Had an animal managed to extricate bones from the rubble? Was someone metal detecting for gold in the tailings? Either scenario was possible. No matter-the boys in blue will never be any wiser without a label to go along with the bones.

Ally felt wonderful, other than being a bit sore and groggy. She had given birth last night to a healthy baby girl, Breanna Erin Sullivan on August 25, 1998; her daughter weighed seven pounds, nine ounces. Ally's labor had been short, lasting only six hours. Ally finished feeding Breanna and placed her gently into the hospital crib. She could not take her eyes off her daughter, watching the rise and fall of her chest as she peacefully slept. Her baby had light wispy hair; her eyes were the blue slate color of a newborn. Would Breanna's eyes remain blue? Ally had been told that eye color can change in infants during the first year. Ally heard the music for the evening news, and turned to watch the television above the bed. She'd been waiting intently for the broadcast because the previews announced, "New developments regarding the unidentified remains found in Horseshoe Bend area."

The female newscaster reported that skeletal remains were discovered earlier this month near the Animas mine workings in Calaveras County. These remains have been determined to belong to a six year old child, Amy George, who was last seen on June 3, 1995. The picture showed a little brown-haired child with green eyes. The newscaster went on to say that the child's family was unavailable for comment at this time. The rest of the newscast faded in a blur as Ally turned off the TV.

Ally was deflated, and confused as she stared blindly ahead. Could the Sheriff's Department have made a mistake in their identification of the remains? No! The authorities would have undeniable proof of the identity before they released the child's name to the media! Was she mistaken? No, absolutely not. Without question, it had been Bree in Horseshoe Bend, and in her subsequent visions. Ally knew beyond any doubt that Bree's body was still up there.

"How's it going, hon?" David said as he entered the room. "How is our angel doing?" He walked over to the crib to check on the baby and reached a hand down to gently cup her head.

"I do say that she is eating extremely well. Did the doctor say what time we will be released?" Ally asked.

"He said any time after nine in the morning. Both you and the baby are doing fine. I can hardly wait to get you both home away from this place, It's so impersonal here." David replied eagerly.

"When is Mom coming?"

"She will be here tomorrow and stay for a week," David responded.

"That will be great." Ally glanced over at the baby; "She is still sleeping, bless her heart."

"She is a real beauty." David said, smiling adoringly at Breanna. He wanted desperately to pick up and hold his baby girl, but he didn't want to disturb her sleep. He gave in, picking up and cradling the infant in his arms, his heart melting. He had his own family.

There was silence for a few minutes. "David, I was watching the newscast before you came in. The authorities have identified the remains of the body we found in Horseshoe Bend. It was some other child, not Bree Jamison. Her first name was Amy; I can't remember the last name right now. I think that must mean that Bree Jamison's body is still up there. The authorities haven't found her."

"What?" David was aghast, he couldn't believe that Ally would bring up that nasty business at a time like this. It just wasn't right!

Ally realized that she was rambling, and slowed down in order to be understood. "David, the skeleton we found was not Bree Jamison. I believe her remains are still in Horseshoe Bend."

"Oh, come off of it already, Ally! Get real! You can't be serious; this is stupid, ridiculous! You really are becoming obsessed with that kid." David's tone was incredulous. "You know, I didn't complain when you asked if we could name our daughter after that child. I thought maybe, it would allow you put an end to it. But truthfully, I found it disturbing...in fact -a little creepy! This whole situation is getting out of control. It has nothing to do with us, our family. It makes me uncomfortable." David's volume had risen and his voice cracked.

Ally stared implausibly, startled by David's outburst. She retorted, "I don't know how to explain this to you..." Einstein, she silently fumed and continued abruptly. "Bree Jamison is missing... murdered! I know her body is at Horseshoe Bend. Should I just forget about it? Get over it? It's a dead child for heaven's sake!"

"Listen to yourself Ally, you've never met this kid. You believe this girl is dead. ...And you're naming our baby girl after her? Does that sound rational to you? You don't know that kid's body is at Horseshoe Bend. You have nothing concrete to prove that Bree Jamison was ever there. You're making all this up in your head."

36

"What do you mean, David? I don't get it, I don't understand you. How you can casually explain away the fact that we found a skeleton of a child up there? Didn't you find that odd?"

"I don't know what happened to that girl or what the circumstances surrounding her death were. I'm sure the police will answer those questions. If there is another body at Horseshoe Bend, I'm sure the police will find it during their investigation. Let them do their job. Why do you insist on being involved in this? You're not a cop." David asserted, trying for a reasonable contention.

Ally took a deep breath, trying to calm down. She didn't want to fight with David about this; she needed him to understand. "David, when I first saw Bree... I subconsciously connected her with our child. It happened as I was starting to feel our baby move. I kept wondering if this tragedy had happened to us, if it were our child. It would be a living hell. I knew I had to do something to bring closure for her family or maybe just for Bree. She needed to be found. I know all this sounds abnormal and crazy to you; but, it's very real for me. I did not search for Bree, she found me. I have to find her before I can bring closure to this situation for me, for us." Her voice had risen several decibels; she sounded on the verge of hysteria.

"Calm down, Honey. You'll have all the nurses over here." He stared at her for a few moments and then said, "What do you plan to do, now? What can you do?"

"Well, I don't plan to wage a massive search of the Horseshoe Bend area, if that's what you mean!" She stopped herself, and then, continued calmly. "'I'm going wait a couple of weeks, Mom's going to be here, and I'll be very busy with the baby. But then, I'm going to contact that Deputy, Neal Bryant and try to explain all of this to him."

"Well, I hope for all of our sakes, that kid is found soon. I need to take a walk."

"David we really need to talk about this. I'm worried..."

"Ally, I need to take a walk to clear my head. I'll be back later." David brusquely left.

A man finished his solitary dinner of steak, and Caesar salad by polishing off his glass of wine. Good vintage. Carefully, he wiped his face, both hands and between his fingers with his linen napkin ensuring that none of the steak sauce spoiled his white button-collar shirt, or his satin tie. Jill, his ex-live-in, always called him obsessive-compulsive during their nicer exchanges; otherwise she'd refer to him as anal.

Well, Jill could always state exactly what was on her mind; it didn't matter whether it was offensive, crude, profane, or just plain obnoxious. The Bitch had left over two weeks ago for a six-week modeling assignment. She had screamed at him that she wouldn't be returning to his house after she completed the job.

"This is over. Do you hear me? Finished, end of story!" He could still hear her words echoing through the empty house.

So melodramatic, what a drama queen! He'd told her that she'd better pack all her shit because the crap wouldn't be here when she got back. Jill screamed at him to fuck off, slamming the door as she left. God, she must be pathetically stupid if she thought he'd ask her to stay. C'lest la vie!

He'd always valued the independence and convenience of their relationship. The long absences when she was gone, on-assignment. Initially, the relationship provided an easy façade, but recently it was becoming more cumbersome; more difficult to maneuver to his liking. The relationship had worn out its' usefulness.

He put his dishes into the sink, mechanically washing all the dishes. He continued to robotically dry every spot of water from the dishes with a tea towel, and proceeded to put them into the black lacquer cabinet without pausing. Then he proceeded to wipe down dark granite countertops and the glass and chrome dining table and chair.

He entered the front room, and noted that it was immaculate. He liked the sharp lines and contrast of the Bentley, black-studded leather couches with the Tangent coffee and end tables. He didn't tolerate clutter. Frowning, he noticed that one of his Ansel Adams prints on the wall was out of alignment and he promptly adjusted it. It was time. He sat down in his Bennett wing chair and retrieved the remote from the stainless steel accessory box on the side table and turned on the evening news.

He sat rigid and alert in the straight-backed chair, his eyes dilated and a small bead of perspiration broke out on his forehead. After hearing that skeletal remains were recovered in Horseshoe Bend, he'd been watching the evening news, every night for weeks, with avid interest. The authorities have now identified the skeletal remains and are in the process of determining the cause of death.

How had those clueless fucks managed to find, let alone pin the correct label on the carcass? This baffled the shit-out-of-him. Those fucking morons didn't even know the nameless maggot was missing. It should have taken them longer, if ever, to make the correct fit. DNA? The science had evolved! They could have made the Nevada connection, but that was a long shot.

Okay, get a grip! It doesn't matter if they have found the discard, and named the bones. Those stupid fucks would never be able to trace the body back to him. He was too smart for that! He was anonymous; totally faceless, that was the magnificence of his work. Yes, Faceless could be his own special code name; his personal handle. He was thrilled with the shadowy and sinister sound of it.

Yes. Faceless needed to follow the investigation; it would make the game more interesting. Locking his fingers together, he made a mental checklist of what he needed to do, but he couldn't dwell on it right now. Checking the gold watch on his wrist, his committee meeting would start in thirty minutes. Glancing at his appearance in the front entry-way mirror, he straightened his tie. He grabbed his Franklin planner, Nokia cell phone, and car keys from a small hall table beneath the mirror as he headed out the door.

CHAPTER 3

Already exhausted, Ally hadn't made it out the door yet to go to the historical library. It had taken her ninety minutes to shower, dress, and put on her make-up. Then she quickly fed, bathed, dressed, and placed Breanna in the baby carrier; she gathered the receiving blanket, the front pouch, an extra set of clothes, and put them in the diaper bag, which straddled her shoulder. When she picked up the baby carrier along with her purse on her way out, a pungent odor stopped Ally in her tracks and made her gag. Breanna needed a diaper change! Ally turned around and dismantled her purse, the diaper bag, and then sat the baby carrier down, removing Breanna to change, and redress her.

"There we go kiddo," Ally said to Breanna as she finished, another twenty minutes had elapsed. How would she manage to get out of the house on time, when she returned to work? It took so much time to do everything with a small baby. Ally loved mothering her infant, but she felt so inept at it. Give it time, Breanna is only three weeks old.

The morning was still chilly, but it was going to heat up into another hot day. The sun was bright; making it difficult to see due to the intense glare. Ally rummaged for her sunglasses within the glove compartment, failing to find them. She sighed with relief as she turned away from the direct sunlight, and found a parking space in the shade. Entering the library, Ally noticed that the Librarian didn't look too pleased upon seeing her baby in the front pouch. Ally was indignant as she gently placed her hand on the back of Breanna's head in response to the Librarian's restrained censure.

"Can I help you?" The Librarian asked crossly, barely concealing her irritation. Ally was glad that she had recorded the dates of the newspaper articles involving Shilo Wilson's death, making this task much quicker because she didn't like the woman's attitude.

"Yes, could I get the microfilm for the "*Lake View Mountaineer*" for September through October 1989?" I'd like to make copies of a couple of articles so could you please show me how to operate the copy machine for the microfilm?" Ally said coolly.

The Librarian retrieved the film and gave her a brief tutorial on the use of the machine. "Thanks," Ally disengaged.

"Let me know if you need further assistance," came the routine reply.

"Where do you keep the back-issues of the '*Lake View Mountaineer*' for May of this year?" said Ally, thinking quickly.

"Over in those stacks, next to the magazine rack. They're listed chronologically."

"Thanks again." Ally replied curtly as the Librarian departed.

Ally quickly located the May 7th article, about the history of child abuse deaths within Calaveras County and made a copy. Ally then, copied five articles, which were dated: September 28, 1989, October 17, 1989, October 19, 1989, and finally October 22, 1989. She returned the microfilm, and the newspaper gathered her copies and other belongings, ready to return home.

Breanna had remained asleep during their trip to the library. Ally carefully removed Breanna from the front carrying pouch and softly placed her in the day-crib. She then placed a call to Deputy Neal Bryant. The clerk told her that the Deputy was out of the office, so she left a message. Deputy Bryant returned her call, two hours later.

"Oh yes, Deputy Bryant, I hope you remember me, Alyssa Sullivan. It was my husband, and I who discovered the skeletal remains of that child in Horseshoe Bend." She stumbled over the words. "Oh good, I'm glad you remember. I was hoping that I could meet with you to discuss this case further. I may have some additional information, which might be important." She paused, listening to his response. "No, I would prefer to speak with you in person, if I may. Yes, tomorrow at ten in the morning, would be fine." Again she paused, "No Deputy, it's not urgent."

Ally carefully prepared for her meeting with Deputy Bryant. She compiled the copies of the articles, the missing child flyer of Bree Jamison, made a note to tell him about the "pom pom bunny", and she made a sequential list of what had happened, leading to the discovery of the body. She knew if not properly prepared; her conversation with the Deputy would become a jumbled mess.

Faceless had spent hours trying to reconstruct the investigation with piss-poor results. By now, he should know everything there was to know, without having access to the god-damn files. He reviewed the newspaper articles; useless, the newspapers divulged minimal information without any real details. The newscasts also, gave the facts, always with the tantalizing promise of "more details to follow in coming weeks." Why hadn't this case been plastered all over the headlines? Was this story being buried?

Faceless advanced to the next level by accessing the new kiosk in the government center; it had information and directories on each department in the county. The activity journal of the Sheriff's Office was available and open to the general public through a direct feed. He perused the daily activity; he began on August 1st and combed through the entries until August 15th. The only possible matching entry occurred on August 8, 1998, when a deputy was dispatched to Horner's grade in response to a caller who had found bones, possibly human. Faceless knew calls like this were common in the wilderness areas, where animal bones were often misidentified as human. Horner's grade bordered Forest service land. But, it was also approximately ten miles out from Horseshoe Bend. Yes, this must be the call regarding his discard, but it was another dead end because no identifying information about the caller was given.

He had made several cursory trips to the Horseshoe Bend region, surveying the area from the ridge through his binoculars. Most of the area appeared relatively undisturbed, yet even with the most superficial glance, one could see that the tailings pile had been entirely overhauled. The boys in blue must have shifted several tons of rock, un-interring the bones. The investigators had scoped in on the tailings pile; the assholes knew exactly where the body was. How? No animal had laid claim to the bones, scattering them about; that's for sure! No mining outfits had even looked twice at this property for at least twenty years. What had caused the assholes to target their search in the tailings? Unfortunately, he concluded that his only option for getting additional answers was to speak to someone in law enforcement.

On Monday night, Faceless entered CJ's Sidelines because he knew this sports bar was a favorite haunt for the boys in blue. At several pivotal junctures, he had taken an ex-girlfriend here so he could eavesdrop on conversations between the boys at the adjacent tables. He seated himself at the far end of the bar so he could keep an eye on the door and on the customers who approached the bar. Faceless ordered his beer and wings, eagerly waiting to strike up a conversation with one of those stupid fucks from law enforcement. Faceless was dangling his ass out further than he had planned to; further than was safe. What a fucking joke! Why? No one was going to connect the dots.

The man knew a fair number of the officers in this county, and was on ostensibly affable terms with them because he attended some of the same meetings and social functions. Occasionally, he would even meet-up for drinks with them, afterwards. There was no one in law enforcement that he was particularly chummy with or that he could call out of the blue, to go out to the bar. Also, Faceless knew that a "chance" meeting would fail to arouse any suspicions as to what his "real agenda" was. So here he waited, getting fucking impatient. You'd think, somebody would come in to watch Monday Night Football. Wasn't it the great American past-time, especially for those jerk-offs! Finally, he spotted Karl as he approached the bar to order a beer.

"Hey Karl, how are you. Long time no see!" He swiveled in his chair towards him. '"What have you been up to?"

"Nothing much, thought I would stop in and grab a beer before heading home."

"Here let me get that for you," pulling out a couple of dollars. "Are you sitting with anyone?"

"No, couple of guys from work stopped in after shift ended, but I got here late. They had to leave, families you know."

"Yeah, it figures. I was bored so I came here to check out the game." He responded as Karl took the stool next to his, glancing at the TV set above the bar.

"Who's winning?"

"The Cowboys, up by twenty, looks like they're going to win by a landslide. Giants can't keep their hands on the ball, at least three turn-overs already!"

"Where's your girlfriend, tonight?"Karl inquired.

"We called it quits! She even took my TV while I was out. God, I miss that TV-46-inches! Had to come here to watch the game."

"Too bad about the break-up; she's a beauty."

"Yeah, but so self-centered, she'd do better dating herself and save any guy the hassle." Karl chuckled as he watched the game intently for several minutes. The Cowboys scored another touchdown. "Man, this game isn't worth watching; the Giants can't do anything right tonight."

"It does seem a bit one-sided; don't care about who wins this game though. I'm rooting for the Broncos; I'm betting they make it to the playoffs," Karl offered.

"Yeah, they have a good team this year. How's work going?"

"Busier than usual; I start my swing shift rotation in a few days. Swing shift is a real bitch; lot of calls and interruptions, hard to get anything done."

"Hey, I heard on the news that you guys found a body, out near the reservoir. That investigation must be keeping you guys busy."

"No, it's under the jurisdiction of the Sheriff's office but that kind of crime makes everyone in the public more anxious. We get more calls regarding suspicious activities, reports regarding strange cars in the neighborhood; you know, everything that goes bump in the night and the like."

"Yeah, I can see it. Anyway it seems like the Sheriff's Office is already making major headway in the case. But I do have a question for you, if you know. It's crazy; I'm just surprised that I never heard that the child was missing through the grapevine or in any of my committees, you know I'm on the board. It's bothering me, this communication breakdown. You know; it should have gone through all the proper channels. I hope no one dropped the ball on this one."

"Nothing like that. Just a crazy set of circumstances, that's all. Never reported; nobody knew this child was missing until some couple, came upon the body while picnicking in the woods."

"Well thank god, that's a relief, at least someone didn't mess up, forget to send out the info. Can I get you another beer?"

"No, I've got to head out. Got to get some things in order before my shift changes. I'll see you around."

"Take care," he said, watching Karl exit.

No fuckin way! No one would just happen upon those bones, and that's a pile of shit, no one has a picnic, next to a tailings pile. What in the hell were those people doing at Horseshoe Bend? It's not even close to the reservoir. Could they have been metal detecting the tailings pile or possibly gold panning in the river? Whoever 'they" were they could prove to be real dangerous but so could a well sighted hunting rifle! Okay, calm down! First, he needed to know who these assholes are.   Then, how had those fuck ups from the Sheriff's office tagged the bones? Obviously he couldn't drill Karl too hard, he didn't want to set off any alarms. Anyway, he strongly doubted that sorry son-of-bitch even knew; it wasn't in his turf. He was too busy lamenting about his schedule. However all the same, Faceless needed more information regarding the investigation; now, before they fucking ruined everything.

Ally waited fretfully for Deputy Bryant in the Sheriff's Office. Breanna was alert but not fussy; she was tucked comfortably in the carrying pouch. Ally arose from her chair as Deputy Bryant entered the foyer.

"Oh, Mrs. Sullivan, how are you? I see you have a new addition since we last met. Is the baby a boy or a girl?"

"A girl, Breanna," and thank you for asking, we're doing fine."

"Would you like to come back this way? I've got a quiet room where we can talk." She followed Deputy Bryant down a long corridor into a small room, which was sparse. There was a metal desk, wastepaper basket; some low shelves stacked with papers, a couple of old fashioned orange vinyl chairs, along with a green tweed desk chair (probably 1970's vintage). The wall over the desk had a corkboard adorned with several public health bulletins, and some "wanted" fugitive posters were tacked onto it. The wall to the left had a blank chalkboard. The desk was barren except for the phone and a yellow note pad with a couple of pens. This was the most inhospitable room ever! Perhaps, Ally discerned, the ascetic environment was intentional because it made the interview process more daunting to anyone who stepped through the door. Deputy Bryant gestured towards one of the ugly orange vinyl chairs; she unloaded the diaper bag and her purse next to the chair and took a seat. He sat in the desk chair directly in front of her.

"Now, how can I help you?"

Ally swallowed hard, gave a little nervous laugh, and continued in a very serious tone. "I'll start in the beginning; this story Is well... a little difficult to believe, so bare with me. I didn't tell you the complete truth when we initially met. My husband and I didn't just happen on that body of the little girl, just by chance, as we told you."

The Deputy's eyes widened slightly; he leaned forward resting his elbows on the desk, and said, "Would you like to tell me about it?"

Ally nodded, and Deputy Bryant continued, "May I take some written notes?"

Again she gave a barely perceivable nod. Ally chronicled her account, starting with last March when she and her husband had briefly stopped to read the road map at Horseshoe Bend and her impressions of the little golden-haired child in the clearing. Then she told him about the subsequent recurrent dreams that she experienced, and learning about the death of Shilo Wilson. She handed him the newspaper article, which referred to Shilo Wilson's death within that area; this information was highlighted. Ally explained her dreams had been so disturbing, that she decided to research the death of Shilo Wilson. She handed him the articles and fell silent as he skimmed the articles. At least, he was still paying attention to her and was actually reviewing the articles.

"As you can see, the child in that photo has dark hair; this obviously wasn't the child I saw. That would have been the end of it; until...I saw this flyer in the Post Office." She quickly handed him the missing child poster of Bree Jamison. "This is the child, I saw in March, and that I've had all the recurrent dreams about."

Breanna started to fuss; she wrapped her arms around Breanna bouncing her gently on her knee. "Well, I really didn't have anything to approach you guys in law enforcement about except some strange dreams or images. I imagined that I would be laughed out of your office if I told you about my visions. I talked David into going back to Horseshoe Bend again, to have a look around.

On our first trip, we found a little child's pom pom bunny, which looked like it came off some clothing or something. It is still there in the shed. I thought we had best not touch it, in case it was evidence or something.

On our second trip, I discovered those bones. I waited to hear any news reports regarding the remains. Then finally when I heard the news report regarding the identification of the remains, the child's name was Amy, and she had brown hair. It definitely was not Bree Jamison."

She looked quickly at him; he was still staring intently at her. "I'm not a psychic or anything, nothing like this has ever happened to me before. However if I'm right, I believe the body of Bree Jamison is still up there at Horseshoe Bend."

Ally concluded her story with Deputy Bryant. He was quiet, absorbing her account of the situation. Encouraged by the silence, Ally continued "I've even been wondering what happened to Shilo Wilson. According to the newspaper, the mother was arrested and charged with her murder. She committed suicide in jail before the murder trial ever began or her guilt established.' She stopped, asking quietly, 'what happened to Amy?"

"The death of Amy George is still under investigation; we're still looking into all possibilities."

Ally stared directly at the Sheriff and asked candidly, "you wouldn't tell me if there were any new information, would you?" She turned her stare to the floor ahead of her and slowly shook her head, feeling empty, drained.

"Do you or your husband have any additional information on this matter? You had better let me know now." Deputy Bryant's fixed stare was unwavering, as were his rigid tone and abrupt manner.   This swift shift in attitude unnerved Ally, making her visibly recoil.

Ally shifted uneasily under his steady stare, her anxiety level steadily increasing as she met his intense gaze. She witnessed the disconcerting transformation of Sheriff Bryant from a friendly and approachable professional to a merciless, steel-hard interrogator. How could he respond in such a manner? Consequently at this moment, she detested him.

"I don't know what you are thinking but I have been completely honest with you! Now, I'm starting to feel like a suspect. How could you even think...think that I could be involved with, with......hurting any little girl!" She stammered, and her eyes began to burn and water, the tears were welling up in her eyes. To her embarrassment, she started to cry; swiping quickly at her eyes. Damn it, she needed him to take her seriously, and not view her as a hysterical female.

Breanna sensing Ally's tension preceded to bawl. Ally stood up, pulling herself together, cuddling Breanna, who was still in the front pouch. She hummed softly to Breanna, steadily rocking her back and forth until the whimpering subsided. Ally continued to rock, side-to-side, at a slower pace, meeting the Sherriff's cold stare with one of her own.

"As I said, I have to check out all the possibilities, you may be covering for yourself or someone else," his flat tone was matter-of-fact. Ally's anxiety rose at an unbearable rate, making her visibly tremble. Then all the stress, fear, and strain of the situation morphed into a surging burst of temper.

"For your information, I relocated to this area with my husband not quite, three years ago. This was months after Amy's disappearance according to the news accounts. Neither of us has any ties to this area or any long-standing connections to anyone else within the area. I'm sure you can verify any of this information. If you need to contact me regarding any information I have given, you have my telephone number and address!" She responded in a forced, harsh whisper as she picked up the diaper bag along with her purse, heading abruptly through the door and down the hallway. Still incensed, shaking with anger, she briskly exited the Sheriff's Department into the sunlight without even a backwards glance. Once outside, Ally stopped to try and collect her riotous thoughts. Her anger dissipated, almost as quickly as it had materialized; leaving her emotionally spent and wary as she walked towards her car.

Despite the warmth of the day, she felt cold and numb after her interview with the Deputy. Her mind replayed their conversation; she regretted losing her temper. If only she had maintained her composure. Oh well! She mechanically placed Breanna in her car seat; quickly and carefully securing the infant restraints. Seating herself in the driver seat, she started the ignition.

Ally's glance kept darting back to the rearview mirror to check on her baby. If her daughter was missing? Oh God! What if she never got any of the answers? Ally shuttered at the morbidity of her thoughts. "Stop it!" she ordered, realizing that she needed to separate the perceptions involving Bree from her fears for Breanna's welfare, which somehow were emotionally interwoven.

49

Relax already! What happened to Bree has no connection, whatsoever, with her child! The nightmares involving Breanna were the result of her misgivings because she'd failed to act on behalf of Bree. Ally now had reported everything to law enforcement and it was their responsibility to follow through on the investigation. She could lay the matter to rest, and move on.

Deputy Neal Bryant sat reclined in the desk chair, staring at the corkboard above the desk. Alyssa Sullivan had to be involved in this murder, protecting the killer, or as far-fetched as it seemed, her account was completely truthful. Admittedly, he had a difficult time visualizing her as a cold-blooded killer or a manipulative accomplice. Mrs. Sullivan's testimony had seemed genuine enough but maybe that was because he could only see her as a new mother. Mrs. Sullivan reminded Neal of his daughter, probably because Jeannie was now pregnant with her first. Neal wanted to believe Mrs. Sullivan rather than accept the alternatives. He couldn't afford to be too sentimental. He would remain objective, keep an open mind, and verify everything.

He'd heard of these psychic connections happening before, but really only in movies or literature. He had never encountered any psychic or paranormal happenings in his twenty-seven years in law enforcement or his personal life for that matter. Assuming Alyssa Sullivan's account was credible, there must be some validity to her story because a 'body' was found. Also, Shilo Wilson was found in that area. What if this other child, Bree Jamison is also, found in Horseshoe Bend? Could she have uncovered a serial murder spree that somehow escaped detection for all these years? God, could there be even more bodies up there?

The cadaver dogs didn't get any other hits, except at the tailings pile, but the area was so spread out. Also, they had brought in a regular cadaver dog team, not dogs specialized for skeletal remains or historic sites. Who knew? Neal picked up the notes he had taken during his conversation with Mrs. Sullivan and headed back to his personal desk in the back section of the Sheriff's office.

He jotted David and Alyssa Sullivans' social security numbers, birthdates, and driver license numbers in the small yellow notebook, which he kept in his front pocket and sat down at the computer. The background check yielded no unusual results, just an employment security inquiry in Alyssa Sullivan's name. She must have had to be bonded at one time. No criminal history for either David or Alyssa Sullivan in California. He wrote a reminder to find out where David and Alyssa Sullivan relocated from, so he could check if for any criminal history in other states.

Neal made some personal notes regarding his conversation with Mrs. Sullivan, slipping the loose sheets of paper, in the case notes section of Amy George's file. He officially documented the method used and the results of his background check on the couple. Tomorrow, he would be stuck at court for most of the day he had to testify in several cases. He penciled-in a four-hour block of time in his calendar on Friday; he would go to Horseshoe Bend, and take a look around.

Later in the evening, Ally filled David in on the conversation she had with Deputy Bryant, giving him a summary version of the meeting.

"Ally, leave this investigation alone now before you're knee-deep in the middle of it!" David urged.

"There isn't any more I can do now, it's a law enforcement matter," Ally responded neutrally. However, she could tell that David was completely happy with her response. What did he want; did he expect her to be more emphatic?

"You know I'm probably the chief suspect; being male. They're probably right now, looking into all my background information. What if they speak to someone at my job? Have you considered what effect that might have? "

"I already told the Deputy that we are relatively new to the area and do not have any significant long-standing connections to anyone living within the area. It will be simple for him to verify that information," Ally responded.

"Ally, I don't like any of this!"

"David, what do you want from me? Assurances that these psychic visions are all over! How in the hell- do I know?" He looked as if he wanted to continue their quarrel, but then he just exited the room in a huff.

Ally silently rebuffed David. Why couldn't David just understand or just accept what had happened?....Because, the visions hadn't impacted him as they had her, dragging her into the middle of this mess. Initially, wasn't she just trying to make this experience go away, get some closure, and bring back her peace of mind? Could she really blame David for wanting the same?

How could she convey to David the diversity of her psychic experience? On one hand, some of her visions were extraordinary, idealistic, and magical whereby Ally felt an intrinsic maternal attraction to Bree. In contrast, other visions were devastating and vile; Ally was impelled to shield Bree from harm. However, Ally knew this innate pull between the supernatural sphere and her everyday responsibilities wasn't healthy. She needed to move on and focus on more practical matters. At least, situations that she had control or influence over because at this point, there was nothing more she could do for Bree. Ally sighed, "Now everything will return to normal."

Faceless was leaving the office lobby of the newspaper, The Acacia Observer, where he had phoned the Calaveras County Sheriff's Office, posing as an editorial fact checker, Zack MacAlvey, for a short filler piece. Smiling to himself at his own brilliance, everybody has caller ID, nowadays. He even got Zack MacAlvey's name from the office directory within the lobby. He wanted more answers, but if he had asked the records clerk any more in-depth questions regarding the investigation, the call would have likely been transferred to a spokesman for the Department. Yes, this brief call had served its' purpose.

Overall, nothing would be suspicious about this inquiry and ultimately, this short conversation had achieved his desired objective. One, David L. Sullivan of Cedarwood, had discovered and reported his discard to the Sheriff's Office and the fuck, investigating the case was Neal Bryant. Just his luck, he knew Bryant could be one tight-lipped bastard; why in the hell did it have to be him?

Once within the city limits of Cedarwood, he pulled up to the phone booth at the convenience store to look-up David Sullivan. There was no David Sullivan listed; however, there was a 'D' and 'A' Sullivan listed on McKinley Circle. He quickly wrote the address and phone number in his notebook. From under his seat in the jeep, he pulled out his county- street and road atlas; and located McKinley Circle. It wasn't too far from here.

As he turned onto McKinley Circle, the Ford Explorer behind his jeep, followed him also, turning into the cul-de-sac. Faceless pulled up to a house with a "Reality" sign posted, it had an attached flyer box. He got out of his jeep and walked towards the flyers. The Ford Explorer pulled into the driveway of the adjacent house that was the Sullivan residence. The garage door raised; there was another car, a Taurus, parked inside the garage. The man who parked in the driveway climbed out of the Ford Explorer. The man, Sullivan? He was about thirty with dark hair and average in height. As the man walked through the garage towards the entry door, Faceless noticed the baby stroller to the right and on one of the garage wall-shelves, there were several boxes of diapers. The garage door slowly lowered, obstructing his view into the garage. He seriously doubted that this asshole could be any threat to him. Most likely, Sullivan found the discard by chance, just a stupid accident. As he climbed in his jeep, he drove slowly passed the Sullivan residence; he could just barely make out the license of the Explorer in the fading evening light. He quickly jotted the number in his notebook, then tossed it in the passenger seat.

Tomorrow, he would call the DMV and see who the vehicle was registered to. But, he would lay odds that this asshole was David Sullivan; he just knew it. He figured he would never have to take any action here. Why take a chance? However if his death did prove necessary, Faceless could easily make this asshole's death look accidental. This house was located within a quiet cul-de-sac of well-spaced homes, which conveniently buttressed against BLM land. Guys often target shoot their guns in the area; the obvious answer: a stray gunshot, that not even the shooter realized- hit a living target. An easy set-up, staging, would be a breeze; case closed. Faceless was a superb marksman, with an excellent rifle scope.

CHAPTER 4

Ally met with Deputy Neal Bryant over a week ago, and she still hadn't heard any more about Bree's case. Ally had promised herself, and David that this investigation was over as far as she was concerned. Why couldn't she just let it be? But intrinsically she couldn't leave this situation unresolved. Was there anything else she could do?

What was the Sheriff's office doing on this investigation? Were they doing anything? Did Deputy Bryant or his office conclude that she was a nut case, and let the matter drop? Ally needed other people to take her seriously! While Ally now accepted her intuitive acuity and owned her experience; she realized that other individuals, including David, would view her as peculiar, unbalanced or just plain hysterical. Her only resolve was to use as much finesse as possible when speaking about her insights. She needed to frame her experience in a rational manner in order to gain as much credibility as possible.

Ironically, Ally felt great, physically; she was more rested than she had been in months despite the regular nightly feedings of Breanna. The psychological mayhem and physical exhaustion that plagued her were gone. However, emotionally she hated to think of any parent desperately waiting for the safe return of their child. In some innate way, she was so close to Bree. As a mother to Breanna, Ally could almost empathize with what Bree's parents were going through: the constant desperation, the continual futile hope, and the complete helplessness to alter the circumstances of their existence. The parents would be isolated in their sorrow from the everyday world, like a piece of themselves was destroyed without any hope of being whole again. Any attempts to regain completeness would be out of reach but baiting them with its promise. Ally conceded that the devastating news of Bree's death would be a lethal blow. At least with this heartbreaking information, the parents could complete the grieving process and not be indefinitely stuck in the anguish of the not knowing the fate of their child.

Ally recognized that Bree had never "caused" her emotional distress or tried to harm her in any way. This beautiful child was only attempting to reach out and communicate with her. Ally intuitively knew all along that there was something unnatural about seeing Bree that day and that some kind of menacing catastrophe had taken place. She had sensed it, even though she tried to rationalize or 'explain away' the experience. Of course, Ally didn't want to be judged as abnormal due to this psychic experience, but her fears went much deeper than that.

Ally hadn't been willing to think about a child being inflicted with deliberate harm. As if by ignoring the existence of missing, abused, or murdered children, this reality would be abolished. It was much easier to ignore the plight of these children, and thus pretend the problems did not exist or minimize the extent of these issues. ...Her apathy was her sin. Ally quickly justified herself, it was not as if she didn't care about these children. She did! It was more about her deeply-suppressed fear of caring too much and not being able to affect the situation. Ally did not want to feel helpless or vulnerable so it was easier not to think about these circumstances at all. She surmised that most people weren't much different than she was. If it's not part of your current reality, the distressful thought of a child in pain is too great to bear.

Sadly, Ally grasped that even as of last week she had wanted to pass this problem on, and forget her experience with Bree had ever happened. All she had wanted was for her life to resume as normal. Ally now acknowledged that Bree had changed her, just as much as motherhood had. Her life had undergone a major adjustment, changed course. She would never be the same again, even if all the long term effects were not immediately evident. She solemnly promised to embrace the changes coming her way.

Paradoxically, Ally realized that Bree actually looked as if she could be her own daughter. Maybe that's why her visions of Bree always stirred-up her fears regarding her own daughter's safety. Just her subconscious mind making a connection between the two girls that's all. Ally quietly laughed at her flow of thoughts. Quit kidding yourself Ally. It's more than all this philosophical rhetoric! In reality, Bree had latched onto her heart. "You know, you have developed some sort of weird maternal feelings for this ghost child! Just crazy- a child you've never even met. Any psychiatrist could have a field day with her." Ally intrinsically knew Bree needed her, had selectively reached out to her, and she would help Bree find her way back.

Faceless sat perched on a stool, and scrutinized his notes in front of him, compiling the various facts of the investigation. To his dismay, he still had more questions than answers. He drained the water from his glass, strategizing his next move. What would be the best line of attack?   The phone rang; fuck it, the answering machine will catch it. He was in no mood to converse in a civilized manner.

"Hi Son, hate to have missed you; call when you get in. I'm planning a belated family dinner for your sister's birthday and I wanted to check dates with you. Talk to you later," came the buoyant voice of his mother, after his brief recorded message. The anger hardened on his face settling like a dark, menacing cloud. He zeroed the message with such force that the answering machine rocked and fell off the small table, the phone was dragged off the table in its' wake. The racket it made failed to draw his attention as he started vehemently pacing the room.

"Well, fuck-you Mom! Isn't that just like you! The birthday celebration must have been an after-thought! Show everyone how much you care. It will be a hell of a production. Good old, Sis. The little queen- Bitch must have made a stink about it after her birthday passed without any fanfare. She called him," son"; had to remind herself of what their relationship was. "Fuck you, Fuck you Mom!" He bellowed out in the empty room. He could not remember the last time his birthday had been acknowledged. The last gift he'd received was for his fourteenth birthday that fucking leather journal that he'd received nine days late! He couldn't forget or forgive the embossed golden letters on the front of it "Courtesy of the Alex Brentwood campaign." Faceless violently flung the notebook in his hand; it slammed against the wall, and narrowly missed breaking the glass within the picture frame on the wall.

More piercing memories came flooding in, he gripped his head as if to force back the tide. The tempo of his vigorous pacing increased. He had to get out of here before he exploded or imploded-whatever. Impulsively deciding to go to the gym, he grabbed his gym bag and headed for the door. He then realized his notes were in disarray on the floor, and an empty glass was still on the counter. He backtracked, placing his notebook in a side-drawer. Next, he washed the water glass with dish soap, rinsed, dried the glass, and then, returned the glass to the cabinet. Noticing for the first time that the phone and answering machine were still lying sprawled across the floor. He picked up the phone and the answering machine, arranging them neatly on the small table. He couldn't get sloppy now. He needed to maintain a clear mind. Again he retrieved his gym bag and headed towards the door.

It is 3:00 am, and Ally is wide awake; she glances at David, who is asleep next to her. Looking up, Ally sees that Bree is once again, looming above the bed. The little girl is gesturing in a forward motion towards Ally. The sweet child has come back to her! Ally gives Bree a warm, reassuring smile, as she reaches out to enclose Bree's hand within her own. Ally silently ruminated. "What can I do to help you, Bree?"

"Please take me home, I want to see my Momma. I'm so scared of the dark. Please....." Bree starts to cry. Ally's mind is flooded with the girl's voice; more than hearing the child but actually feeling her words. Oh Lord, she could feel this poor baby's fear and pain. They were communicating through some bonding of their minds or telepathic means. Incredible, but Ally couldn't examine this communication process right now and just had to accept it. She needed to care for Bree.

"Sweetheart, I want to help you so much, but I don't know how. You have to help me to understand. What can I do?" Ally asked silently and waited eagerly for Bree's reply. She could feel the girl's emotions and responses, as if through some emotional transfusion of thought patterns.

"Come with me, I'll show you." She tugged at Ally's hand." Ally felt the sense of movement. She was floating above the ground with Bree and then, suddenly she was outdoors, where Ally could see the delineation of her yard. Ally looked around in wonder, seeing the high dark boughs of trees in the moonlight; and the pin prick of stars that filled the expanse of the night sky. The still air was fresh, warm, and balmy as Ally listen to the croaking of a distant frog. Ally then began to glide much, much faster with Bree, and the scenery seemed to blur past her eyes as the moments passed. They stopped abruptly, hovering above the ground. Ally looked around at the trees, then the familiar wooden buildings and headframe; they were at the Animas Mine.

Now their movements started to proceed slowly, allowing Ally to mentally process the directions. They were moving in a Northwest direction away from the headframe, past the perimeter of the trees, and towards the loose base of the granite and quartz mounds. Another fifty yards along the base of the hill, and slightly left -up the sloping hillside, and they continued approximately seventy feet. Ally saw the front portal of a mine tunnel in front of her; they had stopped moving.

Bree pointed into the darkness of the mine shaft, "I'm in there; it's like the corn-maze at the Pumpkin patch inside. It has many roads and dead-ends; it is very dark and cold. Can you come back and get me, soon?" She asked fearfully. Ally saw the darkness and silence that enveloped the isolated girl.

"You know I will. I'll bring some help back with me. I promise." They continued their wordless conversation. Then Ally asked aloud as if words were needed. "Will you be okay until I get back?"

"Of course, I'll be fine now," Bree reassured with unspoken confidence. Ally hesitated as she looked into the depths of the old tunnel.

"We can go back now," said Bree and then, no communication just movement. Ally sensed the need for the silence. Just to be present for Bree and not push any of her own questions upon the child. Ally knew there would be time for that later. Ally returned, lying quietly on her bed; Bree was no longer with her. Ally heard her daughter crying and rushed in to take care of the baby. Her daughter was wet and needed a diaper change. Ally felt the sting of guilt that she hadn't been present to tend to Breanna's needs. Ally headed back to bed. How was she going to find a balance under these circumstances?

Upon awaking, Ally was extremely surprised that she had sleep so soundly, after her adventure the night before. Feeling alive, grateful, and oddly guilt-free, she felt confidently exuberant. The events of last night seemed so unreal in the cold, hard reality of day-light. She however, wasn't going to start doubting herself again. Ally would accept these lucid happenings as an unusual form of reality and garner any information she received. She got up to share some morning coffee with David.

"David. Last night, I had another dream about Bree Jamison. I know where her body is. I'm planning to contact and arrange a meeting with Deputy Bryant. I want to go to Horseshoe Bend with him, on Saturday."

"Ally, I thought you were going to stay out of this mess. You're going to get both of us into trouble. It is none of our business!"

Excuse me David, I'm already playing a role in this tragedy whether I choose to or not. Most likely, I'm also, some sort of suspect in any on-going investigation. The only way to resolve this matter is to find out what happened to that little girl." Ally asserted, she needed to be firm and resolute with David, if she ever expected him to take her seriously.

She wanted David to understand how she felt about this situation, as it was so fantastic. She continued in a softer tone, hoping to develop some deeper understanding between them.

"I know it sounds ridiculous but I care deeply about Bree, and need to help her. This is something that I need to do."

David was taken aback by her resolve. "Help 'it' to do what? You're determined to assist a ghost, a vision? Do you realize how crazy this sounds? Tell me about the dream. What happened exactly?"

"Listen David, you wouldn't believe me if I told you! Admit it, you cannot accept what has happened to me as real. All you'd try to do is convince me that what happened was a dream or just part of my imagination. Let me just say that I know where to find Bree Jamison's body," Ally said in an unwavering voice.

"Then why don't you just call Deputy Bryant and give him the information?" David replied stiffly.

"How can I expect you to understand something that I barely understand myself?"

"Not good enough, give me a good reason."

"Okay, it would be difficult to give adequate directions when I do not know the area all that well. I also might sense something while I'm there at Horseshoe Bend that would prove useful in the investigation. Last and the most difficult to swallow, is that I made a commitment, a promise to Bree. Please just trust me and bear with me for a while until this investigation is over."

"A commitment to a ghost for Pete's sake, do you hear yourself, Ally? What about us, the living? Where do we fall into the equation?"

"David, don't you think that I feel torn between meeting the needs of our baby, our family, and helping this little girl? Bree has met a tragic end and no one knows where she is at. I'm the only one who can help her. If you were the father of this child David, how would you feel?" Ally pressed and David looked uneasy with the scenario.

"You already did what you were supposed to do by notifying law enforcement." David retorted.

"You haven't given any credibility to my story. Don't you think that the Sheriff's office may have also dismissed this information? Do you honestly think they're following this lead?"

"Then you do realize how illogical this sounds?" David quipped.

"I knew you wouldn't understand! You won't let yourself. David, I need to do this!" Ally was firm in her resolve.

"I guess I don't have much choice in the matter but I don't have to like it!"

"Are you going to be okay with this or are we going to constantly argue about it?"

"Look, I don't particularly like the idea. I am just being honest with you, but I'll try to hold my tongue. Okay."

She nodded and rested her head on top of her interlocked fingers on the table. "I guess that is the best I can hope for."

David got up from the table and carried his cup to the sink; "I'll see you later."

As David drove to work, he tried to assess this situation. He knew that whatever was happening to Ally, was very real to her. He had watched all the subtle changes in her personality. He wished he could be more open to all of this paranormal nonsense, but it was all so absurd. He liked tangible facts, something solid, concrete. This dream or vision stuff made his skin crawl. He found it irritating that Ally was becoming very comfortable with all this supernatural hocus-pocus. He would just have to wait for Saturday to see what develops.

Ally finished her coffee; Breanna was still asleep. She took advantage of these few moments by making her call to Deputy Bryant. "Yes, Deputy, it's Alyssa Sullivan. The reason I'm calling is that I know where you will find the remains of Bree Jamison. I would like to go with you to Horseshoe Bend on Saturday and I will show you where the body is. Let's just say I had a strange dream. Is nine in the morning good for you? Okay, nine it is. Bring several large flashlights."

Faceless mechanically performed his daily routines and activities, but his mind was fixated on the investigation. What investigative techniques would those sons-of-bitches use on a murder case- this old? They would talk to the aunt of course, but that was a dead-end.   What did Griggs know or suspect? She had only met him once; he doubted that she would even recognize him. He needed to formulate an ongoing action plan, a way to uncover what was in the god-damn files. It would come to him. It had to! He started the relentless pacing but noticed the glances from the lobby. He needed to maintain his composure; pulling himself in check. Putting on his best and warmest smile, he greeted his next client.

It was close to quitting time; he would go hang out at CJ's again. See if he could overhear anything relevant, or stir-up a conversation, and get one of the morons talking. As he headed towards the front lobby, he froze, his astonished gaze followed her sleek progression as she approached the front desk. The petite woman asked if he was available in a lively and amused manner. He stood in rigid stillness and stared at the slender, blonde woman in the classy pantsuit. She swept back her curly blonde hair, though smiling her white teeth flashed deceptively, as she responded with a tinkling laugh to whatever the receptionist had said. Could he leave the building out the back way without notice? What the fuck is she doing here anyway? He thought desperately, then relented to the inevitable encounter. Faceless quickly plastered on a smile, as he headed towards her. The receptionist smiled as she noted his surprise at the unexpected visit.

"Hi Mom, what are you doing here?"

"You never returned my call, Dear," his mother reproached, placing one hand seductively on his arm. She was fiddling with her necklace with her other hand, then brushed her hair away from her shoulder using the same hand. Faceless remained expressionless.

"Remember, I was checking your availability for your sister's birthday dinner?" She said exuberantly, and when Faceless failed to reply, she continued.

"It'll be a small party, the family and a few others. I'm thinking about either October 16th, 17th, possibly the 23rd." He now knew what this dinner was really all about. Mom-could go to Hell, with the rest of the family and all their cronies. He would've forcefully pushed her aside, but he didn't want to create a scene. Noting that the Receptionist was taking it all in.

"Mom, I'll have to check my calendar. Sorry, I've got to run, I'm late for an engagement. You know one of my meetings, I'll give you a call, tomorrow." The man said, giving her a brief peck on the cheek.

"Promise." She said in a lighthearted tone, "I'm going to hold you to it. You're not too busy to call your poor old mother, are you?" she laughed airily, finally letting go of his arm.

"I will, I promise." He said, holding the lobby door open for her. He gave her time to leave before exiting the building. Fuck them all to hell. How dare she. Oh, he knew what the game was! No fucking way was he going to help get that Asshole elected. That Mother-Fucker! He put the screws to Mother-dearest to enlist his support. She'd never have dared come otherwise; he swallowed hard, defeated. He glared straight ahead, his eyes glazed over with a vacant expression, giving him a hallow appearance. The man grabbed at his shoulders and started rocking back and forth. The rocking continued.

Ally tried not to think about David, who was ignoring her as he sulked around the house. Did he really think she hadn't noticed? The tension between them was so thick; you could cut through it, she thought bitterly. Did he think his surly temper tantrum was going to make her change her mind? Whether David liked it or not, she was going to return to Horseshoe Bend with Deputy Bryant this morning. And that was final! So he might as well accept it, she silently asserted.

Ally had fed Breanna, bathed, dressed, and placed her on a blanket in the middle of the floor with the baby gym above her. She bent to give Breanna a kiss on her forehead. The one bright spot of her morning, giving her a fleeting pause in the escalating tension. Oh, her daughter smelled so wonderful; she could still detect the faint smell of baby powder. Breanna held on to Ally's finger; her daughter's hands were so small and delicate as Ally compared the size against her own. Every small movement Breanna made, seemed miraculous and still amazed her. She felt the love and protectiveness surge through her as the tears sting the back of her eyelids. Today more than anything, she wanted to remain home with Breanna and hold her close. Yes, she would endure this day but she kept wishing it would be over soon.

She dressed in her old jeans, flannel shirt, and her hiking boots. She put on a baseball cap, she hoped that she would not run into a family of bats or any other rodents in the mine. Ally thought about what she would need for her trip to Horseshoe Bend. She found a utility belt which belonged to David. She equipped the belt with a sturdy rope, a flashlight, and a can of spray paint. She also brought a steno-pad and pen.

Ally grabbed some granola bars and made a light lunch with a thermos of coffee. The smell of the coffee was so tempting but presently, she could not take the time for a cup. She carefully arranged the utility belt within the nylon backpack so none of the contents would spill out. Then her thermos followed. She placed her lunch in the smaller side pouch.

Ally brought Breanna into the dining room, where David was eating breakfast at the table. David did not look up from his cereal bowl nor did he utter a single word to her. David had continued to avoid her all morning as he subtly ignored her preparations for this trip. How long was his behavior going to persist? She wanted to scream at him, tell him to grow up. She placed Breanna into the baby carrier arranging some toys in front of her. Ally said in a deceptively, casual manner, "Breanna will want a bottle at eleven, and I changed her diaper approximately a half of an hour ago."

Hesitating for a slight moment; then moving more purposefully; Ally shifted her approach. She walked over and put her arms around David, laying her cheek against the top of his head. His soft brown hair tickled her cheek.

"I guess I've got to go now, wish me luck," She said lightly.

Pausing for only a second, David turned in his chair to look straight at her. Anger seething in his eyes, then the expression of anger was quickly squelched as new undefined emotion, flickered in his gaze.

"Be careful, call me if you're going to be late. I love you; "he said catching her eyes.

Ally knew that this was not what David had initially intended to say; she had seen the anger. Furthermore, he had intended to ignore her throughout the morning. Now, he seemed taken aback by his own words. She guiltily noted that fearful concern that darkened his expression. And then, she knew all that David wasn't saying, as they continued to look in each other's eyes. He wanted to protect their family by trying to take control of the circumstances. His fear was that this situation could get out of hand and harm or disrupt their family. He was also afraid that she could get physically hurt out at the mine, today.

She hated what she was putting David through. He didn't want her to return to the mine, but she couldn't yield to what he wanted. Presently, Ally would like nothing better than to renege on going out to the mine with Deputy Bryant; her trepidation was overpowering her fortitude. Yet if she did backpedal, she wouldn't be able to forgive herself, and she would probably even hold it against David. Ultimately, she knew that there was no turning back. Ally recognized their relationship had also undergone a transition and the outcome was still obscure.   Don't think about that right now, she told herself forcefully, for Ally felt she was going to burst into tears. Right now, Ally had to focus on what was about to happen at Horseshoe Bend.

Ally bent to give David a quick kiss on the lips, "I'll be careful. I'll see you, later," as she quickly grabbed the backpack and her purse on her way out the door.

"I'm losing her; I don't know Ally anymore. I don't know how to reach her." David conceded as he stared at the closed door where Ally had exited. He was completely shaken, dismayed by her negligible response to their discord. It was never like this between them before. He was completely devastated by his current thoughts, realizing in his heart that there was only Ally and Breanna (his world). He needed to break down the barriers between them.

David desperately wished he could talk to his mother about this situation with Ally. Memories of his mother surfaced in David's mind; he rubbed the bridge of his nose. David had not thought of his mother in months; he just couldn't deal with the pain and despair of her loss. What would his mother feel about his current problems with Ally? Was he truly listening or trying to understand what Ally was going through? Ally believed she'd had psychic visions; it was her reality. Why couldn't he meet her there and find out what the basis was for this belief? He could have been more supportive. Did he ever really stop and try to talk to Ally to find out what was wrong when she seemed so preoccupied and depressed for all those months? It would have seemed as if he didn't care or couldn't be bothered, and that he didn't even respect her. Ally was shutting him out now, and who could blame her. His mind filled in the blanks of what his Mom, most likely would have said, given the circumstances. David did not care for her tone.

Moreover, what would Mom think about his constant rejection of his father? David knew his mother would be extremely disappointed. Was his father still grieving the loss of his wife? David knew his father had moved here after retiring, in order to be close to him. Lawrence, his father, didn't know anyone else within the area, let alone this state. Yet he hadn't even returned his father's calls or his letters. Dad must feel lonely, even lonelier than he was, right this minute. "You fool!" David silently injected. Suddenly, David felt like such a self-centered and self-absorbed ass. He needed to get his personal life back on track. He would start by having a long talk with Ally.

Ally met Deputy Neal Bryant in the lobby of the Sheriff's office. He eyed her apparel and nodded in approval. "Hello Deputy," she said tentatively.

"How have you been, Mrs. Sullivan?" he replied.

"Oh, please call me Ally. I'm doing as well as can be expected under the circumstances. Did you get those large flashlights?"

He nodded, "Are you ready? First, I need you to sign this release before we go."

Ally quickly read the waiver and signed; it was a standard release of liability (in case of injury or death). She did not even want to think about what could happen! She was already anxious enough, feeling claustrophobic, and they hadn't even entered the damned mine. She hastily relinquished the waiver to Deputy Bryant, who summarily slipped the waiver in a plain Manila folder within his mail file.

Then, Deputy Bryant shouldered his way out the exit, holding the glass door with his back as Ally went through. Deputy Bryant set the security alarm, and made certain the door locked behind him. The gusty wind whipped her hair around her face. Ally rummaged through her purse for a rubber band and secured her hair into a ponytail. Deputy Bryant opened the passenger side door of the Sheriff's car for her. She climbed in and preceded to buckle her seat belt. He got into the driver's seat and made a radio call using the numeric code lingo associated with law enforcement. It sounded official enough to Ally as he set the car into motion.

"Listen, I'm sorry I got so upset, last time,' Ally said. 'I'm sure you're just doing your job. This is just all so new to me."

He was silent, she continued, "Am I under suspicion?"

"No one associated with a case is beyond suspicion. Most accounts have to be verified and re-verified," he clipped.

"Well, be as it may, I believe that Bree Jamison's body is in an old mine at Horseshoe Bend. I don't know what types of precautions are necessary when entering a mine tunnel. I brought some spray paint and rope. "Now, thinking of the mining

68

tunnel, Ally willed herself to relax as she took a deep breath and slowly released it.

Neal secretly wished that Mrs. Sullivan had mentioned the mine during their telephone conversation. Entering the mine, might prove too hazardous without any safety equipment. Neal carefully considered his options. The equipment would be in Building 4 at the county yard; Olsen, from Search and Rescue, would have a key. To contact Olsen and set everything up, would definitely take time and delay this trip... It's Saturday, would Olsen even be home? Meanwhile here is Mrs. Sullivan, who already looks as if she's ready to take flight. He might as well continue on for now; at least, he could weigh the veracity of her story.

She stared straight ahead, out the windshield of the car; she felt tense enough to break. Relax, she told herself again.

"Well for a novice, you'll do." Deputy Bryant turned and grinned at her. Quietly, he decided that it might be better to take some pressure off her. He wanted her cooperation for now, and he wanted to keep a close eye on her. Nothing had surfaced in the background investigation but who knew what the complete story was.

Ally caught the change in Deputy Bryant's tone; she knew he had not undergone another personality change. She sensed that he was testing her. However, she liked the more pleasant exchange even if it was superficial. She felt herself relax a little bit more, she asked semi-sarcastically, "What do you think of the weather?"

He darted her a quick glance and laughed, "Well, my hope is that the rain will hold off until after we are done today."

They made small talk until they arrived at Horseshoe Bend; then by unspoken consent, both fell silent. Ally got out of the Sheriff's car, and steadied herself against the wind. She felt the chill through her flannel shirt; she pulled on her windbreaker and quickly zipped it to her neck. She wished she had brought a heavier jacket but she would warm up once they started walking. She opened the backpack and carefully pulled out the utility belt and strapped it around her waist. She then positioned the backpack on her shoulders. Her purse remained on the floor of the sheriff's car as she closed the car door behind her.

Ally gestured to Deputy Bryant to stop for a moment. She was scanning the landscape trying to mentally reconcile it with the nighttime images from a few days ago. Deputy Bryant busied himself making a radio call to the Sheriff's office giving his location.   She heard him on the cell phone inquiring about the need for a search warrant and then listening to the reply. He gathered additional supplies and equipment from the trunk and placed into a green canvas carry-all; checking the contents: flashlight, camera (equipped with night vision lens), an extendible tripod, yellow police tape, notebook, pens, tape measure, tweezers, rubber gloves, miscellaneous bottles of solutions, a few empty envelopes and empty bottles with self-adhesive labels.

"I heard you talking about a search warrant, is one needed?" her voice carried in the wind.

"No. Luckily all the mining operations around here are on federal lands. No active mining claims have been opened for over twenty years."

"I'd figured no one was actually working out here; this area looks desolate.

Then Deputy Bryant said in an authoritative tone, "Listen, there are a few ground rules. First, I will have to determine the safety and stability of the mine tunnel. Depending on conditions, we may have to abandon the search in order to obtain the appropriate equipment. If cleared and we enter the mine, you cannot touch anything. Next, if we discover anything down there, I want you to stand clear with your hands clasped,' he demonstrated. 'It will take me several minutes to do what I have to do and then, we will leave, understood?"

Ally nodded, silently awed by this whole process. "Then what happens?"

"If there are any bones in the tunnel, we will leave and I'll call the county coroner. The Coroner will determine whether the bones are human or animal and will determine the approximate age of the bones."

She looked inquisitively at him. "It is that easy to determine the age of the child from looking at the bones?"

He chuckled at the simplicity of her question. "No, that takes a lot more investigation as does the gender, especially in the case of a prepubescent young child. Initially, the Coroner can estimate the approximate time that the body has been in the mine by the color of the bones. For example, the Coroner can determine whether the bones are Indian remains or bones from a prior century or more recent bones. After the initial examination, a special group of investigators come in from Acacia to remove the remains and collect any evidence from the immediate area."

"Oh, I thought the County would do that," she replied.

"We really don't have the facilities or man-power for this type of work. So we like other small counties in the region, contract-out this work to a forensic team in Acacia. Are you ready to go?"

She let out a huge sigh, "As ready as I'm going to get. I saw this place in a dream, so it may take some time for me to get my bearings straight."

"I'm here for the duration. Let's go."

She headed towards the Northwest side of the headframe as a starting point. From the headframe, she could see the familiar pines. This was going smoother than she had imagined as Deputy Bryant trailed behind her. It took approximately twenty-five minutes for her to locate the mine portal.

"The remains of Bree Jamison are in there," she said quietly.

"Where in this mine?" he asked.

"I haven't the slightest idea," she responded flippantly.

Her mind was on her last encounter with Bree, such a sweet little girl. How horrible her final moments must have been. No, no, I mustn't think about that right now or I won't be able to do this. I've got a job to do. Relax; focus on finding the remains. It occurred to Ally that if she thought of the bones as "remains," it helped make the task at hand easier to undertake. "Why?" Ally contemplated. The bones were pieces of Bree that conjured images of this sweet innocent girl; whereas if Ally thought of these bones as remains, it objectified the process. The word

71

'remains' seemed cold, distant, impersonal, and clinical. It seemed to put some emotional distance and some objectivity between her feelings and what she needed to do.

Deputy Bryant reached into his canvas carryall and pulled out a lantern-like flashlight and refastened the carryall. He looked at the quartz rock ceiling of the mine to determine the degree of stability. He pulled out his baton and probed the ceiling. A few small particles of debris fell to the ground. He visually scanned the observable portion of the tunnel.

"You should have mentioned that we were going into a mine when we spoke on the phone. I could have borrowed some equipment. We really should have hard hats and maybe even oxygen packs. The air is often poisonous in these old mines. Deputy Bryant hunched down low to the ground, holding the flashlight about a foot off the earthen surface of the tunnel and continued his examination.

"Sorry, I didn't really think about the condition of the mine," said Ally.

"It looks stable enough, but we need to be watchful for any loose rocks especially any instability in the ceiling of the tunnel. Also if we hear any unusual noise or reverberating sound, we are going to exit the mine, immediately. Is that understood?" Ally stood stiffly erect, merely nodding her head in Neal's direction.

"You can go ahead of me," Ally said uneasily. "Do you want to check me for weapons first?" She quipped, attempting to crack a joke to break up the tension, but her voice came out as cracked and brittle. Deputy Bryant looked like he had taken her comment seriously, and was about to respond. She impatiently switched places with the Deputy before he could reply, allowing him to enter the tunnel in front of her.

She followed closely behind Deputy Bryant, carefully watching her footing on the uneven ground.

The temperature in the mine was cool; the air was dry and stale. All she could hear was their breathing and the scrapping sound of their footsteps on rough, uneven ground. Good, no rumbling stones or thundering crashes of caving earth, Ally thought wryly. She cautiously evaded the imbedded metal railings on either side of the tunnel, on which the ore cars traveled earlier in this century. There were broken rails, deeper holes seeped in water, old cables or mechanical workings off to the sides; it did not appear stable or safe. Between the rails, the ground appeared more dry and even. She kept making vigilant glances at the ceiling of the mine, watching for any loose rocks to become dislodged. She noted some small rock debris falling down here and there but no rocks, which could cause serious harm.

Approximately fifty feet within the tunnel, she asked the Deputy to wait. She took the spray-paint out of her utility beat and painted an arrow on the wall. On the ground towards the right wall, she saw a pile of pine needles and feathers; she figured that it was a rat nest. She looked for any visible rodents and saw nothing; she didn't want to stumble unexpectedly on any critters. She did not want to amuse or alarm the Deputy by bursting out in screams.

Neal broke the silence; "Did you see the rat nest back there? That's a good sign if there are rodents or other animals living in this tunnel that means the air is safe down here."

They came to a fork in the tunnel and turned left, again she painted another arrow. As they continued to walk through the narrow tunnel, it was getting so much darker. Ally looked at the light from the flashlight; it was the only light within the dark tunnel, any natural light now long gone. If the flashlight went out, they would be cast into total darkness.

Deputy Bryant was a black-looming, indistinctive shape in front of her. She felt the walls closing in on her as panic increased. She could hear the heavy beat of her heart in her ears and almost felt that her heart palpitations must be visible to the naked eye. Focus on your breathing, breath in, hold, release; she repeated this pattern several times until the panic subsided. She was still in hyper-alert mode; all her senses seemed to be heightened by her fear.

"Are you okay?" Neal asked, listening to her erratic breathing patterns.

"Yes," she responded in a high-pitched screech, trying to quell her fear of being buried alive in this tunnel. This subterranean burrow reminded Ally of an enclosed tomb, as she listened again for any sounds of a possible cave-in.

They continued about fourteen feet to another fork and went left again. This arm of the tunnel dead-ended ten feet in and they turned back. The rock ceiling of the tunnel was so low; ducking, she had a mental image of a cave-in or becoming lost in the mine. Again, she felt the walls closing in on her; her breathing was shallow and rapid. Relax, breath deep, exhale slowly, she told herself; fighting down the panic for a second time.

Ally recalled that Bree had appropriately referred to this tunnel as a maze. It certainly was an apt description. Ally sadly philosophized that this maze was a metaphor for the condition of her life right now. She was traveling in the dark without having any sense of direction; trying to find the correct path, while confronting unknown dangers; and hoping to get safely out in order to return home.

They continued to make their way back to the prior intersection of the mine. This time they made a right turn, she painted her arrow, scarcely able to orchestrate movement of her shaking limbs. At the next fork, they could see the right tunnel ended about five feet in so they preceded left.

She was following closely behind Deputy Bryant, his body temporarily blocking out any light, even the beam of the flashlight. The mine was black; the panic hit her in a solid wave, overwhelming her. She struggled to regain her composure. When Deputy Bryant stopped abruptly and she plowed into him.

"Excuse me," she said in a small voice. Then in the beam of the flashlight, now visible, she saw what had made him stop. There was a red rug abandoned in a heap. In a flash, the sense of déjà vu swarmed her senses. She remembered this old, dirty rug from her dream.

Aloud, she said, "Bree was wrapped in that rug, I remember, I saw it. Her remains must be close by," she was almost hysterical. Okay Ally, she reiterated to herself for the umpteenth time today, calm down. She continued to concentrate on her breathing, slowing it to a rhythmic pace.

Deputy Bryant directed in a sequence of orders, "Stand back, do not lean against anything, and keep your hands clasped.' He noticed her startled expression and said more softly, 'If you touch, drop, or disturb anything; you will contaminate the crime scene or may destroy crucial evidence."

As Deputy Bryant moved quickly around, he placed his carryall on the floor, taking out rubber gloves and pulling them on. Subsequently, he pulled out the yellow crime tape, he pulled the tape around to form a rectangle in the tunnel passage. Finally, Ally could now see what his body had blocked from her view. She could see a scattering of bone towards the center, interlaced with fragments of clothing and towards the right lay a small skull. Above the eye sockets was a hole- the size of a half-dollar with thin hair-like fractures branching off. She knew the child had been bludgeoned with some blunt force object. She didn't need any training to know that.

She watched in quiet as the Deputy laid out a measuring tape. Ally felt the goose bumps rise on the back of her neck, and she knew Bree's presence was with her in this tunnel. Ally knew that the little girl stood next to her; and had taken her hand, even though Ally couldn't physically feel it. Both Ally and Bree watched Deputy Bryant as he continued with his work.

Deputy Bryant worked quickly and efficiently. He took flash photos at various angles, jotting down notes on his notepad.   He quickly made a rough sketch drawing of the scene making notations under the sketch of the rug and the bones, which included measurements of some kind but she could not be sure. Deputy Bryant leaned down to the ground. He took tweezers out of a case in his pocket, gingerly picked up some object with the tweezers and placed it within a small envelope. Returning his tweezers to the case, he used his pen to label the envelope and then placed the envelope in a side pouch of his carryall. He put the camera, notepad, crime tape, and measuring tape back into this carryall and secured the bag. He pulled off the rubber gloves, placing this in the front pouch of the carryall.

Finally, Deputy Bryant turned to her; "I'm ready to head back."

Ally nodded; she could no longer feel Bree's presence within the mine. Their work was done for today. Ally caught the current train of her thoughts, her work was not complete; it was just finished for today. "Really?" "Nonsense!" Ally reassured herself; but in the back of her mind, she knew this was not the end of her involvement. It was the beginning....the beginning of what?

They made their way out of the tunnel in silence. Ally's prior fear of the mine was eclipsed, as the new emotion took its place: overwhelming grief. The full reality of Bree's death submerged her mind and soul, leaving her hysterical, disoriented, and languid as she struggled to keep moving forward. Her chest now painfully tight, Ally felt she would suffocate as she gasped for air to fill her constricted lungs. I knew Bree was dead, Ally reasoned logically with herself but those poor small bones abruptly dispelled Bree's worldly existence.

Her mind was in turmoil as she felt the tears run down her cheeks. She saw a rat, through blurred vision, scurry out ahead of them and into the dark. She reached up to wipe her tears away with her right hand, trying to bring her breathing and emotions under control. As Ally struggled to cope, she accepted that Bree needed to be found and brought back to her family before Bree's spirit could obtain peace. At last, Ally saw the front entrance of the mine tunnel through the darkness around her. She headed for the bright light at the end of the tunnel.

Deputy Bryant had wanted Alyssa Sullivan to be present on this excursion; he did not attempt to deter her from going to Horseshoe Bend. He had wanted to gauge her reactions. At various times, he thought he might have to abandon the mission, for fear she would go into shock. When they discovered the body, Ally appeared half-stunned that a body was actually there. Ally was so genuine, her reactions and emotions were so evident on her face. Deputy Bryant knew she was telling the truth about these psychic episodes; no one was that good of an actor.

He wondered how he would write up this episode regarding someone's psychic experience in an official crime report in a just-the-facts manner. He was entering uncharted territory here, but in actuality, he was rather fascinated by this whole psychic business. It made the investigative process more enthralling; it brought a sense of intrigue to the routine.

Ally and Deputy Bryant finally reached the Sheriff's car; the Deputy placed the green carryall into the trunk along with the lantern flashlight. He walked over to the passenger door to open it for Ally. She climbed in. He radioed his office to send a couple of deputies to secure the mine portal, giving the location by coordinates. He stated he would wait for the deputies' arrival to secure the area. He would need to immediately leave the crime scene, but then would return to scene in approximately 40 minutes to assist.

Deputy Bryant turned to Ally and noticed her red, swollen eyes for the first time. "Are you going to be okay?"

"Yes, I'll be fine; I just want to get home to my baby." She almost started crying again. Her reaction pierced straight through him. It was not what she said but he knew what she was feeling by that devastatingly helpless look in her eyes.

"I know how you feel after seeing that a child has been harmed." Neal searched for gentle reassuring words but failed. He stammered huskily through the dialogue, as he pictured his emotions. "You desperately want reassurance that your own children are safe. You are so amazingly grateful when you see that they're okay. You tell yourself that this type of atrocity couldn't possibly happen to one of your children because you're there to protect them, and keep them safe. Yet secretly knowing this is fallacy, just an illusion so you can sleep at night."

At this moment, Ally knew that Deputy Bryant was likely suffering from the same overwhelmingly grim sense of doom that they both carried. The ultimate knowledge that it was beyond any parents' ability or control to absolutely protect their young from such a horrendous fate. There are monsters, which willingly feed on the pain and destruction of innocent children, without pause or reflection. They live amongst us in a society which houses many such predators.

"How many children do you have?" she asked gently. As if by mutual consent, she changed the course of their conversation.

"Three. My youngest boy, Klay, is a senior this year. My oldest, Roy, is twenty-six and lives in Acacia. My daughter, Jeannie, is twenty-four. She is about to make me a grandfather in November."

"Congratulations on your new grand-baby."

"Thank you."

Deputy Bryant stopped at the main highway to wait for back-up, a couple of Deputies arrived. Deputy Bryant got out of the car to give them some instructions; Ally could see him pointing and gesturing. He handed them his notes and drawings. Then he hurried back to the vehicle.

Ally and Deputy Bryant continued to talk in an easy manner on the way back to the Sheriff's office. It was a little before one in the afternoon when Deputy Bryant arrived at the Sheriff's office.

He turned to Ally and said, "I've got to get back to the scene of investigation. I'll call you later if I need additional information."

She nodded and said, "good-luck." Then she waved good-bye and climbed into her car, thinking about what she was going to tell David. At least she had indisputable evidence that she was not imagining things.

Upon arriving home, Ally rushed into the house. Breanna was sitting in her swing. She picked up Breanna, cuddling her close to her chest, rhythmically rocking her from side-to-side. Ally's face was buried in Breanna's auburn wisps of hair; she had so much hair for a baby. Ally breathed in her sweet scent and continued to hold her closely.

David stood up from the couch, watching her intently. It was several minutes before she could speak. She continued to rock Breanna and look into her small face. All of Breanna's features are so well defined. All Ally could say was, "We found her."

David was rattled, Ally was right. Even though he had decided to be more supportive of Ally; deep down he thought of this psychic business as just Ally's flight of fancy. He had always scoffed at the psychic accounts he'd heard, considering them good practices of guesswork. He considered psychics as well-paid charlatans: vultures preying on vulnerable and overly gullible individuals. This situation challenged and destroyed his belief system. He was an atheist and did not believe that life extended past this realm. You lived and died like any other mammal on Earth.

He had taught, preached, and expounded his point of view. These beliefs he had firmly embraced considering himself a realist, grounded in reality. However, he could not objectively explain away what happened to Ally. How had she known where to find hidden human remains? It did not make sense. Not just one body but now two bodies. One might be a coincidence, but two?

"You must be exhausted," he responded, more calmly than he felt.

"Exhausted, drained, I can't tell you how tired I feel."

"Did you eat any lunch?' She shook her head; he said, 'I'll make you some soup." He brought her some soup, buttered bread and a glass of milk and laid it out before her on the coffee table.

Ally hesitated; she did not want to put the baby down. David resolved the matter by gently taking Breanna into his arms. Ally reflected that motherhood had made her more sensitive, vulnerable, and aware. It must be instinctual; a mother became more hyper-vigilant and intuitive in order to protect and nurture her young.

"Eat," David ordered, noticing she hadn't touch any of her food.

Again, the man had parked on a path, which headed towards the reservoir and walked back in the shelter of the trees, arriving at Horseshoe Bend. He saw that the crime scene tape had been torn down on several sides. Faceless surmised that law enforcement had likely finished scouring the area around his discard. He could determine exactly where the fucks had explored from the foot traffic marks near the buildings and of course, down at the tailings pile. Such fucking morons. It was a wonder that anyone was ever caught, even an idiot. Faceless figured this would be his last trip to Horseshoe Bend for quite some time, the area was severely compromised! He would miss his familiar turf, his own encampment.

Faceless finished this inquiry; yes- the stupid fucks had completed their investigation of this site, making a checkmark on his mental checklist. When he heard the car approach, he barely had enough time to dodge behind the line of evergreens. He saw the Sheriff's car emblem and the two passengers in the vehicle at a distance. One looked vaguely familiar from this distance, it must be the asshole himself, Bryant. The other was a young blond-haired female. The Bitch was not in uniform and did not appear to belong to law enforcement.

Faceless knew that he was at risk of exposure but he needed to find out where they were headed. He mentally visualized where he parked his jeep. No, they wouldn't have seen it driving in.

Faceless was wearing green Khaki pants and a tan tee shirt over his tall, lithe frame. He also wore a brown fleece pullover jacket and well-worn hiking boots. He knew he blended into the tree line, as he made his way to a hiking trail which would take him up the hillside. There, he would be well hidden in the trees but could survey the area for miles. He knew this encampment like the back of his hand; it had always been a favorite spot of his.

He saw Bryant stop the car and the couple got out on foot. Holy shit, they were headed in the direction of the mine portal! The questions fired off in his mind in rapid secession: How come they had parked so far back from the mine portal? What made them return?   They weren't looking anywhere else; how- in-the-hell, had they known exactly where to go? He had made sure that there were no transferences or trace evidence or contamination of the crime scene. For a lightening sharp moment, he felt the flash of fear and adrenaline course through his body, shaking his confidence.   Faceless would clear out of the area as soon as they were in the mineshaft. It would do no good to be found in the area and questioned, his mind continued on irrationally.

He had been home for several hours and still had so much restless energy; he felt it would explode from his being. It was times like these he knew what Jill was good for. He had accomplished several jobs around the house but the tension was not dissipating. He was pacing and highly aware of his agitated state, like a caged lion with its prey just outside the bars, tantalizing him.

He continued to mentally examine the investigation and what the fucking morons had surmised to this juncture. What else did they know?   He realized that he was going over the same questions in his mind for the last several hours and yet, he was no closer to having any real answers.   Damn -it-all-to-hell! He would get the answers!

The morning he spent at Horseshoe Bend had allowed him to experience the killings again, "Man, what a high!" However as the day wore on, he felt the old familiar stirring start building again; he needed to strike again soon. But no, he had to be careful, extremely careful. To act, impetuously, would alert the authorities to his presence. No, he needed to remain Faceless!

"Lay low and wait," he told himself repeatedly. The timing is all wrong. He would need to change encampments, start again in another county.   He would start investigating new sites. Yes that would work. The man started to rock back and forth, and stopped suddenly. No, No, No! He couldn't lose track of any more time; no more blackouts. He had to make his plan.

CHAPTER 5

Still no word! Ally had not heard anything about Bree Jamison from Deputy Bryant nor the media. It had been over two weeks since the child's body had been discovered. Deputy Bryant must be keeping this matter quiet.

She looked at the figurine that David had given her as a gift on her birthday last February. The figurine was a little girl holding a small lamb surrounded by a flock of young lambs. She loved the delicate craftsmanship. It had added to her collection of lamb figurines. The little girl in the figurine reminded her of Bree, sweet and innocent. It was still difficult to believe that someone would deliberately harm Bree.

Ally was still having dreams about Bree, but now the little girl seemed so distant and vague. The messages and images were increasingly more difficult to comprehend, adding to the unsettled aura looming over her.   Where was the quietus, her sense of closure? Ally had a bad feeling or an undeveloped premonition that something was unequivocally wrong. But what? She didn't know.   It felt as if some disruption or catastrophe lurked, obscure, but ready to surface at any moment.

Ally awoke from her dream later that evening. In the dream, Ally saw the image of Bree standing in the middle of a forever mirror, her eternally reflected image behind her. Then suddenly, Shilo steps a little half step to the right of Bree, and Amy George steps quickly to the left.   There is another little girl behind Shilo, and yet again, the image of another, indistinct and shadowed outline of a child is seen in the distant reflection behind Amy. A dark presence, emanating a pulsating evil force, hovers over the children and slowly descends until it submerges the children, leaving only a heavy black cloud visible.

Ally awoke abruptly disturbed by this dream, and laid there restlessly until she heard her baby cry. Ally shivered as she got out from under the covers and pulled on her robe. She went to Breanna. Ally changed a wet diaper and sat down with Breanna in the rocking chair, humming to her softly. Ally was unaware how much time had passed and Breanna had fallen back to sleep, long ago. Ally carefully stood and returned Breanna to her crib, covering her with a quilt.

Ally returned to her bedroom, grabbing the notepad and pen from her nightstand. She recorded the date and approximate time of her dream: The sequence of events, her impressions and feelings that the dream had engendered. In another paragraph, she wrote one heading. "Possible meanings:" She stopped and told herself that she would come back to this after a good night's sleep.

Morning cast a filmy light across the ceiling of her room. Ally was already awake but not rested as the alarm clock signaled the start of the day. She was on the edge, distraught, her emotions ready to burst forth.

"Hey Honey, the alarm went off." She nudged David, who was still sleeping soundly. David stretched his back in an arch, bringing his arms tautly behind him. He rolled towards her in the bed. David could tell immediately that something was wrong. He reached up and pulled Ally into his arms, nestling her head against his chest.

"Want to tell me about it?" He asked in a husky morning voice, and Ally burst into tears.

"David, I had another dream, I thought that this was all over; Bree would be at peace. I'm caught in the middle of this nightmare. Nothing is resolved. It's never going to go away. I can't even make any sense of these images anymore. I don't know what to do." She spoke in this disjointed manner, her sobs lessened in volume but continued on steadily.

David initially had a difficult time tracking the onslaught of her conversation, especially since he had just awakened from a deep sleep. However, he quickly tuned into her thoughts. "Hon, you know that initially I had a hard time understanding and accepting your psychic experience.' He stumbled over the word psychic but continued on. "But when you found that second body, I had to admit that you were right all along. You have some sort of connection or base of knowledge here. It may take you some time to decode these messages, but if you relax, it will eventually make sense to you. You're meant to get these messages."

"David, I don't get it, we found the body. I don't know why the dreams haven't ended? Something really bad is going to happen; I just know it!"

"You're probably having this bad feeling because these visions have spooked you that's all, making you feel exposed and vulnerable. These visions, well, it probably means that somehow you haven't completed your work yet," David grudgingly acknowledged.

"David you just don't get it. You know how I really used to like to read suspense thrillers. I could feel the adrenaline and the sense of fear but if it got too much or I became too unsettled, I would just close the book. I didn't even have to finish the book, if I choose not to. I had power and control over my fear. I'm afraid, and I have no power or control over this situation. I feel that I'm at the mercy of something I don't understand, and I don't know where to find the answers. Anyone I talk to about this psychic interlude will think I'm crazy."

"Well Honey, you're definitely not crazy. Ally, you know I had trouble believing in any extrasensory capabilities, even yours, but you convinced me. You helped find two bodies; this proves that whatever these visions are, they have a factual foundation."

David continued, "Remember that dream you had about the fox? When we were at the Animas Mine, I was examining the headframe. A fox literally stopped right in front of me, then headed off towards you. It seemed to be acting strangely, so I started to follow it. That's when I heard you call out for me; you'd seen those bones. I could've swore that fox was leading me to you and that body.

After seeing that fox, I read up on them. Funny thing is, foxes are only native to the Sierra Nevada range in California but are extremely rare; almost endangered, in these mountains. They fall prey to the coyotes. Most of the population of Red Foxes in California were imported here due to the fur trade or for recreational hunting; so you find large numbers of them in the Central Valley. Also, the few Red Foxes in these mountains are usually found at much higher elevations. Foxes are nocturnal, usually coming out at night, and they avoid contact with people. In other words, it was highly unusual that I encountered that fox, and then after you told me about that dream; I believe it was a message."

"So the dream about the fox was relevant;" Ally paused and then continued speaking. "David, I'm terrified; I feel I have one foot planted in this supernatural plane and the other foot planted in everyday reality, and I'm being pulled in both directions. I don't know how to balance out these two worlds. I'm afraid that I'll be absorbed in the supernatural and lose touch with reality. I have you and Breanna, who need all of me in the here and now. I don't want to be so preoccupied with Bree that I ignore Breanna's emotionally needs."

"I think you focus so much on Bree because you haven't completely figured out what she wants. This fixation will pass once you know what Bree needs from you and bring it to a conclusion. I believe this pull will dissipate. I would help you if I could, but I'm at a loss in all of this. But if you need some practical assistance or common sense,' he said jokingly, 'let me know."

He held her tightly, lightly rubbing her back for a long time. He could hear the baby starting to stir. He pushed her away slightly and said, "I'll go and take care of Breanna, you rest."

She felt a lot better after their conversation, much more relieved. She picked up the notepad she used the night before, and then set it down again. She was just too emotional right now; and besides she had a lot of housework to do. Maybe if she read over her notes about her dream last night, a couple of times throughout the day, something would come to her.

It was after one in the afternoon, and Breanna had settled down for her nap. Ally had just finished her tuna on wheat. Her figure was coming back, slowly. She went to the bathroom and viewed herself in the long wardrobe mirror. Her blond hair was over-grown as she pushed back the bangs and examined the rest of her appearance.

She was still wearing her elastic banded blue jeans. Her pre-pregnancy clothes were still a bit too snug with her belly slightly swollen. Prior to the pregnancy, she weighed one thirty-seven. She was still about ten pounds above that weight but was shedding the pounds quickly. Her gray eyes looked weary, and her eyes were still slightly puffy from her crying fit, earlier this morning. She really needed a haircut. Maybe she could go this evening after David returned from work. This was the first time she'd given much thought to her appearance in a very long time.

She did a quick clean—up job around the house. She was just about finished when she spied the notepad on the dresser. She picked it up and read the notes aloud in the silent room. The color slowly ebbed from her face. The hair at the base of her neck was standing straight on end.

"Oh my god, there are two more bodies out there! That's what you were trying to tell me, Bree." The thought struck Ally like a bolt of electricity; she closed her eyes tightly against the invading tears, opening her mouth and swallowing hard. The rage surge through her. "Who is the brute who killed all of those children?" She crumpled to the ground in a massive heap covering her head with her hands and weeping profusely, rolling over onto her side in the fetal position. She wept until all the tears were spent.

Sitting back up cross-legged, she took several deep breaths to steady herself. Additional tears were close at hand. She reached up to the nightstand grabbing a tissue and blowing her nose. Three tissues later, she was more clear-minded.

She uttered a silent prayer for these children and their families. Ally asked that their killer be caught and then brought to justice before he reaped any more damage and destruction. She tried to imagine what kind of monster could hurt those precious, beautiful children. But try as hard as she might, her mind just could not go there.   She just didn't want to understand this kind of evil. It was as if understanding this predator implied the condoning of his actions. Ally needed to contact Deputy Bryant and let him know what was going on.

Breanna awoke a short time later; Ally fed and burped her. She rubbed Breanna's back gently and slowly rocked her child as she sang a lullaby. Ally got up and gathered the carrier seat and placed the diaper bag inside, carrying it and Breanna out to the car. Placing the carrier seat on the ground, she opened the rear door of her 1994 Ford Taurus. She buckled Breanna into her car seat and placed the carrier and diaper bag, and purse into the passenger seat. "Wow, I'm becoming an old pro at this," She told Breanna.

Looking steadily at Breanna, Ally wrestled with "the truth". She'd been distracted and miserable today, a real basket-case. Was her anxiety was being transmitted to Breanna? She certainly hoped not. Ally needed to establish emotional boundaries, and find balance with her otherworldly concerns in order to protect her family. She knew that she was so incredibly blessed to have her daughter, and she wouldn't allow her baby suffer due to these circumstances.

Upon arriving at the Sheriff's office, she placed Breanna into the carrier seat. Breanna was alert and busily inspecting her hand. Ally approached the glass-enclosed interior office asking the clerk if she could speak with Deputy Bryant; she was asked to wait in the lobby. She sat in a brown tweed, metal-framed lobby chair, which was very stiff and uncomfortable. Ally shifted restlessly in the seat, jostling for a comfortable position. She secretly wondered if all government offices were cloned and copied, as if this level of discomfort was institutionalized. "Geez, could they get something a little bit better? If not welcoming, just slightly more comfortable."

As Ally was bidding her time, a woman exited the interior office door of the Sheriff's station and stopped in the waiting room. She was crying profusely; the black mascara encrusted her eyes, forming dark circles in her rubicund face. The woman had dirty blond hair with black roots; the hair was disheveled. She was wearing an ill-fitting tight, black tank-top with a butterfly silk-screened onto it with worn blue jeans. Ally thought her to be in her late twenties, even though she appeared older. She had a perpetual hard and cynical look etched into her facial features. Ally observed the troubled woman, it would be extremely demoralizing to be that emotionally distraught and have to encounter this dehumanizing office.

Ally kept glancing at her, careful not to stare. There was pain deeply etched onto her face. As Ally sized her up, she wondered what the circumstances were that left her so emotionally devastated. Ally looked down at Breanna, who was still alert but very content in her carrier.

"Thank you for finding my momma. She will be okay now," she heard Bree's voice whisper in her ear. Ally's head came up sharply, but the little girl was not present. Ally eyed the blond woman who was now sitting in a chair, attempting to collect herself. The woman's hands covered her mouth and nose in almost a prayer-like gesture; her eyes closed.

"Oh my god, that is Bree's mother." Ally knew absolutely with clear knowledge that she was right. Ally wanted to say something to this woman but was at a loss as to what to say.

Ally said gently to the woman, "Do you need some help, do you want me to call someone?" The woman barely shook her head in the negative, giving Ally a sideways glance. The woman avoided looking at Breanna at all. "Given time, the pain you feel right now will not be so intense," Ally said quietly.

"What the fuck would you know about what I'm feeling?" The woman said harshly, shooting a steely look at her. She started to get up, almost in a fighting stance. Okay, Ally processed quickly, it was essential that she become more assertive about her insights, rather than just backing away. Also, this was also something she could do directly for Bree, talk to and comfort her mother!

"Listen, I have some psychic abilities. I've had several dreams about your little girl, Bree, and I don't know how or why but I can talk to her." Ally drawing strength from Bree, watched as the woman's eyes widen with a fearful look; she covered her mouth in disbelief and astonishment. Crystal slowly sunk back into the chair.

"You know my baby?" Crystal said uncertainly.

"Yes, Bree told me to tell you that she is fine now. She just wants you to be happy and to think of her in happiness. Then, she will be able to continue on her journey." The woman stared at Ally in a bewildered fashion, unclear on how to respond.

"Look, Crystal that is your name, right? My name is Alyssa. I'm strictly on the level. I don't want anything from you but the promise that you'll try to put your life in order for Bree." Ally was amazed; she had no idea where this information was coming from. It just came out as she spoke, as if Bree was directing her words.

"Do you know what happened to her, who hurt her?" Crystal asked gruffly, and then continued somewhat defensively. "Was it someone, we knew?"

Ally noticed she looked ready to fight again. "I don't know yet, I'm still piecing together the information that I've received. It comes in small chunks. Hopefully, it will eventually all fall into place. That is why I'm here to speak to Deputy Bryant."

"Could you tell Bree that I love her?" Crystal said huskily, in a slurred voice. She had started to cry again.

"Oh, she knows that already," Ally reassured. "But she'd like you to kiss Prince for her. That's her dog, isn't it?"

Crystal happily nodded, "Oh, how she loved her dog! I got the dog as a puppy when Bree was four. She would put that pup in her umbrella stroller and wheel him around. It was amazing that the pup never fell or jumped out. He was soon too big for that kind of treatment, but, Bree didn't seem to notice. My baby didn't have a whole lot of friends; I guess that was my fault. She just didn't have what the other kids had, so that's why she put so much stock in that dog."

Ally smiled and then paused. "Bree is happy that you have Papa. But she is still very worried about you. She would like you to enroll in that substance abuse program that you've been looking into."

"My baby, she knew about the drugs?" Crystal looked extremely guilty and uncomfortable.

"Yes," Ally mouthed softly and nodded affirmatively.

"Mrs. Sullivan,' Deputy Bryant opened the door to the lobby. His glance quickly shifting from Crystal Jamison to Alyssa Sullivan. 'You can come this way."

Ally held her hand out to Crystal, "it's nice to meet you, Crystal. Take care of yourself.' Crystal tentatively took hold of Ally's hand and Ally reached with her second hand to clasp Crystal's hand. 'Believe me, everything is going to be all right in the long-run."

Ally let go and reached down for the handle of the baby carrier and pulled the straps of both her purse and the diaper bag more firmly on her shoulder as she walked towards Deputy Bryant and disappeared behind the closed door.

For a long time, Crystal sat staring at the closed door, thinking about what Alyssa Sullivan had told her. She walked to the pay phone a block up the street at the convenience store. She fished through her pockets for change and pulled out the worn piece of paper from her wallet with a number for the rehab on it. Crystal dialed the number. After a couple of rings, the call was answered, "New Beginnings, this is Laura speaking."

"This is Crystal Jamison, I'm on your waiting list, I was checking back to see if you have a space for me. You do? What do I need to bring? I can be there at 5:00, okay, Thanks." She hung up the phone and stared at the receiver. She'd better hurry, she still needed to go home and get her stuff together.

As Ally followed Deputy Bryant back to his office, she felt her anger rising again. Her head was reeling from the emotional roller coaster she had been on today. She felt the faint beginnings of a headache. They were barely in his office as he turned to face her. Ally had adopted an aggressive stance, despite clutching the handle of the baby carrier.

"What is happening on the Bree Jamison case?" She demanded; her tone was accusatory. Deputy Bryant could see the anger seething in her eyes.

"Whoa, wait a minute. Calm down and have a seat. We can talk about this in a civilized manner," he directed.

He reached to take the baby carrier out of her hand and placed the carrier on the desk. Then he gently caressed Breanna's cheek with his index finger. "She sure is a beautiful baby; it looks as if she's grown a bit."

Watching the Deputy with Breanna, Ally softened her demeanor. She had got off to a bad start; she mentally chastised herself. Deputy Bryant didn't owe her any explanations, nor did he deserve her hysterics.

"She has a well-baby check-up due, next week. Can't wait to find out how much she has grown. Sorry, it has been a crazy day and I'm just about drained."

"Can you tell me about what happened and why you're on the warpath? What made you so angry?" he began.

"I had another dream….vision. The dreams are becoming vaguer, much less lucid. But if I am interpreting the meaning correctly, I believe there are at least two more bodies at Horseshoe Bend."

Deputy Bryant's eyes widened. "Hell,' he muttered lowering his head slightly and rubbing his forehead with his thumb and forefinger. "No wonder you're angry. I'll see what I can do about getting at least a few men to scour the area, again."

"Deputy Bryant… Neal, I don't know how much information you can share with me regarding these cases but I am still receiving visions and impressions regarding Bree Jamison. If I knew more about the case or the children involved or anything to help me piece together any additional information, I would like to help. I could fill out some forms or whatever it takes."

He replied without hesitation, "To start, I could have you sign a confidentiality statement about anything that comes up regarding this case or related cases."

He opened a file drawer in the desk, shifting through manila file folders and pulled out a form. Ally knew he must be worried about the confidentiality issue for he had responded so rapidly. She quickly signed the form that explained that she could be fined or receive a jail sentence if she disclosed any personal information regarding the victims or their families or any material information related to the criminal investigation.

As he reached out for her signed form, Neal stated, "You know that law enforcement officials can take information from a variety of sources, and act upon the information given. It really is unethical to divulge any material information to an individual outside of law enforcement. "

"I see." Ally said gravely, she was being politely dismissed.

Neal persisted, "My main concern at this point is that we likely have a sick bastard still on the streets. Therefore, if I don't do everything strictly by the book, it might be revealed during the trial process, allowing this guy to walk on a technicality. However, I know that you may have some crucial information to add to this investigation; it would be crazy not to listen to you."

"As I told you before," Ally answered, "I've never had anything remotely like this happen to me in the past. The information just comes in waves of…. lucidity. Sometimes strong and easily interpreted, and other times...weak and disjointed. It's hard for me to know what information is important or how this information even fits together. I don't know why these visions are filtered through in such a way or why I received these visions in the first place. I don't even know where to go to find the answers. I just know that I have to help!"

"It's not as if I don't want your help or appreciate the assistance you have already given. You know as well as I do that we would not be this far in the investigation without your help. I will just have to find out if there is legal way to bring you into the process. I will look into getting it authorized but no promises. In the meantime, could you hang tight and try not to let this whole situation take control of you?"

Ally responded, "You know, I thought this would be over once the Bree's body was located but somehow it's not. Initially, I was just trying to buy myself some peace of mind for I felt I was being haunted. Now it is something more, Bree is real and I care about what happened to her and the other children. I want to make sure that the predator who did this is caught and never able to hurt another child."

Neal Bryant could read the pain on her face. He wondered if she could maintain some objectivity. "You know if you became involved in the investigation, you would need to have the ability to hold your emotions in check. If you let your emotions control the situation, you can hinder the investigative process. You just may be too close to the situation to be useful."

Neal watched her reactions closely; emotions flickered across her face, but she did not lose her temper. Good.

Ally responded evenly, "I don't know how to explain these visions to you. Sometimes it's like Bree is right there next to me. I know her as a child. I think it would be impossible to not be emotional under the circumstances. Right now, Bree is a very real person to me, but Bree is gone and I cannot bring her back. Possibly I may be able to help stop the killer before he can hurt any other child or their families I have plenty of animosity for this brute but I don't have an unstoppable rage. Is that what you are concerned about?"

Neal responded lightheartedly, "No, I don't see you as a raging lunatic." Then, he continued in a more serious tone, "Within a criminal investigation, there are legal procedures and protocols which must be adhered to, in order to establish who is guilty of the crime and then, successfully prosecute that person. Often when one is too emotionally involved in an investigation, this person will see only what they want to, act in an irrational manner, or behave impulsively, which can seriously compromise the whole legal process. As I told you before, when I catch the guy who hurt those children, I'm going to make sure the charges stick."

"Neal, I'm just hoping that I can give you some information to expedite the process from an inside source; Bree. I would have to defer any investigative matters to you; you're the expert in law enforcement."

Neal seemed satisfied with her response. "You do have some good instincts for law enforcement work. Have you had any formal education?"

"I attended community college for about a year and a half."

"What type of classes did you take?"

"Mostly general education, why?"

"Did you take any social science, criminal justice, any classes like that?"

"Well, let me think, I took a course called, Law and Society. It was a humanities core course. I also, took a course on Constitutional Law and civil liberties. I think that's about it." Ally paused, "Oh yes, I took a short-course on juvenile delinquency."

"I guess that would qualify as some formal education in criminal justice. I have an idea; I'll give you a call later and let you know what comes of it. Okay?"

"Then I'll talk to you later," she said as she stood up and picked up the baby carrier and the diaper bag. "Thanks for listening."

He watched her departure. He called, Karen, in reception. "Karen, remember that kid from explorers that we hired as an intern, last summer. How did we do that? Could you get me the job description and the MOU for that classification? You called it what, a field officer trainee? And also give me any other forms necessary to hire someone under that classification. Thanks."

"Was it pure lunacy to hire Alyssa Sullivan as a Field Officer Trainee?" Neil leaned back in his chair, pondering this unusual situation. Reluctantly, Neil knew he was going to hire Ally. Yet his decision was giving him pause, and he was hoping to hell he wasn't making a huge mistake.

This morning before going to work, Faceless had seen the white crime scene van heading in the direction of Horseshoe Bend again. He had been parked at a rest stop on the state highway near the turnoff to Horseshoe Bend. The man could barely make out the van through his binoculars; but he couldn't move in any closer and risk drawing attention.

It was a given that the fucks had salvaged his discard in the mine! Faceless had seen the Asshole with the Bitch in tow, enter the mine site. Since then, the crime scene dicks had been out there in Horseshoe Bend, daily for over a week. Bryant-the

Asshole had gone directly into the mine! No, there couldn't be any physical evidence linking the two locations or the two discards. How many more of his discards had been found? What had tipped off those fucks in law enforcement to his discards, anyway? The discovery of his discard in the tailings may have been a fluke, but how did they know about the others? And who exactly was the fucking Bitch with Bryant and how was she involved? Faceless only wished he had gotten a better look at her.

He had mentally gone over each step, in each of the killings a hundred times. Faceless had not left any direct evidence. It was impossible, he had been so careful; vigilant, and painstakingly thorough. This rigid tension was his constant companion; the hours and hours of exercise at the gym, did not eliminate its existence. He only knew one thing that would.....!

The next day, Neal called and asked Ally to come by the Sheriff's office. She agreed to meet him in an hour. Ally fed Breanna, burped her, gave her a bath, and dressed her in a fresh outfit. With Breanna, the baby carrier, and diaper bag in tow; Ally headed for the door.

Ally greeted Neal with a smile as he led her towards his office. As she put down Breanna's carrier, Breanna began to fuss. Ally took Breanna out of the carrier and coddled her against her chest. Neal watched with affection as she held the baby. His daughter, Jeannie, was due in three and a half weeks. He could hardly wait to be a grandfather.

Neal looked directly at Ally, again questioning the wisdom of his actions. Neil took a deep breath and said, "You know Ally, I believe you have seen and felt what you have for good reason. I believe you have had a real and unique psychic experience. It has been truly amazing to hear about your abilities. However, with this being said, main-stream law enforcement and the justice system do not give much credit to psychic phenomenon, feelings, visions, or intuition. When I catch this killer, I don't want a defense attorney destroying the case by bashing holes in your credibility, and confronting you regarding the psychic issue. As you have told me yourself, you barely understand what is happening. Try defending your insights to a jury. Since you have been involved in finding two bodies in Horseshoe Bend, I'm sure that you could be called as a witness in the trial unless we luck out with a confession. When these cases eventually go to trial, I don't want the evidence to be clouded or overshadowed by whether or not psychic ability can be supported in court."

Neal continued, "I don't want anyone in the prosecutor's office or especially the defense counsel to know that any psychic episodes were ever discussed between me and you. Here is what I propose in relation to how you became involved in these cases; you are new to the area and interested in the local history. You researched the Horseshoe Bend area and went on an outing to the area. There, you and your husband discover skeletal remains and notified me; law enforcement. You vaguely recalled that another child's body was found murdered within the area. You confirmed your recollection and came back to talk to me as you felt that it was too coincidental that two girls, approximately the same age, were found dead within the area. You wanted to ask me if I found this suspicious. During the conversation, you told me about a deserted mine tunnel in the area. I asked if you would be willing to guide me to its location, you agreed. During our conversations, I found out that you had a background in criminal justice, and at one point were interested in making a career in law enforcement. After we discover another body in the mine, I realized that this investigation was going to take a lot of time for errands and research; time which I simply don't have." Neal looked her straight in the eye, gauging her reaction. "So, I offered you a temporary per diem position as a 'Field Officer Trainee' under my direct supervision to help me with evidence collection and research."

"What? Are you offering me a job?" She stared dumbfounded at him for a moment before responding to his affirmative nod. "I guess that sounds like a feasible story. I do want to help. What would I have to do?"

"For this position, you would sign a MOU, a memorandum of understanding that you would only work under the direct supervision of a senior deputy, which is me. Also, you cannot investigate any aspect of this case independently without prior permission from your direct supervisor. All aspects of the case are strictly confidential. You do not discuss the details of the investigation with anyone outside the department. You get fingerprinted and go through a basic background clearance and substance abuse testing. Finally, on Saturday, you take a basic 8-hour course at Piute Community College on evidence collection; search and seizure; and arrest procedures, so you can be sworn in as a peace officer. It is the course often given to Juvenile Probation Officers, Social Workers, Constables, bail-bondsman and the like. Are you game for this?"

"It sounds interesting but I don't know how I can manage this. I have Breanna to care for. It's been difficult for me already, trying to balance my psychic experiences with the responsibilities of motherhood, taking care of an infant."

"The fingerprinting and substance abuse test we can do here in the office within minutes. I hope your husband would be willing to care for Breanna while you take the course at the college, it is offered on Saturday. Other than that, this position was set up with students in mind; as an internship. The hours are flexible, and I can work with you around your schedule. A lot of the footwork and research can be done with your baby along. Also, you have the Internet at home, don't you?"

She nodded. "I guess it could work."

"Listen, if it doesn't work, you quit. This position is set-up on a temporary schedule of six-month period. If you'd like, we could do the preliminary business such as fingerprints and the drug test. Then, you could discuss this with your husband and get back to me." Ally nodded relieved.

Ally waited for David to arrive home from work. She heard the door open and David came into the living room. Forgetting

97

the normal greetings, David asked, "So what happened during your meeting with Deputy Bryant?"

"He offered me a job," said Ally. She laughed at the look on his face. She recounted her conversation with Deputy Bryant.

"It makes sense,' David said. "I certainly understand his reasoning. A job helps engender accountability and responsibility to the Department. I think you should accept his offer."

"You are okay with this?" she began hesitantly.

"Of course. I think this will be good for you. So on Saturday, are you going to leave me a detailed list of instructions for Breanna?" he said, half-jokingly.

"You'll manage beautifully."

CHAPTER 6

On October 17, 1998, it was already warm, bordering on a hot, Indian summer morning; when Ally arrived at Piute Community College. Unable to locate her class, she stopped to ask for directions. She arrived at her class, slightly out of breath with only five minutes to spare.

A retired police sergeant, John Kilpatrick, was teaching the class. John Kilpatrick had a mix of red and grey hair, balding on top. He had two-day growth of a beard on his heavy face, and he was about sixty pounds overweight. John had an easygoing manner, which made the instruction material entertaining, as he filtered in stories from his law enforcement career into the curriculum. He used his experience to illustrate points and provide humorous breaks. It certainly shed light onto the material being presented.

The course was information-heavy coming with its own one inch manual. The class could have been easily extended into three days. The first half day session consisted of general classroom lecture on various issues such as ethics, professionalism, general law including probable cause, constitutional rights, and laws of evidence. The second part of the curriculum went through investigations, evidence collection, documentation, and report writing. The final segment was a physical application of arrest, restraining holds and takedown procedures.

After the physical segment, Ally realized just how out of shape she was. She also didn't think she would remember any of these holds or takedown procedures a month from now. At the end of the course, she received a certificate of training with a large gold star bestowing on her the title of sworn peace officer. She was on brain-overload with all the new information but thoroughly enjoyed the class.

Leaving the building, she took a deep breath of fresh air, which dispelled the stuffiness of the old gym. The evening breeze cooled her heated flesh. She was excited to go home and tell David all about her class. And of course, Ally could not wait to get home to Breanna; give the baby her bath and evening feeding. Ally thought emotionally that this was the longest period of time that she had been away from Breanna since her birth.

Faceless needed a plan of action, needed to keep moving forward. He would check out the Sullivan house again, maybe he'd get lucky. It couldn't hurt! He'd never seen the Bitch; the name was Alyssa, according to the DMV. He had also checked the property title for the residence, which was in the name of David Lawrence and Alyssa Joan Sullivan.

It had taken several hours before he saw a woman of medium height with blond hair, leaving the residence. Faceless couldn't see the face from this angle, as she bent down to get into a Ford Taurus. Mmm, nice ass! Wait! Is this the same bitch that was with that asshole-Bryant at the mine? Faceless couldn't be sure. No fuckin way! Why would this Bitch be present at crime scene, weeks later? His imagination was getting the best of him.

Thinking of the mine whet his appetite. "Man, to kill again," his mind returning to his discard in the mine. Grinning excitedly as he visualized the last extinguishing breath before the extermination, tingling. Wait- hold your fire, regroup and focus on the investigation! The authorities were too close right now; their proximity, alarming. As intolerable as it was, he would continue to wait and solicitously plan. He had his new site mapped out, along with a few marks in mind for his next coup. He would opt for one and then dispense with it under their fucking noses.

Ally met with Deputy Bryant on Monday. Neal went over and then had her sign some additional forms, outlining the dos and don'ts of working for the county. Her signature along with the date: October 19, 1998, inferred that she understood and abide by the rules set forth by the department. Neal gave her copies of these rules and guidelines in a folder, which he placed in the bottom of a file box for her.

Neal told her that he'd made some copies of the files involving Shilo Wilson, Amy George, and Bree Jamison for her to familiarize herself with the cases. He placed these three files on top of the folder within the box. Her other assignment for the week was to contact the local chapter of the National Center of Missing Children. Neal wanted records for all missing preteen children within a hundred-mile radius, and he needed her to pick up this information. He told her to keep track of the hours she worked and her mileage for reimbursement, giving her a several blank expense forms and time sheets, in a folder, and placing it on top of the growing pile within the file box.

"Who should I speak with at the Center for Missing and Exploited Children?" Ally inquired, as she wrote notes for herself.

"Eric Morrison; he is a volunteer, who tracks the regional records. I'll give you his message number, and you can arrange to meet him to get the information." Neal said opening his Rolodex and jotting down the name and corresponding number on a yellow sticky note.

"Okay," Ally said taking the contact information and sticking it to her notebook.

"You'll like Morrison. For such a young guy, he's very committed. I call him the 'Boy Scout' because he's so civic minded." Neal said with a chuckle. "We'll meet again on Friday morning at 9 am. Is that time okay?"

"Yes, that's fine," Ally said, closing her notebook and placing it in her purse.

"I'll take you by the supply cabinet to get some office supplies, on our way out. Then I'll take this box out to your car for you." Neal offered, as Ally pulled the straps of her purse and diaper bag over her shoulder and picked up the baby carrier with Breanna inside.

"Thanks," Ally said, as Neal held the door open for her.

Later in the evening Ally put Breanna to bed. David had gone to bed early. She picked up the copies of the law enforcement files on the three girls; she started chronologically with Shilo Wilson. Ally scanned through the crime scene investigation: evidence list, witness statements, the police report, and the foreboding photos.

Then, she started to read the file more thoroughly and take notes. The first entry: On September 27, 1989 at 16:24 hours, Dispatcher Annette Armstrong received a call from Tamara Lee. Ms. Lee reported that her daughter, Shilo Wilson (Date of Birth: October 2, 1982) failed to return home from school. Officer Harold Collins made the initial contact with the mother; Ms. Lee, who reported that she last saw her daughter, Shilo Wilson at 08:05 hours when the child left the house for school. Ms. Lee called the school when Shilo did not return home from school that day. The mother was told that Shilo was marked absent and was never at school. The school, Parkdale Elementary is located two blocks from Victim-Wilson residence at 3465 Parkdale Lane in Sequoia.

Ally cringed, she couldn't imagine what thoughts raced through Tammy Lee's mind when she found out that her child never arrived at school. The horrific images, the mother's mind must have conjured up. Ally could feel her own desperation rising, so many terrible things could happen. Would she ever feel comfortable letting Breanna walk to school or to a friend's house? Ally fiercely pushed aside these troubling thoughts and forged ahead.

Several Officers canvassed the neighborhood to see if the child had been sighted. This activity was reflected by numerous entries with collateral contacts such as: neighbors, school personnel, and then, follow-up with the mother. Each time-dated contact was concisely but thoroughly documented.

Ally avoided looking at the large glossy photos in the file; not feeling emotionally equipped to look at those yet. Instead, she decided to read the official accounts of Shilo Wilson first as detailed within the police report. Then, Ally read various witness statements and other school/agency reports, and Shilo's story emerged. Shilo had lived in the nearby town of Sequoia where she came from a single parent family. Her mother, Tammy Lee, had a mental health condition: Schizoaffective Disorder. Tammy Lee had been reported to the authorities on many occasions for her mistreatment of Shilo. From neighbors' and teachers' reports, Tammy Lee appeared to adopt a very rigid and over-bearing attitude towards her daughter.

What is Schizoaffective Disorder? Ally put a yellow, adhesive tab to mark the section of the file, she was reading. She grabbed her notebook along with her ballpoint pen, and headed to her computer. Ally quickly researched and read about Schizoaffective Disorder, summarizing her findings within her notes: Schizoaffective Disorder is a mental health condition in which an individual experiences a mixture of schizophrenic symptoms such as: unusual behaviors, delusions, and hallucinations along with severe mood swings. It is characterized by rapid or racing thoughts, increased activity levels, agitation, and often self-destructive behaviors. Ally ruminated and wrote the following question in her notes: How would Tammy Lee have reacted when her daughter disappeared, given her mental health condition? Ally picked up her notebook and pen, returning to Shilo's file.

Shilo was a very imaginative and enthusiastic child; it was difficult-to-impossible to confine or contain her spirit. Shilo was removed from her mother's care due to physical abuse for approximately seven months, one year prior to her murder. According to the social worker involved, Tammy Lee successfully completed her court ordered services, and Shilo was returned to her care. The Social Worker monitored Shilo within the home for many months with no evident problems. The case was dismissed.

A month after this case was dismissed, Shilo disappeared. Tammy reported to Officer Collins that Shilo had left for school in the morning, but her daughter never returned home from school. Ms. Lee contradicted her verbal account within her written statement; stating she had walked Shilo to school at 8:05 am and her daughter never returned home from school, that afternoon. The classroom teacher, however, reported that Shilo never arrived at school. When the body was found in the late afternoon on October 16 at Horseshoe Bend, Shilo had been dressed in pajamas. She had been strangled with a bathrobe belt.

Earlier, on October 16th, the duty sergeant received a telephone call from a neighbor of Tammy Lee. This neighbor, Gloria Mosby, reported that an ex-boyfriend of Tammy Lee came to talk to Ms. Lee, concerned that Ms. Lee must have knowledge of Shilo's whereabouts. Ms. Lee became extremely agitated, and physically assaulted the man. Ms. Mosby reported that Tammy Lee was out of her mind. Ms. Lee started ranting and saying illogical and "crazy" things such as the CIA took Shilo because the voices in the game, told them to do it. The young man left in a hurry, seemingly scared away. Then Ms. Lee tore off in her car a few minutes after the young man left. It appeared as if she was going after him. This had all happened approximately fifteen minutes before the call. Ms. Mosby was unable to provide the name of the young man. The woman had agreed to come into the station and give a written statement.

This new information punched holes in Tammy Lee's account of events leading to her daughter's disappearance. Throughout the day on October 17, 1989, several Sequoia police officers tried to contact Tammy Lee to no avail. So far, they had not been able to identify the young man who had contacted Ms. Lee on October 16. Finally, on the morning of October 18th, Tammy Lee was brought into the station for further questioning.

During the interrogation, Tammy Lee had what they called a "psychotic break". She was claiming that the police, with the aid of the CIA, had kidnapped her daughter. Tammy knew that they were trying to keep her child from her, for the voices from the Sego game told her that this was true. Tammy Lee had asserted that she had seen their helicopters. She demanded that they return her daughter immediately. The Detective handling the case had called County Mental Health to ask for help in hospitalizing Tammy Lee in a psychiatric facility.

By the time that the mental health worker arrived, Ms. Lee had de-escalated and was no longer in acute crisis. She was not a danger to herself or others, so the worker refused to 5150 her. The mental health worker stated that this would violate her civil liberties by unlawfully detaining or incarcerating Tammy against her will. Ally quickly recalled from her peace officer training course that 5150- was the California code which allowed a mental health worker to involuntarily place a mentally-unstable person (who was a risk to themselves or others) in a psychiatric hospital for observation. Detective Ryan had wanted Ms. Lee detained in a psychiatric facility after her bizarre outburst during their police interview. However lacking that option, he detained Tammy Lee on a 72-hour criminal hold, not having enough evidence to make an arrest.

Detective Ryan had gone to the courthouse to inform the Judge that their office had detained Tammy Lee on 72-hour hold. They had only circumstantial evidence to hold her as a suspect in the death of her daughter. Currently, the Detective had the inaccurate and/or contradictory statements of the mother about the disappearance of Shilo Wilson and the troubling "incident" accounting of the neighbor. There was also Detective Ryan's report of the bizarre scene in the interview room, which indicated that Ms. Lee was emotionally unstable and volatile, but no physical evidence to link her to the crime.

Detective Ryan garnered a search warrant for Tammy Lee's home and vehicle. He was hoping to find traces of dirt or blood, or any solid evidence to connect Tammy Lee to the death of Shilo Wilson. The search warrant did not turn up any evidence. Detective Ryan was forced to release the hold on Ms. Lee. He called to have her released from her jail-cell on October 21, but Tammy Lee was found dead. She had hung herself with her bed sheets.

Officially, the investigation into Shilo Wilson's death remained unsolved. Unofficially, the Police Department felt that Tammy Lee was responsible for the death of her daughter. The matter was not further investigated.   Ally winced, she couldn't believe that Tammy Lee was responsible for Shilo's death, but it was obvious why the investigators had assumed her guilty given her mental health status and her past CPS history. Tammy Lee - the poor, poor woman! This tragedy must have sent Tammy over the edge.

Ally grieved, as she looked through the 8.5' by 11' inch color glossy photos of the crime scene and pictures of the dead girl. She compared the missing person photo (which looked like it came from her last set of school pictures) with the crime scene images. Shilo looked like a vivacious child who was full of life. That spark, that vitality, was gone in the death photos. It was almost like looking at a completely different child. Then Ally noticed something within the homicide photos and took a closer look. This examination revealed that the bunnies on Shilo's pajamas matched the one in the shed that she had noticed on her initial return trip up to Horseshoe Bend. The pom-pom bunny had come from Shilo's pajama top.

The police had found Shilo's body in the large meadow. Ally noted that this was approximately 300 yards below the mining shed. The police had figured that Shilo's body had been dumped in the meadow, deposited from a stopped car. The crime scene had not extended to the mine property. Ally struggled to remember the term they used in her class to differentiate the two locations in an investigation. Was it the death scene and the crime scene? The death scene referred to the location where the person was killed. The crime scene is where the body is found. In many cases, they are one and the same. Ally was positive that Shilo was killed in that mining shed.

She would call Neal first thing in the morning. Ally's mind was mush but as exhausted as she was, she did not think she would be able to sleep. Maybe if she laid down here on the couch and closed her eyes, she would feel better. Ally surprised herself by falling into a deep, dreamless sleep. She awoke the next morning by David gently shaking her shoulder.

Upon waking, Ally was disoriented to time and place, setting a flat palm onto the couch where she laid. Then, she jerked up with a sudden start, "Breanna!"

"She's fine, I just checked on her," replied David.

"She didn't wake up for her 3 o'clock feeding."

"Hey, don't complain Ally. Maybe she's growing out of the early morning feeding stage."

"I'll go look in on her in a minute. Hey, I may have discovered something important in one of the files; I'm going to call Neal when the office opens. I'll let you know how it turns out."

David looked at her quizzically. "You like this investigation stuff, don't you?"

"Well, only some aspects, like discovering clues and such. I don't know if I could handle the emotional stuff on a day-to day basis." Ally seemed distracted, lost in thought.

David said, "I'm going in to take a shower."

Ally got up to go check on Breanna. The baby had never slept this long. Ally was really getting concerned when Breanna started to stir. "Hi Sweetheart," Ally said, picking up her daughter and holding her close to her chest.

At 8:30 am, Ally called Neal Bryant about her discovery. They exchanged a few pleasantries and then, Ally dived straight to the point. "Neal, the pom-pom bunnies on Shilo Wilson's pajama top in the homicide photos match the bunny I found in the mining shed. I think that Shilo was most likely killed in the work shed at Horseshoe Bend, and her remains were moved to the meadow. Shilo's body was not dumped at the crime scene by the killer in transit as the police thought."

"I will have this investigated..." Deputy Bryant started, but Ally interrupted him.

"The killer took elaborate care to hide the bodies of Bree Jamison, Amy George, and any other bodies that may still be out there. In Shilo's case, the killer did not take the time to hide the body. The killer displayed the body out in the open, where it would likely be found. Why?"

107

"If we hypothetically assume the killer of Shilo Wilson and the killer of the two other girls, Amy George and Bree Jamison, is one and the same; then we have to think in terms of the killer's state of mind when Shilo Wilson's disappearance was being investigated. In 1989, I was working in Siskiyou County, but I remember that the media coverage at the time of Shilo Wilson's disappearance was pretty extensive. The television stations were repeatedly broadcasting Shilo's picture. Volunteers were searching all the remote areas within this county. There was a law enforcement alert sent across the country."

Neal continued talking, almost as if he were speaking to himself and organizing his thoughts. "The killer was likely spooked. But then, why not leave Shilo Wilson's body enclosed within the shed, or even perhaps find a more hidden spot to place the body? The killer risked exposure of being out in the open with the body by moving the child's body to a much more visible location: The killer must have wanted her body to be discovered. Why did the killer intend for this victim to be found but not any of the others? ...I can't give you an absolute answer, but I can pose several theories. Maybe the killer was anxious and made a mistake. He could have started out in an attempt to hide the body and then lost his nerve. This theory doesn't seem plausible because he would have hidden the body at the time of the attack. The body was placed at the crime scene much later. The crime scene technicians made the findings that the child had been deceased for some time, a matter of weeks, before being placed in the meadow. The technicians also speculated that the body had been kept cold to prevent the normal rate of decay. In Shilo Wilson's death photos, she is completely identifiable and remarkably well-preserved."

Neal continued, " Another possibility could be that this particular murder had personal significance to the killer. He may have known the family or killed this child out of revenge or something like that. He may have wanted to send a message to the family by openly displaying the body. Yet another, possible theory is that the delay of discovery of this body could have cast some suspicion onto this killer. It was important for the

108

investigation to be finalized quickly, with suspicion cast elsewhere. I will officially request that the Shilo Wilson case be reopened, and have the key individuals re-interviewed. It may lead nowhere since the killing took place almost ten years ago. Hey, by the way, good job! You've got a good head for this type of work. I had forgotten about the pom-pom bunny. Oh, by the way Ally, I've referred to this killer as a male, probably just a subconscious bias. The killer could be a female. Female serial killers do exist, but statistically the chances are significantly lower."

"Neal," Ally said, "I saw that shed before in a dream. Bree was inside wrapped in the same rug that we found with her remains at the mine. Perhaps the shed has been used for the murders, and later, the killer deposits the bodies elsewhere within the mining property."

"Good call. The killer definitely uses that mining property as a home base, so likely we are looking for a local chap, most likely someone who lives within this county. I'll call for a team of crime scene technicians from Acacia to search that shed from top to bottom, but chances are that any tangible evidence has already deteriorated or been eradicated," he replied.

"I'll see you on Friday, unless something materializes in the meantime," Ally concluded. She hung up the receiver and stared at it for a long period of time, as if some information was going to materialize out of the air and present itself to her. She could only wish.

This work and her entire interaction with Neal and the Sheriff's Office was weighing heavy on Ally. She felt so ill-equipped, out of her depth, and overwhelmed with tension over the enormity of these circumstances. Without really thinking about it, she reached for the file on Amy George and started thumbing through it.

Faceless had scoured all the area newspapers searching for any reference to Horseshoe Bend, the Animas mine or the discovery of the remains within its pages. The newspaper remained where he left it, spewed across the sofa. Where was the god-dammed news coverage! Earlier, he had foolishly started to drive out to Horseshoe Bend but quickly came to his senses. He couldn't believe he'd come close to being that fucking stupid.

The man started pacing back and forth, as he slammed his fist into his hand, scrambling through facts and possible implications. Faceless had seen the fuckers enter the mine! He had seen the crime scene vans in route to Horseshoe Bend for weeks now. Yes, they must have found that discard. Now certainly they are searching for a name to go with the bones, so the fuckers would appear to have their shit together before letting the media know of this dirty little secret.

He grabbed at the news pages on the sofa, wadding up the newspaper into a giant ball and jammed it forcefully into the wastebasket. Was the fucking sheriff office just scouring the area because they tripped over the first body, and figured there could be others? Or did they know about the others? If the second scenario was correct, how had they discovered his trail? How much did they know about him already?

Obviously, Bryant-the Fuck was not onto him, or the cops would have been knocking at his door, hoping for a slip-up or better yet, a confession. Maybe they believed the lack of media attention would bait the killer, drawing him out. They were messing with him, in hopes that he would be stupid enough to put his head on their chopping block. If he got stupid now, he'd be fucked.

He swiped the glass from the table swigging the water as a drop descended from the corner of his mouth and fell unheeded down his chin. He needed the answers now! Maybe he could get the press to do this job? Yes, if I contact the news with a letter or anonymous report, reporter might delve into where the investigation was heading. How would he do this without leaving a paper trail that could lead the Fuckers, right back to his door?

He needed to think; he grabbed his gym bag and headed to the door. As he turned out the lights, he noticed the empty glass on the table. Oh well, he would leave it just this once. As he started his engine, his mind was still obsessing about the empty glass: should he go back and wash it? He decided he would not be able to work out unencumbered if he let the glass go. He went back to his apartment, washing the glass and meticulously drying it. As he reached up to place the glass in the cupboard, he dropped it with a thunderous crash, sending shards of glass into the far reaches of the room.

"Oh fuck," he screamed into the empty apartment as he proceeded with the cleanup. After putting the broom and dustpan away, he headed towards the door. To his amazement, he had left it standing fully ajar. Faceless glared at the open entryway while he exited, closing the door forcefully behind him.

Ally read the file of Amy George in the evening. Skimming through the witness statements and official reports given, a sad, sordid story emerged. Amy George was born July 10, 1988; she had been missing since June 3, 1995. In February 1995, the authorities wanted the mother, Deborah George, for several active warrants related to manufacture and sale of illicit substances and burglary charges; both were felonies.

While Deborah George was trying to evade police, she left her daughter in the care of an acquaintance, Maryann Griggs. Amy went to school with Ms. Griggs' daughter, Monique. Debbie gave Ms. Griggs' a statement on lined paper giving her the authority to enter the child into school and to give medical consent in the case of an emergency.

For Heaven's sake, Ally thought, Amy was left in the care of a stranger. Where was the father of this girl? Where were the grandparents or extended family? There seemed to be a lack of family involvement in both Shilo and Brees' cases too. Ally attempted to curb her exasperation as she continued to study the file.

After a couple of months, Ms. Griggs started to get uneasy about the circumstances, since she had not received any contact from Debbie George whatsoever, since early April. She had no way to contact anyone on behalf of Amy. On May 23rd, she filed legal papers in the local courthouse to obtain non-relative guardianship status of Amy George, and to make Amy's stay in her home, official. The court informed her that she needed to notify the mother of the pending hearing for this guardianship petition, but she had no contact information. Ms. Griggs was told she had to file additional legal paperwork in order to receive an emergency "ex-parte" hearing. This hearing would allow her to explain to the judge why she could not notify the mother or father regarding any pending guardianship proceedings.

According to Ms. Griggs, Amy went to the schoolyard to ride her bike. Monique was visiting her father for the weekend, per the custody agreement. Amy did not come back from her bike ride. Ms. Griggs went to the schoolyard to look for her, but Amy was nowhere to be found.

When Ms. Griggs got back to the house, she found a very brief note on lined paper with a hundred-dollar bill, thanking her for caring for Amy. She hadn't received the temporary guardianship order yet; her ex-parte hearing was scheduled for the following Tuesday. Ms. Griggs believed that Deborah George must have caught wind that she was seeking guardianship and had taken off with Amy.

Ms. Griggs notified the police regarding her concern over Amy George's welfare. However, Ms. Griggs was told that she had no legal standing, since she did not have legal guardianship or even temporary guardianship of the child. Ms. Griggs had called the emergency hotline for Child Protective Services to make a report. She was told by the CPS Intake Worker that Deborah George had left Amy with adequate supervision under her care. Ms. George had even been compensated for Amy's care. There were no allegations of abuse that they could investigate. Ms. Griggs had given the note with the one hundred-dollar bill to Deputy Neal Bryant; it had remained untouched all these years.

The mother, Deborah George, had been shot in a "drug-deal gone bad" situation, along with four other individuals in the middle of April 1995. At the time, she had a false identification on her person.   The law enforcement agency in the state of Nevada ran her fingerprints and matched them with Deborah George from California. Her prints were on record from a previous arrest and conviction; she had spent a year in a California state prison on a prior occasion.

The police detective, Dayton Marks, could not locate any next-of-kin for Deborah George. He knew that she had a sister, Natalie Staples, from her parole contact information in 1987, but Ms. Staples had relocated several times since and they were unable to locate her. The Detective called the missing persons' division in California; no one had listed Deborah George as missing. Detective Marks then published alerts in their website and regional newspapers for any next of kin of Deborah George to contact their Police Department, but no one responded, and the body was left unclaimed.

Ally felt sick, as she realized that the Nevada state authorities did not know that Deborah George had a child, or that this child was missing.   No one, except the killer, knew that Amy was gone until the child's body was discovered in August 1998, three years after her death.   It was unbelievable that Amy George was ever identified, since no one knew that she was even missing. The local school district within Calaveras County along with several school districts from surrounding counties had initiated a safe child program through a federal grant. The local police would fingerprint and photograph all incoming Kindergartners and keep this information in a local database. The parents of these children could sign a waiver if they did not want their child to participate in this program. Amy George had fingerprints and photo within this database.

When Amy's skeletal remains were discovered, Deputy Bryant had little physical information to pursue. The body and the clothes that the child had been wearing had long since deteriorated, but additional evidence was found in the tailings pile. The evidence was a doll in a clear plastic backpack bordered with pink seams.   The exterior of the backpack was very weathered from exposure to environmental conditions.

Deputy Bryant had requested that the doll be fingerprinted, since there was enough humidity within the backpack to prevent any fingerprints from drying out. This hunch paid off. Four distinct fingerprints from both the left and right hands were found on the undersides of the doll's arms.

The thumbs of both hands, Ally surmised, would have been placed on top of the doll's dress; therefore, the prints were not detectable. Ally visualized the little girl swinging her doll in the air to look up at its face; she shuddered at this mental image while choking back tears. Ally rubbed her eyes, demanding that she get a grip, and continued reading.

Deputy Bryant ran these prints against the safe-child database and received a match. Deputy Bryant was able to interview the Principal and teachers of Lakeshore Elementary to discern what had happened. Deputy Bryant had interviewed Maryann Griggs. Ms. Griggs remembered that Deborah George had mentioned that she had a sister, Natalie Staples, whose husband was in the Air Force. He had just been stationed overseas when Deborah George had placed Amy in her care.

According to Ms. Griggs, "Amy was such an endearing child; quiet and introverted. Always anxious to please.' Amy had taken a protective attitude towards her own daughter, Monique, when Monique was trying to come to terms with the divorce of her parents. 'The two of them were just vulnerable little babies seeking security from each other. "

Deputy Bryant was able to locate Natalie Staples, through the Air Force Family Services Division, and to inform Ms. Staples of what had transpired with her sister, and her niece. According to Ms. Staple's testimony, she had a falling out with her sister, Deborah George, over her continued drug involvement in 1994. Ms. George had told her sister to butt out of her life and quit contacting her.

Natalie Staples had tried to encourage her sister to leave Amy in her care. This made Debbie even angrier and her sister severed all communication with her. When Ms. Staples came back to the states in January 1998, she tried to find her sister but had no success.

Until Natalie Staples received the telephone call from Deputy Bryant, she had no clue of what had happened to Debbie and her niece. She had been devastated to learn that no one even searched for Amy. Ms. Staples told Deputy Bryant that she blamed herself. "I should have kept better tabs on Amy knowing how Debbie lived her life. There was no other family out there. I was just so fed up with my sister that I felt I should leave well enough alone."

Why in the world would that woman leave her niece in such a dire situation? The Aunt knew that precious baby was at risk. Why didn't she persevere for Amy's sake? Ally dejectedly looked through the big glossy photos of the crime scene viewing the skeletal remains, mostly hidden by the hundreds of rocks. The excavation of the site yielded a larger view of the skeleton. There was a close-up picture of the weathered plastic backpack with the doll obliterated, hidden from view by the dirt and mud which encrusted the backpack. In subsequent photos, the doll was pictured in a flowered dress, curly brown hair and eyes, remarkably well-preserved in relation to what was left of Amy's body.

The picture of Amy George showed a slight child with thick brown hair and wide green eyes. A hesitant half smile was displayed for the camera. Ms. Griggs gave Deputy Bryant the school photo for the media release. From their statements, it sadly occurred to Ally that both women, Maryann Griggs and Natalie Staples, were suffering grief, loss, and guilt. They were trying to do their best to pull together the pieces of the past.

Ally picked up Bree Jamison's folder, weighing it in her hands. She wanted to continue, but knew that reading Bree's file was going to be emotionally exhausting. She wouldn't be able to stop reading it, and it was already 11pm. She would review this file when she was fresh.

She went through the house, making sure all the windows and doors were locked and secure, and then turned out the lights after making a quick check on Breanna. She pulled the comforter up around her daughter and sat down in the rocking chair staring

115

blankly into space. She sat there for about 30 minutes, devoid of thought, before returning to her room and climbing in bed.

She was tormented by vague dreams, which had no depth or form, just a mirage of shadows. The next morning, she felt as if she had never really obtained a deep sleep cycle. Ally wondered if she would continue to feel out of sorts all day. Ally was grateful to have a day at home, but wished she was more clear-headed because she had a lot of information to process.

As the morning progressed, Ally put in a telephone call and then paged Eric Morrison from the local missing person center. Ally was so involved with the files that she had almost forgotten to place this phone call; it was already Wednesday and her next meeting with Neil was scheduled for Friday morning. Mr. Morrison called back twenty minutes later.

"Hi Mr. Morrison, my name is Ally; Deputy Neal Bryant asked me to give you a call. He would like your assistance in obtaining all records of missing children between ages four and twelve years of age within a hundred -mile radius of Calaveras County."

"Ally, I would be delighted to help, but currently I'm at work. I volunteer for the center, and only spend about 10 hours per month there, updating their computer databases. I should be finished up around here at three, and I'll see what I can find."

"Thank you. Deputy Bryant would appreciate this information as soon as you can give it to him. If you'd like, I can come down there and pick it up. I'll be seeing Deputy Bryant on Friday." Ally felt her head start to pound; she was feeling a little queasy. She had felt "off" this morning when she awoke.

"Yes, that would help save some time," Mr. Morrison replied. "The center doesn't actually have an office. I work out of the Sheriff Substation; this is a small office located at 2415 Jackson Place, suite 2b, just past King's Grocery. I'll meet you there at 5pm."

Ally was grateful to get off the phone. The last part of that conversation came at her from a distance, through the ringing in her ears. She was suddenly feeling very ill. She hoped she didn't have the flu, although she hadn't heard of any bad strains going around. She reclined on the sofa, trying to regain her composure, rubbing her aching head.   For Pete's sake, I cannot afford to get sick right now. Maybe, it's just stress; her emotions had been over-taxed, reviewing those files. After about an hour of rest, Ally definitely felt better. Breanna had been an angel this morning, resting contently in her swing.

CHAPTER 7

David was late! He usually arrived home in the mid-afternoon since he went into work early, around four or five in the morning. This schedule allowed him to meet with major vendors to discuss shipments and to complete paperwork before the store got busy. Ally met him at the door at 4:30. She quickly explained her need to pick up some information for Deputy Bryant; telling David that she would be home in roughly forty minutes. Ally asked David to look after Breanna, who was gurgling merrily in her swing.

Ally entered the Sheriff's substation, calling out, "Hello Mr. Morrison?"

"Right here," he said, pushing back from the computer desk. "You can call me, Eric." He moved forward to shake her hand.

"I'm Ally," Immediately, Ally could see why Neal had nicknamed Eric Morrison, "the Boy Scout." He had a tall, lean frame with wavy dark-gold hair and soulful, earnest brown eyes. He looked like a young boy who had not quite caught up to the size of his frame. He gave her a warm, toothy smile as he handed her a manila envelope full of papers.

"Thank you," Ally said taking the envelope. She was still taking in his appearance; he was so impeccably dressed and well-groomed. Oh my, with those boyish good looks, he could be a supermodel!

"I hope this helps Deputy Bryant. Let me know if I can be of further assistance," Eric said in a well-modulated voice. And so charming too, Ally mused.

"Well thanks, I really appreciate you dropping everything to get this information so quickly." Ally responded promptly, feeling flush. She was starting to feel queasy again, trying to overcome the ringing in her ears.

118

"Could you tell me what Deputy Bryant wants this information for?'" He asked her in a kind manner, giving her a serious, candid look. "I try to keep my information current, so we can accurately track the missing person records. Hopefully, it helps us in avoiding false leads."

"I'm just running an errand for Deputy Bryant. You should speak to him about the particulars," Ally hastily replied. She was preoccupied with her physical malady as she attempted to quell her riotous stomach.

"I've never met you before Ally, and I thought I'd met everyone at the office. Have you been with the Sheriff's Office for a long time?"

"I'm doing a limited internship. Sorry, I have to run. Thanks again for the help," she said quickly, anxious to get back home before she became incapacitated. Ally climbed into the car, waiting feverishly for her stomach to settle down before driving away.

Once she'd arrived home, Ally told David that she felt the flu coming on, and wanted to ward off the attack. She went to bed early, leaving David to care for Breanna. Ally fell into a restless sleep and then, the nightmares began. In her dream, Ally was alone on a path surrounded by an oily blackness; the darkness was so intense that it seemed to take a physical form. She couldn't see where she was heading or differentiate her direction, as she trudged through the heavy surroundings. All of a sudden, Ally discerned that she wasn't alone after all. She couldn't make out any distinctive shape or form, but felt an evil presence just outside of her limited field of vision. Was she being stalked by an obscure shadow?

She quickened her pace to outdistance this pursuing phantom but to no avail. She tried to switch directions, using evasive tactics to elude this unseen shade, but the predator just kept gaining on her. Suddenly, an ominous, evil force was surrounding, and then shrouding her. She shrank into a fetal position, trembling in fearful apprehension, as this malevolent energy sheathed her cowering form, attempting to overwhelm her soul. ...A small hand took a hold of her own. Bree was tugging at her hand, urging her in their unspoken communication to hurry and get away. Ally looked and now could see clearly into Bree's worried eyes and silently followed her lead. The two were running, breaking free from this invisible presence.

"Bree, what are we running from?" Ally bellowed, but Bree was gone; she disappeared as fast as she materialized.

Ally woke abruptly. Her first thought was of escape -to get away from this ugliness, still cloaked in trepidation that lingered from this harrowing nightmare. This was only a quick, fleeting thought, for Ally felt the answers were eminent. Because Ally knew the wicked entity was a shadow or trace of the unseen killer. She willed herself back into her dream world to search for answers.

Ally was back in the swirling darkness -searching for the identity of the killer. "Damn You, Damn You, Damn You, show yourself, you coward!" Ally screamed out into the darkness but received no reply. Instead, she hears a whimper; she finds Bree in the dark shadows. Ally tenderly picks Bree up and cradles her as if she were a small infant, rocking her back and forth until the crying subsides.

"Bree, you're all right now. He can't hurt you anymore." Ally gently told the shivering girl.

Bree turned and met her gaze with her incredibly innocent eyes. She said softly, "I know. I'm crying for the others."

Ally was stunned and taken back by her self-effacing manner; awed by the beauty and strength of her young spirit. "Bree, I need your help to find out who hurt you and the other children so he cannot hurt anyone again."

Bree pursed her lips together and narrowed her eyes as her body stiffened. She was deep in thought considering what she should do. "You know he was hurt badly, too?"

"I didn't know about that. Could you tell me what happened?" Ally probed gently.

"His momma hurt him. Then she got tired of being his Momma, so she sent him to a bad place."

120

"Where was this bad place?"

"I don't know, he called it a grape home." She replied.

"A grape home?" Ally asked in perplexity, "Was the house purple?"

"Maybe," Bree giggled, obviously amused by the question and then laughed louder. "It could be green; I like that color better."

Ally suddenly heard crying in the distance, breaking into the dream. Bree said, "See you later, Alligator."

"After a while, crocodile," Ally replied.

Ally got quickly out of bed, rushing to Breanna's crib. She was soaked. Ally changed her diaper, wiped her down with a warm washcloth, and got her into a new nightgown. She held her, sitting in a rocking chair, humming softly. She wondered what forces of nature could cause a mother to stop loving her child. She could never turn her back on her daughter.

"I want you to have the perfect childhood honey, full of fun, imagination, hopes, and dreams. You will feel my protection, be given security, and love always," Ally quietly vowed to Breanna.

Ally held Breanna as she drifted off to sleep. She continued to hold her for a long time. Finally, Ally placed Breanna in her infant seat while she changed the bedding. Quietly returning Breanna to her crib, kissing the top of her forehead and pulling the comforter around her. "Goodnight Sweetheart, sweet dreams."

Oh my God, how could I have forgot? Ally suddenly remembered as she was turning towards her bedroom, that Breanna was scheduled to have her well-baby exam earlier today. -She was supposed to get her immunization shots. Feeling the dread sink to her stomach, Ally was overwhelmed by guilt. How could she be so neglectful! Damn, there was nothing she could do about it now, except reschedule the appointment first thing in the morning. However, this thought did not ease her guilt or make her feel any better. She needed to keep her head on straight, regain her focus! Ally wouldn't become oblivious to Breanna's needs or allow them to come in second place during this investigative process.

The man should have never called her, just blown her off. The manipulative Bitch had completely sucked him in. Why had he agreed to go to the fuckin dinner anyway, that fiasco? At least the food and wine will be exceptional because it was being held at Cherie's; the plates there were at least fifty dollars a pop. What was she hoping to get from the deal another European vacation or perhaps a new Bentley? It was on Friday; he didn't have to show up. Screw Mom, he wouldn't show! He needed a work-out, grabbing his gym bag as he headed out.

The man had worked out vigorously for five hours, and still was not spent when he returned to his apartment. Faceless had to plan some more. This was no good at all; he was tired of planning. He brought out his pictures. This was boring, he was tired of looking at the same old ones. He would get better ones next time, as he imagined the staging with the various settings and angles. What image would he create? It was time, just do it! He only had to follow his plan. It was a good plan! Then his Mom's gregarious blond image interjected itself over that of the lifeless discards within the photos; he could only see her.

The man sat down in the middle of the front room floor, holding his knees as he rocked vigorously. The rocking persisted. Light now riddled the frozen room, the man looked confused and disoriented, as he sat stiffly upon the ground. How long had he been rocking like this, he wondered aimlessly. The morning light flowed through the half-closed blinds; lamplight was no longer needed. He glanced at the clock on the wall; it was 7:15 in the morning. His first appointment was at 7:30 am; he would have to fly out the door to make it on time!

Faceless swiftly glanced around the room. Fuck, his pictures were spread out all over god-damn floor, anyone could see them. He rapidly picked them up, stashing them away. Briskly, the man entered the bathroom and noted his reflection in the mirror. He absolutely needed a quick shower! Five minutes later, he hurriedly threw on his clothes, his face still unshaven, as he headed towards the door.

On Friday after completing their morning routine, Ally and Breanna were ready to meet with Deputy Bryant at the Sheriff's office. Arriving at the Sheriff's office, the clerk greeted her by name with a warm smile. "I'm Karen," she said brightly as she quickly came around to open the door, giving Ally the numeric code for the entry. Neal had explained to Karen that Alyssa Sullivan had been hired to do some extra errands and legwork for him. Karen wistfully eyed the baby and Ally promised to bring the baby by after speaking with Neal.

As Ally entered Neal's office and the door closed, Karen privately wondered what in the world was Neal's reason for hiring Alyssa Sullivan. She noted that Ms. Sullivan had come to meet with Neal several times recently. Ms. Sullivan seemed so nice and refreshing, but she was a new mother. The baby wasn't even in daycare. It seemed out-of-character for Neal, because he never acted impulsively or in a hasty manner. But knowing Neal, she just had to trust his judgment and knew that there must be a good reason behind his decision. Even though, Karen couldn't help wondering what the reason might be.

"Hello Ally. Have a seat and let's get to work. I've only got an hour before I need to leave for a meeting."

Ally settled Breanna's baby carrier next to her chair on the floor, carefully arranging the diaper bag along the side of it. She sat her book bag on the table, pulling her notebook and the data sheets from Eric Morrison out of it.

She began hesitantly, "Neal, I'm not quite sure what you expect from me, but I did jot down some questions and impressions as I reviewed Shilo Wilson and Amy Georges' files. I haven't had time to review Bree's file yet. I did get this information from Eric Morrison regarding local missing children."

"Don't worry about it, we'll wing it as far as expectations go. If I feel you've done something or said something inappropriate I'll let you know. If in doubt, ask," he gently told her, and then continued. "It's always useful to get a fresh perspective, especially when you're a seasoned old grouch like me."

Opening her notebook, Ally said, "Well, I told you about the pom-pom rabbit and the impression that the crime scene and the death scene might be different. The death of Shilo took place in the mining shed. When reviewing Amy George's file, I noted that her mother was deceased when the "Thank You" note and money were given to Ms. Griggs. The killer must have known the family, or been in the position to have access to intimate information about this child. What types of tests can be run on the note and the money?"

"See, I told you,' Neal replied. 'You're a natural at this. Good pick-up regarding the note and money. It was really too long ago for us to get any valid fingerprints from the note or the money, even if the perpetrator was stupid enough to handle this evidence without gloves. We did complete the fingerprint analysis on the note just to cover our bases. The handwriting expert believed that the person who composed the note deliberately altered his handwriting." Neil opened a cardboard file box behind him. Ally noticed that Amy George's name and a file number was on the box. Neil picked up a plastic bag with a note on lined paper was inside. He held the plastic bag across the desk towards Ally. "Here, smell the bag. You can still slightly detect the smell, the odor- like that of over-ripe bananas. It's Acetate, we use that to detect fingerprints."

"Oh," Ally said sniffing at the bag. Neil pulled the bag away and placed it back into the cardboard box.

"I did notice that all of these children seemed to come from troubled backgrounds. Could there be a connection there?" She asked earnestly.

"That is a definite possibility. However, predators usually seek out vulnerable children. Children from troubled homes have an invisible label of VICTIM written across their forehead. The perpetrators, which pursue these children, are especially attuned to spotting these potential victims. It's like they have an encoded antenna. VICAP (Violent Criminal Apprehension Program) has a new experimental computer software program that can help locate possible suspects based on the background of the victims. We are in the process of entering the data about these victims into the program to see if any profiles are located. However, there are always unknown associations between individuals, especially considering the lifestyle of the parents of these children."

"Hey, I had two more dreams last night regarding Bree," Ally added. "I don't know if it means anything."

"Haven't we already established that your dreams hold validity? Tell me exactly what happened in these dreams." Neal responded gruffly.

"I'm glad I wrote it all down," Ally opened her notebook. "Well in the initial dream, I'm in the dark being pursued by an evil, formless presence. I'm about to be overcome by this force when Bree materializes. I ask her who is after us and she disappears. I woke up. Later, I willed myself back to sleep. I called out into the darkness, demanding that the assailant show himself, when I hear Bree crying. I comfort her and start asking her some questions about the person that hurt her. She told me that his mother hurt him. She said his mother didn't love him anymore, and he was sent to a 'grape' home. That's it," she replied.

Neal scratched his head thoughtfully and said; "She must mean a group home."

"What exactly is a group home?" Ally asked.

"It's a highly-structured facility in a home-like setting for troubled children who have behavioral or emotional problems. There are a lot of rules and regulations, very institutionalized. The type of services the child receives varies per home. There is a level system within these homes, which indicate how structured the home is, and the amount of services that the home is required to provide. Usually the minor stays in this home for 6-12 months, sometimes much longer. Generally, the children are placed in these facilities by juvenile probation or by children's services."

"Does this information help to locate a suspect?" Ally said hesitatingly, this information seemed too vague to be useful.

"Any information helps. This information adds to the profile of the killer. It may lead to some of his motives for choosing these particular victims as targets. However, it is not a clear-cut pathway to the identity of potential suspects. There are over a hundred group homes within this state, alone. Many group homes have several operating homes under their charter. Many group homes start up and are closed for various reasons within a few years. A minor from this area could, and often does, go to a group home outside the immediate region." Neal replied, confirming Ally's suspicions.

"This maybe a ridiculous question, but Bree called it 'the bad place.' Are these places bad?" Ally asked naively.

"The quality of group homes vary; some are excellent facilities and others are of very poor quality. There is much disparity between some of the homes. They are regulated on what services that they need to provide per the level system. The outside monitoring of these homes is lax. Also, the system to enforce changes in the internal policies and procedures within individual group homes is ineffective or nonexistent.

Also, you need to remember that a troubled child is being placed with other troubled children. Sometimes, children within a group home victimize other children placed within the same group home. This victimization includes a wide-range of abuses, such as sexual, physical and emotional abuses. The children have no personal space, and anything they own, which is usually very little, is subject to theft."

"It sounds similar to juvenile hall," Ally balked, she hated to envision any child in such an institutionalized setting.

"For the most part, group homes are less structured and are usually not locked facilities. However, the facilities deal with mostly the same populations. Also, many children experiencing mental health issues end up in group homes. Moreover, many of the children who come from the children's services end are exhibiting extreme behavioral problems due to their life circumstances. Usually, these children are on the fringes of entering the juvenile system, and many times do cross the departmental boundaries. Listen, I've got about 15 minutes before my meeting begins. Perhaps we can touch-base again on Monday?" Neal said reluctantly, glancing at his watch.

Ally asked, "Anything else, you want me to do prior to the next meeting?"

"Just keep doing what you're doing,' Neal answered. 'If you get a chance, review Bree Jamison's file."

"Neal, has the FBI been brought into this case, or does that only happen in the movies?"

"It usually happens when local law enforcement needs additional help, unless there is a federal issue involved, such as crossing state boundaries, something like that. I've been making some informal inquiries and asking for technical assistance. It's not like I can't use additional manpower, but I have been trying to avoid a media circus and a local panic, which generally goes hand-in-hand with a local witch-hunt. In a community this size, FBI involvement is going to attract major attention. It can get pretty ugly in a small community like this: a big can of worms. I'll save that piece for later if it becomes imperative."

"I'll see you on Monday," Ally said, gathering her possessions and then gingerly picking up the baby carrier. Breanna had slept the whole time but was now stirring. She would need another feeding soon.

Friday afternoon after Ally put Breanna down for a nap, Ally hesitantly picked up Bree's file, weighing it in her hands. God, she didn't want to read it, for she already knew the outcome. She kept procrastinating and making excuses to postpone the inevitable. The hopelessness of the situation settled on her like a heavy insurmountable weight. She couldn't change anything. She laid her forehead against the file, wishing for the impossible: that none of this had ever happened. Bree was alive, somewhere, playing with friends in a park with her loving parents proudly watching her. To hell with reality, fantasy was much better. Oh Lord, why me? I can't do this.

Ally threw her head back against the couch, clutching the file tightly with her two clenched fists against her lap. Her emotions - helplessness, despair, pain, and grief surged through her like relentless waves drowning her in their bottomless depths. Her chest felt compressed, like it might explode from the pressure; it actually hurt to breath. Ally couldn't take it, this had to stop or she would lose it, just scream. God, make this stop, help me cope, please, please.

Suddenly a warm calm flowed through her body, gently lifting her to a place of safety and pedestal of reason. A single thought clamored through her mind with resounding clarity: no one wants to work in a sewer, but somehow the shit work has to get done. This situation isn't going to fix itself; someone is going to have to wade through it. Was that her answer? Ally brought both hands up to her face to wipe away her tears, giving a tight laugh. Yes, this task was going to be quite an emotional undertaking but she needed to do it.

It was a strange experience reading Bree's file. She had the constant feeling of déjà vu as she reviewed the file. Much of the information she already knew or had surmised. Ally decided to skip to the background information from March 1993, when Bree Jamison disappeared. The story emerged:

Crystal Jamison had lived on the fringes of society, just one step away from the authorities getting involved. The Sheriff's Office and Child Protective Services had been notified on several occasions regarding drug traffic within the residence or general neglect issues involving Bree Jamison. Usually Crystal had been reported on by a "pissed off" friend who had been slighted by Crystal in some way. The allegations ranged from drug involvement to dirty house, lack of food, inadequate supervision, or poor school attendance. It never was quite bad enough to place Bree Jamison into the child protective services system. There was never enough incentive for Crystal to accept any offered services. Ally had a difficult time visualizing Bree in these living conditions.

On March 7, 1993, Bree had been seen playing with some neighborhood kids for a couple of hours. Afterwards, she had been playing alone outside, unsupervised. It was late afternoon when Crystal, noticed that Bree was missing. Crystal canvassed the isolated neighborhood. The homes were sparse and spread out, there were only three other homes in the general area. She spoke to her neighbors, but her efforts to find her daughter were unsuccessful. Crystal Jamison finally decided to notify the authorities as evening approached.

One female and two male deputies arrived at the Jamison house at 4:45 PM, meeting Crystal at the edge of the property to hear of her child's disappearance. There were approximately 45 minutes remaining of useable natural light before nightfall. The deputies decided to first search the rural property for any signs of Bree. They searched around the abundant piles of debris, broken bottles, used car parts, and gas cans. Deputy Poulsen commented that they needed a backhoe and big dump truck before they could make it to the front door. Deputy Luke Kroff said he was amazed that they did not uncover a meth lab amongst the garbage.

As the authorities approached the house, the stench was unbearable. There were several individuals in various states of dress, found lounging within the household as observed by the deputies through the front door, which stood half-ajar. People were sleeping on sofas or hanging around the house. Two had active warrants and were arrested on sight. The interior of the house was in a deplorable state. There were filthy clothes, household items, intermingled with trash, which laid scattered in heaping piles throughout the residence. The bed where Bree slept, was a dirty, bare mattress with no sheets to cover it. The toilet was inoperable and encrusted with human feces and urine. The sink in the bathroom was covered with grime and grit. Dirty dishes, empty food containers, residual food and other waste were piled on the table, counters, and floor. A thick layer of grease coated the stove and surrounding cupboards. On the stove, a frying pan stood with remnants of a hamburger helper meal, teaming with live maggots. There seemed to be not one clean dish within the house, nor any edible food available.

The smell was horrid; Deputy Kroff started to gag. He had to go outside to get some fresh air. Entering the residence again, he was determined to get pictures of what he saw within the house. He was going to have color copies made. He would even get a magnified photo of the maggots in the pan on the stove. He carefully documented the condition of the house. If they found

Bree alive, she was not coming back to this hell-hole in the immediate future. Ally lamented that poor little girl, Bree had no sense of stability, predictability, or protection during her short life.

Deputy Kroff was pissed off by what he found. He was almost anxious to pin this disappearance on Crystal; however, Crystal had the testimony of her "friends" that she had been in the house while Bree was playing outside. A sympathetic female deputy, Angela Jordan, had been trying to comfort the crying and hysterical Crystal, without success. Deputy Jordan talked privately to Deputy Kroff to encourage him not to charge Crystal with child endangerment. She thought Crystal was going through enough hell at the moment. Ally was aghast when she saw the photos of the interior and exterior of the house and then, felt sick to her stomach. "How can people live in such conditions?" Ally covered her eyes with the palms of her hands, attempting to obliterate the visual imagery which the disturbing photos had firmly etched in her mind.

After Bree's disappearance, several of Crystal's acquaintances were interviewed; many had extensive criminal histories. One possible suspect was interviewed: Jimmy Gilson. He told Deputy Poulsen, "How d'ya know that Crystal didn't sell her for drug money? That's where I'd be looking."

A search was conducted within the area where Bree lived; no clues were found. There was no information on what could have happen to Bree or any information regarding a possible abductor. Authorities speculated that one of Crystal's drug associates might be involved in a possible abduction. Within days, several reports came in. There was a child spotted matching Bree Jamison's description in Southern California. The child was traveling with a short, stocky man with dark hair heading towards the Mexican border. Descriptions of the vehicle varied; maybe the perpetrator was stealing different cars, the authorities assumed. These leads were investigated, but eventually lead nowhere; the trail ran cold. There was one possible sighting in Idaho, but this sighting was quickly determined to be a case of mistaken identity. There were a couple of random reports from unreliable sources. Finally, the trail ended with no further information coming forth. The FBI did not become involved, because it could not be determined whether Bree Jamison ever left the state of California. Bree was officially listed as a missing person, and her flyer was sent out nationwide.

Ally read further on and saw reference to herself and the role that she had played in helping Neal locate the mine. Near her name, she saw the reference number to what was a background check. Ally had a strange feeling, knowing that she was an intricate player in a homicide investigation. This image of herself was completely foreign; some days, she didn't even know herself anymore. To think that her whole life could spin out into a whole new direction: it was a heady experience.

She reviewed the evidence list, and several photos followed. One item on the evidence list caught Ally's attention. Neal had listed a plastic tooth, which housed baby teeth, referenced by a photo number. Ally turned to the photo and studied it, a large plastic tooth with an attached lid, which opened on top. The tooth was buttressed next to a ruler, and measurements were noted at the bottom of the photo. A loose plastic (boondoggle) string was strung through a plastic necklace hoop on the tooth; the ends of the boondoggle string tied in a simple knot.

Something just didn't make sense about this trinket being found with Bree at the time of her death. Ally wondered, had Bree lost some baby teeth? She knew Bree was at an age, at which children generally lost their baby teeth. Ally remembered Neal bending near the body to pick up some small object on the ground with tweezers and placing it in the envelope. It must have been this plastic tooth necklace.

Why didn't it make sense? Okay Ally, clear your thoughts. What is bothering you about that plastic tooth? She aimlessly pondered the question. She decided to sleep on it; closing the file. She turned out the lights and headed to the bedroom, being careful not to wake David.

As Ally was drifting off to sleep, she made a weird connection. Bree disappeared on March 7, 1993. Wasn't the date, March 7, when David and I made our first trip to Horseshoe

Bend? Did she first see Bree's spirit on the fifth anniversary of her disappearance? She didn't even know if this time linkage was significant or relevant in any practical way.

CHAPTER 8

Ally awoke from a deep sleep, aware that she was beginning to understand a sinister correlation between Bree and her killer. The more she tried to recall this opaque connection, the further it eluded her. What did this chilly portent mean? Wait, hold on a moment! What an inauspicious start to her day, Ally admonished herself sternly. She needed to give it a rest because she was becoming far too intense.

It was Saturday; David wouldn't be going into work today. They needed some time together. Ally felt like she never had a chance to speak to David anymore. Between the time demands of little Breanna, her work with the Sheriff's Department, and her psychic wanderings, she had been pretty absorbed by all that had happened to her over the past eight months. She needed to restore some balance in her life by having a wonderful day.

Today, she was determined that they would have a big breakfast together and then, enjoy the day together as a family. She had just finished dicing the potatoes when David entered the kitchen to pour himself some coffee. He had just finished his shower and his hair was still damp; it glistened in the morning light. She wrapped her arms around him and asked "Hey, Hon, how's it going? Long time no see."

He turned around and held her. "Should I introduced myself?"

"Hmm, that would be nice," she mumbled against the warmth of his chest. She savored his closeness, absorbing his clean, soapy scent. David kissed the top of her head.

David said, "I haven't told you the good news. I wanted to wait until it was a for sure thing. But, I'll be taking over as the manager of the Boulevard store. It's going to mean a substantial raise, without much more responsibility."

"Terrific! I know you've wanted it. Is there a downside?"

"Not really. Should be approximately the same hours. But the store has been down on sales and losing out to the surrounding competition, so it needs some good PR and restructuring. It should happen in mid-January after the holiday session is over. How is the investigation going?"

"I think it's going pretty well. I'm now receiving personal information or other nefarious visions involving the killer; feeling his presence. I've got to believe I'm getting these insights because we're getting closer to identifying him. Sometimes, these visualizations seem to be a presage, boding evil. Yet, I keep reminding myself of what you told me. These visions are alarming because I have to face a precarious unknown. I don't have a frame of reference for my psychic experience and it's unnerving. I know none of this makes any sense." She said almost as much to herself as to David.

"Then explain it to me,' David said. 'Now, that I know a real psychic, I'm dying of curiosity." David's words sounded almost condescending, but the tone of his voice didn't. He was serious; he wanted to know.

"I don't understand the metaphysical world, or why Bree just cannot tell or show me, who killed her. The messages come in disjointed spurts through segmented dreams and symbols that I have to decipher. It's like a giant puzzle that I'm trying to piece together, but it always seems like the major pieces are missing. I'm probably just missing the cues," Ally said in a slightly dispirited manner.

"Have you considered that you receive your messages in the method you do because that's the way the information has to be delivered?" David looked at her thoughtfully.

"What do you mean by that? You've lost me." Ally looked perplexed.

"Think about this: each color of light in the electromagnetic spectrum travels at a separate wavelength and frequency. Radio or sound communications also travel by electromagnetic waves. Although I haven't paid attention to paranormal activity until your experience, I believe paranormal researchers use instruments to measure variations of electromagnetic energy. If an energy or spirit is trying to communicate through different space and time dimensions, the transmission of information is probably sent and received at different variations of wavelengths and frequencies. Some of these signals may even be infracted, refracted or inverted; scrambling the message sent."

"Now you've got way too technical for me." Ally looked inquisitively at David.

"Think about computers. Computers use a special language, multitudes of simple commands and codes in order to send, receive, and configure information; to communicate. An energy from another dimension likely uses its own variation of wavelengths and frequencies; its own language, with its own time frame. This time frame may not be compatible with our time lines and doesn't necessarily tie in with your need to know." Ally was aware that David was more comfortable giving a technical explanation to her incredible experience, but his theory was interesting.

"Maybe," Ally said, "the subconscious mind and dreams are used as a medium because the transmission is more easily received when there is less interference and distractions. All the irrelevant daily information that we pay attention to while awake can cause interference or a traffic jam in the transmission of information from this realm."

"Using available receptors to ensure that the message is received. ... Or maybe all these smaller pieces are needed to lay a foundation for the larger picture. The timing has to be right in the cosmic sense," David added solicitously.

"That sounds rather bizarre, but it has a weird logic to it." Ally considered this possibility.

"What is it like communicating with that child?"

"That child is Bree," Ally reprimanded softly. "She does not speak directly to me, but I transpose her thoughts and sense her feelings. I respond to what she is experiencing; I feel her thoughts, sense her feelings, kind of a telepathy....David, what happened to Bree and the other little girls was horrible, but these children had terrible lives to begin with. They were robbed of the opportunity of being children. They had no protection or security

135

when they were alive. They needed someone to advocate for them long before that monster came into the picture. I feel so naïve, but I had no idea what some children encountered in their lives, here in this country."

"Were their situations as bad as all that?" David said, picking Breanna up out of the swing. He bounced her gently on his knee.

"These children were lonely and isolated, ostracized due to their parents' lifestyle. Other children probably wouldn't associate with them due to their environment. I'm sure these children were not being offered play-dates by the PTA mothers, and for good reason, when you consider the health and safety factors."

"What about the child welfare system? Weren't they involved or assisting these children?" David asked.

"With two of the girls, Child Protective Services worked with their families and did all they could legally do and it still was not enough! With the third child, I don't even know if the authorities ever intervened in her life or circumstances. I believe there are two more children out there; and who knows what their situations were. It's all so depressing," Ally finished.

"It seems unfathomable that this could happen here. This is a good community. It's not like the anonymity of a big city."

"David, I'm beginning to see that this can happen anywhere, at least in this country," Ally replied.

"Still, I can't imagine what you feel communicating with Bree, but knowing that the ultimate outcome is that she is gone, and you cannot bring her back."

"David for me, she's not gone. I see and communicate with her as a small child in need of help. Therefore in some ways, it is difficult for me to accept the reality of her death. There is another dimension and surely another beyond that- heaven, the spirit world-whatever you want to call it. It makes the prospect of death, much less scary. Currently, I'm grieving more for what these children had to endure during their short lifetimes and what their family and friends have had to endure, here in the present. I'm working to prevent any more children from going through that nightmare."

"If the experience is so great on the other side, why is Bree stuck here?" David inquired cynically.

"I don't have all the answers, I don't even really know if it is great on the other side. However, I do know Bree and her spirit. She is a very giving child. I believe she wants to fix things before she is ready to move on. "

"Then what, what's next for you?" David asked.

"I don't know. My biggest concern and fear right now, is that this Brute will kill again, and we won't be able to stop it —spare another child, or parent from that suffering. Remember I asked you, what if it were our child, how would you feel? It doesn't matter David, it shouldn't be anyone's child."

"Ally, I know you feel a responsibility and a protectiveness towards any child at risk in this situation. But, you and Neal can do only so much to stop this guy. Some things are beyond your control and you may have to accept the circumstances."

"I know that David, but my heart won't accept that possibility! ...I don't even know if this psychic episode is a one-time connection or if these patterns will continue. Only time will give that answer. But after I finish my work with the Sheriff's Office, I think I will talk to someone in CPS in-depth to find out what the limitations are in the system. Something needs to be done in general to help at risk children. As I read the files, each of these girls lacked a solid support system. It seemed as if their families were broken down. There was no extended family involvement or intervention. These children just fell through the cracks. Children need a strong foundation," Ally stated firmly.

David paused, and then continued gruffly. "Ally, I've decided to contact my father. You know he moved into the area about a year ago."

David had limited, and scarce contact with his father before his mother died. But after her death, David would not speak to his father. His father had tried to contact David on several occasions, even moving into the area to improve their relationship, but David just would not budge.

"David, all this time, you've refused to acknowledge him. What's changed?" Ally questioned.

137

"You just pointed out that children need the security of family bonds. Well, Dad hasn't met his granddaughter. I also realized that I wasn't being fair to my Father. To tell you the truth, we never really got to know each other. He was always gone, away working. When he was home, we were strangers and did not know how to relate. I resented Dad for that. I guess the resentment took its toll when Mom died. I'd lost Mom; she could not be there, so why was he? I guess it was pretty selfish. I should get to know him and then determine whether or not I like him."

"When are you going to call him?"

"Sometime this weekend, when I get my nerve up. I guess fatherhood makes you start thinking about family and your roots." David leaned over and picked up a toy for Breanna from her carrier seat. Cuddling her against his shoulder, he turned her in his arm and held out the toy in front of her.

Also, David mused, "Your psychic experience has helped me to open up to the possibilities of what lies ahead after we die. I'm sure Mom's going to ream me out, real good, if I don't make amends soon! I don't want her brooding about it until I get there. She really could lose her cool. Good thing, she's not a ghost right now-huh!"

"Would you like to invite your father for dinner tomorrow night or would that be too much, too soon?" Ally asked.

"That sounds great," he responded.

"If it's okay with you, could we go to the Harvest Festival this afternoon? I'd like to get seasonal pictures of Breanna with pumpkins and autumn leaves."

"Sounds like a plan. I'll go call Dad now; I'll let you know how it goes."

Later Saturday night, Ally had a very vivid dream. Initially, she saw the back of a solitary young boy, approximately twelve or thirteen years old, in the dim, lamp light. The boy was moving around a small bedroom piling his clothes and possessions into two black plastic trash bags. Ally could sense his isolation and his dejected manner in both his physical movements and his emotional demeanor. The small bedroom housed two twin beds and a dresser. This furniture was cheap and of poor quality. The room was lifeless and dull, with no pictures on the walls, devoid of personal items. Eventually, the boy lifted and placed the trash bags next to the door.

He faced forward as he pulled on an ill-fitting, worn jacket, which was lying upon the bed. Ally looked into his dark empty eyes as he slowly zipped up his jacket. "Fuck them all, I can only count on me;" he said softly, looking lost. He called out towards the other room, "I'm done now; I'm ready to leave." He picked up the two bags, which were seemingly heavy. He was wobbling under the weight of these bags as he left the room. Ally heard his young voice from the exterior room. "Where am I going this time? Where are you taking me?" The boy threw out these abrupt questions in a challenging tone, but his voice faltered at the end of each question with fearful hesitation.

"Don't worry," said an unknown adult's voice from the next room. "You'll like it there."

"But what if I don't?" said the boy in the still wavering voice.

"Well, you told me that you don't like it here, so what's the difference?" came the clipped reply from the adult.

"It's going to be worse!" the boy said with such certitude. She heard the door close with a thud. A few minutes later, she heard a car pull away.

Ally awoke and reflected on this dream. Ally was sure this vision was of the killer when he was a young child. She felt sorry for the little boy, despite her contempt for the killer. His empty eyes were blank, as if numbed to the pain of his existence. He seemed spent...conquered, as if his young spirit had nothing left to strive for.

Ally was disconcerted; she wasn't entirely comfortable with her sentiment regarding this young boy. He was a predator, a vicious murderer! Why was she having more visions involving the killer anyway? Could this mean that she and Neal were getting closer to this murderer? Or was this just wishful thinking? It was difficult for her to even comprehend how in tune she had become

139

to the metaphysical world. It was an adventure, and she was a pioneer embarking into this strange new land. Yet the journey left her exhausted and drained. How she would love a vacation, a break from all this madness! But, she was also anxious to locate this killer. To stop this perpetrator before he could target any more little angels. This ride wasn't over.

    The man chose the Newbury Public library near the University; it was 30 miles from his apartment. Arriving early, the library was deserted; it was much too early on Saturday morning for most of the college crowd. He dressed all in black; his hair slicked back, with several days' worth of stubble growth on his face. He garnished a heavy-duty backpack with several notebooks and a couple of books. He looked like a typical college kid entering the library to do some work.

    He went to the computer, located in the back isle at the rear of library, to compose his letter. He would send the letter to the editor of the public forum section of the local newspaper, The "*Lake View Mountaineer*;" using the pseudo name of Edwin Horace, and a fake numeric address on Lone Pine Avenue. Yes- Lone Pine was the last paved road before entering the dirt back-roads to get to the Horseshoe Bend area. Now, think like an old man, he told himself as he composed the letter to the editor:

Dear Editor:
What are all those damn crime scene vans doing roaring up my road at all times of the day and night? Why are the police always up there at Horseshoe Bend anyway? What in the world are they looking for? Is there a crime wave in this neighborhood? What aren't the police telling me and my neighbors? I'm going to buy a double bolt lock for my door. The world isn't the same anymore. Why do those vans have to come in the middle of the night? Don't they know that decent people are sleeping at that time? All their coming and going has had me up the whole night. Tell them police that we pay their check and they should think

about that, as they are roaring through our neighborhood after midnight. You know, this isn't Nazi-Germany!   -Edwin P. Horace

He printed out the letter and an accompanying envelope. He took his thin knit gloves out of the backpack and put them on before handling the letter. He didn't know if an elderly man would choose to use a computer for a letter to the editor, but he was not going to chance writing it himself. He didn't save the letter before logging off. He was going to take every precaution. He picked up the backpack, and headed toward the front entrance of the library, and placed the letter in the mailbox out front. If this did not get the god-dammed media to sniff around, he did not know what would.

This would make the fuckin Sheriff's Office give up some answers! Yes- they will hate all the media attention! Faceless was unable to hide the smirk on his face as he thought of the Fuck- Bryant, squirming under all the reporters' questions. Hell, they would probably send in a crew from Acacia to camp at the fucking moron's door.

Now feeling much calmer, he went back into the library, and headed up the stairs to the map section. Faceless knew it would be impossible to use the Horseshoe Bend area for any discards ever again. He had already targeted his possible sites, but he needed a better feel for general layout. Faceless made copies of several geographical maps, and circled the locations. He would take a ride to each locale this afternoon, before he picked the winning spot.

As Faceless left the library, he was feeling very giddy. He should celebrate. Then, he remembered it was October 24th, his birthday. Well no surprise, he had not heard or received a card from Mother. He would treat himself to a celebratory lunch. He stopped at one of the local pizza joints near the college and ordered pizza with a beer.

The waitress was flirting with him, which he easily reciprocated. Faceless didn't ask for her number, though. He had to focus on the investigation and what the Fucks at the Sheriff's Office were doing. Maybe later, as he gave his waitress a quick smile. He carefully wiped each finger and his mouth with his napkin.

Ally made a traditional dinner for Sunday dinner; pot roast with gravy, peas with pearled onions, rolls, mashed potatoes, salad, and pineapple cake for dessert. She was nervous about the reunion between David and his father; she wanted to make sure everything was perfect. Ally had only met David's father briefly on two prior occasions: at her wedding reception and the funeral of David's mother, Shannon.

The doorbell rang and she answered. Larry looked much older than she remembered; his dark hair was completely gray now. He resembled David in many ways, but mostly in the way he carried himself. She noted he was slightly taller than David, perhaps five foot eleven to David's five foot ten. He had a similar medium build with honey-gold skin tones and startling blue eyes. Larry's eyes, however, were hooded beneath his heavy lids. He looked weary.

Ally gave Larry a brief hug "Hello, it's great to see you again." He smiled as he handed her a cute teddy bear, "for Breanna." She smiled, taking the bear.

"Thank you, she'll love it. Come on in and let me take your coat." She ushered Larry into the living room where David was sitting.

"Hello Son," Larry said in a husky voice. David stood up as he entered the room. He extended his arm in a downward swing to shake his father's hand, and then hugged his father. Ally felt the tears welling in her eyes as she made her exit to give the two men some privacy. She kept herself busy in the kitchen making final preparations for dinner and setting the table. The warm homey smell of the meal filled the air.

She entered the living room about forty-five minutes later when she heard Breanna fussing. She held out her arms towards David who was holding the baby and asked, "Is she alright?"

He laughed, "She has been entertaining us with grins until a few moments ago."

"Here let me take her, she needs her diaper changed and I'll give her a bottle before dinner." Ally said glancing nervously between the two men but there seemed to be a companionable silence and peace between father and son.

Ally changed Breanna, redressing her. She sat in the rocking chair, gently rocking Breanna as she fed her the bottle. Placing the receiving blanket over her shoulder, she continued to rub and pat Breanna's back to work out the burps. She rocked Breanna for an additional fifteen minutes until she fell into a peaceful sleep. Ally laid Breanna in her Happy Camper (her portable crib) in the dining room. She filled the serving dishes and called the men into dinner.

Over dinner, they discussed local news, sports, and a wide variety of issues. David seemed to be enjoying this visit with his father. There was none of the usual tension between them. She asked David to help her clear the table, and encouraged Larry to sit down and enjoy the college football game.

In the kitchen, Ally asked, "How is everything going?"

"Fine, great, much better than I expected," David replied.

"Thanksgiving is coming up in about a month, David. Should I invite your father to dinner?"

"Yes that would be terrific. I think we would both enjoy that."

They went back into the living room. Ally turned and looked at Larry, saying somewhat awkwardly. "Larry, Thanksgiving is next month. Would you please join us for dinner?"

Ally noticed the emotion in his expression as the tears glistened within his eyes. "I would love to come." Breanna began to stir and Larry said, "Please, allow me." He bent and picked up Breanna from her Happy Camper tenderly, and set down with her in an easy chair. He looked into her eyes and chatted with her in a jovial voice. Ally could see the tenderness in his eyes. She welled with emotion as she watched the exchange.

After several hours, Larry got up and gave David a hug. He turned to Ally and took her hand between both of his, "Well, thank you for the wonderful dinner, I guess it is time for me to take my leave. It was great to see you two and my granddaughter." He looked at Breanna dozing contently in the carrier chair.

"Thank you for the wonderful company. Why don't you come around twelve on Thanksgiving? Dinner should be around two in the afternoon," Ally said, getting up to see him to the door."

"Goodbye Dad, I've really enjoyed seeing you." They walked him outside and watched him climb into the car.

On Sunday evening, Ally reviewed her notes in preparation for her Monday meeting with Neal. "The tooth holder?" What was bothering her about Bree having it? Then the light bulb went off, Ally jotted down her thoughts in excitement, and put her notes away. Also, she wanted to ask Neal if she could try an experiment of holding objects that belonged to the victims. She had seen this done in the movies. Does it really work? Would it work for her?

The following morning when Ally entered Neal's office with Breanna, Neal was on the phone. Ally set Breanna's carrier to the side of the chair, seated herself, and retrieved her notebook from her book bag.

"Honey, you know how worried I get about you. You take care yourself, will you? Okay, I'll call you later after you get home." Neal finished his conversation and hung the receiver.

"Is everything alright?" Ally asked with concern, catching the tail-end of his conversation.

"My daughter, Jeannie, I told you she's pregnant. She had some unusual swelling and was sick to her stomach. The doctor had her come into the hospital to monitor her and the baby. According to Jeannie, it was nothing to worry about, just an allergic reaction or something like that. She is leaving for home now."

144

"I'm sure the doctor would have kept her in the hospital, if it was serious. How far along is she?"

"She's due November 12th; but she had one false labor already. Are you ready to get started?" Neal sounded somewhat gruff as he quickly changed the subject. She could see the concern etched on his face. Ally hoped Jeannie's condition was not more serious than he was letting on.

"Neal, I read the file on Bree. There was one piece of evidence that stood out."

"Yes?" Neal said, very alert and serious.

"This may not be anything, but that plastic tooth, it seemed an unlikely object for Bree to have?"

Neal looked perplexed. "Why, is that? I've seen those teeth holders in children's possession before."

"Think of Bree's environment. The house was a mess! I doubt that anything could be found easily. Objects were quickly lost, discarded, or broken. So if Bree lost a tooth, I doubt her mother would have been able to produce a plastic tooth holder to give Bree to hold the tooth, even if they did do the tooth fairy ritual. Also according to Crystal Jamison's testimony, Bree had been playing for hours outside. It seems weird that the tooth holder would be there, relatively clean, and even intact. You would have thought that plastic cord would have broken or slipped off, or the large tooth holder would have broken away. Bree could have found it lying on the ground, but it seemed like an odd thing to find just lying about. This may sound crazy, but could the killer had it for some reason or given it to Bree?"

Neal looked skeptical. "I imagine anything is possible. I could look into various possibilities. You really think there is something to this?"

Ally nodded her head. "It's not just something you'd pick up at a toy store."

"I'm afraid that I won't be able to keep the wraps on this investigation much longer. I received a fax from the editor of the 'Lake View Mountaineer.' The editor is Mae Ventura; she is a friend of me and my wife. Mae received this letter from a local citizen."

Ally picked up the faxed copy of a letter written by Edwin P. Horace regarding law enforcement activity in Horseshoe Bend. Mae wrote a handwritten note on the letter: "Neal, what's this about? Give me a call. Mae"

Neal continued, "I gave Mae a call this morning at home. The letter was mailed on Saturday, and Mae received it on Saturday evening. She informed me that she is dating the mail carrier who hand-delivered the letter,' Neal said with a chuckle. 'There is nothing like personal mail service. She had to go into the office yesterday, and she faxed this letter while she was there. I let her know that we were investigating the skeleton, which was located within the area, and making sure there were no additional bodies. I promised her an update as soon as possible."

A strange look came across Ally's face as she read the letter again. "Neal, how does this man know you are intensifying your search in the Horseshoe Bend area?" She asked.

"He lives in the area, on Lone Pine, just before you enter the forest service road."

"He specifically mentioned Horseshoe Bend. Those back roads lead to a dozen different locations. How did he know, specifically, that you had concentrated your efforts at Horseshoe Bend?"

"I don't know, but I'm going to find out! Hang tight." Neal picked up the white pages and could not find a telephone listing for Edwin Horace. Breanna had begun to fuss for her feeding. Ally withdrew a bottle from the diaper bag.

"Neal, do you have a microwave close by?" By this time, Neal had picked up the phone and was dialing.

Neal pointed in a general direction, "Out the door and the second door on the right." He was talking to Pat on the other end of the line when Ally returned with the bottle. She picked up Breanna and started feeding her. Ally tried to decipher what was going on from Neal's end of the conversation on the phone. "Could you check again, just to make damn certain? Okay, thanks. Could you connect me to Stella?" He held up his index finger to indicate one more minute. "Stella, this is Deputy Neal Bryant. Could you do me a quick favor and check the voter register, for an

Edwin Horace on Lone Pine Street? You don't have a record? Yes that's all I needed. Thanks again."

Neal hung up the phone and looked directly at Ally. "I think we've had our first contact with the killer!" Ally looked stunned. Neal continued, "I just contacted Pat from the County Recorder's office. There is no such address on Lone Pine and no property tax records for an Edwin Horace. Then I talked to Stella from the Registrar of Voters' Office. There is no record of an Edwin Horace registered with any political party in this county, nor any record of an Edwin Horace voting.

"What's next?"

"I want to go talk to Mae, and maybe find a way to draw Edwin Horace out into the open without tipping him off. Try to get more contact with him. Did you have any other information for me?"

She told Neal about the dream of the young boy with the black plastic bags. "Do you think this dream is related to the killer when he was young?"

"Most likely. That is often a repeated scenario for a large number of children in group home care. It seems like you're getting more and more information about the killer and less about the victims. Hopefully this means that there aren't any more victims that we don't know about."

"I hope to God, I'm completely wrong about those other victims. Neal, these visions of the killer as a child, perturbed me. ...I didn't want to see this predator as a vulnerable child," Ally conceded.

"Ally, killers aren't born that way. Most violent or aggressive behavior is learned, but people do have choices. There are many children who have suffered from abusive histories that go on to lead perfectly productive lives. In fact, many of these individuals work for social or protective agencies; they try to help others."

"I guess what bothers me most is that I don't want to see this guy as human. I just want to see him as some kind of monster or inhuman creature, impervious to normal emotions." Ally confined.

147

"Ally, I don't know what to tell you that will make this process any easier."

"I know," Ally asserted. "Neal, after some of the evidence has been forensically processed, could I handle some of it or anything else belonging to the victims? I've only seen this in the movies, where the psychic touches an article which belonged to the victim and receive visions. I don't know if this is true or if it will work for me, but I thought it was worth a shot."

"I guess we could try it. It couldn't hurt," Neal responded thoughtfully. "I'm going to go talk to Mae now. Let's meet tomorrow at nine to see what develops."

Neal watched Ally gather together her notebook, diaper bag, and then Breanna in the baby carrier. He was amazed she made it look so easy, as he got up to open the door for her.

CHAPTER 9

Ally arrived home from her meeting with Neal and entered the house with Breanna sleeping. She carefully removed Breanna from the baby carrier, placing her in the Happy Camper day crib. She drew the blanket over Breanna's body, careful not to wake her in the process. Ally suddenly realized that Neal had not given her any assignments for this week, but then they had an appointment for tomorrow. Was it an oversight? She would give him a call and ask.

She glanced towards the phone and immediately noticed the flashing red light of the answering machine. She grabbed a pen and notepad and returned listening to the answering machine. Thank Heavens for answering machines, she thought as she fast-forwarded through the message from a telemarketer.

Next, she received a message from her mother, Rene Michael. Her mother's voice was fraught with emotion, which reverberated throughout the room. "Ally, I haven't heard from you. I've left a couple of messages. I'm so worried! Are you, David, and the baby okay?" Her mother's concern seemed a tangible force which hung in the air.

Feeling extremely guilty, Ally called her mother back immediately. She listened to the sharp ring, waiting for her to answer.

"Hi Mom, how are you and Dad doing?" Ally asked.

"Fine. You've been on my mind a lot lately. Are you okay, Sweetheart?"

"Yes, I'm fine."

"Well, where have you been?"

Ally thought her mother had the mind of an interrogator. "Mom, I do have something to tell you. It is going to be very difficult to believe, but it is important. It's a very long story. I will fill in the details later, but for now I'll give you a summary version. Last spring, I saw the ghost of a child in a deserted back-road region of our county." She paused, waiting for a reaction or comment; when her mother didn't reply, she continued. "Somehow, this triggered some psychic visions, which have become increasingly stronger. These visions eventually lead to the discovery of skeletal remains of two murdered children. My visions have been so accurate and strong that the Deputy Sheriff, Neal Bryant, has hired me in a limited capacity to assist with the investigation." She was listening to herself, thinking how preposterous this all sounded.

"Oh my heavens, Ally, are you serious?"

"Yes Mom, it's been extremely crazy. I don't know how this happened, but I know I need to help. Two skeletons have been located, and we believe there may be additional victims. I'm starting to have impressions of the killer. I think this means we're getting close to the killer, but I'm not sure. I'm so anxious... scared."

"Well, I'd imagine so," Rene consoled. "You need to be careful and take care of yourself and your family. What about Breanna? Who is taking care of Breanna while you are working?"

"Deputy Bryant has hired me to do some simple clerical errands. Mostly, I review the files and give him my impressions and observations. I tell him about my dreams or visions regarding these cases. So far, I have been able to read the copies of the files at home. I take Breanna with me when I meet with Neal at the office for updates. He has me keeping track of my own hours. I have been able to do a few things when David is home to watch Breanna."

"Well, that sounds safe enough. I knew something was up; I just didn't know what. You haven't been calling much lately, and you've been so vague and distracted when I do speak to you." She didn't sound accusatory just concerned; Ally felt guilty for not talking to her mother more.

"I'm sorry Mom; I just did not know how to deal with all of this or how to explain or rationalize it to anybody else."

"You never have to explain yourself to me, Honey," she said sincerely. "I believe in you."

"Thanks Mom, I needed that. But that is easier said than done given the circumstances."

"I guess you didn't know, Ally, but my grandmother, your great-grandmother, had a similar gift. She didn't speak of it much, but she never denied her ability either. She was comfortable with it, but knew that some narrow minds could never understand and would ridicule her for it. She told me about her ability when I was old enough to understand, and she explained it in a very eloquent manner. But she made it very clear that it was a private matter that she did not want to share, except with her nearest and dearest. In some ways, I always thought of it as an extremely beautiful form of empathy."

"We've never talked about anything supernatural, or the occult before. I was afraid that because of your strong religious beliefs, you might consider this, somehow immoral or unhealthy."

"Absolutely not. Any such gift, is a gift from God, as long as you use it for good. In fact, your gift supports that there is a world beyond this present one. It lays the foundation for the something beyond our earthly bonds. In fact, you have always reminded me of Grandma. You are an awful lot like her. "Both were silent for a few minutes. "What else can you tell me about this investigation?"

"Not a whole lot," Ally answered. "In fact, I don't want you to tell anyone about our conversation today. One reason that Neal hired me, is to prevent any contamination of the criminal justice process. When the killer is arrested and comes to trial, he does not want the defense or the media sidetracking the judicial process by attacking the credibility of the 'psychic' involved. He plans to present the evidence involved, proving the case, and keep a lid on any psychic encounters."

"Is this job just a facade or is it the real McCoy?"

"A little of both," Ally conceded. "It is a limited internship, which allows me to read the files, and do some legwork for the Department without compromising the outcome of the investigation. Neal has shown great respect for what I have experienced and has never downplayed the validity of my visions. He has been very supportive and encourages me to speak up

151

regarding the investigations, even though I don't have any experience."

"How is David coping with your psychic experience and all that goes along with it?" Rene asked with interest.

"At first, he had a difficult time coping with it, but then, so did I. He seems to have come to accept it."

"As I live and breathe, the atheist becomes a believer. Hallelujah, there is a God!" her mother exclaimed in a mischievous manner.

"Yep, he's a changed man," Ally proclaimed. "In truth, I think it has helped him deal with the loss of his mother. At least now he can talk about her. Also, he has started to mend his relationship with his father. Larry came to dinner on Sunday, and we are having him over for Thanksgiving."

"I'm glad. I talked to Larry at Shannon's funeral, and he seemed so lonely. Ally, I have some vacation time; I'm more than willing to come help you with Breanna if you give me a couple of weeks lead time. What do you think?"

"Thanks Mom, right now I do not know how long it will take until this investigation speeds up, but I definitely will keep your offer in mind."

"I'd better get going. You take care of yourself."

"I'll talk to you later, Mom. Give Dad and Kyle my love." Ally hung up the phone and sighed. Maybe, she didn't know her mother as well as she thought she did. Ally glanced at the phone; she wasn't ready to talk to Neal yet. She would give him a call this afternoon.

Ally and Breanna arrived in Neal's office fifteen minutes late on Tuesday morning. She hurried in, unloaded, and pulled out her notepad and pen.

"I'm sorry I'm late, Neal. Breanna spit-up all over me before I was able to get out the door. I had to clean up."

"No problem. I got your telephone message yesterday, but I was too busy to return the call. Right now, I am working on several new developments in this investigation. I may need your help later on in the week, but as yet, I don't have any new assignments for you. Today, I wanted to give you a few updates. Also, I was able to get a few items that belonged to each of the victims. You wanted to handle them to see if they generated any visions, right?"

"Yes, that's right," Ally replied.

"Mostly, I gathered some personal items that belonged to each of the children; none of which is evidence in the case. I don't want the evidence being handled, because I don't want the chain of custody disturbed. However, I did bring the bathrobe belt obtained at Shilo Wilson's crime scene. I can make the case that I was going through evidence in my office to see if these cases could be related."

"What is the chain of custody?" Ally questioned.

"The chain of custody is maintaining accountability for the evidence from the time it's gathered until the evidence is presented in court. This includes tracking of the evidence. If I had several key pieces of evidence from each case in my office at one time, it could get called into question at court."

"Okay, I'll give it a try. What's new in the investigation?"

"First, I contacted Crystal Jamison. I had to track her down; she went into rehab. I asked her about the plastic tooth. She did not remember Bree having one with her on the day she disappeared. She stated that she had never taken Bree to the dentist. The school had made a referral a few weeks prior, but she had not made an appointment for Bree before her disappearance."

"Excuse me," Ally bend down to pick up Breanna, who had started fussing.

"I called the school," Neal continued, "and they said that they would check their records for that time period to see who made the dental referral. They are supposed to get back to me as soon as possible. However, the school is in the middle of a grading cycle; they have no one available to do the research. They told me that it could take up to several weeks for the school to pull her school records. The records are on microfiche in their school district's archive in Acacia."

153

"Don't they have a school official in Acacia, who could do the research?" Ally asked.

Neal shrugged his shoulders. He looked at Ally and said, "The crime scene unit may have located another body down the shaft of the main headframe. They are trying to shore up the sides so they can safely get down the vertical shaft and excavate the body."

Ally felt a hard stone in the pit of her stomach. She was so hoping that she had been wrong about her dream, that there were no more dead bodies. She felt a sour mood invade her emotions. She held her forehead in her hand and ran her hand down her face to cover her mouth. She needed to get away and regroup for a few minutes. "Neal, excuse me for a few minutes. Could you keep an eye on Breanna?"

"Yes, no problem. Take a walk outside." He watched her leave. Poor kid, he thought. He kept forgetting that she wasn't used to these investigations and was not emotionally equipped to adjust to this type of information.

She returned a few minutes later, looking much more stable and in control. "Sorry about that," she started.

"No need to apologize," Neal said. "Do you want to call it a day?"

"No, definitely not! The sooner we catch this killer, the better. Any more new developments?" Ally asked in a pseudo professional manner.

"No, we've just located the one body; we are still looking for any additional bodies that still could be in the area." Neal admired her determination, he could see that she was struggling to maintain her composure.

Neal reached down and opened a drawer, pulling out a canvas bag. He stood up and began to set various items across the front of the desk, facing Ally. First, there was a hairbrush that had a Disney Dalmatian puppy on it. Second, Neal pulled out a medium-sized plush toy; it was a blue man with a white beard, wearing red pants and a pointed elf hat. Ally had seen this cartoon character before. What was the name? Ally searched her memory bank but could not identify the cartoon character. Third,

154

Neal pulled out a child's crayon drawing, taped to a larger piece of cardboard. The picture depicted a woman in the center, holding hands with two girls, one girl on each side. There was green grass and flowers at the feet of the trio. In red crayon it said, "To: Maryann. From: Amy," in childish, mis-shaped letters.

Neal set down the empty canvas bag and then reached into a cardboard file box behind his chair. He produced a light green strip of folded terry cloth housed in a sealed-plastic bag; it was numbered and dated. Why did this article look vaguely familiar to her? Suddenly, Ally realized that this was the bathrobe belt used to strangle Shilo Wilson. She remembered the bathrobe belt was referenced in the evidence list, along with a large glossy photo of it, in Shilo's file. He placed the plastic bag in the line in front of Ally.

The meeting took on a surreal quality as Ally stared at the items in a row in front of her. She hesitated, oddly wondering what to do next. Ally reached down and picked up the child's drawing, staring at the picture. She closed her eyes and ran her fingertips along the picture, feeling the waxy skittish feel of the crayon marks against the cool, smooth surface of the typing paper. Ally laid her palm flat against the drawing, feeling its coolness absorb into her skin. Colored shadows swirled in her mind. After five minutes, Ally stated, "I'm not getting any thoughts or messages." She lifted her hands from the drawing, and her hand moved towards the plastic bag.

Ally gripped the smooth plastic on both sides of the bag with closed fists, hearing the symphony of the crinkling noise as she moved the bag towards her face. She could feel the soft textured weave of the belt and the grooved indentations of the folded garment below the sleek slide of the plastic surface. Blackness infused her mind and Ally felt an insurmountable feeling of dread overwhelm her. Ally jumped up from her chair, sidestepping it and turned her back to the desk, covering her eyes with her hands.

"Ally, what's wrong? What's happening?" Neal asked urgently, moving around the desk towards her.

"It's nothing," Ally said abruptly, holding up her arm in a non-verbal signal for him to stop. Neal stopped approximately two feet from her and waited silently for Ally to respond.

"It's like everything was enveloped by blackness, and I was overcome by this horrible feeling of hopeless dread. I felt I was drowning in it," Ally said in a childish, broken tones. Ally paused and then continued speaking, now stronger in her presentation. "I had no visions, just an intense feeling. It could have been imparted by the bathrobe belt or just by my knowledge that this was the implement of death for Shilo. I can't say for sure."

"Why don't you take a break and get a glass of water?" Neal said evenly. Ally nodded and moved towards the door. She came back a few minutes later and without a word sat in front of the desk. She took a quick look at Breanna, reassuring herself that the baby was comfortable. She looked at the row of possessions. Ally noted that Neal had discreetly removed the evidence bag, containing the bathrobe belt, from the desk; it was nowhere to be seen. Neal must have returned it to the cardboard file box.

Ally looked at the remaining two items, she had not handled: the hairbrush and the plush toy. Neal watched Ally intently, studying her slightest movement. She deliberated and slowly reached out to pick up the hairbrush with her left hand. She held it out for a second before drawing it in towards her body. Then she balanced the hairbrush within her hand as if taking in its weigh. The hairbrush undulated gently in her hand. She turned it over with her thumb so the bristles were pointed downwards, and she closed her eyes.

Ally ran her thumb slowly over the lower portion of embossed Dalmatian on the back of the hairbrush. She could not take the full measure of the Dalmatian with her left hand, so she brought up her right hand and cupped the back of the brush. She started to slowly rub the embossed figure in a circular motion before tracing the outline of the Dalmatian with her right thumb. Her right hand encircled the hairbrush grasping the sides of the hairbrush from underneath, the bristles of the hairbrush pressed into the palm of her hand. Ally held onto the brush in that manner for several minutes before opening her eyes and replying,

"Nothing." Returning the hairbrush quickly to the desk, her eyes moved towards the stuffed toy.

Ally stared intensely into the eyes of the toy on the desk, as if it was going to speak to her. She reached out and grasped the toy with both hands, holding it above her lap as she continued to stare downwards into its face, as if she were in a trance. She shut her eyes and continued to cup the plush toy with her palms. She remained in this position for about seven minutes without movement, except that her fingertips seemed to press into the back of the plush toy increasing her grip on it. Neal was uncomfortable as he shifted restlessly in his chair. He found Ally's actions and behavior weird, and the room felt somehow eerie.

Ally opened her eyes, continuing to stare down at the stuffed toy. She did not look up as she spoke to him in a barely audible whisper. Neal strained to hear her, for oddly, he did not want to disturb or unsettle her. "This plush toy is called a Papa Smurf," Ally said, as if to herself. "It belonged to Bree; she often slept with it. Papa Smurf brought her a sense of comfort and security, like a beloved grandfather who knows all your heart-felt wishes and dreams. Bree thought that Papa Smurf was magical and could read her mind. Neal, you got Papa Smurf from Crystal Jamison. She had it in her suitcase at the rehab. Crystal keeps Papa Smurf with her as a memoir of Bree, to give her strength during the difficult times. It holds a faint scent of Bree. Neal, you need to get this back to Crystal as soon as possible; she needs it! It was painful for her to hand this toy over to you; it was like she was losing Bree all over again. I received this information as I held Papa Smurf and looked at the toy." Ally placed Papa Smurf back on the desk in a sitting position.

Ally continued to speak. "When I closed my eyes, there was blackness, but a bright purple fog floated through this blackness. In the center of this fog, there was an expandable screen, which would expand and contract indiscriminately. I knew that this screen contained visions, but I was at a loss of how to access the information. I only received one clear image. It was as if I was Bree, and I were bound and gagged on the backseat of a car. It was still light outside, and there was a man wearing a maroon

157

long-sleeved shirt with faint checkerboard striping. He was wearing what I believe was a baseball cap. I saw him glance into the backseat through the rear-view mirror. He had mirrored sunglasses on. His image was blurred and distorted, because Bree had been crying. The image disappeared and I tried to retrieve more images, but couldn't. It seemed the harder I tried, the more distant the visions became.

"Was there anything within your vision to give up more specific details like the make or model of the vehicle, the identity of the captor, or the location?"

Ally thought his question through and shook her head. "There was daylight left, and I got the feeling that Bree knew the captor, so this was very confusing to her. She did not understand what or why this was happening to her. That's all I can say."

"Well, thanks for your effort," Neal said uncertainly, unsure what to say.

"I'm a little tired. Is there anything else we have to cover today?" Ally said in a distant, monotone voice.

"No, that's all for today. I've got some telephone calls to make. On Friday, I'll touch base with you, here in the office, unless something urgent comes up in the meantime."

Neal watched Ally walk out the door, shutting it behind her. He let out a huge breath of air. It almost felt like he had been holding his breath for the past half-hour. He picked up Jeannie's childhood brush and slipped it back in his coat pocket. After witnessing Ally's weird trance-like state as she intently handled these objects, Neal felt slightly guilty over "testing" her with his daughter's brush. On the other hand, he had been curious about whether she would get a read on it or not. Neal placed the rest of the items in his canvas bag, so he could deliver them back safely to where they belonged. Neal's first stop would be at the New Beginning Rehabilitation Center. It was only a few blocks away.

First thing in the morning, the man bought a paper. Faceless did not know what to expect: to read his letter in the editorials, or

158

to see a media blitz regarding the investigation in Horseshoe Bend. It was anti-climactic when nothing occurred. Let's see, he mailed his letter on Saturday, the twenty-fourth, and today was Wednesday, October 28th. It was possible that the letter had not arrived yet. He would keep looking for it the next few days.

Faceless wanted to drive out to Horseshoe Bend and find out what was going on. Fuck, he didn't want to be seen in the area, but the temptation was too great! If he drove to one of the side trails, then he could park behind in the trees, off of the main vein, and hike up the backside of the ridge. Likely, he could get there without being seen, and if seen, he could claim that he was hunting for gold. He pulled out a metal detector, which he bought used twelve years ago when he first started going to Horseshoe Bend. He dressed the part: his old Khaki pants, flannel shirt, and a baseball cap. His versatile backpack was now emptied of books. He filled it with a hand-sized pick shovel, several cloth bags, an extendable shovel, and binoculars, along with a water bottle and a sack lunch.

He called his receptionist, Julie, and told her to reschedule his appointments for Friday, if possible. He told her that he was coming down with something, and did not want to come to work for fear he might be contagious. He would try to get into the office tomorrow, but no guarantee. He donned his headphones for the metal detector and his sunglasses, and headed for the door.

He went around the regular roads to get back to the dirt trails; he pulled off on a small-narrow dirt road and continued for about three-fourths a mile with branches brushing up against his jeep into a deep pocket of trees. No one would come in this direction this time of year. He was trying to figure out if deer hunting season was over yet, but he had not noticed any other vehicles on route. Besides, any deer hunters would be closer to a water source, and it was late in the day for hunters. If he headed east roughly two miles, he should be able to connect with the ridge trail that overlooked Horseshoe Bend. He considered the time it would take to hike the ridge: it would be another two and a half miles each way. He'd better make some time; it was about eight-thirty in the morning.

It took him longer than he expected to get to the top of the ridge: an hour and a half. He sought the shelter and the shadows of the trees, staying away from the main trail. He got to the top of the trail, looking up at the sky. The gray clouds were coming in with the wind; he hoped that the storm would hold off until this evening because by then, he would be back home. He found a spot to sit on a fallen log within the shadows, and took out his water bottle, taking several large gulps. He set the water bottle next to the log as he retrieved his binoculars. He did not want to risk going any further up the ridge.

He spotted the Crime Scene Van and several individuals in heavy dark-blue canvas jumpsuits with matching ball caps. They had taped off about a half a square mile with the standard "CAUTION DO NOT ENTER" yellow police tape. Below the headframe, he saw the tech-boys within a square cage that was being lowered into the shaft by a large crane. Faceless fell back on the log as if the air had been knocked out of him. How had they managed to find the crypt? And how in the hell are they ever going to get down there to retrieve that discard with all the water in the shaft? He watched as the cage was lifted out of the shaft, filled with equipment to be sent down to the technicians.

He watched the crew down below for roughly twenty minutes, engrossed in the crime scene investigation below him. Which areas had the pricks processed and which areas hadn't been? Faceless saw a sheriff's car approach. The Chief Fuck-Bryant was on duty, and acting the big shot -talking to the lead crime scene Dick. As Bryant talked, his eyes visually scanned the ridge above.

Faceless made an involuntary movement and somehow his action must have alerted Bryant to his presence. Oh Fuck, Bryant was moving in his direction, and motioned one of the pricks to follow. God, he had to get out of here, quick! Right now, or he would be detained for questioning.

Faceless grabbed his backpack, shoving his binoculars in the front pocket, slinging it over his shoulder as he grabbed the metal detector. Quick, think, which is the quickest way down the ridge? A third of the way down, he could cut through the trees and could shave off about three-quarters of an hour in getting back to his jeep. God oh God, how was he going to get out of these back roads before they had the area covered? All the morons had to do was to head back on the main trail towards Lone Pine Road and radio ahead to have another dick coming in the opposite direction. They would have him boxed in. He needed to get back to his jeep on foot and then make his escape. Damn, Damn! What was he going to do? He started mentally rehearsing his story as he made his way down the ridge at a record pace.

About one-third of the way down, he made a break from the main trail and tried to negotiate the rough downward terrain through the tree-laden forest floor. He felt sick from the heavy smell of the thick underbrush. Fuck, why had he even came up here? Stupid, stupid, thing to do! His foot caught on the exposed roots of a wild oak tree, sending him sprawling into the thicket of trees. He reached out to catch himself as he grabbed hold of a tree-trunk to prevent him from falling, but he twisted his ankle in the process. The metal detector went flying, making a huge racket, which thundered through the silence of the ridge. His ankle was throbbing, but he could not stop and inspect the damage, not until he was out of here. Man, his ankle hurt like hell; perspiration beaded his forehead. He carefully picked his way down the ridge to retrieve the metal detector.

He could not see the main road yet. He hadn't lost his bearings coming down the ridge, had he? He felt the panic well up, along with the adrenaline. He felt like a frightened little boy, and he didn't like the feeling. He mentally put a reign on his emotions. He wasn't going to lose it now. Instead, he focused on how he was going to explain away his presence here, if he got caught.

He spotted the main road and figured another mile and a half to his jeep. He needed to keep moving, but the pain in his ankle intensified. He quickly glanced in all directions before coming out into the clearing to cross the main road. He headed straight for the tree line again to avoid direct exposure.

It took him approximately forty-five minutes to make it from the ridge back to his jeep. He sat in his jeep trying to formulate a strategy. Now what? If he went back the way he came, he would surely be detected. It was risky, but he needed to continue on this back road around the reservoir and exit into Tuolumne County, another fifteen miles on these fucking dirt roads. Hopefully, no one would notice his vehicle. The rain started to fall; it was not muddy yet. He couldn't afford to get stuck out here. He also didn't want to leave any tracks.

Oh fuck, the thought hit him like a jolt of electricity. I left my water bottle up on the ridge. Damn, he was sure they could get a DNA sample from the top of the bottle, or that his fingerprints could be lifted. "Damn, Damn, Damn!" he screamed out loud, grasping his hair with his fingers; he started to rock in a short rapid motion. Now he was longing for rain, so it would wash away any evidence of his presence there before law enforcement located that water bottle. Was it possible that they wouldn't locate it? He clenched his arms to his chest, his hands balled into fists against his ribs, his head bent towards his arms as he rocked furiously back and forth, trying to alleviate the tension, trying to figure out what to do.

He was uncomfortably aware that much time had passed since he got back to his jeep. How long had he just sat there? The rain was coming down in pelts. Fuck, how could he have lost track of time like that? He turned over his engine to read the time on the display: 3:10 PM. He had taken off his watch before leaving to go to Horseshoe Bend, because he didn't want to scratch it up. He had been sitting here, just sitting, for over three hours. How could he let this happen? Stupid! He had so much at stake. There was no use in the recriminations, right now. He needed to get out of here before dark, and before he got stuck in the mud.

He did not see any other vehicles as he traversed the muddy roads. Maybe his little sabbatical had served its purpose. The boys in blue would believe that any person would be long gone by this point in time, but he needed to careful. Despite the muddy conditions in most areas around the reservoir, he was able to maintain an average speed of twenty miles per hour. It took him about an hour to reach the state highway.

He was home free.   In another hour, he would be back at his apartment. He continued on for about ten minutes, and then noticed a county mountie following him.

The flashing lights came on and he pulled to the side of the road. Relax; don't panic, he told himself as the Deputy approached his vehicle door.

He rolled down the window, feeling the drops of rain hit his face. "What's wrong, Deputy?"

"Did you know that one of your taillights is out?"

"No, sorry I wasn't aware."

"Could I get a copy of your vehicle insurance, registration, and driver's license?" The Deputy looked at his registration and insurance card before handing them back. He took the driver license to his vehicle to run a check.

He returned a few minutes later with the license in hand. "Looks like you've been four-wheeling by the looks of that mud on your jeep."

"No, just thought I might try my luck with that thing with the rains and all," he said, gesturing towards the metal detector.

"Any luck?" The officer asked.

"None whatsoever, don't really know why I bought it. Just heard there is gold in dem dare hills," he replied in a jovial manner.

"Listen, I'm just going to give you a fix-it ticket. After you fix your taillight send proof to the county, they will remove the ticket. You have two weeks."

"Thanks," he said.

"Oh, by the way, did you see anyone else while you were up there?"

"Mmm, no, I didn't, but I was off the beaten trail, down near the stream,' He quickly lied. 'Why do you ask?"

"Just looking for someone. Thanks anyway." He pulled away. This wasn't good, but he would survive.

CHAPTER 10

Ally checked the doors again for the third time, wishing she could dispel her uneasiness. The meeting with Neal on Monday had been alarming, and left her feeling exposed, as if she was being watched. This foreboding lurked on the periphery of every waking thought and was firmly embedded in her disturbed sleep. Ally couldn't believe she'd been immersed in this investigation for less than two weeks; it seemed much longer. She decided to go grocery shopping to get her mind off of this persistent anxiety. Ally returned home an hour later with the groceries and started putting them away.

Breanna seemed to be enjoying herself in the front pack; she kicked her feet and squealed with delight as Ally moved around. Ally was amazed; this was new for Breanna, and she couldn't wait to tell David all about it. Determined to keep her mind in the present, she chatted with Breanna as she worked, and soon the job was done. Sitting with Breanna in the rocking chair, Ally read the story of the "Big Red Hen" to Breanna, in an effort to relax both of them.

Ally was in the process of reading the second story to Breanna when the phone rang. Ally reached over and hesitantly picked up the receiver from the end table.

"Hello Darling, calling to make sure you're okay." Good. It was her mother, Ally sighed. Her angst-ridden presentiment had her anticipating the worst.

"Oh, hi Mom. Everything's fine. You should see Breanna; she is cooing, grinning and squealing. She gets excited about everything. I just bet she will be an early talker." Ally said with forged cheerfulness, which barely veiled her trepidation.

"I just can't wait to see her; I already know how adorable she is. What's going on in the investigation?" Rene inquired, not fooled by Ally's blitheness.

"The investigation is speeding up. Deputy Bryant found another body," Ally intoned.

"Oh, how horrible!' Rene paused, took a deep breath, and then continued to speak. 'Ally, I'd like to come visit you the second week of November, and stay throughout the Christmas holiday. Dad would not be able to come until December 20th, and I am hoping that I can get Kyle to come for a few days, if it's all right with you."

Ally was very emotional; she did not realize how much she missed them, especially Mom, until just that moment. "I can hardly wait to see you. That would be simply wonderful."

"Ally, I want to see you and your family, but I am also really worried about you. Please take care of yourself; I've got a bad feeling. While I'm down there, I'll help in whatever way I can. Look after Breanna."

"Thank You Mom, I appreciate your help and I love you too." Ally was emotional, and her voice broke as she spoke to her mother. She suddenly realized how much she needed her mom here with her, during this nightmarish ordeal.

"Where is Breanna?"

"I'm rocking her now, but she is sound asleep. She looks so angelic." Ally said softly.

"Give her a kiss for me. I'll let you go; I'll call you later with the flight details. I love you, Ally."

"Love you too. Talk to you, later." Ally placed the receiver back into its cradle and shifted her weight slightly, so she could stand up without disturbing Breanna. She took Breanna to her crib and laid Breanna down for her nap. She decided to rest also and went to lay down on her bed.

Ally slipped into an altered-state of consciousness. She was neither deeply asleep nor quite awake. She could see a vague outline of Bree sitting cross-legged, but she couldn't distinctly see any of her facial features. Bree seemed so distant, but her message came through. "The man, he was there, today, at the mining place. He was above the pumpkin maze. He was just watching the men work. I saw him. I don't think he was supposed to be there; he got scared and ran away, when they hearded him. He looked scary."

"Bree could you tell me what the man looks like? Then I would know him if I met him."

"He is big. He has yellow hair and brown eyes. That's about it."

"Is he taller than me?" Ally asked, trying to get a more specific description.

"Yes, he is much bigger."

"How much bigger?" she pressed. She could see the vision of Bree, become less defined, less distinctive than before. She was leaving.

She called out, "Bree, do you know the man's name?"

No response.   Bree was gone.

Ally got up and poured herself a glass of water. She sat down at the kitchen table. To think that he, the killer, was watching and following the investigation; it made Ally's flesh crawl.   She called Neal at the office and was told that he was out of the office. Karen did not know what time Neal was expected back. She asked Karen to leave him a message.

Around three O'clock, Neal called back.

"Hi, "Ally said quickly. "I just called because I had a brief vision of Bree. She told me that the killer was at Horseshoe Bend today, watching the technicians work. She said he seemed to be hiding.   He was scared off when he was discovered."

"I thought that was him," Neal said.

"You mean you were there?"

"Yes, I went to see how the search was progressing," Neal answered. "Also, I wanted to determine if there was any place to watch the investigation undetected because of that letter we received. When I looked up at the ridge, something moved. I wasn't sure if it was an animal or a person. I asked for patrols to stop anyone leaving the back-roads. In this county, there is only one paved road out of the area, Lone Pine. In Tuolumne, there are two exits onto the state highway. We haven't received any news back yet."

"I tried to get a description of the killer," Ally told him. "The only description is that he is much taller than me with brown eyes and blond hair."

"I will see you bright and early, Friday. Eight-thirty sound okay?" Ally confirmed and hung up the receiver, mulling over their conversation. Somehow, the discussion with Neal served as a cathartic release, giving her a needed reprieve from her agitation.

Ally prepared chicken breast with wild rice and salad for dinner. She couldn't wait until David got home to tell him about Christmas.

David walked through the door, and Ally ran to hug him. "David, Mom called. Mom, Dad, and hopefully Kyle are going to come here for Christmas. Mom will likely come early and spend more time; help out with Breanna during this investigation."

"Hon, that's wonderful news. We'll have to think of some things to do while they are here." David had always gotten along well with her family, despite David and Mom's conflicting views on religion.

"You should have seen Breanna today,' Ally said. 'She started something new: She's squealing with delight. You should have heard her while I was putting groceries away." David walked over to Breanna, who was on the floor lying on her blanket. David knelt down and picked her up, bouncing her gently up and down.

"Are you going to show Daddy what you can do?" Breanna started to grin back at David. Soon, she was squealing and gurgling. It was wonderful to watch David with Breanna. They relaxed into dinner and enjoyed a terrific evening together.

Later that night, Ally slipped into bed. David hungrily pulled Ally into his arms, holding her gently and securely against his chest. Ally let go of all her thoughts of the investigation, and all her fears evaporated as their kissing intensified. Their lovemaking was desperate, urgent, and primal, rooting in their mutual longing and desire; reaffirmation of their physical and emotional needs.

For the first time in months, Ally felt at peace, she was completely safe within David's arms as she slowly floated back to earth. Ally laid in her contentment, nestled against David's chest, feeling at one with David and at home in time and space, completely encompassed in the moment. She could hear the deep, steady beat of David's heart blending in with his rhythmic breathing as he drifted into sleep. It was the first time in many months that she escaped her emotional isolation, able to be free and open. Watching David tenderly as he slept, she wondered if he felt as alone as she had been. She suddenly realized that she and David had briefly lost their "togetherness." She never wanted to feel as alone as she had been throughout this ordeal. She vowed never to lose that emotional contact and commitment again with David. Ally did not want to lose her emotional connection to all the people that she loved and valued in her life.

Faceless knew he had almost gotten caught today. It had been damn close. He felt as if his head were going to explode. "Damn it, I'm in control!" He declared in the empty room. He was finding it increasingly more difficult to dissipate the tension. He had lifted weights in the gym for a couple of hours, but his ankle was swollen to twice its normal size. He had elevated his ankle and iced it, but it was still swollen and throbbing. "Damn you Bryant, it's your fault, you son of a bitch!" He would make sure that Bryant was publicly humiliated. "Yes, you'll have egg on your face, just wait and see."

He noticed the mess around him. This wouldn't do. He started cleaning up on autopilot, his movements automated. When finished, he rewarded himself by bringing out the photos of his kills, and the teeth that he kept from each one. One from each discard was kept in a small velvet bag. He smirked thinking ironically that the teeth are the last body part to decay. He mentally replayed each kill in his mind, going through his preparations to the final conclusion. His mental recollection of each kill brought him a wave of ecstasy. He basked in the afterglow; rapidly however, the delight faded, and a hollow feeling prevailed. Isolation and dissatisfaction invaded his joy; the fantasy wasn't enough.   The silent compulsion steadily rose to an imminent necessity, he would kill again soon.

Meanwhile, he was going to take special care to hide these photos and teeth; because he did not want any physical evidence around his apartment or person at this stage of the game. That's it! Faceless knew exactly where to place his keepsakes for safe-keeping.

He had to deal with Bryant first, and figure out a way to send him packing. How to discredit Bryant: He played out possible scenarios in his mind, but quickly lost interest. He started planning his next kill, the anticipation of the hunt. He enjoyed the planning phase, and he took meticulous care in flushing out the details.   Faceless got out his map, studying his chosen area-his winning spot! His finger traced the route he would take on the map, lazily circling the disposal site. What would she be like this time? Tomorrow, he would start looking for his next target. He could only look, he reiterated; but soon when he had a solid plan, he'd go in for the kill.

Ally woke up to the sound of the rain pelting the windowpanes. She could hear the drumming of distant thunder and the branches of the maple tree brushing up against the roof. She prayed the tree could withstand the storm. She had discussed cutting it down with David in the past, but it was so truly beautiful. Jeez, it felt as if the house was coming apart at the seams.

Ally saw the red digital display of the alarm clock go out, leaving the room in total darkness. It came on again in a couple of minutes, flashing like a neon beacon as warning, a precursor to the power outage that lay ahead. Ally turned over and nudged David.

"David? David? Where are the flashlights? It looks as if we're about to lose the power." David mumbled something incoherent and turned over in his sleep. Ally crawled out of the warmth and comfort of her bed, grabbing her robe. Groaning, she went in

169

search of the flashlights. Two were in the garage with the kerosene lamp, which she promptly brought back into the room along with the matches. She then picked Breanna up out of her crib in the adjoining room and brought her into their bed, snuggling back underneath the warmth of the covers.

David turned back over in his sleep, throwing his arm in their direction. "Careful honey, we have a visitor." This comment seemed to penetrate David's sleep fogged brain and he half opened his eyes, taking in Breanna's presence in their bed.

"What time is it?" he mumbled in a deep hoarse whisper.

"About 3:30 I suspect. This storm is a beaut, there may be damage to or from that maple tree. Don't say I told you so."

"I will check for damages at first light." David turned over, and as if on cue, a rumbling crash trumpeted through the dark stillness.

Both David and Ally bolted upright and looked at each other. David said, "You'll be safe here. I'll just grab that flashlight and assess the damage."

He dressed quickly, finished by pulling on his coat and hat. Ally said, "Be careful out there."

David came back about ten minutes later; he was soaked. He was systematically removing his wet clothes and hanging them to dry in their bathroom. Ally hovered in the doorway as David spoke over his shoulder. "There were some split limbs and the tree doesn't look too stable, but it should hold out the rest of the night. There doesn't appear to be any damage to the house. I will call into work and take some time off, in order to take out the tree. I don't have anything immediately pressing at work."

"Did you need any supplies or do you have what you need?" Ally asked.

"I think I've got everything I need,' he responded. 'Just going to wait for first light and the rain to ease up a bit before I can do anything. Guess I'll try to get a little more shut eye."

David climbed into bed and pulled the blankets up to his shoulder, turning onto his side. Breanna had stirred but not awakened. Ally thought of the phrase, "sleeping like a baby." The storm didn't bother Breanna in the least.

David was outside at the crack of dawn, trying to cut away the limbs to avoid any property damage. About 9 am the phone rang, and Ally answered.

"Hi Ally, it's Larry. Just called to ask what you wanted me to bring for Thanksgiving Dinner."

"Just yourself," she quickly replied.

"How are you? Is the baby keeping you up nights?"

"Not the baby this time, but the storm. It wreaked havoc on our maple tree out front. David is in the process of taking the tree down before it can damage the house."

"You think he could use a little help? I can be over in fifteen minutes to help the cause."

"You really don't have to," she said.

"Oh but I insist, I'd love to help. I'll see you in a few."

Larry arrived, and Ally stepped out of the house to greet him. The rain was just a small drizzle now. Larry gave Ally a hug and called out to David. "Came to see what you have here. Thought you could use a little help."

Larry went over to assess the situation, as David climbed down the ladder to join him. The two were involved in deep discussion, making hand gestures, and strategizing where to cut the limbs. Ally went back into the house.

It was late morning and all that remained of the maple tree was a stump, and a very large pile of debris. David still had to cut many of the larger branches in the pile into more manageable sizes. Ally put on a fresh pot of coffee for the men. David started calling around to get a local guy to haul the debris of the maple tree to the dump. Ally fed and changed Breanna and laid her down for a nap.

Ally began preparing lunch by placing hot rolls in a basket and covering them with a napkin. She took a deep breath; you could smell the scent of fresh baked bread throughout the kitchen. She was serving up clam chowder into bowls when the phone rang. She called David and Larry in to eat and picked up the phone. The voice that greeted her sounded vaguely familiar.

"Hello, Ally?"

"Yes, this is Ally," she said, trying to place the voice on the other end of the line.

"This is Eric Morrison. I hope you remember me from the Center of Missing Persons."

"Oh yes, how are you?" Ally asked.

"I'm fine. I'm calling because I have some additional information for Deputy Bryant. I realized that I missed a computer cue when I searched for children within the area. I went back to the Center to set some new perimeters for the search in the database. I re-entered the information and I came up with two more names for you. Did you want to pick up the information?"

"Yes, of course. Are you at the office now?" Ally said calmly, hiding her distress.

"Yes, I'm here now, but I'm busy this afternoon. Could you come by within the next hour?"

"Yes, I'll leave right away. See you in about fifteen minutes." Ally hung up the phone; she was feeling slightly queasy again. Was this sickness, an emotional reaction, connected to her dread of finding more victims? She turned, feeling a wave of nausea rush through her. Then, the thought struck her like a tidal wave: Could she be pregnant again? No, she couldn't be. She just couldn't be, it was way too soon. She swallowed hard and tried to quell her riotous thoughts. While she was out, she would buy a pregnancy test just to make sure.

"David,' she said entering the kitchen. 'I need to do a quick errand; I should be back in half an hour to forty-five minutes."

"Okay, where are you going?" Ally gave David a furtive look, as if to say do we really want to discuss this? Larry looked quickly at Ally and then at his son. David explained, "Dad, it's a long story but Ally is doing some work for the Sheriff's Office. She is employed as an intern to do some assorted research and errands."

Larry looked mildly surprised but said nothing. Ally said quickly, "I need to pick up some information from the missing persons office. I'll be back." Dropping a quick kiss on David's cheek, she glanced at Breanna, who was sleeping peacefully in her swing; she hated to wake her. The baby however, stirred only slightly as Ally got her ready to go. Grabbing her coat from the front closet and her car keys from the coffee table, Ally headed out the door with Breanna.

Arriving at the office, Ally tried to quell her nausea as she shifted the baby carrier in her grasp, and knocked quietly at the door of the small suite.

Eric Morrison called out for her to come in. Ally entered, she saw Eric in the far corner of the room. He was intensely absorbed by the computer screen he was viewing as he contentedly pecked away at the keys. "I will be with you in a minute," he said not even glancing up from the screen with complete efficiency.

Ally glanced around, taking in the barren environment. The small, impersonal suite sported a couple of desks with computers. Situated around the desks were a heavy-metal filing cabinet and a five-shelf metal bookshelf. On the bookshelf were various atlases, a zip code locator, a reverse directory, and several phone books from across the state. A long rectangular table skirted the sidewall, above was a very large dry erase board. The other wall was covered with a corkboard, littered with flyers of the missing. Beneath, there was another long table, which was fronted with chairs and phones. This inert office was void of people except for her, the baby, and Eric.

Eric Morrison deftly finished up his work on the computer and stood up from a solitary desk in the rear corner of the room. Eric looked at Ally, and stepped towards her. Then seeing the baby carrier, he stopped abruptly, eyeing Breanna in astonishment as she cooed and excitedly kicked her feet.

"I didn't know you were a mother. Maybe someday I'll plan to have one of those, "Eric replied.

A little taken back by his response. Ally said incisively, "Waiting for one in a sports model?"

Eric grinned, "And a full warrantee."

"Where is the rest of the staff?" Ally asked, surprised by this deserted and austere workplace.

Following her gaze around the unaccommodating office, Eric replied casually. "Can't afford to keep it staffed. We have a list of a few local volunteers, who are willing to come in when something needs to be done. The local sheriff and police departments use this facility occasionally, for meetings or trainings. But mostly, it's used as headquarters for search and rescue if we have missing hikers, or as an immediate response center if someone is missing. I don't know how local law enforcement has managed to maintain this suite through various budget cuts, but they have."

"It is good of you and the others to volunteer your time." Ally responded as she dismally thought: an immediate response center without anyone to respond to a crisis.

Eric shrugged, "The work needs to be done."

He shuffled over and handed her a large manila envelope. "I made a pot of coffee, would you like some?"

"That sounds wonderful."

"Over this way." He poured her a cup and pointed out the cream and sugar containers. "I did not locate much more info but I found two names to add to the list."

"Thank you for your efforts," Ally said, taking in his appearance. He looked more disheveled than when she saw him last. Last meeting, she remembered he had looked so GQ, not a strand of hair out of place. Now, she noted he must have skipped shaving this morning. His tie was hanging loosely around his neck, and his hair was tussled. He seemed preoccupied, with a rather intense look on his face. She silently mused that he must have had a fight with his girlfriend or wife, but somehow she did not see him as being married.

"Has Deputy Bryant found a body?" He asked suddenly, taking her off guard. She quickly regrouped as she responded impassively. "For any information, you would need to speak with Deputy Bryant."

"I'm sorry, it's just that I often speak with the families of the missing." He explained. "The anxiety, restlessness, and sorrow are just too much to bear. If I can't bring back their loved one, at least I can help give them closure so that these families can begin the healing process." Eric was speaking passionately, his candid face fully animated.

"You know I'm just an intern," Ally said. "I'm still so uncertain about what I'm allowed to say and what I'm not. It's best if you speak to Deputy Bryant."

"I know sometimes I get carried away. It's just working with these families, sometimes for years, you get so close. Especially if it's a child." He looked at Breanna, then back at Ally. "I'm sure you understand." He looked earnestly at her, silently pleading with her to give it up.

Ally feeling pressured, responded quickly, "I really can't. Listen, I've got company at home, I'd better get going. If I were you, I'd give Deputy Bryant a call."

Ally got to the car feeling a bit unnerved. Eric had known Neal for years from the sounds of it. So why was he so reluctant to call him for additional information? Was Neal and Eric at odds with each other? Neal hadn't indicated any problems. Office politics at play? Ally started the car, glancing in her rearview mirror and over her shoulder as she backed up.

She knew that Neal would hesitate to give out any information, other than the mere basics, to further the investigation. Neal would play it by the book, except for maybe hiring someone like herself. Neal giving her a job seemed a bit out of character, but she could understand his reasoning. Maybe Eric thought he would get a complete answer from her if he got her talking.

David looked up as Ally entered the house. "How did everything go? Breanna have you been a good girl, today?" Breanna squealed in respond to David's voice.

"Fine, Breanna slept until about fifteen minutes ago and then she started to get fussy. She now, needs her diaper changed," Ally stated.

"Here let me take care of that," David took Breanna, then the diaper bag from Ally. "Dad left about twenty minutes ago. He

175

had some things to do, but he said he would see us at Thanksgiving. How did your meeting go?"

"I got some additional information from Eric Morrison, but he was pressuring me to give him information about what is going on. I'm sure he's concerned given his position. I just kept referring him back to Deputy Bryant. I'll have to ask Deputy Bryant what he wants me to tell him, or maybe I can get Neal to give him a call. Anyway my next meeting with Neal is tomorrow morning."

"It sounds as if you handled the situation just fine," David reassured. He was struggling with Breanna's diaper and looked completely bewildered. Adeptly, Ally came to the rescue - completing the task, giving Breanna and David, a big smile.

CHAPTER 11

It was very early on Friday morning, when Ally arrived at the Sheriff's Office. She wasn't overly conscientious; it was because she'd barely slept the night before. Ally didn't know if Breanna was teething, colicky or coming down with some virus. She would doze off and then within a half-hour, be up and crying again. Ally could not determine what was wrong. She tried every comfort technique she had learned or heard of, but nothing seemed to work. As a result, Ally was exhausted and feeling like failure as a mother.

Breanna, however, was resting like a little angel this morning. "Go figure," Ally thought wryly to herself. She continued to check Breanna's temperature with the palm of her hand against her forehead and the side of her face for the umpteenth time. Breanna didn't have a fever.

Ally sat down Breanna's baby carrier as she punched the security code into the keypad and entered the interior of the Sheriff's Office. Coffee? The smell of fresh-brewed coffee overwhelmed her senses, leaving her in a state of intense longing. She stopped at Karen's desk to greet her and the record's clerk. "Is Neal in?" she asked.

"He's on the phone; he should be off in a minute," Karen said.

"Do you mind if I grab a cup of coffee? Breanna kept me up most of the night and I'm exhausted."

"Go right ahead. The cups are underneath the coffeepot in the cupboard," Karen offered. Ally retrieved a cup of coffee and came back to Karen's desk sipping off the cup. "Boy, I can remember those days; my children are older now," Karen said as she chuckled.

"How many children do you have?" Ally asked.

"Four: John is fifteen; Ben is twelve; Emily is nine, and Nathan is seven. Here is a picture of all four of them together."

"They're beautiful. Your daughter looks just like you. A full house, I bet. Right now, it is hard for me to imagine going back to work. It seems like there is no spare time. I'm supposed to go back to work full time after the holidays. I'm not looking forward to it."

"It's a balancing act, that's for sure. But thankfully, my kids are old enough to help out a bit. I can't remember how I managed when they were babies." The door opened, and Neal stepped out.

"Hi Ally; I'm glad you're here." Neal said; he looked weary and drained. "Come on in," Neal ushered her in and closed the door.

Neal sipped at his coffee as Ally adjusted the baby carrier at the base of her chair. Setting down the diaper bag, she stopped to pull out a manila envelope out of her shoulder bag.

"Eric Morrison did some further research, and asked me to give this information to you," she said, holding out an envelope. Neal choked on his coffee.

"Hey, Neal, are you okay?" Ally asked. She was already in a half standing position.

"When did you see Eric Morrison?" he asked sharply.

Ally began hesitantly, watching Neal's reaction. "Yesterday - around lunchtime, I received a call from him. He had thought of another way to expand the perimeters for the database search, and he had come up with an additional two names for you. He asked if I could come to the office and pick up the information."

"What did you talk about while you were there?" retorted Neal.

"Mostly about the Missing Persons Headquarters, but he did try and obtain information from me about who you are looking for. I just told him that he needed to speak to you about it."

"Good, good. Was anything else said during your visit?"

"No, not really. He talked about the center and how it isn't fully funded, stuff like that. I did feel like he was starting to pressure me about this investigation, so I told him that I needed to leave. Neal, what's the problem?"

Neal rubbed his eyes with his hands, clasping his hands in front of him as if trying to determine how much he should relay to her. He glanced up at her over his clasped hands, eyeing her intently.

"Neal, did I do something wrong, something I shouldn't have? Tell me what's going on, please!"

"No, you did nothing out of the ordinary," he answered. "Remember on Wednesday, I told you that I'd asked highway patrol in both Calaveras and Tuolumne counties, to watch for anyone leaving the Horseshoe Bend area. Well, yesterday afternoon: I got a call from Deputy Holt from Tuolumne County. He pulled over Eric Morrison merging onto the state Highway in Tuolumne County at approximately 3:45pm on Wednesday. That dirt road is one route out of the Horseshoe Bend area. Morrison told the Deputy that he was metal detecting near the stream, which is plausible. Holt almost thought it wasn't worth mentioning."

Ally being quick on the uptake, responded, "But you're suspicious?"

Neal nodded, "Did you know that Eric Morrison is a local dentist? He works with a group of dentists down near Center Street. It got me thinking about that plastic tooth, Bree had; something available to a dentist. The other thing is that it's common for serial killers to integrate themselves into the investigation in some manner, like working for the Missing Person Bureau. Moreover, if Morrison is our man, he could have used his position at the Missing Persons Bureau to plant false leads or derail our investigative efforts, especially in the cases of Shilo Wilson and Bree Jamison. This evidence is all circumstantial, nothing that would even give us cause for a search warrant, but my suspicions are definitely aroused."

Ally was initially engulfed by her consternation of this disclosure and then, a flash of scorching anger, blazed unchecked, as she replayed all of Eric's manipulations. She now recognized how Eric had skillfully tried to entice and wheedle information from her during each of their encounters. How ironic: she bought into his phony concern for the victims and their families. She'd

179

been worried about his emotions! ...For God's sake, the onset of her visions involving the killer had been launched when she first made contact with Eric. Each time she called or met with him, she'd became physically ill. "I must be an idiot! How could I have missed all the cues?" Ally mumbled incoherently to herself.

However, her anger was rapidly replaced with a crippling fear. This chilling fear knotted up her stomach, sinking deeper, as the realization dawned on her. Breanna was there with me when I met with Eric! Did I talk about David in his presence? The knot grew larger, and Ally now felt sick to her stomach. She closed her eyes against the invading fears and tears, feeling hot tears press against the back of her eyelids. The tears squeezed out of the corners of her eyes and ran down her cheeks.

Ally's breath was shallow, burning in the back of her throat as she tried to swallow the knot there. She struggled to speak, "Neal.... Breanna was with me yesterday, when I met with Eric!"

"Take it easy, Ally! I said I was suspicious; he may have had nothing to do it." Neal calmly reassured her as he sensed her panic. She arched her head back and swallowed hard, trying to quell her desire to run. She wanted to distance herself from this wicked situation, but knew that she couldn't. From the moment Neal gave her this news, Ally knew that Eric Morrison had hurt those children.

"It was him! ...How could he? How could he?" She said between tears. "What he did to those little babies, their fear and pain. Then, he had to see the parents and families of those girls afterward. ...Playing his perfected role as a trusted, caring, and concerned authority." Ally sobbed, choking back additional tears. She wiped her eyes with the palms of her hands, sniffing loudly. "Their pain, loss and desolation. Oh God, I cannot think about it."

Neal got up and brought her a box of tissues. This made her cry even harder. Neal frequently forgot how close her emotions were to the surface. She was making him choke up. Neal couldn't help but think how jaded he'd become. First and foremost, he'd thought of the possible apprehension of Eric Morrison and procedurally how he could accomplish this task. He'd ignored all other factors including the human victims involved. He had not even thought of the victims and their families or the role of the pseudo-professional, which Morrison had assumed. If guilty, Morrison is one extremely cold bastard.

Neal placed a reassuring hand on her shoulder and said authoritatively, "Ally he may not be guilty."

"Neal, I know he did it. This may be just hindsight talking, but Eric Morrison seemed so kind and caring. On the other hand, whenever, I have been around him, I have been anxious to leave. I have felt physically sick; I thought I was coming down with something, but now, I think it has been my subconscious mind trying to tell me something about him, warn me."

"Ally, you know I trust your intuition and instincts. But believe me. You need to keep an open mind." Neal counseled but Ally was lost in her own thoughts.

"Neal, what makes an individual become a monster like that? He can't have a conscience. I just don't understand how he could watch and experience the pain of those children, and then, watch the parents and families agonize as he questions them about their missing children without tipping his hand. I don't even know how to put all that I'm thinking and feeling into words at this point."

"It is hard to say.... I'm not a psychiatrist. In the case of a serial killer, it is the eternal question; everyone tries to take a stab at. "

"Do you have some information on serial killers which I could read, anything which would help?" Ally asked.

"I'll look for any information I have around here," Neal responded. "You can find some information in the library and on the Internet."

"I'll do some research," Ally replied. Now that Ally had calmed down, she realized that her outburst was not appropriate within the law enforcement arena. It could make Neal weary about utilizing her help.

"Neal, could you please keep me in the loop? I will try to keep my emotions in check, okay. Maybe just becoming a mother, myself, has made me even more sensitive to these children and the pain of their families."

181

Neal was aware at some level, that Ally's reaction was much more normal and healthy than his own was. He wished that he could reach that genuine innocent place within himself once again. Her fresh, untainted impressions, unsophisticated comments, and reactions were what he needed to break this case open. She had already pointed out key pieces of evidence or factors in this investigation; she was so green -she questioned everything and took nothing for granted. She forced him to think in terms of rudimentary factors in an investigation, in victimology, and in the psychological profiles of a killer.

"Well, you're part of this team aren't you? So far, you know just about as much as I do," Neal remarked.

"Okay, where do we go from here?" Ally asked.

"I'm definitely looking at Morrison as a possible suspect," Neal replied. "I found out this morning that Morrison had a juvenile record. I've ordered a hard copy from Juvenile Probation. Hopefully, the records haven't been sealed, or they haven't destroyed any of the records. I'm not sure how many years the Department has to maintain the hard files. If not the actual file, I should be able to obtain his file on microfiche."

"How long will it take to get these records?" Ally asked.

"Early next week, I'm glad his record is local. I'll review this information and see where it leads. Listen, I have an idea. Why don't you take a break? When you get back, I'll give you a summarized version of the training on serial killers that I give at the academy.   It will give you the basics and then, you can do your research."

"I'll get Breanna taken care of." Ally said, picking up the baby carrier and diaper bag on her way out the door.

"Are you done already?" Karen asked, seeing Ally come out of Neal's office.

"No just taking a break. Figured I'd use the time to change Breanna's diaper and give her a bottle," Ally responded before heading to the restroom.

Karen watched as Ally left. She had noticed the puffed eyes and the anxiety etched on Ally's face. Concerned, Karen again wondered why in the world Neil had hired someone like Ally.   It's none of my business; she acknowledged as she started her filing.

When Ally returned to Neal's office, he had note-cards out which he was reviewing.

She quickly sat the baby carrier down and pulled out a notebook and pen from her shoulder bag.

Neal looked up and nodded. "Ally, the training that I give is usually two-days; I use a slide projector and give handouts. This information might be confusing but I will give you some of the major points." Neal lectured:

"We are looking at a profile of an organized serial killer. This means he meticulously plans out and executes each killing. No death is random. He stalks his victims, often weeks or months in advance. The body is often moved from the place of death, so is the murder weapon, and other evidence. He enjoys exerting control over the victim, then, over life and death. He enjoys watching the victim's fear and suffering."

"That sounds like Eric. After victimizing the children, he could relish the devastating effect it had on their families." Ally said bitterly.

Neal shifted his cards and continued. "He is likely to keep trophies or souvenirs of his kills: keepsakes of the events, allowing him to relive the pleasure of his experience. Usually, a major stressor will set the killer off. This stressor threatens the killer's sense of control, shaking his feeling of superiority. He or she decompensates, which means this person will find it increasingly more difficult to function at their standard level on a daily basis. This will initiate a new phase of the killing cycle. The killer will begin to plan his next kill, orchestrating every move until he kills again. With the new kill, the killer will feel at the top of his game again, and will behave accordingly. He has a delusion of grandeur, believing that he is smarter than anyone else around him."

Neal drew a small diagram for her, depicting a stressor that lead to a dip in the emotional state of the killer. As the killer plans his next attack, his emotional state improves. After the kill, the killer reaches a state of emotional equilibrium, which Neal labeled as the plateau. The cycle continued.

"Organized serial killers demographically are often white, male, with a higher than average IQ, and employed in a highly skilled or technical field."

"Eric fits this criteria." Ally asserted and caught Neal's expression. "Yes Neal, I'm aware that Eric is only a possible suspect. I believe he's responsible, but I'm willing to keep an open mind, the evidence might exclude him."

"These serial killers are likely to study investigative procedures and keep up with current technology and advances." Neal continued without pause. "These killers are not insane; they know what they are doing and they know that it is wrong. They take pains not to get caught, hiding or even planting evidence, and often follow the police investigations into the crimes."

Neal broke the lecture-mode with his commentary remarks. "I will tell you what I tell my class at the academy. The mass media, Hollywood and books often create mysticism around a serial killer; an image of a super-killer with unmatched intelligence and ability. The truth is these killers are generally equivalent to other killers, who skillfully plan out their crime, but serial killers hide behind their anonymity."

Neal continued with his lecture. "The serial killer hones their skills with each murder; a serial killer will make more errors and leave more evidence with their first few victims. In the majority of serial murders, the victim is a stranger to the killer. Whereas in approximately eighty percent of all murders, the victim knows their attacker. This makes the investigation into a serial murder case, procedurally more difficult. In a typical murder investigation: Initially, law enforcement evaluates the crime scene for any possible clues or evidence and gets a timeline for the crime. Law enforcement is taught to follow this trail of evidence and timeline. Look for people who saw the victim last, look for motives. Once you identify a suspect, you start to determine if any evidence and/or alibis include or exclude this person. For example, a married woman is found murdered. You find out that the husband has taken out additional life insurance on his wife within the past few months, you have a possible motive. You start to question the husband about his whereabouts at the time of the murder, check alibis, and verify all the information to look for any discrepancies to substantiate or disprove his involvement in the murder.

Neal glanced at Ally and asked, "Any questions so far?"

"No," Ally shook her head. "I'm still trying to absorb the information, I'm sure I'll have more questions later."

Neal returned to his lecture. "In contrast to other killers, the serial killer does not have a clear, or at least easily defined, motive. There is often no relationship with the victim, and the killer often hides the body. These crimes are naturally more difficult to solve, for you don't know where to start looking. Unfortunately, law enforcement often inadvertently facilitates the ability of these killers to remain anonymous for a variety of reasons. Some of these reasons are not flattering, such as the law enforcement officer's ego and turf wars between various agencies such as the FBI and the local police." Neil paused and then said, "There's your quick overview of the material."

Neal broke into commentary about their case. "In this investigation, I have tried to provide minimal information about these deaths and this killer to outside agencies. My intent is to keep this investigation as quiet as possible and out of the media spotlight. I don't want this investigation to turn into a media circus event, and cause a huge frenzy. If the media sensationalizes the case, the public and local politicians demand immediate answers, and this can hinder the investigative process. A case can be rushed to closure before you have an enough solid evidence. Rushing leads to mistakes! Mistakes can cause a case to be lost in the court system, or it can result in an innocent person being convicted."

"Neal, going back to what you said earlier about the killing cycle," Ally questioned, "you said that a serial killer decompensates before the killing cycle begins again?"

"Yes. Then it is almost an obsession or compulsion to kill again to obtain a euphoric plateau again." Neal stated, impressed by the speed of her ability to absorb this information.

"Neal, can you see physical manifestations of this decompensation, such as a change of grooming habits or a sudden carelessness in appearance?"

"Organized serial killers are very adept at gauging other people's reactions and responding in a socially competent manner. Yet, the killer like I told you, is unraveling; he will have a more difficult time, functioning at 'his normal level.' He can become increasingly reckless and foolhardy when under pressure or feeling threatened. I would guess it was possible to see such physical changes in some cases, especially at the end of the cycle," Neal commented.

"We may be in for trouble," Ally lamented. "He could be planning his next kill, soon."

"What do you mean?" Neal asked quickly.

"The first time I met Eric Morrison, he looked as if he stepped out of a GQ magazine. He was very polished, not a hair out of place, creases in his pants, the works. When I saw him yesterday, he hadn't shaved, his tie was loose, his clothes wrinkled; he looked disheveled. He seemed edgy and tired. I was struck by the contrast."

"Damn, you're right. That doesn't sound good. Come to think about it, he's always seemed well put together when I've seen him. I'll see if I can call in some favors and get a few men to keep him under surveillance. I need to figure out how to get enough evidence to obtain a search warrant." Neal quickly glanced at his watch and said, "Ally, I've got to wrap this up. I've got another appointment. I'll give you a call later to let you know how it's going."

"I'll talk to you later then. Meanwhile, I will do my research." Ally picked up Breanna, who was sleeping peacefully. She exited the office, closing the door behind her. She called out her good-byes to Karen and Maggie as she exited the interior door.

After her meeting with Neal, Ally was drained. Before she arrived home, Breanna started crying in the car. As they arrived home, Breanna was howling, echoing Ally's own mood and her desire to give way to her emotions. Ally fixed Breanna a bottle, then, propping the pillows on her bed; she sat and fed Breanna.

While she was burping her daughter, Breanna fell back into a peaceful slumber. Then Ally quickly followed suit, waking hours later. She was disoriented upon waking, not knowing whether it was day or night. She panicked briefly until her eyes settled on her daughter, calming her anxiety. Breanna was sleeping peacefully by her side. It was 12:30 in the afternoon. She had only been asleep two hours. She got up, placed Breanna in her crib and did some housework in slow motion trying to dispel her lethargy.

Around mid-afternoon, Ally secured Breanna into the car and hustled off to the library near the university. She found a couple of books about serial killers and checked them out. After arriving home, Ally laid out a blanket on the floor along with the baby's play gym setting Breanna beneath it. Sitting next to Breanna, Ally skimmed one of the books, stopping to peruse specific sections. Reading about these killers while sitting next to her daughter was disconcerting. She decided this research could wait until later.

As the afternoon wore on, Ally felt that she had her emotions well in check. However, almost as soon as David walked through the door that evening, he asked her what was wrong. Ally choked up again. "Neal has a suspect in the murders, but he has no proof or not even enough evidence for a search warrant. It was just an extremely emotional day." Ally kept the fact that she knew the 'suspect' to herself. She didn't want David to worry or to stress him out, anymore than necessary.

David took Ally in his arms and gently drew her towards the couch. He sat down on the couch next to her, holding her closely. Breanna had been playing contently with her previously abandoned baby gym; now she began to fuss.

David got up and brought Breanna back to where they were sitting before Ally could even move. They just sat there as a family, not moving or even speaking for about an hour. Ally could not ever remember David being this attentive to her needs; she liked the change. Ally got up to finish dinner preparations.

Later that night, after Breanna was laid down for the evening. David and Ally went to their bedroom. David drew Ally into his arms and they held each other tight. As Ally breathed in David's scent, feeling his strong arms around her, supporting her. Rapid heat seared throughout her body, and she was engulfed in an intense longing. She placed her hands on both sides of his face as she drew his head down for a long lingering kiss, cherishing his closeness. Her body pulsated in its need. Ally felt bereaved of air, felt as if her heart had expanded and was radiating outward. They made love as never before, Ally desperate to reaffirm life, taking joy and wonderment in being alive. Afterwards limbs entangled, David and Ally stayed wrapped in each other's arms, unwilling to let the moment go. Ally whispered "I love you, David," as they drifted off to sleep.

Sometime in the twilight hours, Ally awoke. She was wide awake, but did not know what had awakened her. She sensed Bree's presence in the room, but she could not see her. "Hi Bree," she said softly.

Bree giggled and said, "How did you know I was here?"

"I felt you right here," Ally said, rubbing her hand over her heart.

"You felt me in your heart? How did you do that?" Bree asked in half awe and half wonder.

"Sweetheart, when you love and care for someone, you don't need to see them to know that they are there."

"Do you think it's that way for my momma?"

"Honey, I know it is. She always has you in her heart."

"Wow," Bree said. "I'm there all the time?"

"Yes, you sure are." Ally paused. "Bree, are you trying to hide from me?"

"No, it's just that I have a harder time seeing you. You are far away." Bree's voice started to quiver.

"Why is that?" Ally continued on gently.

"I'm in a dark hallway, like at the pumpkin patch. I think I'm supposed to go to the lighted room, but I'm scared. So I'm just sitted here on the ground, thinking. Can you go with me?" Bree begged in a quivering tone.

"Bree, I don't think I can. I don't know how to get to where you are to help you. But Honey, try not to be too afraid. In the lighted room, there are many, many people who love you. You will feel safe, warm, and oh so, loved in there."

"You really think so?" Bree asked.

"Yes Honey, I really, really do."

"Okay, I'll think about it," Bree said uncertainly.

"Bree, do you know how many children are with you at the pumpkin patch?"

"This many!" Ally could imagine Bree holding up her fingers.

"Remember Bree, I cannot see you very well; can you tell me how many fingers you are holding up?"

"One, two, three, four,' (as Bree counted off her fingers), 'four!" Bree said finally.

"Do you know their names, Bree?"

"No, I just saw them."

"Could you tell me where you saw them?" Ally asked.

"I don't know how to tell you. Maybe I can show you?"

"No Bree, it's okay. I'm just trying to find out who else is there so I can tell their mommies."

"I know Shilo, but she left. You know she was the first one to come here," Bree said importantly.

"Thank you, Bree that really helps me. I think we have found out who hurt you kids, but we have to be sure." Ally could feel Bree's presence leaving. "See you later, Alligator."

"After a..." her voice dissipated and her presence was gone.

This encounter with Bree had given Ally a measure of serenity and contentment. Ally believed her visions of Bree were more indistinct and abstract because Bree was moving on. She would soon be at peace. She had read about near death experiences; the tunnel with the bright light of all encompassing love on the other side. Deceased loved ones waiting for the entrant with open arms and hearts, ready to embrace and welcome this soul into their fold. From what she'd read about this experience, it was beautiful.

Once Bree "crossed over to the other side," would she still be able to access psychic insights? Ally just hoped that she and Neal had gained enough information to proceed in this investigation without any further psychic intervention. She prayed that investigative skills and expertise were enough to break open and solve this case.

Ally got up, pulling on her robe. She went in to check on Breanna. She was sleeping peacefully in her crib. Ally watched the ever so slight movement, the rise and fall of her head and chest as she slept. She crept back to her bed, careful not to disturb David.

Faceless had picked up the October 30th copy of the "*Lake View Mountaineer*" en route to his first morning appointment. He finally had a break between appointments at eleven in the morning. He sat down with his coffee, flipping through pages until he came to the editorial section of the paper; his letter should be in today's paper. Most of the letters written were about a local political corruption scandal. Another opinion article was about the neck-to-neck campaign for a congressional seat between the incumbent, Roy Sommers, and his opponent, Jonathan Whitley. He continued to skim through the letters. He found one written by the Editor of the public forum addressed to Edwin P. Horace:

Dear Mr. Edwin P. Horace,
In response to your letter written on October 24, 1998: Could you please contact our office? We would like to have a reporter speak to you regarding your concerns about recent police activities for an upcoming article in the newspaper. Please contact me at 1(800)242-7000 extension 398. I appreciate your input on this matter.
Sincerely,
Mae Harris, Senior Editor

He felt his frustration level peaking as he stared dumbfounded at the newspaper. Fuck. He had never anticipated this maneuver. He closed his eyes tightly, rubbing his forehead, while he tried to strategize his next move. So they wanted to interview Edwin P. Horace. Were they on to him, or was the newspaper just searching for a juicier story? He knew what to do. Edwin P. Horace would just have to write another letter indicating a police cover-up. He strongly doubted that they would bury both letters. They had their subscription rates to consider. He felt better with making a clear plan. He would feel a lot better once he executed it.

Another option to consider was whether he should try to get additional information from law enforcement by talking to Bryant-he doubted the Asshole would tell him anything. Should he contact the families, get them to demand answers? If he did this, it could backfire, pushing law enforcement harder to supply answers. Maybe the Pricks could piece together more than he bargained for. Then what? He continued to run various scenarios through his mind. He still had three appointments to go before he could head to the library to compose his next letter.

After completing his appointments for the day, he headed home to change into his student's attire: jeans, tee shirt, and zip-up fleece jacket. He grabbed his knit gloves, sunglasses and trusty backpack, heading back to the library near the university. He went to the same computer located at the end of a deserted aisle and began to compose his letter to the editor:

Dear Miss Harris,

I don't want no trouble. Since I sent you my letter regarding the police goings on, I have received nothing but trouble. The police come by my place at all times of the day and night shining their lights in my windows. I see their police cars parked in front of my place, watching my doings. They must not be up to anything good, I say. You might have talked to the police and used my name that's the only thing I can figure. That is why I can't meet with your people.   - Edwin P. Horace

He typed the envelope and placed the letter within, placing his gloved finger in a nearby drinking fountain then running it along the gummed edge. After he sealed the envelope, he put a self-adhesive stamp on the letter. He was careful not to leave any evidence as he mailed the letter. Again he stopped at the same pizza joint, flirting with the waitress as before. He took her number, promising he would give her a call once he was through with his mid-term exams.

CHAPTER 12

Ally called Neal on Saturday morning, and had him paged. Neal promptly called back.

"Hello Ally, what's up?"

"Neal, I had another vision. Bree indicated that there were four children besides her at Horseshoe Bend, confirming my interpretation of that dream. Also, Bree told me that Shilo was the first. She even called Shilo by name. Has Shilo's case been reopened with witnesses, or neighbors being re-interviewed?"

"Yes, I've unofficially reopened Shilo Wilson's case, believing her to be a victim of our killer, but I haven't re-interviewed any of the original witnesses. It happened nearly ten years ago. It's possible that many individuals will not remember the particulars, or that time may have distorted their memories of the situation."

"I checked out several books regarding serial killers as we agreed," Ally said. "I read that the first killing is usually the closest to the killer, where the killer is the most likely to make mistakes. Hypothetically, if Shilo was the first victim of our killer, she was the only victim to be found at the time of her death. She was left out in the open to be discovered, as if the killer panicked. Maybe more evidence was overlooked at the time because the mother was the main suspect. What if we take a closer look? Is it worth a shot, or is this just an exercise of futility?"

"Either we find something or we don't," Neal replied practically. "It doesn't hurt to ask some questions."

"Anything new with the investigation?" Ally asked.

"We are having a difficult time pulling that child's body from the mine shaft. She's caught in a crevice under some dislodged timber. We're being ultra-careful so as not to put any of the technicians at risk." Neal continued, "There is another even-more lethal problem, which we've encountered while trying to dislodge the body. The technicians detected garlic-like fumes emanating from the shaft. This odor means that the rock within the shaft contains Arsenopyrite."

"What exactly is Arsenopyrite?" Ally questioned.

"Arsenopyrite is a natural occurring mineral in some quartz mines. It's often found in proximity to gold. The Arsenopyrite, after being exposed to oxygen, has been leaching arsenic into the standing water of the mine. Hence the standing water, within the shaft, has very concentrated levels of arsenic; it's very toxic. You've heard of Arsenic that is found in rat poisons? It's processed from Arsenopyrite. This poison is in the standing water. We have called in the Environmental Protection Agency and hazmat crews to assist in the recovery of this body. There is a whole list of procedures that the techs must do to protect themselves while trying to extract the body from the shaft."

"Any guess on a timeframe?" Ally asked.

"Right now, your guess is as good as mine. If Morrison is our killer, I've been trying to think of a way to lure him into making a big mistake. I may need your help for it to work. Are you up to it?"

"You bet I'm in on it. What would I have to do?"

"Whoa Ally, I'm still trying to come up with the details. I'm sure I don't have to tell you, but if Morrison calls, let me know right away. Remember, if you're in contact with Morrison, you cannot let your feelings show or you'll tip him off. He's not dumb. We don't want Morrison packing up and starting somewhere else."

"I'll keep that in mind. Did you want to meet Monday or Tuesday?"

"We'll meet Monday. Hopefully, it will give me enough time to come up with a plan."

Ally hung up the phone and absentmindedly looked at the clock on the wall. It was 9:45; David said he was going to work until around two this afternoon. He was always so busy during the holiday season. Ally felt anxious and unsettled; she needed to do something. She grabbed the baby holster from the hall closet. Ally placed Breanna in the front pack, which held her securely against her chest as she completed some housework.

With the housework completed, Ally decided to take Breanna for a long walk to clear her beleaguered mind. The sun was out, but the air was crisp. She took a deep breath and held it, feeling the sweet rush of its release. She still was having a difficult time dispelling this sense of foreboding. Definitely on edge, but she also felt a sense of excitement as the investigation forged ahead. Should she feel guilty about anticipating this cat and mouse game with Eric Morrison? It just wasn't like her. But then, she had changed; her life had changed in such a short time. A few months ago, it seemed her biggest worries were what she would wear to work, or what she would make for dinner. Her prior everyday worries were so marginal in comparison to her present concerns.

Ally returned home in time for the afternoon news. While feeding Breanna, she listened to recaps of the political debate last night between the incumbent, Roy Sommers, and his challenger, Jonathan Whitley. Roy Sommers was expostulating on the beneficial effect some new legislation would have on family values, children, and the educational system. Jonathan Whitley shot back that he needed to put his voting record where his mouth was; because Mr. Sommers had opposed some highly significant legislation concerning these very issues in recent history. Mr. Sommers contended that the so-called legislation that Mr. Whitley referred to carried additional clauses which would have had a devastating impact on the economy, while doing little to support children or families. Again, Mr. Whitley responded that it would have only been devastating to his special interest cronies. Who was being truthful? She had been prepared to vote for Roy Sommers; however, she made a silent pledge that she would look into the voting record of Roy Sommers and actually read those legislative measures before she cast her vote.

Ally laid Breanna down in her bassinette, looking meditatively down at her sleeping daughter. Ally sat in the rocker next to the bassinette, and shut her eyes, seeing shrouds of purple fog, vivid in its intensity. She watched as a small spot began to enlarge, presenting as a screen in her mind's eye. She watched as the vision became more precise and intensified.

A young boy, roughly thirteen years old, was sitting on a beat up couch staring out the window. The weather outside was overcast, but no snow or rain was coming down. He stared intensely out the window; as if by his sheer will he could make whatever he wanted magically appear. All was silent; the boy did not even appear to twitch a muscle as he continued to stare out the window in front of him.

She saw the shadow of an adult in the doorway and heard a male voice say, "Okay, it's time to do your chores."

"What time is it?" the boy anxiously implored.

"About a quarter past four."

"She's not coming. Mom promised me that I could come home for Christmas break, but she won't come." He spoke in a matter of fact tone, but his intense gaze undermined his words. He was desperately hoping, praying that his mother would prove him wrong. "I don't give a fuck anyway," he said in a monotone voice; because he knew displaying any hint of intonation at all would cause a maelstrom of emotions to surface.

"Watch the language! Next profanity I hear you use, you'll lose level."

"Yes Troy, I'll watch my words," the boy mocked, as he continued to stare out the window. Now, the snow had started to slightly fall. "Maybe she was delayed by the weather?"

"Listen, she was to pick you up at noon. She ain't coming." Troy seemed to check his attitude, a little. "Listen, I know you're upset, but it's time to start getting ready for dinner. Your counselor should be in tomorrow. I think you should talk to Nancy about this. Okay?"

"Fine, just great. I knew he wouldn't let her bring me home," the boy said as he hit the door jamb with his fist.

"Who are you talking about?" The man seemed primed and hyper-vigilant, as if expecting the crisis to escalate.

"My stepfather. He doesn't like me." The boy continued on in the same emotionless tone, but Troy seemed to hear the slight quiver in the boy's voice.

Troy asked softly, "When was the last time you saw your sister?"

"You mean their daughter? It's been almost a year. I don't care anyway; she is very spoiled."

"How is she spoiled?"

"They dote on her. Their whole world is set around what she wants, what she needs. She doesn't have to do anything; they baby her to death." His voice trailed off and then he demanded, "What do you want me to do?" The boy was solemn, resolute, his lower lip drawn tight.

"Why don't you start by sweeping the Rec Room?" The boy trudged off and the worker sighed in relief.

A woman's voice could be heard from the adjacent room. "How did it go, Troy?"

"Fine so far, he didn't have a melt-down. That's just what we don't need. Several of the boys seem on the verge of a breakdown. Keep a close eye on him tonight. He may run." Troy answered, as he approached the open doorway.

"Where is he going to run to?" She asked.

"Damn if I know! But he has managed to run to nowhere before. So keep an eye on him, okay? He's a tough little guy," Troy said admirably.

"He's just managing to bury the emotions deeper," she answered. "When he blows, it's going to be a big one. Last time, he really managed to hurt Justin. I thought I might have to take Justin to the hospital. If he hurts anyone this time, I want us to give 7-day notice to remove that kid. Okay Troy?"

"We told him last time, no more chances. He knows the consequences."

"Just so we are clear on this," she responded briskly.

"But remember Barbara, what his counselor said, 'his anger is a thin disguise for his pain, fear, and frustration.' That boy is in a world of hurt!"

"Don't you think I know that? But we've got the other boys to consider. We have to protect them too." Barbara countered.

"I'm well aware of that fact; as I said earlier, I know we can't give him any more breaks."

Ally opened her eyes and stared momentarily at the wall in front of her. She reflected on her vision. How could parents be so clueless and irresponsible? How could a mother be that detached from her child? Only God knows! A mother is supposed to nurture, support, protect, and love her child unconditionally; that young one was denied any of these emotional fundamentals from his mother. His father was just as bad, probably even worse. That boy was truly a feral child. ..."Which grew into a ferocious beast." Ally uttered rancorously, feeling betrayed by her sympathy for Eric. She got up; rubbing her eyes and then, stretched out her back trying to dispel the vision, and get back to the present.

She needed to run to the store and pick up some candy, she thought suddenly. It was Halloween. Ally didn't think they would get many trick-or-treaters, but it was good to be prepared just in case. She had been disappointed last year that they didn't have many children come to the door. She had decorated the house and wanted to see all the little ones in their cute costumes but only had a handful of kids came around. She now understood how strange and frightening the world can be, when you have small children. She hoped she wouldn't become too paranoid and over-protective with Breanna.

On Monday, Ally entered Neal's office with Breanna in tow. Breanna was fussy and Ally was hoping that Breanna would make it through the meeting. As soon as she set down the baby carrier, Breanna let out a big whooping cry. Ally picked up Breanna and methodologically started to rock side to side, adjusting Breanna's position in her arms to maximize her comfort.

Neal watched her automated movements. Silently, he wondered how she could be neck deep in this investigation and just carry on with the normal everyday functions of new motherhood. Besides being horrifically stressful, it was emotionally crippling. He could not imagine being novice to law enforcement, and being launched into a serial murder case involving little children, while dealing with all the emotional and physical demands of being a new mother with an infant. He couldn't have done it.

God, what was he doing? Neal had another fleeting doubt about his wisdom in bringing Ally into this, but he seriously doubted that she could have kept herself at bay. Even though her involvement was technically less than ideal, he reasoned, Ally had been instrumental in making significant inroads into this investigation. In addition to her visions, Ally had a good natural instinct for police work. He also enjoyed her company and thought of her fondly, as if she was his own daughter. So, he thought to himself, who cares if these circumstances are a bit unorthodox?

Breanna's cries had subsided, but Ally continued her methodological sideways rocking as she began to speak. "Anything new?"

"Yes, my granddaughter. My daughter, Jeannie, delivered a healthy baby girl, Kayla Jean Shaffer, born on Saturday afternoon. She was seven pounds, two ounces and twenty-one inches tall."

Ally could see that Neal was in seventh heaven. The joy on Neal's face was indescribable. Ally wondered if Larry had the same reaction after meeting Breanna for the first time. Ally flashed Neal a huge smile. "Congratulations on your granddaughter. Give her a kiss for me."

He returned the smile wholeheartedly, "Thanks."

"How is Jeannie doing? You were worried about her?"

"She is doing wonderfully, no complications. The hospital released her and the baby yesterday. My wife is going to stay with Jeannie and the baby for the next week."

"That sounds great." Ally said, "She is likely going to need the help for next few days until she is back on her feet."

"Well, we'd better get started; I've got a lot on the schedule for today. Have you received any more visions?"

Ally described her vision to Neal, who nodded to show that he was taking it all in. "Neal, I believe this boy in the vision is the killer, but I can't be sure. I don't know why I would be able to see images of the killer's past."

"Ally, all of this psychic business is new to you. Maybe this is normal? "

"Maybe," Ally said unconvinced. "I think there must be some reason."

"Anyway," Neal continued, "I received the file back on Morrison. It's an interesting read. I also spoke to his juvenile probation officer, Charles Stills, who still works in the system and has a steel-trap memory. I am convinced that Morrison is our man. His background fits like a glove for this killer. Eric Morrison spent a year in juvenile hall, and then years in various group homes until he emancipated from the system. He went to Job Corp where he learned some technical skills and continued on to college. He entered the school of dentistry before obtaining his undergraduate degree, which is highly unusual, but allowed."

"Well, we know he's not dumb; he can maneuver or manipulate the system."

Neal gave Ally a stern stare, cleared his throat, and continued. "As a kid, Eric was arrested for kidnapping his younger sister and then submitting a ransom note to his parents. Charges were dramatically dropped from kidnapping to custodial interference and child concealment. At the time, Eric had no other juvenile history and he was a good student. The prosecutor felt sorry for him. The boy had just turned twelve and the situation was viewed as a pathetic but dramatic demand for attention from his mother and stepfather. The stepfather gave Eric no slack, and would not allow him to return to his mother's home, even to visit. You'll never guess who his stepfather is. He is the lieutenant governor of this state, Alex Brentwood, and the mother is his wife, Susan Brentwood."

"Did he harm his sister?" Ally asked quickly.

"No, his sister, Caitlin, had told him that she was planning to run away. She was six years old at the time. Eric offered to help her. He hid her out in an old abandoned workshop and composed a ransom note. Eric started to unravel as the police and media became involved in the situation. A young officer noticed his agitation and sat down to talk to him. Eric confessed to

200

everything. He told the officer that the whole situation had 'snowballed out of control,' and he didn't mean to scare anyone."

Ally moved to lay Breanna down in the baby carrier. She had fallen asleep.

"During his stay in Juvenile Hall, Morrison was seeing a therapist on a weekly basis. During treatment, Eric seemed to allude to some emotional abuse from Brentwood. Eric also claimed that he was an incest victim. He indicated that his mother was responsible, but then, quickly clamed up."

"Incest was not dealt with very well back in the mid 70's, and isn't even today; we have a hard time giving proper support to male victims. Male victims often do not report these situations, and female offenders are rare. The majority of female offenders have many extensive psychological problems and truly are mentally ill. Stills, the probation officer, stated that one moment Eric would vilify his mother and then the next he would have complete adoration for her. Stills believed that there was some validity to Eric's allegations."

"So Stills believed that Eric was not simply trying to manipulate him?" Ally inquired.

"No. Even though, Eric's mother, Susan Brentwood, denied the allegations, stating that she didn't know what would make Eric say such a thing. The famed stepfather, Alex Brentwood, was hot, calling Eric ' a little punk, and a pathological liar' who would say anything to get out of trouble. Eric had been jealous of their relationship, and would stop at nothing to break up their marriage. Brentwood emphasized that Eric was completely self-centered, and indulged by his mother. To have his mother's sole attention, he would do anything, including causing physical harm to his baby sister."

"The matter was dropped, and Eric Morrison never disclosed any information about any sexual molestation or abuse again. Stills tried to talk to Eric about the sexual abuse, but Eric would just sit there, staring straight ahead, arms crossed, refusing to say a word."

"You can't be serious. No one made any further inquiries?"

"No, Eric refused to talk about it, so there wasn't a complaining witness to pursue prosecution. Also, due to the charges against Morrison, the prosecutor felt he would have a difficult time establishing the boy as a credible witness. ...After these accusations had been made, the stepfather and mother had very little contact with Morrison. According to Stills, the mother would send a cheap, inappropriate gift at Christmas time to keep up appearances. She usually forgot his birthday or sent a gift after the fact. At one time, Stills tried to get Eric's mother and stepfather involved in family counseling. Alex Brentwood was outraged, stating that neither he nor his wife had a problem, and the state needed to concentrate their efforts on the boy!"

"What happened to Eric's biological father?" Ally inquired.

"Eric seemed to be really close to his father, Randy Morrison. Susan Brentwood reported to Stills that Eric used to follow him around constantly, mimicking all he did. The father would use a wrench to fix a faucet, and then, Eric would get a wrench and pretend to be fixing it at the same time. When Randy Morrison mowed the lawn, there was little Eric following behind him with his toy lawn mower. "

"On Eric's fifth birthday, the couple separated and later divorced. Randy would work under the table to avoid making child support payments. Susan Brentwood did not want to allow visits if she was not receiving any support money. The state put pressure on Randy Morrison, and was about to revoke his driver's license for lack of child support payments. He skipped state. He did not remain in contact with his son."

"When Eric was about to be released from Juvenile Hall, Stills tracked down Randy Morrison to talk to him about possibly taking custody of Eric after his release. Randy told Stills that Susan had interfered with his relationship with Eric. Susan would never let him see his boy; now Eric was a stranger to him. He was not in the position to raise his son on his own, and he made lots of excuses why this would not be a good idea. About a month after this conversation, Stills thought he would give it a second try. He called Randy Morrison's telephone number and it was disconnected. He sent a letter and it was returned from the post office, stamped: 'Recipient no longer at this address, no forwarding address available.'"

"What a jerk!" Ally responded as Neal continued.

"Stills looked for other relatives to provide a home for Eric, but relatives were few and far between. The available relatives did not want to get involved, especially with that child, who had deep emotional problems. Stills was given the impression that Susan Brentwood had been talking to anyone who would listen about her troubled son, and how the state could give Eric, the appropriate mental health and other therapeutic services that he needed. Susan had pleaded with her husband to place Eric into a private hospital, but Alex was livid over the danger Eric had exposed their daughter to. According to Susan, Alex felt that Eric must pay his dues for his unjustifiable behavior, and Alex was not going to rescue Eric from his own actions."

"Stills told me that he was extremely happy when Eric really started to apply himself just wanting to get out of the system. Eric had become physically assaultive towards some of his peers during the first couple of years in the system, resulting in additional juvenile assault charges being added to his record. It didn't seem to take much to set him off during those days; a look was enough provocation. Moreover, he just didn't seem to care; he had no one to impress. Suddenly, Eric appeared to turn around completely. He got good grades, focused on avoiding others and staying out of trouble."

"It seems as if the pieces are falling into place," Ally said disjointedly.

"I also spoke to a cousin of Tammy Lee," Neal added. "I forget her name, but it will come to me. She said that Tammy Lee had a relationship with a man which had fizzled out before the tragedy. She thought he was a dentist, but she couldn't be sure. She was going to contact her mother and her sister to see if they knew the name of Tammy's boyfriend. Her mother lives here locally but is currently on a cruise. Her sister moved to Arizona."

"When will you hear something?" Ally asked.

"Possibly Wednesday. I heard back from Park View Elementary where Bree Jamison attended. The school secretary said that there had been no doctor or dentist listed on her emergency card at the school. They documented that she received a dental referral in her school records, but the individual who made the referral was not referenced. They have a regional list of local medical providers, such as dentists, chiropractors, opticians and the like who will provide services or will talk to the student body as a lecturer. However, the school does not keep records beyond a two-year time frame of when a specific medical professional provides services. They keep the two-year records for income tax purposes. The providers can claim their time as a business or promotional expense. Therefore, most local providers have their name on the list whether they provide services or not. Of course, Eric Morrison's name is on the list, but so is every other dentist or hygienist in this town."

"There is no way to show what dates and how often Eric was at the schools?"

"Not really, " Neal said. "However, a receptionist did say that Eric Morrison likes to help out as much as he can. In Amy George's school records, a physician was listed on her emergency card but no dentist. I could not find any evidence of a dental referral being given to Amy George from her school. So far this information is too circumstantial to pursue as a lead, but we do know he has plenty of access to children and he would be in a position of trust. I know many of the teachers around here and how some of them love to discuss and gossip about the children and their families when they are in the staff lounge. There are all kinds of tidbits Morrison could have picked up about the children hanging around the school office and the staff lounge."

"Could you question Eric Morrison?" Ally posed.

"There is not enough evidence to directly implicate Morrison. We just have some vague circumstantial evidence. We need more. I could informally speak to Morrison, but that would serve no useful purpose at this juncture. It could frighten him off, and he could start over fresh somewhere else."

"So what are we going to do now?"

"It's what you're going to do," Neal said watching her eyes widen.

CHAPTER 13

"What...What are you talking about? What can I do?" Ally was baffled, and quite sure that she had misunderstood what was said.

"Listen Ally, I have a plan to draw Morrison out into the open. You are an instrumental player in this plan if it is going to work. Please hear me out," Neal began.

"What would I have to do?" Ally shuddered; fear and excitement co-mingling to send an electrical jolt up her spine.

"You're going to tell Morrison that I needed to leave town to be at a conference for three days in Acacia, and I left instructions for you to contact him. I want missing children reports on all girls from age 5 to 10 for all of Northern California, even if it is a suspected parental abduction. While you are there, you will be carrying a tan envelope addressed to you from me; you are going to find yourself with an urgent need to leave the office temporarily, leaving the envelope behind. Your departure is going to be long enough to give Morrison an ample time to spy."

"Okay?" Ally prompted, encouraging Neal to continue.

"I would do this myself, but I believe it would make Morrison suspicious since all of his dealings have been with you. Are you sure you want to do this? You know it isn't too late to back out, and please, back out if you don't think you can pull it off."

"No. I don't want to back out," Ally said firmly. "I want this guy caught and out of commission as soon as possible. I will pull it off, don't you worry about that. What is the memo going to say, and how is it going to help us catch him?"

"The memo is half-truth, half fiction, but I'm willing to bet that it will bring Morrison back to the scene of the crime. This plan will only work if Morrison believes that we have no leads on a possible suspect. I'm hoping against hope that Morrison doesn't understand police procedures completely. If he knows general practices in crime scene protocol, he may become suspicious.

Perhaps he will just regard us here in Calaveras County as country bumpkins; let's just say this plan would be a departure from normal procedure. I can only hope he buys it. Well, here's the memo. Read it for yourself." Neal had an 8 ½ by 11' plain manila folder that was secured by a black hinge paper clip. Neal carefully removed the hinged paper clip, opening the manila folder with a handkerchief that he removed from his pocket. "Here, take the letter," he told her.

"Can I touch it?" She asked in bewilderment.

"Yes, but I only want your fingerprints on the memo. I used latex gloves, both when I put new paper in the printer, and when I removed the memo, placing it in that folder."

Ally picked up the computer-generated memo uncertainly. There was a blue stamp on the page which said, COPY with a handwritten note next to it: original in the memo file dated November 2, 1998. She began to read:

TO: Alyssa Sullivan
FROM: Deputy Neal Bryant
Sorry to miss our weekly case conference, but I forgot a lecture session that I scheduled for this week. I want to fill you in on the latest developments on this investigation, and give your instructions on how to proceed in my absence.
Developments:

- The case of Shilo Wilson has been reopened with the perpetrator listed as unknown. This means our suspect is likely involved in at least four murders.

- Mae Harris (senior editor of the "*Lakeview Mountaineer*")) researches the name and address of individuals submitting public forum letters to the paper, to ensure legitimacy. She received two letters from an Edwin P. Horace, inquiring about our investigation. This was a fake name so the person who submitted the letter maybe a suspect in these murders.

- I took both letters with their original envelopes directly to the forensic lab in Acacia. The composer of these letters used gloves and left no fingerprints while handling these letters. Also, this person used a water bottle and self-adhesive stamps on the envelope, and was careful not to leave DNA. However, the letter writer didn't realize that he dropped an eyelash onto the envelope, and it was sealed beneath the stamp, preserving the evidence. This eyelash is being analyzed for its DNA, and this sample will be compared with the statewide database.

- The killer had possibly a bloody nose or some other injury while at the 'tool shed'. We found a single tissue with dried blood on it. Judging from the amount of blood on this tissue, there were others. Our suspect must have bent over to retrieve the other tissues, dripping blood onto the floor of the shed. None of this blood is usable for DNA purposes, since it has dried out, and been exposed to external factors. However, some of this blood seeped into an elbow-pipe, and pooled at the bottom. This blood, being at the bottom of this elbow-pipe, has not been compromised, and will likely yield some DNA evidence. Hopefully, we can match the DNA sample to the composer of the public forum letters. Once a suspect is identified, we can demonstrate his DNA link to the crime scene and his attempts to subvert the criminal investigation. This will definitely strengthen our case.

- The crime scene technicians missed the pipe. Last night, I detected and located this blood evidence using luminol within the area where the tissue was found. I didn't have a complete evidence kit with me. Therefore, I haven't removed the pipe from the crime scene for fear of destroying or contaminating the evidence. I'd like them to analyze it in the mobile CSI lab which should be back down at Horseshoe Bend tomorrow, Tuesday.

Assignments:

- Contact Allen Saunders, he comes on at 3pm. Ask him to guard the shed until the techs arrive. I don't want to remove the two officers from their posts. I just wish I could post a surveillance crew to watch just the shed area, but I don't have the manpower. One deputy is watching the headframe and the other man is attempting to watch the rest of the one-mile perimeter. It is difficult to secure the entire area due to the openness of the National forest lands.

- Call Cynthia Arnold to make sure that the DNA sample from the letter gets top priority. I want this DNA analyzed and results back prior to the Thanksgiving Holiday.

- Finally, contact Eric Morrison and ask him to run a search for all missing girls between the ages of 5-10 within Northern California, even if parental abduction is suspected. If we can identify the victims, perhaps we can link them with a potential suspect.

I will meet with you next week on Tuesday at 8 am. Perhaps by then, we'll have more to work with. You can contact me by pager, if you run into any problems.

Ally finished reading the letter, the excitement mounting. "Neal, how much of this is true?"

"We did find an eyelash on the envelope from Edwin Horace, and we did find a tissue with dried blood at the crime scene. I planted the elbow-pipe in the pile of debris at the shed. I plan to camp out at Horseshoe Bend, and hopefully Morrison will come back to the scene of the crime to retrieve the pipe. I have also set up several surveillance cameras. If caught, trespassing behind police evidence lines will give me reason to arrest Eric Morrison for at least a 72-hour hold, and it should secure a search warrant of his vehicle and residence. Ally, can you place that memo in this envelope?"

He carefully opened the manila folder again, displaying a tan envelope marked: TO: Alyssa Sullivan, FROM: Deputy Neal Bryant. The envelope had a big red CONFIDENTIAL stamped across the envelope. Ally knew Neal had deliberately chosen the stamp to draw Eric's attention to the envelope; it was like a beacon in the night, quickly drawing one's focus. He knew Eric would not be able to resist the invite.

Ally secured the letter in the envelope. Neal nodded and said to her, "I only want your fingerprints on the letter. If Morrison reads the memo, his fingerprints will also be on this letter. Later, I will fume this letter which will permanently display the fingerprints on this document for evidentiary purposes."

"How will this play out?" Ally asked, taking the envelope and placing it in her book bag.

"I will not have any of the deputies following you for many reasons. Currently, I'm not taking any cases and the other deputies have had to cover the rest of the load and also do surveillance duty at Horseshoe Bend. Also, I don't believe that Eric Morrison has any knowledge that he is a suspect at this point; we don't want to alert him in any manner. I don't believe you will be at any risk. Are you still game to do this?"

"Of course. I did not expect to have any surveillance."

"Okay, I need you to take detailed notes on the following. Make sure the following instructions are not with you during your meeting with Morrison, or anywhere he can view them." Ally pulled out her notebook and pen. "Ready?" Neal inquired, and Ally nodded affirmatively.

"I do want you to carry this tape-recorder. It will be in the pocket of your sweater during your meeting with Morrison. Before approaching Morrison, and while still in your car, lean over as if finishing a call on this cell phone. Turn the tape recorder on and make sure the red record light is on. Then, you state your name, date, time, and that you are about to meet with Eric Morrison at the Office of Missing Persons. If we go to a hearing on this subject, I want to prove that you neither gave nor asked Mr. Morrison to read the memo. Also, I need to prove that you did not discuss the case with him, other than to give him my instructions. This maneuver is to avoid any entrapment defense." Ally responded with a nod as Neal continued.

"Then, after your meeting with Morrison, I want you to say into the tape recorder your name, date, time, and that you just finished your meeting with Eric Morrison. If Morrison is watching, pretend to be using the cell phone. During this recording, I want you to check that the memo and document are there. This is a very important procedure: First, say into the tape recorder: 'Regarding reference number 10324, I am opening envelope (#4), to verify that the original memo is stamped with the word, COPY in blue with a handwritten notation by Deputy Neal Bryant.' Second if true, state: 'Verified original memo (#3) is secure in envelope (#4), reference number 10324 on this same date.' This is to verify that you have the initial letter in your possession. Return the letter and tape recorder to this office. Ask for the Duty Deputy, John Bowden. He will have a big plastic bag waiting for you. I want you to place the envelope and the tape recorder in the plastic bag and seal it for evidence. This procedure will ensure the chain of evidence. "

"Okay, then what?" Ally asked.

"The Duty Deputy will be instructed not to touch either the envelope or tape recorder. He will take the evidence bag and then document the transaction for the chain of evidence form in the handling process. You will write on the form that you verified your possession of the original memo (evidence -3), which was secured in an envelope (evidence -4) after the transaction. Then, write the following: I, A. Sullivan, took the evidence from location B to location A. Placed (evidence-3) memo within (evidence-4) envelope, and tape recorder (evidence-5) with (evidence-6) tape in an evidence bag, reference number 10324 at location A -on this date. (See attached report for complete description). You must sign, then date, and put the time on your entry. You will sign off on the transfer of the evidence to the duty deputy, John Bowden. I've just given you extensive instructions. Do you need clarification or do you have any questions?"

"I was able to follow the reasoning, so it all made sense," Ally said. "You want to ensure the integrity of the evidence in court, so nobody could have contaminated the evidence during and after the transfer, right?"

"Bingo! I told you that you're a natural. Are you going to be able to find a sitter for Breanna today when you meet with Morrison?"

"Could I borrow your phone?"

"Of course."

Ally picked up the phone and dialed Larry's number. Larry answered right away. "Hi Larry, could I ask you for a favor? Would you mind watching Breanna for me at 11:30 for an hour or two? I have an urgent matter to attend to. You don't know how much I appreciate your help. I'll meet you at the house at 11:30. Thanks again." She hung up the phone and answered Neal's unspoken question. "Larry is Breanna's grandfather. Should I call Eric Morrison now?"

"Give me one minute first." He took out a small tape recorder with a thin black cord from the top drawer of his desk. He plugged one end of the black cord into the tape recorder, and placed the suction cup on the receiver of the phone. He pressed the record button on the tape recorder and said, "Okay, you can call now."

She picked up the phone and started to dial. "Hello Eric Morrison? Yes, this is Ally. Could I get your help again at lunchtime? Deputy Bryant had to go out of town, but he left instructions for me to contact you. He needs another search of the database. It's really urgent. I hope this isn't an inconvenience. Good. I'll meet you at the Missing Person's Office at noon. Thanks again, your help is appreciated." She hung up and looked at Neal. Neal stopped the tape and pulled the suction cup from the receiver. "Let me guess," she said nodding at the

211

tape recorder. "That is evidence -1 and -2?" Not waiting for an answer to her rhetorical question, she asked, "Are you all set to go camping?"

Neal chuckled, "I'm on my way out the door, now."

Ally gathered her stuff together, picking up Breanna in the baby carrier and said, "Good luck." Neal opened the door for her.

Ally fed Breanna and bathed her before Larry arrived. Larry rang the doorbell just as was finishing up. "Hi Larry,' she said upon opening the door. "You don't know how much I appreciate your help on such short notice."

"Sure, no problem. What's up?"

"I told you that I'm working for the Sheriff's Office doing some errands and research. Deputy Bryant has an urgent errand for me to run. Hope you don't mind?"

"Not at all. Do you mind if I take Breanna to the park to feed the ducks?"

"Not at all." Ally pulled out a coat for Breanna and took her stroller out of the closet. "Her diaper bag is packed. Here's her bottle; it just has to be warmed. I doubt that she will need a bottle; she just had one. I should be back in an hour, maybe two."

Ally's nerves were getting the best of her as she arrived at the Missing Person's headquarters; Eric Morrison was waiting for her on the sidewalk. Ally already had the cell phone up to her ear. She held up one finger to Eric that indicated she was going to be another minute. She set the tape recorder, made the appropriate verbal notations, and slid it back into her sweater pocket. Then she placed a newspaper, a blank lined notepad, pen, and day timer in the open book bag, which contained the memo in its tan envelope. She didn't want to make Eric suspicious by just carrying in the envelope. Ally grabbed the book-bag and her keys as she got out of the car. Ally gripped the door of her car as she got out, bending her head to collect herself. She said hoarsely, "I'm sorry. I'm not feeling so well; I'll be alright in a minute." Ally didn't have to act; she was sick and dangerously close to vomiting due to her fear.

"Where's the baby? You're not getting tired of her yet, are you?" he joked.

"No. I'm adding to my fleet! "Ally quipped. "It's just my morning sickness can't tell the time of day," Ally lied, easily falling into her part.

"Oh, I see; you're pregnant." Eric responded, and Ally noted the strange look on his face, which caused a fearful chill to radiate throughout her body.

"Deputy Bryant had to go to Acacia to lecture at the academy, but he left word that he wanted me to contact you. He said it was top priority." Ally rushed on, anxious to end this charade. Take it easy or you'll give yourself away! Ally continued casually. "He would like all the records of missing girls between ages 5-10 for Northern California, even if it's a suspected parental abduction. I hope it's not too much information to ask for. Did you want me to come back?"

"No, that shouldn't take long to compile if you care to wait." Eric said politely. Ally nodded. Her face was pale as she followed him in and sank into a chair. She pulled off her jacket and draped it over the chair. Ally hoped the tape recorder was still operating; she had seen the red record light come on while she was in the car. It was still operating prior to her slipping it into the pocket of her sweater, but she could not see if it was still on. She couldn't re-check it here in the office.

Ally leaned against the back of the chair, her head raised and eyes closed as Eric plugged away at the computer. She could feel her breathing becoming heavy and labored. Oh God, control yourself, Ally thought nervously to herself. She tried desperately to control her breathing. She had to maintain control and keep the panic at bay. He worked for approximately fifteen minutes before calling, "That should do it. It should print over there."

Ally got up suddenly and then started to swoon; she knocked over her book bag, spewing the contents across the floor. She gripped her hand over her mouth and ran toward the bathroom. Eric could hear her gagging behind the closed door. He saw the envelope with CONFIDENTIAL stamped in red. It was lying on the floor, along with several other items and a newspaper. He walked

213

over to the envelope, and hunching down, picked it up. He glanced swiftly at the bathroom door; he could hear heaving sounds. How long did he have before she got back? Eric quickly released the flap of the envelope, folding in the restraining prongs and pulled the sheet of paper out from inside. He desperately wished for some gloves but there was no time to spare; he had to seize the opportunity. He read the memo hastily; his face pale and registering shock. She was still discomposed in the bathroom, so he reread the memo. He put the paper back into the envelope carefully refolding the prongs. He opened and scanned her day timer. Well, well, well, he couldn't believe it! Ally was Alyssa Sullivan of McKinley Circle. He could hear the toilet flush and the water running. He immediately placed the day timer, envelope, and the remaining articles back in the book bag. Her washed face still pale, Alyssa Sullivan exited the bathroom. Had she given him enough time? She glanced nervously from the book bag to Eric Morrison and back again.

"I put your stuff back into your bag for you. Don't worry, I did not even peek at your stuff; shut my eyes the entire time. Your secrets are safe with me," Eric said teasingly. "Are you feeling better now? Do you need me to call someone?" He sounded concerned.

"No, thank you. I will be alright now. If we're finished, I'd better go home for the rest of the day. I appreciate your help." Ally carefully picked up her sweater from both sides from the back of the chair, being careful not to tip it. She almost knocked her sweater over in the process; her hands were shaking so badly. She snaked her first arm through the sleeve and pulled it around her body, inserting her second arm in the other sleeve. She smoothed down the front of her sweater to ensure that the tape recorder was still present; it was. Her heart was pounding so hard she hoped he could not hear it. God, she had never been this afraid; she was alone with a killer. She reminded herself she could not let the fear show, or it was over. "Sorry to be such a bother," her voice quivered slightly. Damn, thought Ally. Control it. He would probably chalk it up to her being ill.

Ally could not read his face, but he had a wild look in his eyes. His movements seemed much more animated; she could almost see the tension emanating from him. He walked over to the printer, grabbing several sheets of paper. He stapled them together, placed them into another tan envelope, and handed it to Ally. She nearly jumped as he approached. A chill ran through her body.

"I'm glad you could do this on such short notice," Ally said. "Again, thanks for your help." She proceeded hastily, almost too fast, towards the door. She climbed into her car; wishing she could just peel away, and put a hundred miles between her and that man. Ally breathed deeply as she leaned her head back on the seat. She sat there for a few moments, collecting her wits. Ally had been so nervous that she actually lost her breakfast in the bathroom. So much for her academy award winning acting job; reality had its own reactions. Picking up the phone, she dialed the number for road conditions. Eric would think she was making a phone call, but she actually made the final verbal notations for the tape recorder and pushed end on the cell phone. She quickly turned off the recorder before starting the car, noting that Eric was watching her from the glass entryway.

CHAPTER 14

After watching Alyssa Sullivan leave, Eric Morrison used his cell phone to call the office. "Hi Julie, you'll need to cancel my examinations for this afternoon, or see if Phil can fill in for me. I cannot get my jeep started, and I'm having it towed into the dealership. I should be okay for tomorrow. If necessary, I can get a loaner car. Thanks."

He drove home to change; he had to move quickly. He had a brief window of opportunity; after 3:30pm, it would be impossible to lift the pipe. He slammed his fist repeatedly into the steering wheel. "Fuck!" He shouted out into the open space. Damn Tammy. Damn that fucking whore! I should have had the whole damn thing planned better. It could have easily been concluded as a murder-suicide. I should have just killed the kid and then stuffed those fucking pills of hers- down her throat. I should have left her crazy notes scattered around the place, or even torched the apartment, for that matter. If I'd done that, no one would even look twice at me. If it weren't for Tammy, there would be no solid connection between me and any of the discards.

It just occurred to him that he might run right into one of the two boys, guarding the area. What if the crime scene dicks were on-site? From what he read in the memo, the Crime Scene Technicians had left the site last night, and the van would not be back until tomorrow. But did this mean that the techs wouldn't be back until tomorrow either? He wasn't sure, but Bryant was worried enough about securing this pipe to send someone out there to protect it. The techs must be busy, elsewhere. If he ran into anyone, he could shoot the breeze; maybe obtain more valuable information on the premise of metal detecting. Faceless didn't want to run this risk, but he sure as hell didn't want them to be able to extract DNA from that pipe. They couldn't track the DNA back to him, could they?

After he had changed into his old clothes, he grabbed a flashlight, pick ax, rope, bags, and stuck it in his old backpack. Yes, he had his gloves in the pocket of his fleece jacket. He grabbed the metal detector again, as a prop if he was questioned. Many people check out old mines with a metal detector; it was the perfect excuse. What would he say if he were to get caught behind the crime scene tape or with the evidence in hand? He was struggling with that one.

He quickly thought back to what he had read in the memo; it didn't sound like too many people associated with this investigation knew about the pipe. If he got caught with the pipe, the Deputy or the Tech would likely be clueless as to the significance. He searched for a plausible explanation for having an elbow-pipe in his possession. He would have to cross that bridge if he came to it. No. He had to be prepared with an answer. He couldn't be caught off guard or he would appear suspicious. That's it: the perfect answer! He could say he was using a steel pipe to set and test the metal detection scale, which distinguishes between ferrous verses non-ferrous metals on his detector. Great.

Eric parked on the same deserted road as before and started hiking back towards the ridge. He did not have time to hike clear to the top of the ridge, but he managed to get up far enough the hillside to get a good visual of the area. He could see the sheriff deputy, who was guarding the crime scene at the headframe, but he could not determine where the other deputy was posted. He slowly made his way down a back trail towards the mining shed.

He knew he was out of the field of vision of the roadway. Moreover, he had not seen anyone as he approached the mining shed. He hid in the shadows up against the shed, pulling on his gloves as he scanned the terrain for the second prick. He couldn't see anyone; the place was deserted. He made his way towards the front of the shed. There was no lock on the exterior door of the shed, just some crime scene tape. Fools, he thought. He silently entered the shed. He saw a smaller area squared off within the shed and proceeded to this area. He bent and grabbed the elbow-pipe. Suddenly he heard, "Freeze and put your hands over your head. Don't give me reason to shoot."

Eric jumped. His arms went up; the pipe flew out of his hands, clattering down in the pile among the debris. "Place your hands behind your head and slowly back up three large steps." The Deputy quickly padded him down, finding only a pocket knife on him. Eric was handcuffed and turned around. His eyes widened, and adrenaline flooded his body when he saw Neal Bryant. Eric knew without a doubt that he had been had. The perfect set-up.

Fuck! It had been so perfect, he thought in bewilderment. How in the world did they key in on him as a suspect? He had been so careful, so meticulous, during the killings. Eric felt himself drift and zone out. He felt as if he were listening in at a distance as his Miranda Rights were being read. Then he was led in silence toward the waiting sheriff's car just hidden out of sight. He heard Bryant call over his shoulder, "Saunders, grab the film." Neal bent Morrison over, placing his hand on his head, pushing him slightly to get him into the back of the sheriff's car.

Oh Shit! They have it all on tape. What would he do now? Get a grip, he thought frantically to himself. He was struggling to maintain his composure and keep control of this situation.

Deputy Neal Bryant started the conversation on the way out of the area by saying, "Do you want to talk about it? I hear confession is good for the soul."

"Go fuck yourself!" yelled Morrison. "I want a lawyer. By the way, what am I being arresting for: scavenger hunting?"

"Cute, Morrison," Neal said curtly. "Try tampering with evidence, crossing a police barricade, interfering with a police investigation, even a trespass violation, if I can make it stick. I suspect those are just the appetizers. I can hardly wait for the main course." Neal's jovial tone was belying the steel gaze in his eyes. Morrison didn't respond. Neal glanced through the rear view mirror; by god, Morrison was pouting. He looked like a little boy caught smoking. He might just have to rethink his interview strategy.

"Listen, you can contact your lawyer when we get down to the substation," Neal told him.

Morrison did not respond but stared blankly ahead. Eric thought, "Man, I fucked up! What's Mom going to do?"

After a taxing silence, Neal glanced again through the rearview mirror. Morrison was rocking methodically back and forth, his eyes fastened on the back of the car seat, staring blankly. He seemed to be in another dimension. Was this guy unraveling, or was it all part of the act? Morrison did not say another word on the way down into town, but he was relentless in his perpetual rocking. Neal wondered if Morrison was working on an insanity plea, or if he had definite problems. At least he wasn't claiming to hear voices.

They arrived at the Sheriff's booking station, and Neal went to the rear of the car to retrieve Morrison. He was still rocking. Neal reached down and grabbed his arm, "We're here," Neal said as he pulled him towards the door. Morrison's eyes flashed, and he suddenly looked disoriented. "Let's go inside," Neal said calmly as Morrison looked at him in confusion. Neal led Morrison into the booking station and handed him over to the junior deputy, John Bowden, for processing. Neal said, "I want a drug and alcohol screening as part of the processing. Then, he can contact his attorney. I will be at the desk in the rear office working on the search warrant."

After Bowden had booked Morrison, the junior deputy led the detainee to a jail cell. Morrison watched in bewilderment as the cell door closed automatically, and he stared densely at the man's retreating back. Lost. After a long pause, he proceeded to pace in a frantic frenzy, as he tried to grasp the change in his circumstances. What was his plan? What could he do? He repetitively banged his closed fists against his skull, roughly keeping pace with his jagged strides. He stopped abruptly, where is she? Has Mom found out yet? He looked up and down the deserted corridor, but no one was there. Eric sank down into a fetal position, clutching his head tightly, and the rhythmic rocking ensued.

Approximately forty-five minutes later, Neal was finished with the court documents asking for a search warrant of Eric Morrison's apartment and vehicle. It was dicey whether or not he would be granted a search warrant, since there was not yet any direct evidence to tie Eric Morrison to the death of any of the children. It was all circumstantial evidence: first his having access to children, he knew Shilo Wilson, and finally, there is strong evidence to suggest he was very worried at what might be found at the crime scene.

Joy Pouls, Tammy Lee's cousin called. Joy's mother had told her that Eric Morrison was living with Tammy about six months before her death. They broke up around six weeks before the tragedy. They had known each other from adolescence. Both had been briefly placed in the same co-ed receiving home while they were awaiting group home placements.

Neal was also working on a petition for a sample of Morrison's DNA; if the court granted it, it would be the mother lode for this investigation. He would wait before submitting this petition; any findings on the search warrant would make his case for a DNA petition stronger.

"Deputy Bryant, could I interrupt you for a moment?" Deputy Bowden said hesitantly as he entered the room.

"Yes, what's up?" Neal said without looking up from the computer.

"That guy you brought in, Morrison, he hasn't said a word and he keeps rocking. I asked him if he wanted to contact his lawyer; he did not even seem to hear me. What do you want me to do?"

"Keep a close eye on him. I don't know if he is suicidal or not. If he has not responded within another hour, call county mental health and ask for a licensed psychologist to respond to the jail. Keep me posted, I've got my pager on. I'm going to the courthouse."

Ally was holding Breanna comfortably in her arms, singing softly to her while feeding her a bottle. The phone rang breaking into Ally's peaceful repose. Placing the bottle on the end table, she placed Breanna on her shoulder and picked up the phone.

"Hi Ally, it's me, Neal. Just thought you would like to know we arrested Eric Morrison when he tried to lift the pipe up at the shed in Horseshoe Bend. The Judge just granted me a search warrant. It was somewhat difficult, since we had no direct evidence to tie Eric Morrison to the homicides. I only have strong evidence to demonstrate that he purposely entered a crime scene with the intent to contaminate evidence or obstruct justice. Thankfully, I have a great credibility record with the Judge.

"I hope we find something to link Morrison to these children, or my credibility is going to take a beating. There are some politics at play here, since Morrison's stepfather is the lieutenant governor. Additionally, Morrison has a public service record and good guy image; it was a tough sale. I'm about to head to his apartment. Saunders remained at Horseshoe Bend to search for Morrison's vehicle. I'll call you tomorrow if we find anything. Thanks for your good work."

"Thank you, for letting me know. I appreciate it," Ally said. She sat back down with Breanna, patting her back. She felt numb and incredulous. Ally held Breanna a little more securely. "Breanna, what are you going to encounter in your lifetime? I just pray that you are always emotionally, physically, and spiritually healthy. Please, please God," she quietly pleaded.

Ally continued rocking Breanna for the next hour. Breanna gave her solace, and a sense that the world was still a good, wholesome place. A sense of peace enfolded her. She did not believe this was over, but she would sleep easier knowing that Eric Morrison was behind bars, unable to hurt another child. She got up and placed Breanna in her crib, pulling the blanket over her and kissing her forehead.

Ally went to her bedroom and laid down on top of the bed. Relaxing her body and mind, she was hoping that she could willfully summon Bree. Her motivations were unclear. Maybe to get validation for her belief that Eric Morrison was the responsible party? Maybe to find a clue to where the remaining body may be hidden? She was unsure of her intention, and Bree did not come through. Was it over? She felt slightly depressed; she would miss her interaction with Bree.

Ally heard the front door open; David was home. She slowly drew herself up into a sitting position and rubbed her fingertips over her eyes. She stood up and exited the room to tell David the news.

Later that night, Ally had a difficult time relaxing. She awoke frequently from shadowy dreams, with only a vague recollection of each dream's content. Finally, mentally exhausted, Ally fell into a deep sleep.

"Hey Ally! Ally, wake up! You need to see the news." Ally could hear David's voice intruding upon her sleep-fogged brain. She snuggled deeper into the pillow trying to escape the sound. The sweet softness of her bedding sent warmth cascading through her being; she closed her eyes into the delicious dark recesses of her mind. She was so relaxed and insulated from exterior worries, floating back into her dream world. David persisted, "Ally, you really want to see the news."

Ally rubbed her eyes and tried to focus as she sat up in bed. She stood wearily, resting her head against the palm of her hand. "Okay, what do I have to see?" she said in a gravelly voice. David came up behind her, placed his hands on her shoulders, and steered her gently towards the television in the front room. The blaring news narrative formed meaning, and Ally was vaulted into the bitter, harsh reality of the morning.

The news was filled with stories about the murders of several small children, the skeletal remains, and the main suspect, Eric Morrison. It was a frenzy. Ally picked up the television remote, clicking through the network channels. Each of the major news stations was running various stories regarding serial murders in Calaveras County.

Ally listened as a female newscaster reported. "The skeletal remains of two children were found in an isolated region of Calaveras County known as Horseshoe Bend. The authorities believe that the same suspect is tied to a child found murdered at Horseshoe Bend in 1989. This unsolved case was recently reopened. The main person-of-interest in all these murders is the stepson of our lieutenant Governor, Alex Brentwood. Let us go to our news correspondent in Acacia, who is currently speaking with Alex Brentwood."

Ally studied Alex Brentwood's appearance on the television screen. He appeared (at least-on the television set) to be a tall, imposing man in his early sixties. He had dark hair, silvered at the temples, with hard, impenetrable dark eyes. Alex Brentwood had a muscular frame and appeared to be fit, not an ounce over or under weight. He wore his business suit as armor; impeccable, unyielding and forceful. She continued to study his image as a cheeky female reporter announced who she was. "This is Sheila Trenton with Enterprise News interviewing Alex Brentwood. Mr. Brentwood, you are aware that your stepson, Eric Morrison has been arrested in connection with the homicides of several children in Calaveras County?"

Alex appeared to be a formidable man, given his calculated response to her words. "It is my understanding, Ms. Trenton, that the local authorities have not arrested Eric on any charges related to homicide. It appears Eric was just unfortunately in the wrong place at the wrong time. Ms. Trenton, you do need to keep your facts in order." Sheila seemed ruffled by his dismissive tone. "Excuse me, Mr. Brentwood; hasn't law enforcement implicated your stepson, Eric Morrison, as the prime suspect in this serial homicide case?" Sheila carefully emphasized the words, stepson and prime suspect, in order to regain control of the interview.

"I have not personally verified whether Eric is a suspect, let alone the prime suspect. If so, it would be certainly foolhardy, since they do not have a shred of direct evidence to link Eric to the murders of those poor children. Eric was out with his metal detector doing some gold mining, he accidentally trespassed onto a crime scene. How law enforcement managed to finesse an arrest warrant out of these conditions is beyond my comprehension. I would hate to think that my political foes would attack my family, but I just cannot see any other justifications for this travesty. Eric has no such enemies; he has been a pillar of strength in his community with a reputation which is above approach."

Ally noted that his speech was impassioned, but his tone was hard. Little, if any warmth was reflected in his demeanor. He was saying what he needed to say under the circumstances with his current campaign held in the balance. God, Ally thought to herself, his voice did not even show a hint of inflection when he mentioned "those poor children."

"You believe this arrest is politically motivated? Who do you believe is behind this arrest?"

"I have my suspicions, but I intend to have concrete proof before I speak out. I have hired Stephan Connor, with his sterling reputation as an attorney, to defend Eric in this matter. Then perhaps law enforcement can really do their job instead of wasting their time on such petty misdemeanor violations. They need to do some real police work by finding the culprit in the deaths of those small children."

"Back to you Connie," said Sheila.

The camera flipped back to the anchorwoman sitting at the desk. Connie was saying, "The local authorities and the chief prosecutor in Calaveras County are unavailable for comment."

Ally clicked off the television, turning to David. She stared at him, dumbfounded. She was feeling completely overwhelmed, and her eyes teared up. David put his arms around her and kissed the top of her head. "Congratulations, Ally. You have driven this investigation full throttle into an arrest."

"I still don't believe that we are quite there," Ally sighed. "It doesn't feel complete. I guess it won't feel quite right until there's been a guilty verdict and a sentence given. If Alex Brentwood has his way, it won't be happening. I need to call Neal and find out what's going on. Did you check on Breanna?"

David grinned at her. "Sleeping as deeply as her mother was. She's fine. I'd better run or I'll be late." He kissed her before making for the door.

Ally called the sheriff's station and was placed on hold. When Neal answered, Ally rushed him with her questions. "Neal, what's going on? What did you find? I've seen the news this morning!"

"Ally, it is crazy around here. The phones are ringing off the hook. The reporters are swarming in front of the stationhouse. Tell you what, lets' meet at Carrie's Coffee House; we'll have breakfast and I'll fill you in. Do you know where it's at, on Largo Avenue?"

"Yes, I've seen it. What time?"

"Give me forty-five minutes, I've got a few things to do and then I'm going to sneak out of this place. I'm going to enjoy the break. Talk to you later."

The restaurant's maroon carpeting and forest green and maroon floral seats gave the restaurant a dim-evening look, even though it was barely nine o'clock in the morning. Ally could smell the sweet aroma of coffee and bacon ever lingering in the air, whetting her appetite. Neal came up from a long corridor aisle, which hosted booth seats on each side. "Hi Ally, I'm seated over this way," he said as he ushered her to the end of the aisle.

"Wanted to sit back here, I doubt the press is going to hunt me down, but you never know." Neal said unconvincingly, and then continued. "We have the additional benefit of privacy in these seats."

Ally placed the carrier seat on the far end of the bench; quickly checking on Breanna, as she settled into the booth. Neal picked up the menus and handed her one as he scanned the corridor at regular intervals. He scanned his menu clinically as if his decision regarding his selection was of great importance. Ally got the impression that his mind was not on his breakfast. Ally looked at the menu and spotted a spinach and cheese omelet. She closed her menu, and asked Neal what was going on.

225

Neal stretched out his back, suppressing a yawn. "I've been going hot and heavy on this investigation for the past 24 hours. As I told you, Morrison tried to lift the pipe, and we arrested him on the spot. Upon an arrest, he was acting strangely. He was zoned out and he kept rocking; did not respond to his surroundings. Later, he started acting more normally, demanding an attorney and asking to make a phone call. His drug screening came back clean. I don't know if his strange behavior is a prelude to an insanity defense, or if he really does have some mental health issues. But I think the insanity defense will go down the drain with all the efforts he has made to subvert the investigation."

"During our search of his apartment, we found a huge stack of violent pornographic magazines in the back of his closet but it wasn't child pornography. We also found several porno magazines on a bookshelf. You won't believe it; these magazines were flanking a framed photo of his mother. And on top of these magazines, we found pictures of both Bree Jamison and of Shilo Wilson. The children were alive at time of the photos, so no big smoking gun there. However, at least we have a link to these two children and Morrison. It might make some fair innuendo on his propensities in court."

"On his computer, again, we found more pornographic material, but nothing illegal. We found a digital camera and hundreds of photos on his computer. It seems like he is an amateur photographer but no photos with children. I bet he has some photos of the children hidden somewhere, since he is rather visual. It seems to be one of his passions. I'm combing my brain to try and figure out where these photos could be hidden, but so far nothing." He looked at her inquiringly and she shook her head in the negative.

"We also found some children's incisor teeth. We have sent the teeth to Acacia for DNA processing. We are also going to have to get DNA samples from Crystal Jamison and Natalie Staples to see if we can match any of the teeth through Mitochondrial DNA."

Ally looked inquisitively at Neal and said, "What is Mitochondrial DNA?"

"There are primarily two types of DNA: Nuclear and Mitochondrial DNA. One can generally derive Nuclear DNA from fluid samples. You can get Mitochondrial DNA from bone and hair follicle samples. It has no nuclei, but you can have multitudes of these cells, and they survive longer. From Mitochondrial DNA, you can determine the likelihood of the skeletal remains being maternally linked to another individual. Thank heavens we have maternal relatives to test. It will take about three to six weeks to get the results back. If those teeth belong to any of our known victims, we have a strong case against Morrison. If not, we are going to have to build a huge bridge to link Morrison with these murders. Hopefully, more evidence will surface. "

"Morrison did have ropes, rags and tape found in his vehicle, but these items were new and we cannot compare them with any recovered samples from the remains. All the materials are generic ones that you can buy at any hardware store. It all sounds incriminating, but a good defense attorney can give a hundred reasons why someone exploring the backcountry may have these items. I have many of the same items in my truck. Here comes the waitress." Neal fell silent as the waitress approached.

Neal nodded at Ally and she said, "I'll have the spinach and cheese omelet with Monterey jack with the English muffin and coffee please."

"I'll have the special," Neal said, "eggs over medium, bacon and white toast. I'll have coffee, too."

The waitress turned over the coffee cups on the table, filled them with the coffee from the decanter, and left the decanter on the table.

When she left, Neal continued. "We have booked Morrison on tampering with material evidence in a police investigation, criminal trespass, and obstruction of justice for crossing the police barriers. We have not formally charged him on any homicide charges. Those charges will not hold felony status if we don't obtain more concrete proof of his complicity. I want to keep him out of commission on the lesser charges while strengthening my case on the murder charges. Morrison will have his arraignment and bail hearing on Thursday."

"What do you need me to do?"

"I need you to do a lot of telephone and scheduling work. I compiled a list of the labs and contact names. I need you to keep on top of getting DNA results back on that eyelash we obtained. Also, I need you to schedule appointments between the lab and the girls' relatives, Natalie Staples and Crystal Jamison. I want proof-positive of Bree Jamison and Amy Georges' identity before we get to court. I've got an outline for you." Neal grabbed a manila envelope from his briefcase and handed it to her.

Ally promptly placed the envelope in her book bag. She noticed that Breanna was awake now. Breannna was alert, looking around, but not fussing. What a sweetheart! She was busy chewing on her small fist.

"The only other thing I wanted to tell you," Neal added, "is that we almost have the human remains from the shaft dislodged. We had to hire a pumping outfit to pump out some of the water from the shaft. It has been a difficult undertaking to say the least. I'll let you know what happens. I'm just guessing but it may be difficult to make identification. I may have some more phone-work for you to do at that time. Oh, it looks like our food is coming, just on time."

The waitress placed a delicious looking omelet in front of Ally and then placed Neal's breakfast in front of him. "Is there anything else, I can get for you?" she asked.

They said no, and the waitress made her way back towards the front of the restaurant. By silent consent, they stopped discussing the case even though it was on both of their minds. Instead, Neal talked about his grandbaby, Kayla, and how his daughter, Jeannie, was fairing. Ally filled Neal in on Breanna's developmental milestones. They let the conversation take on a lighter note.

"Breanna is sure a calm baby; she has not fussed at all during breakfast. Kayla is having problems with colic. Jeannie's doing everything she can think of to calm her, but as of yet, nothings worked. Kayla cries for hours at a time." Neal commented.

"I heard that a little bit of peppermint, like from a broken dinner mint dissolved in a bottle of water, sometimes helps."

"I'll let Jeannie know. It's worth a try," Neal said, getting up and picking up the check. Ally reached for her pocketbook and Neal waved her money away. "My treat. By the way, you must have done a wonderful job with Morrison. The look on his face was priceless when I arrested him.

CHAPTER 15

His carefully, cultivated mask had been ripped away; he was Faceless, no more! He was 'out-of-the-closet,' so to speak; the fuckin bitch had exposed him. Yet he was surprisingly relieved, because now he could do whatever the fuck he wanted to. Eric's manic pacing became even more rapid in the small, cramped cell, as he ruminated on the bitch's duplicity. She was going to get her pay back before long.

He had just finished his initial conference with Stephan Connor. So dear old Alex had bought him the best. He knew it wasn't out of sentiment. Alex must be sweating bullets over his upcoming election and then this. Eric laughed in delighted merriment, this was a cloud with silver lining after all. Eric just hoped that it cost Alex a pretty penny besides the lost sleep. Sweet, a great pay back after all this time! Eric sat down on the bottom bunk, his mind spinning in different directions. At least for now, he did not have to share this jail cell. Hot Damn, his luck was changing after all. Eric started rocking vigorously back and forth, viciously giggling.

The arraignment and bail hearing were scheduled for November 5th. But Stephan Connor was returning today with an affidavit for Eric to sign. The affidavit stated that he, Eric Morrison, was unclear regarding the reasons for his arrest, since he was merely testing the setting of his metal detector in that mining shack before continuing to the mine in search of gold. He didn't know the police were conducting an investigation there. He believed the police tape to be a relic of the past for he saw no police activity in the area. Connor would submit an affidavit, along with a petition to the court. The petition said that these negligible offenses placed the petitioner, Eric Morrison, erroneously 'under a cloud of suspicion' for a deplorable series of criminal acts. The longer it took to adjudicate these infractions, would inevitably cause irreparable harm to Morrison's reputation and standing in the community.   Connor stated, "If we get lucky, the judge will dismiss the charges and throw it out of court before the arraignment hearing.   If we get a hearing on the petition, I'm shooting for Wednesday. It's a long shot but worth the effort." Yet was Connor right, is that what he actually wanted? Which persona did he prefer?

Eric smiled and laughed heartily in jubilation again. It had been fun, putting one over on everyone for years with the Good Samaritan act, his perfected, good guy image. But wouldn't 'being under a cloud of suspicion' be much better? Funner. Maybe a change-up was in order. He'd have everyone, especially the bitches, intimidated and tip-toeing around him; afraid of what he may do, his dark predilections. Especially the "Bitch," he could cast her a baleful stare, leer at her, and make her shit a brick; if he didn't have to play the good, little boy anymore. Of course, he wanted an acquittal; he didn't want to spend any more time than he had to, in a stinkin hell hole like this one. He'd have to figure out how this should be played out.

God love the media! Alex — Caitlin, and last but not least mother — must be feeling some heat. I just hope those reporters are jamming microphones in their faces day and night, asking them why they thought this had happened. He could just see mother primping herself for the cameras, playing the tragic heroine.   Privately, she would be agonizing about being late for her nail appointment. Would "Mother Dear" make a grand premiere visit to the jail-house? That remained to be seen. He stared blankly out the bars at the empty corridor, waiting. He crossed his arms tightly, and started rocking.

He knew Bryant was working his ass off to find evidence to hang him for the murders. The prick must be spinning his wheels in his circumstantial mire or he would have added the charges by now. The fucking Idiot didn't realize that he was too smart to leave any direct evidence to link him to the murders. And in his apartment; hell no! The Morons must be busy analyzing those teeth; that would cost them two to four weeks of wasted effort.

He had substituted the incriminating ones with the decoys. Christ, the law enforcement dicks were so predictable. They think they're so smart; I'll show them. The show would begin tomorrow, and they certainly won't like it.

Was his mother going to come to the jail? How long had he been in this cell now? Not good, he was losing track of time. He walked towards the bars, looking up and down the corridor before returning and sinking down

Roughly rubbing his face to clear his mind, he needed to stop this damn rocking and slow down his rapid thoughts. He did get blind-sided by the motherfucker-Bryant and that Bitch. No wonder she nearly jumped out of her skin whenever he came within ten feet of her. It was her fault that he was so hyped up and stuck in this cage. A malicious smile formed on his face as he thought of what he would do with her and a knife, if only he could get her alone. It was enough to give him a hard-on. Yes! He definitely was going to get that Bitch, make her suffer. You had your laugh, but you're going to pay for it. He'd never killed a woman before. A new experience, the Cunt would be his first! What would it be like fulfilling his fantasies with her? More difficult, maybe; but much more gratifying! The Cunt wouldn't be like his discards, blind and stupid to the situation. No, the Cunt would be apprehensively anticipating his every move, along with the inevitable outcome of her predicament. The horror would be evident and locked in her eyes; the fear emanating from her skin. It whet his appetite!

He needed a solid action plan because he didn't want to lose track of any more time. He couldn't afford any more voids at this stage. .... He'd have to plan it all out clearly, as sadistic images flooded his mind. Dissatisfying, because it was too delicious...certainly not enough, all these dark impulses without having the opportunity to act upon them. Soon, he'd be out; the Morons couldn't keep him locked up much longer or jack-up the bail on minuscule charges. He then would seize his opportunity.

Still obsessing, engrossed in the mental pictures; he was breathing hard, much harder. He reached down into his orange jumpsuit pants and grabbed himself, pumping harder and harder as he imagined the reaction on Alyssa Sullivan's face, as he eviscerated her fucking little maggot baby, right before her eyes. And then he'd fuck her. If she is pregnant again, wouldn't that be bliss! Three in one go! He envisioned her mutilated body and that of her maggot sprawled-out in front of him; his hands covered in blood. Yes, yes, he was coming, his skin and the atmosphere around him was super-charged, tingling with electricity. "Holy Fuck, I feel alive, on top of the world!" He cleaned-up, and laid back on the bunk, interlocking his fingers behind his head. The electricity, like the atmosphere around him, sizzled. Much better than his flat, bland magazines or his dry, worn out photos! Oh man, it will be so much better when I have the real thing and not just this watered down, dismal fantasy. Then, I'll be able to taste that fear.

Eric walked over to the bars, scanning the corridor. What did I expect? Of course, Mother won't come until Alex-the Asshole gives her a thumbs-up.

"What time was it anyway? He gripped the bars tightly, unconsciously rocking back and forth. He swung around, kicking at the cell door. ....Okay, he needed to plan, focus on the plan I will stake out the Sullivan house, find out her schedule. She lives in a secluded area; it should be easy to grab her without being seen, if I act quickly enough. Or would a store parking lot be better? He would decide after surveying the house. The jeep will be just out of sight, but within a short distance. I will attack her from behind, cover her mouth and nose with a rag soaked in anesthetics. He had a small vial hidden which he obtained from the office. It had been a very easy lift, especially in such a low dose. He just knew it would come in handy one of these days. It will daze her, but not for long, enough time to place her and the maggot into the back of his jeep.

He visualized the scene. I will bind her wrists, her ankles, and then her mouth. Bind her with duck-tape; no, several layers of duck-tape (especially across her face), so it will make it more difficult for her to breath. I will wait until she regains consciousness and is aware of her surroundings. Aware of the maggot's presence within my arena! I'll look her in the eye, running my tongue over my lips, bringing out my knife to display to her. I will run the edge along the maggot's neck, pressing the edge into its skin. I will say, "It won't happen that quick, my dear."

He would return his knife to the scabbard, and then he would drape a blanket over her body, including her head, to blind her. He knew what the Bitch would experience exactly! Her breathing will be labored. She will only have her imagination and fear to supply any visual stimuli. She will only hear her own breathing in her ears. He was dizzy with delight, as he imagined her senses intensifying, hyper-vigilantly, swamping her in fear. He would drive, a long time but not too long, so as not to lose the effect. He didn't want her emotionally numb to the experience. Just long enough to let the terror submerge her in the reality of her nightmare.

Yes, I will take her to that other abandoned mine in Tuolumne County; wishing he could look at his map of this area. Once parked at the site, he would loudly collect his tools and supplies, letting her fear supply the information of what he was gathering. She would be listening for any sounds from the maggot.

I'll dump the Bitch along with her maggot into a wheel barrow, and proceed to the mine. He would have the metal poles strategically staked in a triangular pattern beforehand. The camera would be adjusted to the perfect angle and timer set. Only then, would he remove the blanket, unveiling for her vision, his sacrificial altar. If she was so concerned about slaughter of his discards; then she simply could take their place. How fuckin noble of her! The Bitch! Pretending to be so ingenuous, acting a part, but she was a selfish, calculating mercenary like the rest of the whores. If she believed her own diatribe, she was better off dead than stupid. He'd heard eating the heart of your enemy makes you stronger; he was feeling invincible already.

Shaking himself, he needed to flesh out his plan: First, he would use rope to tie her hands above her head to the first stake. He would look into her eyes, as the fear overwhelms her in its intensity. Then slowly he would drag both legs to the second pole, securing one leg tightly to the pole with a rope, making sure the grated pole and ropes press tightly into her skin. He would cut the duct-tape from the inside leg, grazing the skin as he did so, leaving a bleeding gash. It would hurt like hell as he secured this leg to the third pole, the grated pole imbedded into the gash, bound heavily by the rope. He'd look into her face the entire time; surely she would be sobbing hysterically and literally choking in her terror. Man, I hope she faints from the pain and terror so I can revive her again.

Eric felt his thighs and dick began to tauten, as he continued with his fantasy. He would remove some sheet metal shears from his bag, cutting up the seams of her pants, nicking her skin along the way, drawing blood. He would continue only if she was conscious so he could experience her pain. Then he would cut up the center of her shirt. Maybe he would cut off her breast. No, don't rush it! Besides, the maggot must be the first to seriously bleed because he wanted the Bitch completely conscious during the exhibit. The photos of this event will be truly spectacular! He would run his knife along her stomach, pausing at her ovaries, nicking the skin. Pausing long enough for her to anticipate what he was going to do, and letting the knowledge grip her. He would run his knife up her chest to her neck. Setting aside the knife, he would choke her out, looking into her face as she fell unconscious. Yes at this point, I'll remove the maggot, hide it away. As he revived her, the reality would dawn in her face that she was still alive, and the maggot was missing. She wouldn't know if I disposed of it yet or not. He would taunt and toy with the Bitch about whether or not he'd crushed the fucking maggot! Eventually he would return with it, to continue the fun.

The Bitch will be under my complete and utter domination. Mine to torment, use, and abuse! Closing his eyes, he started to masturbate again as he visualized her fear; anticipating his next move. He'd take her, withdraw, and then ejaculate all over the fucking maggot. Suddenly, his mother's image flashed in his mind, as his release came.

The guard came back mid-stream, rudely disrupting his rehearsal. The guard looked at him, rolling his eyes towards the ceiling, and said irritably, "Your lawyer's here to see you again. I hope you are this hot when you are out of isolation. The boys in general lock-up will have a good old time. I hope they get you good. When I think of what you did to those children, I'd like to cut your balls clean off!"

Eric Morrison grabbed a towel to clean himself up. He said to the guard, "Hey man, I'm innocent."

"Yeah sure, you're the Pope. Just framed so your step-daddy will lose the election. Hope you know nobody's buying that crap."

"Only a jury has to," Eric sneered. Hopefully this lawyer would be good enough to get him out quick. He knew that this guard was itching for any excuse to do him in, and he was sure there were others like this guard out there. He needed to watch his back; both on the inside and outside of this cage. Where was his mother right now? She was probably just posturing for the media.

Neal Bryant was frustrated as he counted the minutes lost waiting to testify. It was a motion hearing for Eric Morrison. He had so much to do, but everything seemed to be in a holding pattern. He had spoken to the county prosecutor, Andrew Williams, approximately two hours and twenty minutes ago. Sir Williams, as he called their self-important county prosecutor, told him all about it.

Stephan Connor submitted a motion to have all the charges against Morrison dismissed. The premise was that his client did not intentionally violate any laws; he just demonstrated poor judgment when entering that shed at Horseshoe Bend. Mr. Connor indicated that Morrison felt any police investigation would be long over, since he did not see any law enforcement personnel until he was, in fact, arrested. Connor contends that to keep Mr. Morrison detained any longer would violate his procedural due process rights and constitute illegal constraint.

The Honorable Judge Natrisha Owens contacted Andrew Williams, to ask whether or not the county had any evidence to offer as proof that Mr. Morrison knowingly entered an active crime scene. Williams indicated that they did have proof. He would be able to present this evidence in the preliminary hearing, since the case would be tried as a felony.

Mr. Connor told the judge that this was not good enough, each day that passed caused incredible harm to his client and his good standing in the community. Judge Owens asked Mr. Williams whether he could present a prima facie case to support the need for a preliminary hearing. Mr. Williams stated that he could not get all the witnesses in the court with such short notice, but he could present the investigating officer, Sheriff Neal Bryant, to testify on the matter. Neal received the phone call from Sir Williams with instructions that he should be prepared to testify at 1:00 this afternoon. It was now 2:30 and not a peep. It was Wednesday and he had so much to do before the weekend. He shouldn't be wasting his time here.

Sir Williams had presented this information to him in outline form as if he had taken the information straight from one of his damn legal summaries. The attorneys never gave any consideration to anyone's time but their own. Couldn't they have called him right before he had to take the stand? He really needed to talk the County into a laptop computer so he could utilize his down time. He had tried previously, but they claimed to be hung up on the confidentiality and security issues. Neal thought these were lame excuses used to cover financial constraints. The Board of Supervisors really didn't want to authorize extra expenses to agencies that weren't profit producing, except maybe during election years.

Neal was getting edgy. He hated just standing in this shabby hallway wringing his hands. Finally, he was called in to testify. Neal entered the courtroom and was called to the stand. "Could you raise your right hand? Do you promise to tell the truth, the whole truth, and nothing but the truth, so help you god?" the female bailiff said.

"I do," Neal Bryant said decisively.

"Could you state your full name and occupation for the record?"

"Neal Jacob Bryant; I am a sworn senior deputy sheriff employed by Calaveras County."

Sir Williams stepped up in front of his prosecutor's table, glancing at his yellow note pad. He turned in the direction of the witness box and met Deputy Bryant's glaze. "Hello Deputy Bryant," Neal nodded at the acknowledgement. "This is an informal hearing to demonstrate to the court why the defendant should or should not be bound over for a preliminary hearing to answer the charges presented to the court. This hearing will determine whether the defendant is released from holding, or if the court will need to proceed to the date of the arraignment and bail hearing. Hearsay evidence will be allowed, and you may allude to any evidence in your possession. Keep in mind that any evidence mentioned within this proceeding will have to be produced during the preliminary hearing. Do you understand the scope and nature of these proceedings?"

"Yes, I do," Neal responded evenly.

"Deputy Bryant could you tell the court in your own words, what led up to the arrest of Eric Morrison?"

Neal answered: "The Sheriff's Department located the skeletal remains of three bodies in the Horseshoe Bend region of this county. In addition, the body of another murdered child, Shilo Wilson, was found in this area back in 1989; the case was never resolved. I attempted to limit information about these skeletal remains to the media until I had some understanding of what had happened to these children.

During our investigation into these deaths, the Department became aware that some unknown party, who had knowledge of our interest in the Horseshoe Bend area, was scrutinizing our investigative efforts at a distance. It also became apparent that possibly the same individual was making serious attempts to hamper, contaminate, or sabotage the ongoing investigation into the deaths and identities of the skeletal remains in the Horseshoe Bend area. Some of the evidence to support this claim is still being processed.

During this juncture, Eric Morrison was asked to produce names of missing children in a 100-mile radius of Calaveras

County by my intern, Alyssa Sullivan. Mr. Morrison works as a volunteer coordinator at the missing person center for our region. Ms. Sullivan reported back to me that Mr. Morrison was intensely inquisitive about our current interest in these missing children.

On October 28, while I was at the crime scene, some unknown person was secretly observing the recovery process from a ridge above the crime scene. This person took off in a hurry after I discovered his/her presence, but we were unable to get up the ridge quick enough to question him. Later that day, Eric Morrison was stopped by Tuolumne County, Deputy Holt. It appeared as if he was leaving the Horseshoe Bend area by an alternative route."

In the course of my investigation, I found that Eric Morrison knew the child, Shilo Wilson, whose body was discovered in Horseshoe Bend in 1989. Mr. Morrison had a romantic relationship with the child's mother. Much of what I suspected in terms of Mr. Morrison's obsessive interest in our investigation was circumstantial and perhaps innocent in nature. Therefore, I devised a sting operation, which would provide proof of whether Mr. Morrison's interest in this investigation was illicit.

Ms. Sullivan asked Mr. Morrison to complete some further research for the Sheriff's Department regarding missing female children of a particular age range within the Northern region of California. Ms. Sullivan met Mr. Morrison at the Sheriff sub-station in order to pick up this information. We tape-recorded her conversations with Mr. Morrison to establish that she did not coach Mr. Morrison, or ask him to read a confidential document in her possession. This private memo was in a prong-sealed envelope clearly marked confidential, addressed to Ms. Sullivan from me. Ms. Sullivan left the envelope unattended when she made a supposed emergency trip to the restroom. When she re-entered the room, Morrison had placed the envelope along with other items in her book bag. Before leaving the sheriff's sub-station, Ms. Sullivan verified that she had the original memo in her possession. This document was later fumed for fingerprints. Two sets of prints were found; Ms. Sullivan's and the second set of prints belonging to Eric Morrison. I had only touched the document with latex gloves. The Department filed additional charges of 11143 PC, Unauthorized person receiving record and 618 PC-Open contents of a sealed letter, upon receiving the fingerprint results this morning.

The letter to Ms. Sullivan fictitiously indicated that there was unprotected DNA evidence in a pipe at the crime scene, which is a utility shed within Horseshoe Bend. In less than two hours after his meeting with Ms. Sullivan, I arrested Eric Morrison at the crime scene with the pipe in his hand. Two surveillance cameras documented this: one monitoring the activity to the exterior shed, and one monitoring the interior of the shed. Both films show that the area was clearly marked with yellow police tape, marked 'Do Not Enter.' Signs were also posted on the door of the shed, indicating that the police forbade entry into the shed, and any violators would face criminal prosecution. I arrested Mr. Morrison and read him his Miranda Rights.

Additional evidence is being processed and may become available to demonstrate that further efforts were made to sabotage this investigation. At this juncture, I do not have absolute proof that Mr. Morrison made any additional efforts to sabotage the investigation, but the evidence to substantiate or eliminate Mr. Morrison as a suspect should be forthcoming in a couple of weeks.

"Thank you, Deputy Bryant. I've got no further questions for you." Sir Williams said as he eyed the defense.

Stephan Connor moved stealthily around the defense table, eyeing his prey. "Deputy Bryant, do you usually entice unauthorized individuals to enter a crime scene during an active investigation?"

"I take exception to the word entice," Neal snapped. "Neither I nor my intern encouraged or instructed Mr. Morrison to read the memo or go to the crime scene. He did that of his own accord."

"Do you not worry about preserving the integrity of your evidence in an ongoing homicide investigation? If my client went to the crime scene on your pretense, for whatever curiosity reason he may have, you now can claim that you found trace evidence tying him to the crime scene. Sounds as if you are trying to manufacture evidence in this case by establishing a link between my client and your homicide investigation!"

"I resent your implication," Neal shot back. "Again, I did not instruct or encourage the defendant to enter the crime scene. I just presented the opportunity for him to get caught on tape doing so."

"Deputy, you did not answer my question, so I will repeat myself. Don't you worry about preserving the integrity of your evidence by securing a crime scene in an ongoing investigation?"

"Our Department had already processed the existing evidence at this crime scene." Connor actually gave him a Cheshire cat smile as he followed up with the next question. "So are you telling me that you no longer had an adequate reason to prohibit entry into that so called shed? It was no longer an active crime scene?"

Oh shit, Neal thought to himself. He could see the trap he had fallen into. It would read one of two ways. It could look like he compromised an ongoing investigation, and possibly contaminated evidence in the process, by his efforts to arrest Morrison on weak charges. Or it could seem like he had been lax in clearing the area. If it were no longer a crime scene, Eric Morrison's presence would not constitute criminal trespass. This didn't look good. Neal carefully phrased his answer. "The shed, the contents of this shed, and any evidence within this shed was examined by our crime scene technicians. Any evidence which was unearthed was carefully preserved, documented, and dated, through the chain of evidence procedures for criminal investigations. Any additional evidence collected from that particular area would be after the fact and dated accordingly. Of course, any evidence and all questions related to that evidence would be examined and subject to court examination during any future proceedings.

This shed is one crime scene among several crime scenes within that locale. Several sets of skeletal remains were found within the area. At this juncture, we are still searching the area for additional remains, if present. This was why I was extremely

241

concerned when it appeared that some party might be compromising our investigation by spying or attempting trespass. Any trespass could easily contaminate any remaining evidence. Any clearances of any crime scene within this locale would be extremely premature, since we have not completed our investigation within the surrounding area.

The Department assigned a two-man crew to secure the area. The Department does not have the large manpower or resources to hire additional people to stake out this locale, which is approximately one square mile radius. Therefore, when I put this operation in motion, I was extremely careful to monitor all of Eric Morrison's movements within the area with two surveillance cameras and my own close monitoring of the situation. I hope this adequately addresses your concerns, counselor."

"No! This does not address my concerns, Deputy. If your Department now dramatically discovers physical evidence to link my client with this crime scene, you know it will be intensely scrutinized."

"I have no doubts, Sir. However, I carefully monitored all of Eric Morrison's movements on the date in question. If he has not strayed into this locale and/or any other area within Horseshoe Bend on any other date in recent history, no further evidence should appear, should it?"

"I have no further questions at this time," Stephan Connor said dismissively. Neal studied Connor as he exited the witness box. Connor acted like he had already won by discrediting him before the Judge and the legal community. On the other hand, Neal felt that his testimony had gone well under the circumstances of having extremely weak charges. Was Connor's attitude all posturing and jockeying for position?

The Judge decided in the Department's favor, but Sir Williams was not happy as they exited the courtroom. Williams had let Neal have it immediately after the motion hearing. Williams informed him that any future evidence from the crime scenes at Horseshoe Bend would be weakened, because the Chief Investigator had admitted on the stand to allowing entry by an unauthorized person into a secured area. Williams further fumed that he, Bryant, had clarified that the County did not have enough manpower to properly secure the area in the first place. The defense could lay a solid foundation of the argument that any evidence collected from Horseshoe Bend was severely compromised. Moreover, Neal had indicated that an unauthorized individual could possibly access the site for it was not completely secured by using two officers for a square mile of terrain. He had even suggested that Morrison could have been there some other time. The Sheriff's Office better drum up some uncontroversial evidence in these murders. If all they had was physical evidence from the crime scene, then they would have to kiss any prosecution in these murders, good-bye."

Great! He, a veteran, had stepped in it; tripped over his own tongue! How could he have stepped into Connor's trap without even realizing it? He tuned Andrew Williams out as he continued to derail him. Neal knew he may have compromised this entire investigation, and was feeling gravely ill with the enormity of the circumstances. "How in the world am I going to keep this Bastard off the streets?" he muttered as he turned and walked away from Williams. So much for his Perry Mason moment. He should have known better.

Eric sat in compressed stillness, his rock solid mass barely concealed the ravenous energy of his unfettered rage. With feral eyes, he stared at the blank cell wall in front of him. Mother never came to see him. She must not have been given a pass by Alex-the prick. Why had he even expected it? Ha! His mother was a fucking whore, just like all the other bitches out there, pimping out her services for money and status. At least, his discards were better off dead than finding out what the world is really like. He'd found out early enough.

Eric sprang to his feet in a rampant rage. When was Connor going to get him released from this cage? Alex had put up the bail money; it would've tarnished his image, to not do so. He needed to get out and prepare his harvest by ferreting out his kill; the

243

Bitch's days were numbered. After he killed the Bitch, nothing would be able to hurt him again. She could've left well enough alone; his discards were forgotten long ago. None of them belonged to her, so why in the hell did it matter to her anyway? "Hell, it shouldn't be taking this long." Eric howled out in frustration.

"Shut up already, your attorney has bailed you out." Startled, Eric looked behind him at the guard, who opened the cell door. "You're free to leave." Eric decided to make a brief stop at his apartment; but he would quickly move on to his headquarters.

CHAPTER 16

Ally was trying to plan for Thanksgiving, as she drove to the Sheriff's office on Tuesday, November 10, for her weekly meeting. She didn't feel very festive. The Morrison situation loomed over her like a dark cloud, troubling in its intensity. She prayed for relief from this crippling anxiety, which colored everything in her life.

It felt strange and sadly amiss, traveling alone without the baby. Breanna was home with David. He had readjusted his work schedule today because he would be working late into the evening. Tonight, the store had a special promotion, tied into the Sub-for-Santa program. David needed to complete some of the paperwork and then he was going to help wrap some of the gifts, scheduled for early delivery. The store was going to fill orders as soon as possible to avoid shortfalls, and the last minute scrambling before the Christmas holiday.

Neal looked surprised when Ally arrived in his office, empty-handed except for the book-bag hanging idly from her shoulder. "Where's the babe?" he asked as she seated herself.

"Left Breanna home to baby-sit David. She's in the process of training him," Ally quipped. She then noted a dull, lifeless look in Neal's eyes. "Neal, what's wrong? What happened?"

"Ally," Neal began. "Eric Morrison was released on bail late yesterday."

Ally sucked in and held her breath; her reprieve was over. "Are you serious?"

"Unfortunately, yes. Morrison was granted bail, last week, and the bail amount wasn't too steep given the current charges. Brentwood bailed him out. Guess it was better than face the embarrassment of having Morrison incarcerated."

"Now what?" She whispered deflated, feeling sick to her stomach, as the grave news sank in.

"He still has a preliminary hearing to contend with and he is

245

under scrutiny. Meanwhile, we keep plugging away at our investigation. There has to be some answers out there. You will probably be called to testify at the preliminary hearing. It's on December 30th. County Counsel, Andrew Williams, needs to meet with you to go over your testimony."

Ally was trying to listen to Neal above the concert of her irrepressible thoughts. There was a faint ringing in her ears as she tried to retain focus on what he was saying.

"Are you okay?" Neal asked solicitously. Ally had a vacant stare, as if she was beyond attempting to figure out what happened or what went wrong. God, Eric, is going to kill again, she cried silently. Her energy evaporated quickly, sitting stiffly as inertia shrouded her body.

"Yeah, I'm fine," she retorted. "I just thought he would be locked up longer." Ally froze; Eric wouldn't try to harm her or Breanna, would he? No -that's just crazy. He wouldn't do anything risky while he's being investigated.

"That is what we all hoped for, but it didn't happen that way. Now, we focus on the present and keep working the investigation." She was struggling to emulate his detachment, but felt the anger welling up inside her. The pressure was mounting.

"Great, fine, whatever," Ally clipped.

"Ally, listen. Our maneuver was a gamble and a risky one at that. I'm going to have to do damage control with the integrity of all the evidence. Any evidence in this investigation will need to be rock solid. You need to keep going and not give up. It isn't over until we get it to the jury and the verdict comes back. This is all part of the procedure in investigating a case. Sometimes, you win and other times you don't."

"Okay, I get it," Ally responded curtly. "I'm thinking how hard it is on me emotionally that Eric was released. ...That he is free and able to kill another child! I'm not considering how this legal debacle affected you and your reputation, as well as the Department," she baited. Ally was aiming for a spark of emotion: anger, just anything to show her that it was not just another case for him to solve. Show that those children and what they went through had a significant impact. It can't be just another case!

She felt like she was crumbling. She swallowed hard, then harder, trying to push down the hard knot in her throat. The tears were welling in her eyes, her nose starting to run.

Neal handed her a tissue. Otherwise, he seemed immune to her emotional state and continued calmly. "I know you want this guy out of commission. We all do. We didn't get what we wanted, so we keep plugging away. Hopefully through our persistent efforts, we win in the end. However, we never give up at the first sign of pressure."

"Okay, I get it! The investigation isn't over."

"You missed the whole topic of procedure. We need to have a very solid investigation, so we get a conviction, and keep this killer off the streets. I know you believe Morrison is the killer, we both do. However, at this point, we have no evidence to back it up. Ally ...Usually before you're intimately involved with a murder investigation, you have a number of years in the field to prepare you for all this madness. It's not surprising that you're overwhelmed, and the lunacy of the legal system can throw anyone into a tailspin occasionally. Just try to trust in the process. Usually if you give these perps a long enough rope, they will hang themselves with it." She wanted to scream; to shout at Neal for being so calm and matter-of-fact about this horrible business.

"When do I meet with Andrew Williams?" She said quickly, trying to get the meeting done and over with soon. At this moment, she wanted to get as far away from this place as she could and not look back.

"Can you meet with Williams on Friday, December 11th, in the afternoon?"

"Yes. You know I've never testified in court before?" Ally gained some hard-sought composure, struggling to maintain a conversational tone. Her voice was stilted, shifting from high to low in accordance with her internal struggle.

"I know that I haven't had time to prepare you for the court system. It's never easy the first time you testify," Neal coached. "Answer clearly; take time to think before answering. If you get confused by a question, don't hesitate to ask for clarification. Andrew Williams can walk you through the procedure and then give you some better advice. Don't worry, you'll do fine."

"Yeah right." How in the world did I wind up in the middle of this mess, Ally thought pensively. It was by your own choosing; she reminded herself sternly. She shouldn't be taking it out on Neal.

Ally's mind was a whirl when Neal asked, "anything we haven't covered before we wrap it up?"

"Caitlyn," Ally stunned them both by replying.

"What?" Neal asked in confusion.

"Caitlyn, the half-sister of Eric Morrison. No one has spoken to her, have they?"

"No. Do you feel someone should speak with her?" Neal tried to grasp her quick change of gears.

"It all started with his sister. Caitlyn has known Eric a lifetime. She may have an interesting perspective," Ally offered.

"I can track her down if you want to speak with her," Neal said gingerly, hating the thought of a confrontation with the Brentwood family.

"I do," Ally said with resolve.

Neal stared at Ally. She had some great instincts for police work. It was no time to start doubting or undermining her now. "I'll get you some contact information and let you talk to her. You can give me a report back. I don't want to tip off Alex Brentwood that we want to talk to his daughter, especially since we have nothing solid to tie Morrison to the killings yet. I remind you to proceed cautiously; just tell her that we are just gathering some background information on Eric Morrison. If she mentions needing legal counsel, get the hell out of there. The city can't afford any lawsuit. Alex Brentwood is a dangerous man to tangle with personally and politically. He can be very nasty. It may take a couple of days to locate an address and phone number for her. I don't even know if she is married or not."

"I won't make the department look bad. I will be very discreet," Ally assured him.

"Well, it would be far more of a challenge to Alex Brentwood if I spoke to Caitlyn personally. Maybe, if you speak to her, the slight will not be as devastating to Brentwood's insurmountable ego. I'm sorry for the turn in events, just bear with the changes the best you can. I'll call you with Caitlyn's contact information as soon as I am able, but its low priority in terms of the current investigation."

Neal watched Ally waiver out the door. Well, that was easier than I thought, but so are root canals in retrospect. Was he wise to give her this much lead? She did not know the normal course of investigative work. This unsophisticated approach was his ultimate blessing and curse. She expected the grunt work and didn't complain about any humdrum task that he presented her with. She always thought outside the box, because ultimately she didn't have a clue as to what the perimeters of the box were.

This was one investigation that could not have the slightest amateurish overtones. Neal might have failed at this already. Am I losing perspective? He knew there were already some fatal flaws in the course of this nightmarish investigation. Am I letting Ally influence my thinking too much; evoking too much emotion, stifling my objectivity? Was he the captain of a ship, who had put the cabin boy in charge of the helm? Neal needed to regroup and pull in the reins on this investigation. He was not going to let the psycho get away with killing those babies.

Neal was looking for that proverbial key of indisputable evidence to turn the investigation around. He silently vowed, "I hope it exists, because if it's there, I will unearth it. So help me God, I will. Let there be that smoking gun because I'm going to nail that bastard."

Ally had arrived home in an emotional, crying frenzy. She unloaded the pain and hurt of her morning appointment onto David. He took her in his arms and rocked her until her tears subsided. He didn't speak; he just let her unravel. She fell asleep, spent from the emotional upheaval. She awoke to find his note: "Ally, had to go, even though I hated to leave for work knowing how upset you are. We'll talk this evening or not, whatever you like. Take care, until later, David."

Ally still hadn't told David that she'd even met Eric Morrison, let alone about her intrinsic role in his arrest. He could be so overprotective at times; she didn't want him to worry. But, was it fair to keep this information to herself, given the situation? She felt safe enough while Eric was a suspect and in the public eye. But, what if they couldn't produce any evidence of his involvement in the murders; then what? She didn't want to contemplate this possibility. She could only hope that the evidence was forthcoming.

Ally went to check on Breanna, wondering when David left. Breanna was sleeping peacefully. Ally checked her diaper; she was still dry. David must have changed her right before he left the house.

Heavens, he was so wonderful. She hoped he wasn't harboring any hidden resentment over her involvement in this investigation. He hadn't expressed any disapproval over the past couple of months, but she remembered his initial reaction. She also knew she had changed; she had never been so emotional, sulky, or intense before in her life. "I just hope he loves the new me as well as the old. If we can get through this, we can get through anything together. Let's face it -a psychic interlude, her involvement in a full- blown serial homicide investigation, and trial was not part of their original five-year plan." She mused.

Ally jumped when she heard the phone ring, and quickly answered the call.

"Neal." Ally was surprised that he was calling her back so soon. It was barely three hours since she left his office; a long three hours, but three hours all the same. She wondered what was up.

"Ally, I've got a number for Caitlyn, she's expecting your call."

"What do mean? You've already found and talked to Caitlyn."

"Yes. I hadn't even started making some tentative inquiries. I decided I had better return some of my phone messages before I drowned in the pink sheets. I was about six or seven down the pile and picked one up from Caitlyn Mathews. I didn't recognize the name, so I called. Low and behold, Eric Morrison's sister called because she wanted to talk to us. The truth is stranger than fiction. Are you psychic or something?"

They both laughed, "So I'm told," Ally answered. "What did Caitlyn have to say?"

"She told me that she wasn't even sure why she wanted to call. She just needed to talk to someone about her brother. I told her that I was backed-up for several days, but I would be more than pleased to have my intern meet with her to discuss any concerns. I gave her your name and told her that I would have you give her a call."

"Wow. Talk about perfect timing," Ally said. "It can't hurt that she contacted us first; I know that thought must have crossed your mind, too."

"You bet, I hate to tell you, but I'm greatly relieved. We just need to tread carefully with both Alex Brentwood and his high-rent lawyer, Stephan Connor. You know I hate to keep reminding you, Ally, but I do have to let you know that if we are not extremely careful, the killer of those children will walk. I'm trying to make darn sure that doesn't happen. To catch a killer, you have to think objectively and detach yourself from the emotionality of the circumstances. I hope you can understand this."

"Yes," Ally sighed, "Logically it makes sense. I will maintain my composure, but it's difficult at times. It has been personal for me from the onset, since I saw the first image of Bree. If I'm doing anything to compromise the investigation, let me know; I'll stand aside."

"Ally, I don't want you to quit, but I do want more objectivity. As I've told you before, visions or no visions, you have some great instincts for investigative work. The problem is that sometimes you need to slow down the process; evaluate and re-evaluate the information you have. Decide what information is supported by evidence, in order to build a strong foundation for the prosecution. I'm hoping for a damning piece of evidence to materialize; but short of this, I need to build a multitude of circumstantial evidence to support murder charges. If I rush in and fail to deliver a good investigation, like it or not, Morrison or the unspecified killer will go free. Remember that it could just as

251

easily not be Morrison. Just think: this killer has killed at least four children, maybe more. I don't think he'll stop if we don't get him convicted. Most likely, he will relocate and start all over again."

"I understand," she said. "It makes perfect sense. Initially, when you were talking so objectively about the hearing and the procedural process, I felt the children were not being validated. They were being objectified and discounted; I reacted with emotion. I know this isn't the case. I'm sorry for the outburst."

"No need to apologize, your reactions are normal. The rest of us in the system are jaded."

"Are you regretting that you hired me? Are we good again?" Ally asked sheepishly.

"I have occasional doubts about the wisdom of involving you in this mess. This one is as dirty and disgusting case as anyone could ever receive in a lifetime. I hate to bring you into a horrific serial murder case along with all the political undercurrents. All elements surrounding this case are dirty pool, and you don't have the experience to equip yourself to handle all the nuances, heartaches and pitfalls. You have a beautiful young family, and that should be your focal point right now."

"I was enmeshed in this case before I met you," Ally told him. "I could not leave the children behind once they had been discovered. Whether I was hired or not is inconsequential. I am haunted by what took place at Horseshoe Bend. I believe I was meant to be part of this investigation for the long haul. I just want to make sure my being here positively effects the outcome. I keep reminding myself that finding four of these children has helped the families find some closure.

"Ally, let me give you a word of caution: A case like this can be damaging. I don't want this case to tear you to pieces, because sometimes you cannot put the pieces back in order to come back whole again."

"Okay, I'll keep that in mind."

"We will meet again on Tuesday and go over developments. Let me give you Caitlyn's phone number so you can arrange a place to meet. I would go to a public place. Do not meet her in her home! Find a place where you can speak privately but not unobserved. I don't foresee any problems, but it is always better to air on the side of safety. If anything makes you uncomfortable, leave. Call if you have any problems. Caitlyn Mathew's number is 724-1332; she lives in Acacia, so it's the same area code."

"Thank you Neal, I'll see you next Tuesday."

Ally hung up the phone and dialed Caitlyn's number.

"Hello, is Caitlyn Mathews there?" Ally asked.

"This is Caitlyn Mathews," said the pleasant even voice.

"Hi. I'm Ally. I'm working with Deputy Neal Bryant; he said you wanted to speak to someone about Eric Morrison. When would be a good time to meet?" Ally wanted to arrange a time when David was home from work to care for Breanna. Then the thought hit her like a lightning bolt: tomorrow is November 11th; Mom's going to be here. She felt guilty; it had completely skipped her mind that mom was coming this week. She had done nothing to get ready. Oh well, She figured Mom would understand.

Caitlyn's reply brought her back to the present conversation. "I was hoping that I could meet with you in the evening, tomorrow night. I work during the day and need to make arrangements for my husband to pick up the kids."

"Yes, tomorrow night would be fine. I thought we could meet at the Mill Coffee House off of Highway 60."

"That would be wonderful," Caitlyn agreed. "It's about half-way between Acacia and Cedarwood. I dreaded the thought of driving all the way to Cedarwood and back on a work night." I'll meet you out front at 6:45, okay?"

"I'll see you then." Ally hung up the phone, thinking that Caitlyn sounded, well, so normal. Ally didn't know what she had expected, but it was hard to imagine a regular person like that could have a serial killer as a brother. "What Ally, every member of the family had to be weird or wired differently?" Yet with what Ally had learned about the Alex and Susan Brentwood, she couldn't help but wonder what Caitlyn Mathews' childhood had been like.

Her head was throbbing; it's probably all the tension. Taking two aspirins, Ally laid down, waiting for the medication to take effect. She closed her eyes and slipped into a dream-like state. Ally sees the thickset back of a man with dark hair, prowling within a kid's darkened bedroom. The intruder clamps his heavy hand over the mouth of the sleeping child and then straddles the youth. The young child awakes, eyes full of fear. A boy? The brutish man places duck-tape over the boy's mouth, and continues to secure his wrists and ankles. The abductor quickly rolls this child up in the bedspread, slinging the frail kid roughly over his shoulder. Ally can hear his muffled cries as he is carried off. The child is taken into some room. A cellar? It is very dark and cold for Ally can see white vapor form, as the man breathes in and out through his mouth. The wrapped child is dumped in a heap on the ground. Through the young boy's diminutive sobs, Ally can hear the man's mirthless laughter. In a brusque voice, the vile man says, "That will teach you. You stupid Ass. Don't fuck with me!" He departs, and Ally can hear the door being locked from the outside. The laughter gets acutely louder, shriller, and it won't stop, chilling Ally to the bone. Then, the child's cries are mixed with the laughter, each competing to drown out the other, completely unnerving Ally. Breanna's cries, mix in with the chorus of the other two sounds. All rationality is suspended, as raw emotion overwhelms Ally. She covers her ears to drown out the noise, screaming hysterically in frustration, "shut-up, shut-up, stop, can't you just shut-up!" Leave me alone!"

Minutes pass, Ally rolls over and opens her eyes, Breanna is still crying. Reason emerges through her frayed senses, leaving Ally, shaken-up and mortified by her outburst. She shamefully got up to care for Breanna. How could she have disengaged from her baby like that? Ignored her needs. Never again! She couldn't lose control like that. She had hated that feeling. She didn't know if she'd been screaming at the man, the boy, or for little Breanna to shut-up and leave her alone, maybe all of them.

And what was going on in her vision? She couldn't make sense of it. Who was that man? He was stocky with dark hair, unlike Eric. And the child, looked like a boy. Who was he? One of the victims? Ally realized that she didn't get a clear image of either the man or the child. The room where the child was taken to, certainly wasn't the shed at Horseshoe Bend. All she could do is pass on the information to Neil.

Eric was living out of his camp trailer; his private headquarters. He hadn't returned to his apartment since the first night after his release. He had managed to out-maneuver the media personnel and make a quick escape. So far, no one had disturbed him here.

Over a week ago, when he decided that he needed a new hideaway for his keepsakes. In the 'worst case' scenario, he also planned a safe haven for himself. He had pulled this trailer from the storage lot. Then, he had found the ideal spot to park his trailer, outside the national forest and just off a deserted trail that ran from the main dirt road. His headquarters couldn't be seen from the main road, since the surrounding trees and bushes hid it. However, he could see anyone coming for miles. With his amazing foresight, he had even stocked up on provisions.

Eric looked around at the sparse, interior cavern of the burnt out trailer. The soot etched ruts riveted the blackened dingy walls, and the ambiance was embellished by the scorched cupboards. This 1987 Prowler, Lynx trailer had caught fire and had been damaged in a fatal traffic pile up. His 'headquarters' had been purchase from a salvage auction. Eric was thrilled because this camp trailer didn't exist on the books. Over the years, he had restored the melted wiring and hoses to make this hovel functional again. It wasn't much to look at, but it definitely met his needs

He laid back against his sleeping bag; the pictures of his deceased discards were fastidiously arranged and attached to the ceiling. He stared intensely at the images, as they hovered above his head. But, his new target would have to wait until he took care of business. The Bitch was his "top priority," as his rapid pulse heralded the start of the hunt.

255

While Ally drove to the airport to pick up her mother, she told Breanna all the fairy tales that she could remember. She wished that David could have gone with them, but the holiday season was a very busy time for his store. She was disappointed all the same.

Ally watched a plane landing as she headed towards the short-term parking lot. She liked to watch the arrival and departures of each plane, imaging what places they were traveling from and where their final destination would be. It was difficult to find a parking spot with the holiday travelers running amuck. She saw red backup lights up ahead, waited for the car to pull away, and then parked in the stall.

She pulled on her gloves, instinctively hunching her shoulders within her jacket as she opened the car door. It was a very cold and windy day. She released Breanna from the car seat, and worrying about the cold draft, quickly zipped up her snowsuit. Ally placed her in the front pouch, wrapping a thick blanket around her. "Well Breanna, it's been a long time since you saw your grandmamma."

Ally was able to locate the arrival gate quickly and easily. Her mother's flight was on schedule, and that meant she would only have to wait twenty minutes more. Breanna was fidgeting, and started to fuss. It had been several hours since her last bottle. Ally headed towards the restrooms to heat the bottle. She found a vacant seat, and sat down. Removing Breanna from the front pouch, she cradled her in her arms and began to hum. Breanna's mouth desperately sought the nipple of the bottle; she was definitely hungry. Ally was unaware of the serene, wholesome image she and Breanna made as she fed her daughter, oblivious to the smiles of strangers around her.

Ally just finished burping Breanna when her mother's flight arrived. She placed Breanna back into the front pouch of the halter, placed the strap of the diaper bag and purse around her shoulder, and headed towards the gate.

Rene Michael emerged from departure gate doors with her arms already spread wide in an ever-ready embrace. She wrapped her arms around both Ally and Breanna in the same instant, while caressing her daughter's cheek with her own. Ally felt the tears surface, knowing how much she needed exactly this very thing. Rene held her at arm's length, looking at her from head to toe in an ever-vigilant assessment. "You look very stressed!" Rene stated frankly.

"You look absolutely wonderful," Ally said in a quiet, sincere voice. "It is so, so very nice to see you." Ally's glance wandered over her mother's five foot, four inch frame. Her mother was not skinny in stature nor over-weight. She had womanly, soft dimensions. Rene had short ash blond hair and cloudy grey eyes. Her eyes sparkled with merriment, but at the same time she seemed able to look deep inside of Ally. Rene's persona radiated warmth and comfort.

Rene made another brief assessment of her daughter and said, "Let's get my bags. You can tell me what's going on in the car. Meanwhile, let me hold my granddaughter. I've been dreaming of holding her since I left in September." Ally handed Breanna over to her mother as they continued towards the luggage carousel.

By the time they had arrived at the house, Ally had told her mother the entire story, from the ghost sighting in March to the news of Eric Morrison's release. Rene listened intently, only asking a few clarifying questions. They continued their conversation, non-stop, into the living room.

"Mom, I believe whole-heartedly that Eric is guilty; I get the hibby-jibbies whenever I'm around him. But I'm worried, there may not be enough evidence to connect him to these murders, since the deaths happened so long ago. We're at a precipice, if Eric isn't locked up soon, he'll kill again. Here I am, in the middle of a serial murder investigation, armed with nothing. My knowledge of police procedures is minimal at best, and I rarely get any psychic images anymore. I feel so damn helpless!"

"Ally, I believe everything happens for a reason. Neal is still relying on you and trusting you with the intimate details of this investigation, despite some of the problems. Therefore your help must be worthwhile. Also you may not want to hear this, but God is utilizing you in his service. He trusts you with this gift, knowing that you'll do the right thing. Just have faith that everything will come together in the end. It was meant to happen at this time. Look at all that has happened in a few short months, after nothing materialized for ten years."

"David basically told me the same thing, weeks ago. I'm trying to convince myself."

"David, the confirmed atheist! Halleluiah," Rene joked. "The convert speaks."

Ally was speaking in a broken fashion, trying to put words to her thoughts. "I'm trying to have faith; but I'm afraid, and I don't know when I'll feel safe again.   Since this all started, I've had nightmares about Breanna, and now, I'm worried that Eric Morrison will harm her, somehow." Even talking about this fear made a huge knot materialize in the pit of her stomach, and Ally suddenly felt sick. "I know it's probably irrational, since he is currently under investigation, but that doesn't alleviate the fear. It's like I'll always be looking over my shoulders, and I'm worried that I'll smother Breanna in my effort to protect her."

"Honey," Rene soothed, "You're meant to be where you are today, but you can't always predict what's going to happen along the way. I know that God is directing you in this endeavor, and I'm sure he'll protect you along the way. You just need to ask for his protection and guidance.   Listen and trust in your intuition. If you let your fear over-ride your senses, you may miss or may tune out some essential messages. Fear is a lousy fellow to have as your compass; to provide direction. I know it is easier said than done, but you need to relax and go with the tide. Have faith that it'll work out the way it's meant to."

"I'll try, Mom. I feel better already. More at peace than I've been in months. I guess I needed to talk it all out."

"I'm glad we finally have a chance to talk; I knew there was a lot that you weren't telling me. I'm not psychic, but I've still got my mother's intuition.   I cannot tell you how worried I've been for you.   What time is David going to be home?"

"He should be home around six. I was hoping I could leave you with Breanna. I have an appointment tonight with Eric

Morrison's sister. I hate to ask on your first day, but..."

"You know I'd love it," Rene interrupted. "You also know that I came here to help you out. Do what you need to, but make sure you give me a call before you leave from your appointment so I can be looking for you."

CHAPTER 17

Ally arrived at the Mill coffee house about ten minutes early. Caitlyn Mathews was nowhere in sight. It was too cold to be waiting outdoors, but ultimately, Ally did not want to miss her. Twenty minutes later, Caitlyn arrived, out of breath.

"You must be Ally. I'm Caitlyn Mathews. Sorry to keep you waiting; I got tied up at work. Let's go inside, it's freezing out here."

"What sort of work do you do?" Ally inquired.

"I'm a public health nurse," Caitlyn replied as a waitress came to lead them to a table. "I'll just have a coffee and look at your desert menu." Caitlyn said to the waitress.

"That sounds great to me," Ally responded. She now got a good look at Caitlyn. Caitlyn was in her late-twenties, but she was self-composed and presented herself as someone much older. She was of average height and weight, her long dark brown hair was pulled back in a loose ponytail and framed her oval face. Her eyes were green, in sharp contrast to her dark hair. She was wearing a worn brown-leather bomber jacket over a red button up shirt and Levi's. She had on ankle-high leather boots.

Caitlyn's naturally warm personality was evident, even within the first minutes of their brief introduction. Ally felt comfortable around Caitlyn, and she sensed that Caitlyn would be very easy to talk to, despite the situation. Caitlyn came across as self-reliant and confident, but she emanated a streak of vulnerability. Ally wondered if this vulnerability was evident because of the nature of their meeting. It was difficult to discuss private family matters with a total stranger.

The waitress came back with coffee and desert menus. By the time, Ally turned over her cup; Caitlyn was already drinking hers. "Boy, I needed that." Turning to the waitress, she said, "I'll have a slice of your chocolate fudge cake." Ally's liking for this lady was increasing by the minute.

Ally said, "I'll have the same."

After the waitress had left, Ally looked directly at Caitlyn and said, "You want to talk to the Sheriff's Department about your brother, Eric Morrison?"

For the first time this evening, Caitlyn hesitated, an undefined emotion etched itself on her face. She looked down at the coffee in her cup. "I don't know what I wanted to say exactly or even where to begin. What I'm about to say will only make sense, if you understand our family background and Eric's childhood."

Caitlyn began, "My father met my mother when Eric had just barely turned six. They married less than eight weeks later. My father immediately staked his claim by impregnating Mom. As soon as I was born, and they had established their own little family, Eric might as well have been an unwanted guest in our home. He could have disappeared for days, and they would have hardly noticed for he was practically invisible. The only cardinal rule was that he never embarrassed or disgraced my father."

"This was a rule that Eric would never adhere to; in fact, he deliberately went out of his way to antagonize my father. Eric hated my father. Eric thought that if Father and I were out of the picture, he would get his mother back. In the beginning, I believe he felt that if he were bad enough, my father would simply pack his bags and leave."

"Even if he had succeeded, it wouldn't have done him much good. Sadly, Eric lacked insight into our mother's character. She is very histrionic and dependent personality. If it weren't my father, it would have been some other man. My mother will love as long as it meets her needs. If the relationship no longer gets her what she wants, it ceases to exist in her mind. Eric was so damn smart; it simply amazed me that he could never understand this. Even at the age of six, I got it: my mother is very superficial; and will conveniently use other people to meet her own self-centered needs."

Ally remained silent, nodding encouragingly for Caitlyn to continue with her account.

Caitlyn sighed in acquiescence. "My father had his own egocentric needs. In my mother, Dad found the perfect mate: someone shallow, who could play the charming hostess, dutiful wife, and mother; while catering to his every whim. Dad also wanted a family-man image to build his political career. Initially, he loved me, but only as an extension of himself, or a possession. Eric, as a resentful, angry stepson, never did fit into my father's picture of what an aspiring politician should have in a family."

"What was your relationship like with Eric, while you were growing up?" Ally questioned, urging Caitlyn onward.

Caitlyn took a deep breath and reminisced. "Early in my childhood, I hero-worshipped Eric. He was a handsome, charming young boy. He had a good sense of humor, and could make me laugh. I thought he was the center of the universe. Whereas, Eric resented me intensely because he felt like I had the unconditional love of both my parents, and he had no one. He believed that I was chosen over him by Mother. Therefore, he often played mean, nasty tricks on me or he broke some of my toys, but I always forgave him. Even at six years old, I knew how extremely hurt and lonely he was. I truly loved him. I was full of anger at both my parents because I could see how badly they treated him."

Caitlyn fell into a deep silence as if dredging this up had exhausted her.

"What finally happened? It couldn't have been good?" Ally gently encouraged her to continue.

"One day, my father was particularly nasty towards Eric, berating him for some sarcastic remark Eric made to his teacher. Eric directly confronted my father, saying that he was only worried because someone may write about it in a letter to the editor of the paper. Then Eric said that yes, he just might write the letter himself. My father's face turned an ugly shade of purple, and he said he would not have some snot-nosed brat making trouble for him. They had military boarding schools for the likes of him."

I couldn't stand it anymore. I started screaming at my father, to leave Eric alone. I hated him. I ran behind the rocking chair,

262

refusing to come out, sobbing hysterically. My father stormed out of the room. I grabbed a piece of paper and started writing a runaway note. Eric was still in the room, so I asked him how to spell some of the words."

"Eric told me if I was going to run away, he would help me do it right. He knew a place that I could stay. We would bring some food, and he would bring me more food later. We would make them sorry. He helped me pack a bag, and we took a long walk to a deserted workshop. He said he would come back and check in on me. But, he never did. I was scared and lost, but I did not want to leave because Eric would come back. Sadly, I expected him to return, and rescue me. I had a loaf of bread, peanut butter, jelly, a bag of chips, cookies, and a blanket. I was there for about two days before a police officer picked me up."

"What did the police officer say when he found you?"

"The officer told me I had nothing to worry about: Eric was in juvenile hall. He wouldn't be able hurt me anymore. I was very confused: I thought I was in trouble too for running away, and was being taken to jail. Then, the officer told me that he needed to stop to drop off some papers at juvenile hall. I panicked. I told him that I did not want to go to juvenile hall. He told me that the juvenile hall was just for boys and girls who get into trouble, to get them the help they needed. I insisted that I wasn't that bad. He just laughed; promising me that he was not going to leave me there. I was quiet for the longest time. Then I told him that I supposed juvenile hall wasn't that bad, but still, it was quite sad. I remember the stunned look on his face as I told him this like it was yesterday. The officer must have thought my statement was rather profound, that sadly children would need to go to juvenile hall in order to get the help, they needed."

"Eric had defied my father, and he was sent away, never to return. I felt that I had gotten away with it once, but it would not happen again. If I ever screwed up, I would be sent away. My parents would abandon me too, as they had Eric. I spent my childhood trying to avoid my father's wrath."

"As soon as I was eighteen, I ran away and got married. Amazingly, the marriage and relationship survived. My husband is everything that my father and mother are not. I truly love Chris. His family is full of warm, loving, and wonderful people; I adopted them as my own. We have three children: twin seven-year old sons, Jordan and Austin, and four year old daughter, Lizzie. They are my family, not my parents or my brother."

"How do you get along your father, now?" Ally asked.

"Once I would no longer agree with my father's opinion as bible, or at least pretend to, he did not have much use for me. He wants my presence at family functions to support the ever-important political image, but that is as far as his emotions extend. Both my father and I know where our relationship stands. We tolerate each other. I keep up appearances at family and social functions, because my father is a vindictive man. There is no use in unnecessarily stirring up trouble. Chris and I have talked about moving to another state, but Chris's family is here. I told him that I am an adult and have no need to run away from my problems or my parents. I am old enough to stand up for myself now."

She looked up, staring straight into Ally's eyes, and stated bluntly, "You may be on right track if you suspect that Eric murdered those children."

Ally felt the bolt of electricity shoot through her body. Shocked, she couldn't believe the abrupt statement Caitlyn just made, without any hesitation. Ally asked, "What leads you to believe that your brother is responsible for the deaths of those children?" She carefully paraphrased her response to make sure that she hadn't misunderstood her.

"I'll level with you and I'm never one to beat around the bush. If you can't tell already, I'm a straight-to-the-point type person. I don't have patience to dance around what needs to be said."

"Okay," Ally said, "but we need to back up. Do you have any direct knowledge of your brother's culpability?"

"Absolutely not, or I would never have stood by and let any of this happen.

"Let me help you to understand why I believe he may be responsible. Over the years, I have slowly seen the anger, resentment, and bitterness eat away at Eric, destroying the wonderful boy he was. I promised myself that I would never let the same thing happen to me. I escaped for my own self-survival. I have no use for either of my parents; however, Eric has never been able to rectify his early memories of our mother. He idolizes, and he hates her. He despises my father and me. I am able to feel this hatred whenever I'm in the same room with him. The brother I loved is gone. In his place, the monster my parents created is thriving. I am the only one who noticed the changes, for I am the only one who truly cared about Eric. I hate the man he has become."

Caitlyn paused, and then said. "I tried to discuss Eric with Mother on several occasions, but since it's not about fashion, the beauty parlor, or the county club, she simply wasn't interested. When Eric was arrested, Mom was truly upset, complained that it disrupted her European vacation plans. Father couldn't leave because he had to do damage control on his campaign. For what it's worth, I hope this helps. I'm afraid of how far Eric has gone with his hatred, and how much further he's willing to go. I'm still surprised that he has never tried to hurt anyone in our family. I've got survivors' guilt that he may have killed those little angels to get even with my parents and me."

"Thank you," Ally said softly. "Your information, certainly sheds light on the situation." Ally was trying to respond professionally to the overload of information, she just received.

"You know he did it too, don't you?" Caitlyn asked. "You're a mother. I can tell by the subconscious way, you were rocking from side -to-side, while you were waiting outside for me. And you've got that maternal protective instinct." Ally nodded, but remained silent and let her continue. "I hope this helps you stop him. For the record, I am more than willing to testify to anything that I just told you. You don't have to hide my testimony or cover it up. I'm a stand-up lady. No matter what hell may come of it."

"Thank you again for talking to me, Caitlyn. It must have been difficult for you to come forward."

"No more difficult than living with it. As I said, I'm a mother of three." Caitlyn responded giving Ally a knowing look.

They left the table in silence, going to the front to pay the bill. "Take care of yourself," Ally said, as Caitlyn walked out into the night.

Eric waited until nightfall to drive up to the house. He re-verified the Sullivan address from the interior cover of her daytimer. He had glanced through the daytimer, hoping to find some useful information about the investigation, but he'd been too rushed. Hah! At the time, he'd been worried about getting caught 'spying', so he quickly stuffed it back into that hideous book bag.

"What day is it?" he thought restlessly. Damn, how could he prepare a detailed plan if he couldn't even remember the fucking date? He couldn't keep track of his days, and worse still, he was losing track of large periods of time. This wouldn't do! He pressed his palms against his thighs, drawing his shoulder blades together as he replayed the events of the past few days. Yes, that's right. It's Wednesday, November 11th. Now, he could prepare for the hunt.

He couldn't believe he let a cunt play him like that! She'd thrown him off his game; that's all. The stupid Bitch will pay fucking big time for that set-up. It's just a matter of time. As he replayed the fantasies he'd had about her in his jail cell, he felt the excitement and tension mount. No quickie! He'd make the pain last a long, long time. He could hardly wait! Hell, he was already hard in anticipation.

That dick head, Bryant, will suspect him, of course. But there would be no crime if a body isn't found, and hers won't be. Her case would be just another simple missing person report, to be filed away in a dusty gray cabinet, only opened occasionally when a Jane Doe turns up. Eric smiled to himself, licking his dry lips.

He thought about relocating, but why? He'll enjoy the game all the more. Bryant would glare at him in passing, but unable to relieve his frustration. He bit his lip in delight. Bryant was already looking like a fool. What a joke! They will laugh him out of the legal system, then eventually, out of his office. The pathetic fucker! As if he was smart enough to mess with the pro. Eric gripped the wrist of his left hand, leaning his elbows against his thighs, rocking rapidly trying to contain the exultation bursting within him.

"Oh ho, there she is, coming to me! Yes, yes, keep it coming baby. I'll play you all right, much better than you ever played me; just watch and see. You're mine. You're just so fucking stupid that you don't realize it yet.   Aww, you're leaving the house. All Alone, Sweetie. Are you just waiting for me to come?   Uh huh, you'll feel me cut you right through there." He said, focusing his intense stare at the targeted area.

He watched as she drove away; he needed the full command of his discipline. If he was not meticulous, thorough, the cops might just trip over something. Yes, yes- it was all in the planning. "I'll just have to watch you for a while, and wait!" He continued to survey the house until he saw her return. Good, still all alone with nowhere to go. He would come back and watch; get her routine down. He was so excited that he was tingling with it; his ass hopping like a Mexican jumping bean. Oh hell yes, it will have to be soon!

Ally reflected on her interview with Caitlyn Mathews during her drive home. Caitlyn had painted a very vivid portrait of her family. The players in this family saga, trekked across Ally's mind, each demanding her deliberation in turns. On the surface, the Brentwoods and their adult children must seem so fortunate: the all-American family. They had it all, affluence, respectability, status, and good social standing. Whereas, the reality of their familial dysfunction is so contrary to public perceptions. Reality clashes violently with fiction!

Rene looked up from the couch as Ally entered. In the dim light, Ally could see that Breanna was still nestled in Rene's arms.

"Just getting to know my granddaughter," Rene said. "It's my bet that she will be an awful lot like her mother. How did your meeting go?"

Ally sighed. "It was so terrible that it was great, at least in terms of the investigation. I'm debating on how soon I should call Neal back. Maybe dispatch will connect me tonight. I don't know if this justifies an after-hours call."

"Ally, you won't sleep until you talk to him. If it's not okay, I'm sure he'll tell you. That's really the most he can do, isn't it?"

"How do you manage to make things so simple?"

"Because, Love, most things are actually rather simple if you think about it. People draw in complexities that are really non-existent, and agonize over the trivial, which is a horrendous waste of time. It's just our ever-present desire to act as if we know it all that stops us in our tracks. However, it's the real tough issues that we allow to fester, spiral out-of-control, and reap the most destructive havoc. Therefore, it's usually best to deal straight forward with most issues and concerns in a timely manner."

"Okay, I give up. I'll call." Ally picked up the phone and dialed dispatch. Identifying herself, she asked to be patched through to Neal Bryant. Without much persuasion, the dispatcher complied.

"Hello Neal? It's Ally. I hate to disturb you at home.....Yes, I just met with Caitlyn Mathews. I met her at the Mill Coffee House, public place like you suggested. Let me fill you in." Ally found that she could practically repeat the conversation back verbatim, despite not taking any notes, for she had been completely absorbed in the narrative.

"Neal, Caitlyn was also, emphatic that she would be willing to testify if called upon to do so. I was not sure if this warranted an after-hours call, but I thought you would like to know. Yes, I will see you on Tuesday." She replaced the receiver.

Rene said, "That poor family. I cannot imagine a lonelier, desolate existence. They are all so isolated and immune to normal emotions and familial interactions."

Ally nodded her head; her mother had a unique way of viewing information. She would need to look at it from her

268

mother's perspective every so often. She would never have thought to feel sorry for either Alex or Susan Brentwood, but her mother had compassionately included them all.

"Well Ally," Rene added. "David called. He said the shipment that he was waiting for was delayed by weather in the Midwest. It should be coming in within an hour. He'll be home about eleven. He asked me to have you call him, when you got home. He wanted to make sure that you got home, safe. I couldn't help myself; I teased him unrelentingly about his conversion to non-atheism. He did take it as a man."

Ally burst out laughing, and her mother joined in. "Should I make some popcorn?" Ally asked. "We can pop in a video. For now, I think I'm all talked out."

"That sounds wonderful. Just let me put this little angel to bed. I'm going to spoil her beyond endurance for you. Any light-hearted movie is fine with me. I think we could both do with a dose of good humor."

Eric Morrison arrived extremely early the next morning. And then later, he watched as Sullivan pulled out of the garage, stopping his vehicle in the driveway. Sullivan left the garage door open as he retrieved some garbage cans, and continued to the curb. Looking through binoculars, Eric noted that Sullivan was wearing a red manager vest of the Smart supermarket chain. Which store? He'd follow him to work today; it would help in the planning. Sullivan got back into the car, closed the garage, and started down the road.

Eric followed Sullivan's car at a distance, almost losing sight of it a couple of times. It looked as if he was headed in the direction of the Smart store near Grant Street. Morrison pulled into the parking lot and hurried into the store. Not too many people were around this time of the morning, but he did not want to attract attention. He headed towards the juice cooler at the rear of the store. He noticed that the corridor towards the restrooms posted framed photos of the store's employees. He looked over the photos, reading the name placards at the bottom of each photo. He found the photo of David Sullivan and studied it intently. David Sullivan had a serious demeanor with a perpetually pre-occupied expression on his face, as if he constantly had a long daily to-do list and not enough hours in the day to complete even half the list. A typical fucker. Eric heard some employees heading from the back storage room into the main hub of the store. He hurried over to the juice section grabbing orange juice and headed to the check-out. He observed Sullivan, talking to some delivery driver at the front of the store. Eric quickly paid for the juice and headed towards his car.

He was thankful he wasn't recognized, with the news media splashing his face over the airways. He had started to grow a beard, and he let his hair hang straight down instead of being combed back. He donned a pair of non-prescription glasses and wore his clothes baggy, rather than his usual tailored fit. These small changes had grossly altered his appearance, making him appear much older. Ultimately, he had managed to keep a low profile. He used to be Faceless, after all.

Back in his car, Eric opened the juice and took a long swig. He needed to decide what to do next. He decided to drive to the office, and work on some damage control. It was Thursday, and Julie should be there by now. He knew that Julie usually arrived an hour or more before anyone else arrived at the office. She had told him that she used this time to work on billing and filing without interruption. He would speak to Julie alone. He knew that Julie, a single mother of two, had a thing for him. It would be too easy. By the end of the workday, everyone would know his version of the story; it would spread like wildfire, taking a life of its own.

He parked two blocks down the street from the professional building, which housed his office. He walked the back way, using the stairwells. He knew the media hawks might be watching, and he did not want to encounter anyone until he was good and ready and in a strategic position. Then, he would be more than willing to play with them. He silently entered the office.

He stopped at the half-door entrance to the reception area. Julie had not even hesitated in her paperwork; she hadn't heard him enter. He needed to play her to the max; he already had rehearsed this scene. He cleared his throat, shifting his weight from one leg to the other with a downward sheepish glance.

"Hi Julie," he began nervously. "I wasn't sure if anyone expected, or for that matter wanted, me to come in. Have Phil, Stan, and Chuck been able to cover the load? I'm sure there must be a lot of cancellations. Oh man, I'm sick about all that has happened."

Julie looked startled and eyed him apprehensively. He could read her like a book. She did not quite believe he was guilty, but was struggling to find any reason that he would deceive her when he told her that his jeep had broken down that day.

He covered his face in his hands, his body quaking. His deep tormented breathing made his shoulders arch and rapidly withdraw. Julie wondered if he was actually sobbing. She had never, ever seen him like this. He had never appeared vulnerable; just the opposite, very sure and confident of himself, arrogant.

Julie knew this was Eric, but it wasn't. He was always so polished and poised. Now he was disheveled almost sloppy in his appearance. Oh poor Eric, he must be at the end of his rope. She wondered if he was going to have a complete breakdown. She did not know what to say to him. She continued to stare at him in astonished awe.

He seemed to compose himself, but when he spoke his voice quivered. "First, I have to say I'm sorry for lying to you. It's all so complicated..." His voice trailed off. He came back abruptly, "Hell, I can't believe anyone could ever suspect that I could do anything so, so despicable... so horrendous. This is a damned nightmare." He choked back a sob.

Julie was feeling awkward witnessing his raw emotion, but her curiosity was fired up. She did not want to appear nosey, but he was telling her about it, wasn't he?

"Eric, what's going on? This fell on all of us out of the blue. Why did you go up there? Why did you lie about it?" Her tone was inquisitive but not accusatory.

Good, he thought, I have her positioned. She'll believe anything I tell her. "Do you mind if I sit down, Julie? It's rather hard to explain, rationally. I wish I would have thought it through logically, rather than letting my emotions take over. Maybe I wouldn't be in the mess I'm in right now if I really had thought it through, but you know what they say about hindsight."

She nodded, still apprehensive, but not so fearful. He went through the half door, plopping down on a chair.

CHAPTER 18

Julie could not believe what had materialized in front of her eyes. Eric Morrison was before her, looking abashed and self-conscious. He was slouched down, his hands clasped, arms resting on his knees and his eyes downcast. He looked and acted like a little boy making a confession, fessing up to the lie he told. He reminded Julie of her own son, Brandon, when he was afraid of the trouble he gotten himself into.

"Eric, I want you to tell me what is going on," She said sternly in a very mother-like way.

Eric started to laugh ironically. "This is one of those life story confessions. But I have to start way back in my childhood in order for what happened to make any sense at all. I got into some trouble as a kid and spent a year in Juvenile Hall. Later, I lived in several group homes."

He stopped shifting his eyes upward to gauge her reaction. "Not really because I was such a bad kid, but I could not get along with my stepfather. He had connections, and did not want me to live under the same roof with him."

Julie was silent, encouraging him to continue. After several moments of intense silence, Julie said, "What does this have to do with your current problems?"

"During my stay in one of these group homes being, oh, about fifteen, I met a girl named Tammy Lee. We were tight and looked out for each other's backs. After about eight months, Tammy returned home to her mother. We wrote for a while. However, her mother wanted Tammy to put her troubled past behind her, and move on. I was part of that troubled past. As a friend, I wasn't considered a wonderful influence at the time. We stopped writing to each other."

"My relationship with Tammy was a turning point for me. I decided I was only hurting myself by continually getting into fights, running away, and engaging in other inappropriate behavior. I didn't want adults to consider me trouble anymore. My behavior just helped my stepfather justify his actions, because he really didn't care one way or the other what I did. He just wanted me out of his way. I turned my attention to school so I would have a good job when I got out of the system.

On my seventeenth birthday, I took my GED test and passed. I started vocational school two weeks later, not sure of the direction I wanted to go. I ran into Tammy again in a temporary receiving home. Again, she seemed to give me direction, even suggested that I think about dentistry. Tammy said dentistry was a very reputable and profitable profession. She said I even looked like a dentist."

"Tammy told me that she had really screwed up after returning home: she went wild and got into trouble with drugs. But Tammy was determined to clean up her act because she just had a baby girl. It was tough being a mother at sixteen. She told me her daughter, Shilo, was living with her mother. She had to get her act together so she could get her baby back. I wished her well and told her to keep in touch; that didn't happen."

"That's too bad, she sounds like a good friend;" Julie said softly.

"At nineteen, I had received my Associates Degree. I started working as a dental hygienist. It was a good job, and I got my own apartment. I was plenty high on myself. I figure most of the guys from the group home had graduated into jail or prison, so I was ahead of the game. I was also proud that I did it on my own, without any financial or emotional support from my family. In other words, life was good."

"I continued to attend college at night to become a dentist. At twenty-four, I had finally got accepted into dental school. It had been a slow process since I was a part-time college student, I scored high on the DAT, the dental aptitude test. I was also able to get grants and scholarships to support myself while attending school."

"What happened to Tammy?"

"I ran into Tammy again during my first semester of dental school. We started living together. It didn't take long to realize that Tammy's problems ran far deeper than I ever imagined. She had serious mental health issues. She could be a sweet, giving, pleasant person one minute, and then be full of rage and hostility, the next. Vindictive as hell, her illness made her into the nastiest person. Tammy was wonderful when she was on her medication, but she would never take it unless forced to somehow. She would call you every name in the book and use every available profanity to tell you she wasn't crazy.

A couple of months into the relationship, I dropped out of school. Whenever I was gone, Tammy would accuse me of cheating on her and all kinds of other atrocities. She accused me of talking to her social worker behind her back, in order to get Shilo placed back into foster care. Truth is, Tammy was right on this fact. I was concerned about Shilo because Tammy was out of control. I felt I could care for Tammy, but I could not be constantly present to protect her daughter. A social worker was looking in on Shilo, and Tammy was able to control her behavior during the visits. This control was only good for short intervals, maybe an hour or two at best; afterwards, she would be raging, even more erratically. I only wish the social worker would have listened to me.

I finally had enough and told Tammy that she needed to get back into therapy and take her medication faithfully, or I was history. I realized that Tammy was dragging me down; back to a life and into a person I no longer wanted to be. I felt a loyalty towards her, but felt we could make a go of it only if she would get the help she needed.

This ultimatum resulted in the worst confrontation of my life. I actually thought she might kill me. She told me that if I went to sleep, she would cut me deep. She was going to make me sorry I was ever born. I would try to walk out the door, and she would barricade the doorway. She also informed me that if I left one mark on her, she would make sure I was arrested for domestic violence. I was afraid to move her out of the doorway or push past her.

To tell you the truth, this was the only time I felt I could actually hurt a woman; I was scared of myself. This fight continued throughout the night and into the next day. For the next couple of days, we had strained harmony between us. Tammy was on her best behavior for fear of losing me, I guess. I never wanted to go through a scene like we had, ever again."

"I can't blame you; it must have been rough," Julie responded.

"Yes it was. You can't imagine how difficult the relationship turned out to be. The first time she left the house after that fight; I packed up and left without even leaving a note. Needless to say, Tammy was livid. She sent me scalding letters without signing her name. I left work one night to find that all my tires had been slashed. She even ran up a huge bill at the video rental store, checking out videos under my name without returning them. She posted a flyer near my office stating that I was a registered sex offender. You know how well that went over, since my practice mostly was children.

I thought Mike Diaz, the pediatric dentist I was working under, would ship me out on the rails. I had to remind him that in order to receive admission into the dentistry program I had to be fingerprinted and cleared. I explained that I was having girlfriend problems. He told me I'd better get it straight and soon; he wasn't having any of this.

I could not tie any of this harassment directly to Tammy. I contacted the police and was told they couldn't do anything about the situation because I had no proof that it was Tammy. They suggested that I get a restraining order; I was embarrassed and did not follow through with the protective order. You know: young stud afraid of his ex-girlfriend."

"After six weeks, the harassment finally stopped; I hoped she had moved on. I was relieved but still doubtful, looking over my shoulder all the time, half-fearful...anticipating her next move. Approximately three weeks after the harassment stopped, Tammy's daughter, Shilo, was reported missing. My heart sank; Tammy knew that I was placed in Juvenile Hall when I was twelve for helping my younger sister to run away. My stepfather had pushed to have kidnapping charges issued on me; it was adjudicated as custodial interference. I knew in my heart of hearts that Tammy was behind the disappearance of her daughter and that she was going to try and have me arrested for it. I was sick with grief and fear for Shilo; and of course, myself. At the time, I did not know what had happened to Shilo.

I went to talk to Tammy at her apartment complex to try to reason with her. I was at her front door, promising I would come back to her, but she needed to tell me where Shilo was. Tammy's eyes were wild and unfocused. She was very aggressive, and she was acting more bizarre than ever. Remember I told you that Tammy was very mentally ill, but I'd never seen her this irrational and unbalanced before this time. She was swinging her fists at me as I backed away. Then, she started talking crazy. Tammy said she knew that Shilo wasn't coming home because she heard the voices in the Sego game, said so. She screamed at the top of her lungs that I was responsible. She didn't want to 'exchange' Shilo for me. Then she said, the police had shot me because the voices in her radio told them to. It didn't make any sense; she must have been hallucinating. I was standing right in front of her, when she said that I'd been shot. She continued to talk irrationally, and I ran away in fear."

"That's disturbing, all those things she said!" Julie exclaimed.

"Yes." Eric looked downward in dismay and then said heavily. "Shilo's murdered body was found in Horseshoe Bend. ...It was an area that I loved to explore, and I had told Tammy about during better times. Later, a mutual friend in the loop told me that the testimony Tammy gave to the police was that her daughter had gone off to school and never returned. Shilo was found in her pajamas. I also learned that a neighbor heard our exchange and reported it to the police. For these reasons, the police decided to re-interview Tammy.

When the police talked to Tammy again, she flipped out. They called it a psychotic break and took her to the state hospital. There were no beds available at the facility, so they held her at the county jail. They placed her on a seventy-two hour hold for safety concerns, but also for further questioning. She committed suicide in jail. I don't believe any official suspect was named in Shilo's case.

I always felt that Tammy somehow fatally injured Shilo and panicked, or, sad to say, deliberately killed her daughter with the intention of blaming it on me. I knew how she could be; very smart in a crazy way. She would have planted evidence to cast the suspicion onto me."

"It's so horrible; I can't imagine what you were going through at the time," Julie empathized.

"I began working with the missing persons division when Shilo was missing. I found a way to give back; somehow I was trying to do something positive from the ashes of tragedy. I also approached the dean of my dentistry school and begged to be re-enrolled," Eric responded.

"In late summer this year, I heard on the news that another skeleton of a child was found in Horseshoe Bend. Later, I inadvertently learned that law enforcement had linked Shilo's death with this other child. I believed that the connection was circumstantial; the bodies were linked just by location. I truly believe Tammy killed Shilo in one of her rages.

I was, and I always have been, fearful that Tammy might have left something in the Horseshoe Bend area to implicate me in the murder of her daughter. I was scared and desperate, so I had to take a look myself. I know this was wrong. It seems that my whole life, I've been trying to run away from my past, and it just keeps catching up with me."

Eric agonized and rushed on desperately. "Now, the worst has happened; I believe I am the prime suspect in these murders. Law enforcement has found several bodies. I had just thought there was one other. God, I'm stupid; I just should have left it alone. If questioned about Shilo, I should have answered honestly. I just didn't think anyone would listen. I guess most of this is going to come out in the trial anyway."

Eric looked directly at her, lost. His unspoken question hung between them: "What should I do?"

"Oh Eric, it's a mess," Julie said, "This is one time that the truth may dig a deeper hole for you. I doubt the police will believe you now at the end of the day."

He clasped his arms tightly over his chest, gripping his arms; he looked skyward towards the ceiling unseeingly, as if in prayer. He was silent. He clamped his eyes tightly and swallowed a large lump in his throat. Then he responded tightly, "You don't think there is anything I can do?" He sounded hopeless and forlorn, so desperate.

"Listen," Julie responded, shaking her head from side to side trying to focus her thoughts. "I'm not good at this, I'm probably not a good person to seek advice from. I don't know. Maybe you could talk to the media?"

"Oh, no, I couldn't do that," he said suddenly, his eyes wide and earnest. He said it in a manner that implied he knew this would help, but it was out of the question. Eric hoped she had picked up his lead.

"Why couldn't you speak to a reporter, tell them your side of the story?" Julie asked.

"No, it's out of the question. Just wouldn't do," he said finally.

"Okay Eric, I may be slow on the uptake. So help me understand why you can't talk to the media. They are already talking about you anyhow. You can shed new light on the situation," she persisted.

"You know what I did was illegal," he sighed.

"God, yes, it was illegal, I'm not stupid," she answered. "You'll have to take some lumps for the current charges. You know it came out that you had a connection with that child, Shilo. Sooner or later, your whole past will come out. You know the press will be digging into your background. When your connection with that child is fully exposed, it will make you look guilty as sin. Wouldn't coming clean publicly be ultimately better than being a suspect in those murders?"

"I've thought about it, but I can't! I just can't!" Eric had a determined set to his jaw; the stubbornness presented itself.

"And why can't you? You know it's going to eventually come out anyway. I already heard on a news brief this morning that there was some connection between you and the mother of the first victim."

"Because...." Eric stopped closing his eyes tightly as if to close off the reality of the situation.

"Okay Eric, directly or indirectly, you asked for my help. Now you can't even give me a good reason you can't talk to the media. If it's a bad idea, let's figure out an alternative, but you haven't even given me a good reason for rejecting this idea. I can't help you, if I'm unaware of what the problems are."

"The answer is not logical, but emotionally based," Eric explained. "I put my mother through a lot, as a kid. I resented my step-father, so I became oppositional and defiant. Always, Mom was caught in the middle, trying to reconcile the differences between her husband and me. What I did when I hid away my sister, put her under a lot of strain; she had a hard time coping. During this time, Mom almost had a nervous break-down. You know she's not a strong woman; she has had a tough life. Now I'd be dredging it all up again and spotlighting the problems we had as a family."

"Your family would prefer that you remain the primary suspect in all those murders?"

"My stepfather hates that I may be considered as a suspect in the deaths of those children because it would taint his political career. He doesn't give a damn about me or what happened to those children. But, if I went into my personal history and it reflected badly on his parenting and his role as a father, Alex would be outraged. He will not tolerate it! For years, he has built his political image as the ever-concerned father and family man. In many ways, I'm his dirty little secret: the dark skeleton in his closet. ...And my mother would be caught in the middle again, torn apart. I don't know if she can handle the pressure."

"You've got to be kidding. Your step-father is that obsessed with his political career?"

"Oh, believe it, Julie. I've lived with his hypocritical rhetoric, most of my life. It doesn't bother him in the least that he might not have been the best parent in the world; it's having the public find out that he failed in the role that bothers him."

"But your mother, she put up with this?"

Eric sighed again, "You just don't understand the type of person my mother is. She's very susceptible to a forceful man like Alex. She always believed that he knew better than she did about how to raise a boy. She relied on his judgment. She felt that maybe because she was my mother that she was too soft on me; that I needed a male influence."

"Okay, that was back then, but what about now? Doesn't she know that you need her support?"

"There must be some truth to the fact that love can blind you to reality. I think my mother sees her husband, as a strong, proud, principled man. She believed that Alex was someone she could depend and lean on. It would be hard to be married to such a guy and have a different perspective of reality or difference of opinion. Alex is very narcissistic man. He would tell my mom how to behave appropriately, and she would listen.

"You're more accepting than I could ever be," Julie said. "I would expect more from my mother or in being a mother, myself. I guess people view their responsibilities differently."

"You might understand if you met her," he said lightly.

"You probably should give the reporters your story, or the media will make it up as they go. You don't need the press putting their unique slant on things. You can be notorious or the tragic hero in the eyes of the public. You may not have a choice in the matter, but I wouldn't chance it to luck."

"I guess I need a little more time," Eric said. "You don't have to tell me that I don't have much of it. Let everyone in the office know how sorry I am for all the publicity. Thanks for letting me spill my guts. I've just had no one to talk to. I told you that I broke up with Jill, didn't I?" Eric said in a sheepish manner. He looked directly in Julie's eyes. "Thank you, I appreciate your help."

She saw Eric's defensive wall come up again. He was shutting down, distancing himself. "Take care," she said awkwardly as he walked through the door.

Eric grinned to himself as he walked to his jeep. He knew just how much gossip there was around that office. If Julie didn't tell an excellent sob story to the media, it would be one of the other cows in the office. Somehow, he'd always known it would be beneficial to stay in the good graces of their herd; you never knew when you might be able to use them to your advantage. He knew the story would be more enticing and believable if he didn't deliver it personally, and if he appeared reluctant to have it aired. He was happy to play the martyr. Eric reflected on his past relationship with Tammy.

Eric had learned to lie effectively, he stuck as close to the truth as possible. He believed it was Tammy's fault that Shilo was dead. Tammy should have chosen him. Early on in their relationship, he tried to ensure that Shilo was taken back into foster care, thinking he and Tammy could build a relationship, but CPS simply dismissed the case. Finally, he told Tammy that he didn't want to have a kid. He gave her a choice that night, Shilo or him. What was the big deal anyway? Shilo would've gone into foster care; he had, and he was just fine. But Tammy's choice was Shilo, her mistake! He walked; so she should've taken the cue and left him alone.

Tammy thought she could diss Eric like that, and he would be a pathetic little wimp taking all she dealt out. She just had to keep pushing it; didn't know when to stop. How dare she? Who did she think she was anyway? Tammy was just a pathetic tramp. He couldn't believe that he had ever thought they might share a future together, if only Shilo were out of the picture. He had been so fucking stupid to get involved with a whore. She had even messed up his career for a year and thought he would just timorously walk away.

When he grabbed Shilo from her room that night, he had acted impulsively. It really wasn't like him at all to behave so rashly. He had trashed himself for that mistake many times since; he knew planning was paramount. Despite his critical error, he had felt so alive. He knew what he was missing; he hadn't had that feeling since he kidnapped Caitlyn.

Afterwards, he knew Shilo would have to die. He wasn't going back to any fucking institution. He just didn't expect it to be such a rush. Shilo had been his first; he had made some serious blunders. If he hadn't been smart, law enforcement would have been shining their light down his throat right away. After the excitement of the kill wore off; he knew that he'd screw himself good if he didn't think quickly. He had placed Shilo's body on ice in his large ice chest in his camp trailer, which remained hidden in the mountains. After news reports of the disappearance, he helped in the search for Shilo. Crazy Tammy had unwittingly helped him with all her half-truths to the fucking pigs.

When the timing was right, he had returned to Tammy's apartment and played her right. Spit it back in her face that Shilo was dead and gone; man, it felt great. He had also prodded and poked at all her warped ideas and her crazy-assed theories, engaging her fucked-up thinking. A sly sneer formed with his reminiscences:

After Shilo was returned from foster care, Tammy initially believed that CPS hadn't returned Shilo, but replaced her kid with a replica. She insisted that the CIA and the police were working in concert with CPS, to keep Shilo away from her. The crazy-assed notion actually had a name, a psychiatrist has called it -Capgras Syndrome.... Eric told Tammy that he worked for the CIA and had been sent to spy on her. His recent assignment was to dispose of the impostor child because they planned to keep the real -Shilo forever. They needed to run tests and experiments on her. Therefore, Tammy would never be allowed to see Shilo again.

Tammy cried out hysterically that he was lying, pummeling Eric around the chest and shoulders. Eric grabbed Tammy by the shoulders. He told her to listen to the voices because these voices were ordered to tell her the truth. In fact, she could probably convince the voices to tell her where Shilo was being held. Then, he had seen the old hag of a neighbor, that perpetual busybody, heading up towards her apartment. He already had Tammy riled; she played right into it, just as he had planned it. The neighbor thought Tammy was crazy.

"Please Tammy, please tell me where Shilo is? If she comes back; we can be a family again. I'll stay with both of you, just tell me that she's safe." He pleaded contritely. Tammy started striking Eric again around the face and chest.

"Shilo is not coming home, because I didn't exchange her for Eric. The voices say so, they told me the truth. The police shot Eric because the voices in the radio told them to do it. They sent you here instead to capture me; they need the host plant for the validation of their experiment...." Tammy spewed out her all too familiar, delusional rant. Fuck , Tammy was such a social moron, and pathetically stupid to boot. She didn't have a fucking clue that you couldn't say things like that in public. At the time, he had to abruptly leave the scene, before he burst out laughing.

As soon as he left Tammy, he dumped Shilo's body in the meadow. An hour later after getting off the phone at the substation, he told a straggling group of seven volunteers that an officer had just requested that a few locations be searched again. He added the meadow at Horseshoe Bend to the list.

It was early morning, before dawn. Upon hearing her cries, Ally got up to feed Breanna only to discover that Breanna was very hot to the touch. Ally hoped it wasn't serious; Breanna had not been sick before. Oh Lord, she had never bought a thermometer, or any other baby medication for that matter. Ally picked up Breanna along with a new diaper and nightgown. She headed towards the kitchen to phone the 24-hour medical hotline. Ally was waiting on hold, when her mother entered.

"Ally, what is going on? Who are you phoning this time of morning?"

"Breanna is running a fever. She hasn't been sick before. I'm on hold waiting for the nurse." Ally was weary with concern.

"Relax, take it easy." Rene tried to hold back her amusement. "Babies run quite a few fevers during infancy. You just want to make sure it doesn't remain unchecked or too long in duration. What's her temperature?"

"I'm not sure, I don't have a thermometer," Ally said, mortified. Rene walked over and placed her hand on Breanna's forehead and then her palm against the side of Breanna's face. She repeated the process with Ally comparing the body

284

temperatures. The gesture made Ally feel warm and secure; protected as if she were a little child again.   She was so glad to have her mother here with her.

"Yep, she is a little warm. Let's give her a lukewarm bath while you're waiting on hold. That should help bring the fever down. I might be a bit rusty, but it's coming back." Rene poured water into the sink, taking a wash cloth and gently dampening Breanna with the water. The nurse came back on the line. The nurse advised Ally to call back: if the fever continued for several days, was over 102 degrees, or would not break. She suggested alternating the infant medicinal formulas of Tylenol and Motrin every few hours, giving her the dosages for an infant of three months.

By the time Ally had finished talking to the nurse, her mother had enveloped Breanna in a towel.   Ally felt Breanna's forehead and she did feel much cooler. "Thanks Mom," Ally thought to herself. "Now, are you going to tuck both of us in?" Ally said with a laugh.

Rene chuckled. "Do you want me, to?"

"Right now, more than you'd imagine," Ally answered.

"I would, but I just might give poor David a heart attack, looming above your bed." They both laughed. "You do look exhausted."

"You're right. I'm headed back to bed, but I'll take Breanna with me. She just might start fevering again."

"Maybe she's getting a cold.   You might want to keep her indoors for a couple of days."

"Good night, Mom. I'll see you in the morning." Ally yawned and headed towards her bedroom. In the morning, she would need to pick up a thermometer and some baby medication.

The next morning, Ally was tired as she got out of bed, suppressing a yawn. She might as well get up; she wasn't doing much sleeping anyhow; due to her fear that Breanna might start fevering again. Ally's ears would catch the slightest difference in breathing or noise that Breanna made. She had laid her hand on Breanna's chest several times during the night to make sure she was breathing steadily. "Heavens," Ally thought, "I haven't been this anxious since I brought her home from the hospital. Breanna is fine." Ally subconsciously checked Breanna again for fever.

Ally placed Breanna in her infant seat in the kitchen and poured herself a cup of coffee. She sat the cup down and stretched out her back. She rubbed her red, stinging eyes. Her mother entered the kitchen, already dressed, and as cheerful as always. God, there were things that she wished she had inherited. How did one perpetually maintain a good mood and that high of an energy level? Ally didn't know the secret.

"Ally, didn't you let yourself get a wink of sleep? You are not going to feel like yourself all day."

"I'll be all right," she said. "Just let me get a second cup of coffee down."

"Heavens girl, you need to take care of yourself. I'll take my mother's prerogative and order you around a bit. Why don't you go and take a nice hot shower?"

Ally started to argue, but it sounded just too good. She might as well enjoy the pampering for the next couple of weeks. It was Mom's way.

She felt a hundred percent better as she entered the kitchen after her shower. Mom had cooked some scrambled eggs and toast, which Ally ate hungrily. Ally helped clean up the breakfast dishes and then went to check on Breanna, who was sleeping peacefully in her infant seat. "Mom, I think she is starting to get warm again. I'm going to run to the store and get a thermometer and some medication. I'll be back in a few minutes. There is a pharmacy about three blocks from here."

"I'll hold down the hatches," Rene called after her.

CHAPTER 19

Eric had maintained a regular vigil of the Sullivan house. After his meeting with Julie, he had done some research. Eric had checked county recorder records in the city offices and found the property maps of all the homes on this street. He printed the map, and he compared the visual layout of the houses with the parcel maps he collected yesterday. The map even depicted the BLM land adjacent to the cul-de-sac.

He had parked his rental car near the corner of the neighboring house; the same one from which he had taken a flyer. It hosted a Ready Real Estate sign with a small attached "sold" sign placed above it. He surmised that the neighbors would believe his rental car belonged to the new owners. The new owners would believe this car belonged to one of the neighbors. It would take time for anyone to realize that this car did not belong in the neighborhood. He had taken the extra precaution of lifting some license plates from a car parked in long-term parking at the airport. He exchanged the plates so the vehicle could not be traced back to him. He had rented a Honda Accord, for it seemed that every three out of four houses within this area had one.

Eric had decided not to use the old county car which he had bought from surplus about eight years ago. The timing of that purchase had been perfect. Marvin, from Fleet Management, had been retiring when he bought the car. Marvin had let him take the car with the "State Exempt" plates in order to have the car's transmission worked on, and to have the vehicle detailed. Marvin had told Eric to drop off the plates when he had the vehicle registered. Then Marvin retired, and no one knew Eric had a county car with government plates. Obtaining a county car and getting a volunteer position at the Office of Missing Persons had been brilliant maneuvers on his part.

This county car had truly been a windfall: he used it to snatch his discards. Everyone noticed the county car when he entered the neighborhood, but no one dared look long enough to see who was driving or which house it was approaching. If he drove slowly past, the neighbors would believe that he was looking for an address. He could also linger for periods of time, pretending to be filling out paperwork or taking a phone call while he surveyed the area. However, in this neighborhood, he feared the county car might draw attention.

Eric had watched David Sullivan leave at 4:30 this morning. He made a mental note that it was roughly the same time as yesterday. There were no signs of life until he saw the Bitch pull out of the garage at 8:30. He could see the side of the infant seat, but he could see no other children with her. He cautiously made his way across the roadway to the house.

The trees and shrubs around the house gave him ample cover. He could easily approach the house without being observed, except from the neighboring house, which was vacant. Eric silently wondered when the new owners were going to move in. He would have to keep an eye out for them, so they never got a good look at him. He would have liked to talk to the real estate office about this house, to learn as much as he could about the owners, but it was too risky. He could be recognized, and he had to attract as little attention as possible. He could not leave any witness trail.

He walked through the unlocked wooden gate, into the back yard. He walked the perimeter of the house; there were no swing sets or children's toys lying about. He had never asked the Bitch if she had any other children, besides the maggot. He didn't expect any. He had never heard children's voices or children's television programming in the background when he had spoken to her on the phone. He also hadn't seen any other kids with the Bitch when she left the house.

Eric had checked her mailbox yesterday and had not found mail in anyone else's name besides hers and her husband. He would check again this afternoon if possible, but he assumed no roommates. He couldn't believe his luck: there were no dogs,

288

either. There was no doghouse or doggie door, and he didn't hear any barking within the residence.

He tried to look through the windows, but the blinds were drawn on the lower windows. He could not hear any television or radio on within the house. He presumed it would be just Alyssa Sullivan, her husband, and the maggot in the house. He was glad; it would be much cleaner and easier this way.

Eric was through the gate when he heard a vehicle approaching the house. He pushed back up against the exterior wall. He slowly eased along the side of the house, until he could peer around the corner into the garage. He saw Ally exit the car, holding a pharmacy bag. He ducked out of sight again, to wait until the Bitch was out of the way. She didn't even glance around, when she got out of her car. How perfect. She feels completely safe in her neighborhood. It would be easy to sneak up on her. A smile played on his face as he reviewed his fantasy; fuck, it would be good.

Eric discreetly made his way back to the rental. He silently opened the car door and then slumped down in the front seat, making an adequate diagram of the house and property. He noted his findings in his journal. He would burn these pages after he completed the task; just as he had burned his earlier records. About thirty minutes had elapsed since Alyssa returned from the pharmacy. Eric attracted no attention when he left the neighborhood.

Ally answered the phone on the third ring. She had been talking to her mother about childhood Christmas memories. Ally could not wait to show Breanna the Christmas lights downtown. She knew Breanna would not get much out of it, but she was still excited: Breanna's very first Christmas.

"Hello? Yes, Neal I can hear you. You found a what? ...A mummy! Neal, what in the world are you talking about?"

Rene continued to stare at Ally inquisitively, raising both her eyebrows. "This I've got to hear," she mouthed.

"Are you serious? I've never heard of such a thing before! Can you make an initial identification?" Ally continued to listen to the conversation over the phone, and the gloom and weariness etched on her face lifted. Rene watched the transformation in eager anticipation. She knew the news must be positive, at least in terms of capturing the perpetrator. Ally desperately needed relief from her mounting stress."Oh Neal, this sounds like the major break we've been waiting for. Please let me know what happens. Thanks again. I appreciate the update." Ally stared at the phone for a moment after placing it back on the receiver.

"C'mon Ally do tell! I want to know what just happened; it's gotta be big," Rene burst out.

"Oh Mom, it's so completely unbelievable...surreal. Remember how I told you the crime scene technicians, in cooperation with the EPA, were attempting to dislodge some skeletal remains from the vertical shaft of the mine? Remember how the arsenic levels within the ground water of this shaft are very high? Well, from what Neal was just telling me, the body was lodged in the shaft in close proximity to the standing water, but it wasn't submerged. Arsenic agents prohibit or hinder bacterial growth. The arsenic concentration within the water was so high that it was bacteriostatic, which means it prevented bacteria from growing in the vicinity. Bacteria causes a body to decay. Arsenic preserves a body better than a freezer does. This being said; the mummified remains of a child have been found and excavated from the shaft. The features are still recognizable."

"Oh my dear god," Rene said covering her mouth with her fingers to smother the audible gasp. "I can't believe it."

"It's true! Neal was telling me that the ancient Egyptians used arsenic in their mummification process. Also during the American Civil War, soldiers were embalmed with an arsenic compound, which preserved their bodies so they could be returned home upon the trains. However, this practice was soon discontinued when many of the morticians started to die from exposure to the arsenic."

"And Halloween is over."

"Neal has compared photos of the child's remains with photos of missing children within this region without a positive match. He arranged for a police artist from Acacia to come down and make a sketch, so he can air the sketch on the evening news."

"This is obviously important news, Ally. But how is locating and identifying this body, going to help break the case? I heard you tell Neal that this discovery was possibly the major break in the case."

"Well, I assume the killer believed this body would be submerged in a hundred feet of water and was unlikely to be discovered. Neal found a pink toothbrush wrapped in cellophane on the body. It was embossed with the name of Eric Morrison's dental group. Neal is working on a search warrant for Eric Morrison's dental offices. It is worth a shot, since they have yet to find any direct evidence in his home or vehicle.

We're starting to show a pattern or connection between the children and Eric Morrison, but the connection is still very shaky. Hopefully, we can obtain a search warrant for his office and find something more concrete. Neal believes Eric must have kept photos of these children, or that he took something belonging to them. Most serial killers keep some 'souvenir or trophy' linked to the killing. Neal said that Eric is an amateur photographer. He strongly believes that there must be photos hidden somewhere."

"Well, I hope for everyone' sake he is caught soon. I know that I would sleep easier knowing this killer was off the streets!"

"Mom," Ally hesitated. "I should have told you -told David...You know I had a couple of meetings with Eric Morrison before he was considered a suspect. What I didn't tell you was that I helped Neal with the 'sting' operation that lead to Eric's arrest. I set him up!"

"Oh Ally, you must be out of your mind with fear!" Rene cried out aghast.

"Full of apprehension -yes! But Mom, I honestly don't think he'd try anything right now; he knows he a suspect. If anything happened to me, he'd be the first person the Sheriff's Department would interview. But if we can't make these charges

291

stick or connect him to the murders, I don't know what Eric may do."

"Baby, I'm terrified and worried about you! I wish I could stay here throughout this whole trial process. I know how much this situation must be weighing on you. It would be ridiculous to tell you not to worry. Please, please be careful and watch out for yourself."

"I will be careful; there isn't much more other than that, which I can do." Ally paused, then continued hastily, changing the subject. "Neal is hoping that he will be able to have the artist sketch available before the Department's 3:00 news conference. Sheriff Tim Garrison is going to address some media questions regarding the investigation." Alarmed, Rene continued to assess her daughter's emotional state, but decided to let the matter drop. She didn't want to escalate Ally's distress by dwelling on these precarious circumstances. Heavens, she couldn't even dispel her own, let alone Ally's anxiety, managing not to tear up in reaction.

Eric picked up the local newspaper and the main paper from Acacia; he skimmed the headlines to find any news related to the criminal investigation within Horseshoe Bend, or any articles pertaining to him. There were a couple of articles in the Acacia paper, and the local *Mountaineer* seemed to have nothing else to report on. He knew the Sheriff's Office was going to hold a news conference at 3:00pm to give the latest updates. He could go to an electronics store at the mall in Lake City to watch the broadcast.

Eric read the numerous letters to the editor; he was a central topic. The *Mountaineer* must be accepting letters at their front desk or by fax: he could not believe the speed at which these letters had appeared. How fitting; equal numbers for and against him were posted. Anyone, who posted a letter needed to submit a name, but could request that their name not appear in print.

Eric read a letter, which summarized the story that he'd given to Julie. It must be from Julie, herself or one of his other "Faceless" co-workers. This letter delineated his troubled childhood and expounded on his challenging relationship with a woman who suffered from mental illness. He skipped along reading: A long time after their break-up, the woman's daughter disappeared. Eric feared his past would be used against him, and he mistakenly tried to uncover the details of this investigation to ensure he wasn't a suspect. ... Eric Morrison is a positive role model, who has done so much to improve the community, blah, blah, blah...Eric snidely lamented.

Connor was going to have a shit fit when he hears about this. Eric would play dumb and innocently tell him he had no idea who had written this letter; maybe it was his sister. Eric would act indignant, but it would help Connor understand why his client had not been upfront with him. Eric would give the lawyer something to ease his troubled mind, if it needed easing.

Now what? He needed to be doing and planning. He was going to pop a gasket if he didn't keep up the momentum. He would do a drive by of his apartment and office to gauge how much action there was.

There was little to no activity at his apartment, aside from a guy milling around who might be a reporter. Guess the press got tired of waiting for him to make a showing. Now onward towards his office. Eric could not believe his eyes; there were at least three police cruisers parked outside his professional building. He stopped at a small coffee enclave across from his building. He had never frequented this business before. He avoided looking directly at the clerk and asked, "Hey man, what's going down over there?" Eric jerked his head absently towards the police cruisers. He tried his best imitation of a spaced out ex-hippie.

"One of the women from the office over there told me that the police had served a search warrant on the offices of that dentist, the suspected serial killer. His office is over there, you know."

"Man if he's not guilty, he's fighting an uphill battle. I'd hate to be in his shoes. That guy's in deep shit! Later dude." Eric directed his gaze at the coffee cup and still almost dropped the cup as he made his way out the door.

"What had the assholes found? Damn it, Damn it! What in the hell is going on?" He wanted to call Julie, but he couldn't risk it while the pigs were combing through the place. Grasping his head, he started rocking back and forth while he tried to logically reason through what they may have found. He had not been sloppy; he hadn't given them much to work with. He climbed into the front seat of his rental and grasped his knees, beginning to rock. No, no, he couldn't go there. He needed to keep focus, keep the momentum. He just couldn't lose track of any more time.

He turned the key in the ignition and could hear the engine squeal; it didn't turn over. This couldn't be happening. He wouldn't let it. He counted slowly back from ten to zero out loud to help refocus his mind. He turned the key again; he could hear the engine turn over and the regular hum of the motor. Good, good, everything is in order. He gripped the steering wheel tightly before shifting into reverse. Steady, steady, he continued to speak calmly to himself. Did he dare proceed with his plans? His plans were already a production in motion; there was no turning back now. Besides, if he was going down, that Bitch would be going down first. She wasn't going to be on the outside mocking him; that was for damn sure. But when?

He was still half-rocking. He mentally tried to cease the motion but to no avail. He needed to move, yes, he needed to go to the mall. He would listen to the news conference. He needed to know what they knew. How would he find out what they didn't want the general public to know? None of the boys in law enforcement would talk to him anymore. They would close ranks. He was one of them, but separate. He was never a major player in their group since he was not a member of their forces. Now the defenses would go up.

How much did that conceited bitch know about the investigation? He relished the idea of torturing the information out of her. Fuck, she was probably just a glorified go-fer, yes, an eager beaver, hiding behind their guns, trying to impinge some of their power for herself. They would tell her as little as possible; unsure whether she would run her mouth. Give her just enough information to get their shit work done, while she pretended to be a genuine police bitch. He could imagine her telling her stupid college groupies about her big assignment with the Chief Deputy Sheriff, while her assorted groupies stood as carp with their big mouths drooping open.

He couldn't wait to slaughter the Bitch. Why wait? He'd love to string her up, create a public spectacle of her demise. Like, stake her decapitated head in a communal spot as conquerors did to their enemies in bygone ages. He couldn't do anything like that without taking an incredible risk, but oh how he wanted her humiliation to be broadcasted for all to see. Wasn't there a way? Eric thought hard, biting his bottom lip. Okay, okay to the mall.

Rene and Ally stiffly watched the news conference, absorbing every detail. Rene watched with growing horror as the reality of the situation alerted every dark crevice of her being. A deep-seated premonition struck her to the core. She just knew there was danger around them all, especially since Ally spoke of her involvement in the arrest. She didn't want Ally detecting her fright, thereby placing more of a burden on her daughter. She felt so completely helpless, unlike her usual capable self. Oh Lord, if only, she could do something, anything, to protect her family.

The news conference was a summarization of all the events that had been coming out in isolated pieces during the recent days. Local law enforcement had found the remains of three bodies in the Horseshoe Bend region near the old Animas mining site. They were still in the process of determining if there were any more bodies in the area. Authorities believe a child discovered within this area in 1989 may be related to these unsolved murders.

The chief investigator, Senior Deputy Sheriff, Neal Bryant, is currently following several leads in the apprehension of this killer. The Department was not ready to name a prime suspect yet.

When asked if Eric Morrison was a suspect, the spokesman stated that it was too soon to name suspects in the case. At this time, no one could be ruled out.

The news conference ended with a police artist sketch of a small child with dark hair and wide spaced eyes. The spokesman asked anyone who could identify this child to call. The broadcaster from Acacia came on to recap what was said during the news conference; then, several legal experts gave their opinion on how the authorities would proceed in the investigation. Ally turned to her mother; Rene's face had lost its color. Rene said breathlessly, "This is just awful, that poor little angel."

Ally reeling in shock from the impact of the news, stood shaking her head, rubbing her eyes, walking back and forth without purpose. Right now, she was stuck with the all too familiar numbness, which left her feeling totally exhausted. In general, Ally had always believed that people were basically good and decent. These killings tore at her and violated her basic principles. How could one human being do such terrible things to other human beings, let alone innocent children? You couldn't even call him animalistic, for animals were never that cruel.

"Mom, I have to go to the morgue. I have to see this child for myself," Ally trembled. "God, I'm terrified." Emotion breaking through; her throat closed up and became very tight as the tears escaped her tightly clamped eyes. She let out an audible sob. Rene rushed over, pulling Ally into her arms. Ally's quaking legs were unsteady beneath her; Rene pulled her towards the sofa. Rene cradled Ally's head in her arms as she had done when Ally was a small child. The two remained that way for a long time.

"I'll make you some tea," Rene said and made her way towards the kitchen.

"You have no tea. I guess we'll have to make do with coffee." Rene called out. But Rene was back before Ally realized she was gone.

"I'm going to call Neal," Ally said in a temporal tone; steel-hard resolve had replaced her earlier emotions. Ally came in a few minutes later to report that Neal was not in; she had left a message. She didn't want to bother him on his cell phone, especially at this juncture.

Ally sat down to sip her coffee. She tried to make small talk with her mother, but Rene knew Ally's mind was somewhere else. Rene didn't know if she could speak without giving herself away. She didn't want to worry Ally by transmitting her penned up fears. Consequently, they both fell into a strained silence.

An hour later, the phone rang. Ally grabbed it before the second ring. "Yes Neal, I'm glad you called back. I have to go to the morgue to see that child. I'm not sure if I will get a reading, but who knows? It is worth a try. I'll see you at 7:45 then."

Ally re-entered the front room, watching her mother as she rocked Breanna. "Mom that was Neal. We arranged to meet at 7:45. David's working long days during the holidays. You won't mind looking after Breanna, right?"

"As I told you, I'm here to help. I just hope this terrible business is finished before I leave."

Eric Morrison drove toward the Sullivan residence, thinking of the news conference, he had watched at the mall. He was incensed: They weren't supposed to find this discard, except as a relic of an archeological dig. He couldn't fathom how the pigs were deciphering his stratagems so fast. Fuck, he wished he still had an inside line.

After the news conference, his mind went blank; he had lost track of time again. He was getting sloppy. He needed to score to get back on top again. How could he just misplace two fucking hours? He pressed his palm tightly against his forehead in an effort to recapture what was not there. He knew he needed to move soon, he had to make it click. He snapped his fingers repeatedly. Get his rhythm back.

He arrived on the Bitch's street. It was a dark, cold night. A sliver of the moon provided no natural lighting to the dead blackness of the sky. No wind stirred the trees in the unearthly stillness. It was unnatural; he could not even hear a car or a dog in the distance. It would be perfect.

No, no, he had to wait, wait and watch. He needed a clear head, no vague remembrances clouding his mind, no time voids. Tonight was wrong, give it time, take time, do it right. He breathed deeply, holding his breath as he counted slowly in an effort to gain control over his rapid thoughts. Great, he was clearer. He parked in the shadows, outside the luminance of the sparse streetlights, watching and waiting.

Eric made a furtive surveillance of the neighborhood; no apparent activity. He quietly got out of his rental car with his flashlight, softly closing the door and making his way over to the outside wall of the Sullivan's garage. He quickly glanced around at the neighboring homes, making sure all was clear, before he turned on the flashlight. He aimed its dull beam at the ground, and then tucked the flashlight in the waistband of his jeans. Eric carefully climbed on top and balanced himself on the gas meter in order to look into the high garage window.

After he grabbed the window trim with his left hand to balance himself, he removed the flashlight from his waistband with his right hand. He quickly surveyed the garage through the window. He extinguished the light of the flashlight. There was no car in the driveway; David Sullivan's SUV was gone. The Bitch's car was in the garage. No sign of the hubby. Good, very good.

There was a light on in the house; he continued his vigil. Eventually, the garage light came on, as the Bitch made a move towards her car. He'd snuck a fleeting look but ducked quickly out of sight. She left the light on in the house. Was there anyone else there or was it to provide light for her return, he silently questioned. He watched her leave and then carefully made his way around her house. He looked for shadows or any signs of movement within the residence, and listened for sounds of the radio or television. Nothing. The stupid cunt had left the light on; the poor dear was afraid of the boogey man. The light wouldn't do her any good, anyhow.

He studied the front entry of the house, the driveway, and the sides of her residence, looking for the best line of attack. He noticed she generally pulled her car into the garage rather than leaving it in the driveway. He planned to wait until she was parked in the driveway. It would make his attack, easier to manage. Less chance of her seeing him approach and she would be further from the house. About five feet from the driveway, a tall hedge grew parallel to the driveway and along the outside wall of the garage. It was separated only by a small strip of surmountable lawn where he could possibly be observed. This hedge obstructed the view from the neighboring house and from the street to the right of the house. If he stood next to the shrubs, she would surely see him as she approached. He followed the hedge; it ended just short of the wood-slab fencing for the backyard, about ten feet back. The hedge had been cut back near the fence to allow access for the gate to open completely. It was a perfect hideaway, giving him the full view of her driver-side door. He could come up from behind as she unlocked the car. He knew he would strike under the cover of darkness; it was the only reasonable course.

Clearly the attack would be visible from the left side of the house, but the new owners still had not started to move into the adjacent house. Hopefully, they would not start moving in until his mission was completed. Straight across the street stood a shed. The accompanying house across the street was built in an L-shape, with the garage perpendicular to the front of the home. Their garage blocked the view of Sullivan's driveway. Logically, the only time those people could witness the attack would be if they were backing out or entering their garage. Eric had already noted that they were an elderly couple. During his surveillance, he had never seen them step out, let alone leave their residence after nightfall.

He made his way forward to the driveway and then outward to the street. He could park here on the street to the right of her driveway, just past the hedge. This hedge would also obstruct her view of his car. He would remove the interior overhead light bulb in the car and leave the rear passenger-side door of his car slightly ajar. This plan would allow him a quick escape.

He needed to tie her up, but it would be too dangerous here on her street. How long could he expect her to be unconscious from the anesthetic? He had never used the anesthetic straight from the bottle without an oxygen mask. She also wouldn't have a steady supply like within a surgical procedure. He would place a waded rag on duct tape, douse the rag immediately prior to the attack, and secure it to her face as he dragged her into the back of the car. He could stay on top of her until she fell unconscious, but where would he take her to bind her? It had to be close, since he was unsure of the time span for the anesthetic. He wanted her bound and gagged before she had regained consciousness. Before, he headed to Tuolumne County. He knew that behind these houses was BLM land; there had to be an access road nearby. He thought he saw the road just past the turnoff to her cul-de-sac. He needed to go back out that way, check it out and review his sketches of the plat maps from the Recorder's Office.

His planned encounter with Alyssa Sullivan was surely fated; she sure had jumped and squirmed whenever he was in her vicinity. He played his fantasy in his head again like a repeat of a favorite story; enjoying his hardness against his thigh as he visualized himself seeped in her blood.

Eric was unaware of Rene's quiet presence. She was curled up on the sofa reading her book while Breanna slept peacefully within her swing in the room. Just like Ally, Rene could not bear to have Breanna outside of her sight. Rene was so uneasy; she needed to be able to see Breanna to be ensured of her safety. Rene wasn't paying much attention to her book. Her reading was just a pretense, as she looked up at the clock again. It was almost nine. Shouldn't Ally be home? She prayed a silent prayer for her daughter's safe return. Covering her face in her hands, she released her pent up tears, unburdening herself, as unrelenting questions without answers saturated her mind. This perilous predicament had no straightforward solution, no simple resolution. Given the gravity of the situation, her homespun adages were fruitless in consoling or reassuring her daughter. She had never felt so utterly useless in her life.

CHAPTER 20

Slowly, Ally maneuvered her way through the maze of county buildings. The night was inky black, which made it extremely difficult to read and follow the county signposts guiding her to the morgue. Finally, Ally found her way; driving up behind several county buildings to an isolated, red brick building situated at the very rear of the lane, tucked against the hillside.

The morgue stood formidable and isolated, outlined by the florescent wide-base street lamp. The wood-vented patio cover, which veiled the front entrance, cast eerie shadows over the cement walkway. Ally exited and locked her vehicle quickly; she rushed up to the entrance of the morgue only to pull herself up short as she approached the door. Her legs turned wooden as she consciously willed herself forward, step after stiff step, in the surreal light of the shifting shadows.

All was silent except for the heavy pounding of her heart and her audible breathing. Ally stood there for what seemed like an eternity, listening to the evidence of her fear. Her hand reached for the handle of the exterior door. It was very cold to the touch as she paused, half-surprised and half-annoyed, to find the door unlocked. She had been more than ready to turn around and go home. Chastising herself for her cowardice, she entered the florescent panel-lit lobby to approach a deserted reception desk, which was sheltered by protective glass. She felt like she was entering a scene from the Twilight Zone. Feeling the dark stillness behind her, she felt the sharp, fresh, tingle of fear crawl up her spine. Glancing to her right was a door leading to the inner workings of this office building with a numeric keypad to secure the doorway.

She made her way to the door; maybe knocking would alert someone, anyone, to her presence. Feeling her anxiety rise to a hysterical level, the apprehension was gnawing in the pit of her stomach. Then she noticed the intercom box to the left of the doorway. She pressed the buzzer button without response, then tried to speak into the small speaker.

"Excuse me, Miss, can I help you?" The deep timbered voice came from behind her. Ally surged upright, jumping as the fear and adrenaline coursed swiftly through her body like an electric current. It took her several stunned, startled moments to process the question as she turned slowly towards the man. He was tall, over six feet, wearing a black and white security uniform with the corresponding service hat. He laughed gruffly, "I'm sorry. I guess you didn't hear me coming up. I didn't mean to startle you."

Ally swallowed hard, her hand was at the base of her throat, attempting to recapture her voice. Her voice quivered as she told the man, "I have a meeting scheduled with Deputy Neal Bryant; he is expecting me."

The security guard picked up his cell phone, which must have had a radio function for he was speaking directly to someone inside the office without dialing a number. He was telling the person on the other end of the line about her presence. "I was asked to show you back. Follow me." He stepped between her and the door, his body initially shielding her view as he entered the code and opened the door. He led the way down a darkened corridor, for only the center row of ceiling lights was powered. The lack of substantial lighting gave the building a deserted, nightmarish quality. Ally was sure this was a cost-saving procedure, but if she were in charge, the place would be ablaze with lights.

Ally surveyed her surroundings. There were several closed office doors, which hosted posted nameplates. Opposite the offices were restrooms, employee break room, and the door to the conference room, which stood slightly ajar. Ally proceeded to follow the guard towards the rear rooms. She curiously tried to take in what she saw as she followed the guard's quick steps. She reminded herself that this was a morgue; she was supposed to feel increasingly uneasy.

Ally saw Neal talking to a man in a green hospital uniform. She could not make out any distinguishable features, since he was covered from head to foot, sporting a paper hair net, goggles, plastic gloves, and shoe covers. His face mask was pulled low so he could speak to Neal. The only thing that Ally could make out was that the man was tall. Neal looked up as they approached, holding up a hand to stop them without hesitating in his conversation with a medical technician.

"Ally, I will be with you in a moment."

"I will leave you here, then," said the guard, making a hasty retreat towards the front of the building. He did not appear comfortable, being in this part of the building, the morgue and autopsy rooms. She shifted her weight from one leg to the other as she surveyed the area. Despite her sweater, she was cold as she gripped her arms in an effort to warm herself.

She walked a few yards back to inspect the room she had just passed. This room, she guessed, was a typical autopsy room with three workstations. White linoleum covered the floors, which seemed typical of most medical facilities. The ceilings were very high with three long horizontal windows framed in blue along the back expanse of the room. Below the windows, along the far wall, was a blue Formica counter which stretched the length of the wall with built-in white cabinets below and above the countertop. The blue accents were a nice touch, creating a lighter, less-dismal atmosphere to the stainless steel workstations. In the center of the far right wall, there was an industrial-size ground scale; she figured it must be used to weigh the bodies coming into the morgue. Beyond the scale, there was a solid metal door with a round temperature meter to the right of the metal doorframe.

Each workstation was equipped with a stainless steel sink, hoses, liquid-filled bottles, and plastic containers with accompanying stainless steel cabinets full of various supplies. Each also had a scale like one sees at the produce section at the supermarket. Ally shuttered as she made the mental connection of what it was used for: it must be used for weighing various organs. It was a very sterile environment, devoid of anything non-essential. Glancing behind her, she saw two doors: one labeled Men and the other Women. There must be locker rooms with showers.

The room was cool but not cold; the air smelled very fresh. She suspected the building was equipped with an excellent ventilation system.

Ally returned to her earlier position, standing near the doorway of a small narrow room. Neal was still talking. He stood further back in this small room. Behind him was a large window with a protruding ledge lining the window. Swivel chairs faced the ledge. Across the expanse of the room, there were two desks equipped with computers and phones. A tall white bookcase separated the two desks. It was filled mostly with medical reference books. Ally looked beyond Neal's shoulder through the window. She could not see much with Neal and the other guy blocking her field of sight. She was able to make out what looked like an operation room. It had two big satellite dish sized lights attached to mechanical arms. She really could not see anything else.

"Well, thanks Mike," Neal said to his companion, as the man moved passed her and exited out of the room.

Ally looked back through the big window. She saw a child lying isolated on a gurney. The girl's face looked pale blue in the artificial light. Ally could see bright purple-red marks around her throat. Ally felt her legs start to give way beneath her. She was silently demanding herself to be strong so she could handle this.

Neal looked up from the notes he was composing to find Ally almost crumbled in a heap on the floor, her knees giving out beneath her. He sat his notebook on the ledge before him and in one swift move he placed his hands under Ally's elbows, hoisting her up and into a nearby chair. Ally said in a thick husky voice, "I'm all right."

"Shush, before you hurt yourself. Keep your head bent to your knees like this and breathe deeply." Ally felt like she was slumped over in her chair for an eternity. She finally heard Neal's voice through the thick, cotton-wool feel of her head. Has your lightheadedness passed?"

"I'd better stay this way for a few more minutes." Ally responded in a halting tone.

"Mike, can you grab me some water from the break room? Have a fainter here," Neal shouted through the doorway. He came back with a paper cup full of water.

Ally sat up, clearing her throat. "Sorry to be such a problem."

"Don't worry. It's happened to the best of us in the force. I know twenty year veterans of the force which still cringe whenever they enter the morgue." Ally steeled herself in her seat and turned to look through the window again.

Ally didn't know what she expected to find or learn from this encounter, but so far, nothing. What am I doing here, she rhetorically demanded. Was this just another useless, but emotion-wrenching, endeavor to leave her sick to her stomach? Was she working it too hard, trying to force supernatural information to surface? Or was her part in this investigation over, and she was just too stupid to realize it?

She closed her eyes against the invading image of this child isolated on a cold steel gurney. Ally worked on making her mind go blank. Neal turned to look at her and said urgently, "Ally are you okay? You look strange."

"I'm okay Neal, just trying to relax my mind to see if any information surfaces."

"I need to tell you Ally, I have Sanders bringing over Lily Martinez. She may be able to identify this child. She saw a recap of the news conference on the six o'clock news when she got home from work and called into the station. She stated that this child might be Priscilla McCabe. Why don't you go sit in the family group area? If Ms. Martinez identifies this child, I will need to get some background information. You can sit in on the interview."

"That sounds okay." Neal led Ally across another hallway into a brightly lit room. There were high horizontal windows that must provide much natural light during the daytime hours. The ceiling was vaulted, but not as high as in the autopsy rooms. A half partition wall divided the large room into two subsections. One side had a couple of family style dining room tables with comfortable looking chairs around them. A small side table hosted a decanter of coffee with condiments and hot water for tea and Cocoa, along with a box of single serving packets of hot chocolate mix and a variety box of tea bags. Napkins and Styrofoam cups were provided. There were a couple of vending machines, one which had soda and juice, and another filled with food items, such as yogurt and muffins.

On the other side of the partition, there was a couch, coffee table, and some colorful disk-shaped chairs. Ally noted that the side tables held house plants, magazines and a box of tissue. Ally was refreshed by the comfortable surroundings, and appreciated that some considerate administrator was in-tune with the emotional needs of the families of the deceased. She saw an office across the hall for grief counseling. She poured herself a cup of coffee and sat down at one of the tables, absently leafing through a magazine.

About a half-hour later, Neal entered the family room with a woman. Ally stood up as they entered. The short woman was in her mid-to-late 50's with dark hair, deep brown eyes, and a medium frame.   Ally felt the woman's concerned expression was a perpetual characteristic of her face. Currently, the woman's eyes were red and swollen, but she was not crying as she looked at Ally with a guarded, distrustful look. Ally wondered what she was thinking: dismissing her as too young or too inexperienced to have much merit.

Neal turned to Ally, "Alyssa Sullivan, this is Lily Martinez. Ms. Martinez, this is Alyssa Sullivan. She has been working as a case aide in this investigation and has given me invaluable assistance." Ms. Martinez still regarded her with a dismissive glance.

"I'm sorry that we have to talk to you under such tragic circumstances." Ally said, as she held out her hand. "Could I get you a cup of coffee or tea before we begin?"

"No, no thank you," Lily Martinez replied as her expression softened a bit.

"Well, let's get started. Are you okay to talk right now, Ms. Martinez? We could schedule an appointment at a later date, if you wish." Neal was assessing her emotional state.

"No, I'll do fine. I'm all right," she said gruffly, which contrasted dramatically with the pain-filled expression etched on her experienced face. Her harsh tone was belied by the tears brimming in her eyes. Ally could tell Ms. Martinez was not given to public demonstrations of emotion. By keeping her emotions private, her expressed thoughts were more concrete and contained.

Neal asked, "Ms. Martinez, can you tell us the name of the child and your relationship?"

"The child is Priscilla McCabe." Ms. Martinez stated bluntly. "I provided foster care to her mother, Debbie McCabe, when Debbie was a teenager. I also had Priscilla for a time." Her voice cracked.

"Do you have a number or address for a parent or relative of this child?"

"No, no, I'll explain," Ms. Martinez said in a matter-of -fact manner. "Debbie was taken away from her mother when she was twelve years old. Her mother, Delores, was an alcoholic who died from liver problems several years ago. Debbie had been sexually molested by several of her mother's boyfriends, when her mother was too inebriated to know or care about what was going on. Her father was never identified. I never heard of any relatives. If there were any, they were long gone and out of the picture when I became involved." Ms. Martinez paused when neither Neal nor Ally spoke, then continued on.

"When Debbie arrived in my home, she was fifteen but not, she was so street-smart. She had seen a lot, that one. Debbie was a wild one, always running away, always getting with the boys. I tried to talk to her, but she wasn't listening. She had been in seventeen foster homes before she arrived in my home. She never really settled, always had her bags packed, ready to move on. She was ready to take on and challenge the world. About five months after she arrived in my home, she ran away for the sixth time. She hooked up with a twenty year old, Wade Warren, and got pregnant."

"Wade Warren claimed he did not know how old Debbie was. But he was arrested just the same for statutory rape. He served a year of jail time and had to register as a sexual offender. To tell you the truth, Wade Warren was much less street smart and much more naïve then Debbie. He didn't have much going on up here," Ms. Martinez said tapping a finger to her temple.

"Debbie, she had the baby. She agreed to behave and quit running so she could live with the baby in my home in foster care. Debbie named the baby, Priscilla. She tells me that the name means, "Giving honor." She said the baby made her honorable, whole. I said it gave her work. She did good for the better part of a year; then adios," she waived her hand away. "I had the baby; I called her Cilly."

When Debbie turned eighteen, she asked Children's Services to place Priscilla with her. She was working at a discount store and had a small apartment. She was always dolled up in pricey clothes. Her work didn't provide enough cash for what she was sporting, but no one asked me. I always wondered what she was up to. The baby was placed with Debbie.

She still was living on the wild side, hanging out with the biker boys. Got a tooth knocked out in a drunken brawl, wore hoochie clothes down to here, and wore pointy-heeled boots up to her knee. She even got several tattoos and pierced body parts," Ms. Martinez said, shaking her head.

Debbie brought the baby to me when Cilly was five. She tells me that she's scared. She caught the girl dressing up in her lacy under things with make-up all over her face. Debbie told me she slapped the shit out of her daughter, but she loved her. She said she was scared that she was going to mess up Cilly's life, like the mess she had made of her own. She wanted to do better for her child.

She asked me to keep Cilly for a couple of weeks while she got her head straight, and I agreed. She moved in with a more reserved female friend, who would look after Cilly while she worked evenings, and she brought Cilly back home. She still did her own thing, but kept the guys away from her home and child.

More than a year ago, Debbie was charged with second degree murder after a bar room fight. I went to find out what happened. She tells me that she's at the bar, minding her own business. A woman grabbed her from behind by the hair, yanking her backwards in her chair, pulling her and the chair to the ground. Then she jumped on her. The woman was pounding on her and telling her to stay away from her man. Debbie didn't know who the hell she was. Debbie's friends pulled the woman off her, and Debbie pulled out a knife. The woman pulled away from the others who were holding her back, and Debbie stuck her with the knife. Debbie was charged with voluntary manslaughter.

She pled down to some other charge. I went to get Cilly but the authorities had located Wade Warren, and had given him custody of the child. I went to the jail, told Debbie that Cilly was placed with Wade. Debbie got mad at me, saying that she don't want to talk to me no more.

One night, I get a call from Wade, asking me if I stole his child. I tell him I don't know what he is talking about. He is rambling that if I didn't do it, Debbie surely had someone do it. He wasn't going to take the rap and be a sitting duck for the police again; he being registered and all. I tell him if Priscilla is missing, he needed to call the cops right away. He hung up.

I called the police. They do a child welfare check and find that Wade had moved two weeks ago. Then, they tell me they can't do a damn thing. They have no proof that the child is missing or in danger. It could be that the father relocated with her. If he failed to register within a thirty days' time frame, they may be able to pick him up on a probation violation. I kept calling to see if the school records had been transferred, but since I'm not a relative, no one can give me any information. I tried to locate Debbie, but she was transferred from jail to prison. No one can tell me where she's gone. I've got no rights, no need to be asking, and no one wants to listen.

Then, I see the news tonight. I already knew it was bad. It shouldn't have happened. You in the government wait for bad things to happen and then shake your heads and say how sad. I say how stupid, how unnecessary. You say that you want to protect the privacy rights of the parents, but what about the rights of that precious child? Are you through listening to me now? I want to go home."

Neal responded, "Just a couple more questions, please. Was Priscilla born in this county?"

"Yes, at County General, but she attended school in Lake City." Neal took this information down in his notes. "Do you know if she had seen a dentist or been referred to a dentist before her disappearance?"

"I don't know if she had a dental exam, but I suggested to Debbie that Cilly have a complete physical, dental, and optical exam, since she was going into the first grade. Priscilla's birth date missed the cutoff, so she started school at age six. She repeated kindergarten since she was pretty small and introverted for her age. The teachers told Debbie it would give Priscilla an advantage down the road. Debbie was ready to take them all on, but after she settled down, she must have taken their advice."

"Do you have any demographic information on either parent or child, such as birth date, social security number?"

She gave him a veiled contemptuous look, like he had not heard a word of what she had said. "Yes, I have the information for you, right here. I took the dates from my records." She opened her notebook and retrieved several folded pieces of lined paper, which Neil unfolded. Lily had full names, birthdates, and social security numbers for Debbie and Priscilla McCabe. She also had a birth date and social for Wade Warren, in addition to his arrest and release date. Lily provided the dates of birth and death for Debbie's mother, Delores McCabe, and her obituary notice. She had copied dated logs of her conversations with Debbie McCabe, Wade Warren, various police officers, and school officials. A brief summary of these conversations were recorded. She even had the criminal identification number for Debbie McCabe, including arrest and disposition dates. Lily had saved Neal at least twenty man-hours with these pages alone.

Neil looked directly at her and said sincerely, "Thank you for all your help. I'm sorry for your loss."

Lily gruffly nodded.

"Could I please have your address and phone number, Ms. Martinez, in case I have any additional questions?" She nodded reluctantly, and gave him the information he wanted.

Neal walked Lily Martinez to the lobby where the Deputy Saunders was waiting to give Ms. Martinez a ride back to her car.

When Neal returned, he was flicking the top of his ball point pen. "Well, I will be able to put Debbie McCabe's criminal identification or CII number into the system. I'll have no trouble finding her. But what a hell of thing to have to tell Debbie: Sorry to inform you, but your child is not living with her deadhead father. Her father abandoned her to our local serial killer, and she has been lying in the bottom of a mining shaft for the past year."

Ally had never seen Neal this upset before. Ally asked, "Why was Priscilla placed with her father? He was a registered sex offender."

"Warren was never charged with any sexual abuse or other abuse against his child, and he never lost his parental rights to Priscilla through the courts. Therefore, the legal system and child welfare would consider his offender status irrelevant."

"Sad," Ally replied.

"The killer obviously does his homework," Ally pondered. "He chooses his victims carefully. If Lily Martinez had not come in, who would even know that child was victimized? Same with Amy George. Is it that easy to get information regarding these children's backgrounds?" Ally was speaking her thoughts aloud, only half-conscious of Neal's presence.

"Dental applications contain a lot of confidential information," Neil explained, "like parents' income, and medical histories. School records have teacher's concerns, comments, and notes about the child's living arrangements. Also, in communities this size, some families are known to multiple agencies. Some cases are even staffed by multi-disciplinary teams to access the best services to meet the family's needs." His voice trailed off. "Ally you're amazing. I think you may have discovered a missing link in this case." Neal was obviously excited; Ally was dumbfounded.

"Neal, what is it? I obviously tripped over something."

"The CAP (Child Abuse Prevention Council) is made up of private citizens (usually in a professional capacity) who volunteer

311

to serve on the board to administer various programs that provide services to children at risk for abuse and neglect. One of their umbrella programs is the multi-disciplinary team. A teacher or agency representative makes a referral to the team regarding a particular child they might have concerns for, feeling that this child might need services from various agencies. A judge signs a waiver of confidentiality for the team to meet and discuss a particular child. Representatives from several programs within the area meet to discuss best services and to create an intervention plan to assist a child or family. Parents participate in the process and help identify areas of need. The team reconvenes periodically to discuss progress on the intervention plan.

When the team first convened, it was mostly for teenagers who were at risk of going to juvenile hall or being expelled from school. Over the past ten years, the services have extended to younger children, to assist them before serious problems develop. Intervention services include referrals to public health immunization programs, mental health, food and nutrition, parenting education, and district tutoring.

It is my bet that our friend, Eric Morrison, serves on this board, and that these children were referred to the council due to their problematic home lives. If true, we have a strong link between Morrison and the victims. It would explain how he got so much information so quickly about his victims. It's another nail in his damn coffin."

"Is this our smoking gun?" Ally asked.

"If correct, it's definitely strong circumstantial evidence. Service on the CAP board is part of public record. I can easily get a court order to find out if those children were referred. It's a point of circumstantial evidence that the prosecution will have to submit to without argument. Let them try to shrug off."

"Oh... by the way, I was able to discuss this investigation with a FBI profiler, Avery Brezo. He couldn't give me much information without reviewing the files, but he offered some insights: Brezo theorized that our killer, was traumatized as a child. The killer's response to the trauma was externalized rage. He views the world as a wicked place and he's wicked. He will now seize the power and control that he didn't have when he was younger. He also suggested that our killer could be categorized a Malignant Narcissist rather than a true psychopath. True psychopaths are generally disconnected from their emotions, and without conscience. For example, they often coldly and objectively analyze their crimes to the interviewers, giving a rather dispassionate or text book accounting of their actions. A Malignant Narcissist has emotions, but only his emotions are relevant; everyone else's are insignificant. A Malignant Narcissist shows a pattern of vicious destructiveness and inhumanity. He enjoys and takes pleasure in the pain of others; a true sadist. A Malignant Narcissist is just as cold and dangerous as a true psychopath for he has no morality. Personally, I believe Morrison probably had a conscience at one time, but it was damaged beyond repair, early on.

"Did you find anything to implicate Eric in his office?" Ally asked.

"It's too early to tell. There was nothing obvious," Neal responded. "Appointment records for just the past year are kept in the office. The office manager has appointment schedules for the past five years transferred to microfiche and stored in their corporate offices. She needs to request the information. It will take at least a week just to see if our known names are on the list. It will take much longer to view the entire schedule. We did find pictures of Morrison at the schools with various children, but none of these were with any of our known victims. I requested personnel records to see if there was a pattern of vacation or sick leave used around the time frame of the known disappearances. Again, they have this information in their corporate office, and the office manager doesn't know how long this information is stored.

While I was conducting the search, some unusual techno artwork kept drawing my attention. There were several 24" by 18" inch framed art pieces of young children in cute poses. There was a small girl resting her chin in the palms of her hands, watching the flight of a butterfly. Another child was floating a blade of grass down a river stream, and a third was blowing the spindle off a dandelion. The pictures were a mosaic composed of thumbnail "cut and paste" pieces from other images or photos. I asked the office manager where these art works came from. She wasn't positive, and she was not sure who the artist was. A receptionist thought the art pieces might have been a public recognition gift for their community services involvement.   No one else in the office seemed to know where the pictures came from.

I asked to borrow the pictures and received permission. I FedExed the prints to an agent at VICAP. VICAP is a support agency through the FBI that provides help and information to apprehend violent criminals. They keep a database of unsolved serial murders to link a suspect to similar crimes. The agency has the latest and greatest software. I was hoping that one of their photo enhancement programs could defragment and reorganize the pieces within the mosaic, and bring it back to the original prints. They may need the original software program or the owner's hard-drive to do this. I'm not sure yet. Hopefully, if they need those items, they can write a strong enough recommendation to secure a seizure warrant. You know, I suspect if Morrison is our killer, he has photos somewhere. Wouldn't he just be arrogant enough to publicly display these photos in such a manner? To rub it in our faces?"

Ally sighed, "Is there anything else? I'm ready to head home."

"Not really. I don't think I will find out anything more over the weekend. "

"My Mom's in town and has willingly volunteered to help me out with Breanna. So, if you do need extra help with the leg-work let me know."

"Thanks Ally, I just might take you up on the offer. I may need someone to retrieve some of the records I was telling you about or make copies. I'll walk you to your car."

"Thank you. This place is rather spooky at night," Ally said gratefully.

CHAPTER 21

Eric remained hidden, watching from his lookout post behind the hedge. It was close to ten, when she turned into the driveway. He was so close! It would be too easy to grab the Bitch now; it would only take a few seconds. It was a shame he didn't have his equipment with him. Perched restlessly with indecision, he knew that he wasn't properly prepared at this time, so he might make clumsy mistakes. Yet if he hung around too long observing, he just might attract attention to himself. The garage door closed, he'd waited too long. Maybe tomorrow, Bitch.

He felt like doing something, anything. Slashing her tires? If he did anything destructive now, it would send out an alert. They'd be on the lookout, and watching for him. He would have to be content with his plan. He slowly went through his rehearsal from the point of contact to the discarding of her body.

The disposal site was a difficult to find mining tunnel. This tunnel was a little more than a hole in the side of the cliff. Its rusted metal bars were secured with a padlock prohibiting access. He had cut and replaced the previous padlock with one of his own. The track to this tunnel was up a steep incline of loose rock, and the under-ground ceiling of the tunnel was just as unstable. The wide spaced metal bars would provide easy access for various rodents and other scavengers. In no time at all, little would remain of her decomposed body, not to mention that of the maggot.

If only he could watch for himself, as each incremental level of decay led to the complete putrefaction of her body, but he wouldn't! The boys might be watching, and tailing him at that point. It wouldn't be good to be caught with the body at the disposal site; in fact, it would be the height of stupidity. He watched the shadows casted by her body, as she passed the shaded windows. His thoughts had the desired effect; he was completely aroused.

Reaching down, he took charge of his arousal as he continued to watch her shifting, hazy shape. He wiped himself off in the cold, wet grass. Yes, tomorrow he would be back, this time prepared. Then if fate offered him an opportunity, he would seize it.

He heard a car approach and jumped back to his post, quickly zipping up his jeans and giving them a final snap. The garage opened, and the interior light of the garage illuminated the front of the house. He didn't feel comfortable with the light, and his anxiety began to rise steadily as the minutes passed. What was the fucker doing, and why was it taking so long? Was anyone aware of his presence? He didn't see anyone look out of the house. Finally, the garage door descended slowly, cloaking him in darkness.

Ally arrived home bone-tired, dreaming of a hot drink and a warm bath. The house was dark except for a small circle of light from the end table lamp. It was so quiet and calm; Breanna must be sleeping peacefully. Walking through the door, she was startled by Rene's verbal onslaught.

"Ally, where have you been? I've been worried sick, half out of my mind. Couldn't you have picked up a phone for crying out loud?"

Ally felt like a guilty teenager as she sought to pacify her mother's anger. "Mom, I'm sorry you were worried. I should have called, but to tell you the truth I didn't even think about it."

Rene took a deep breath and checked her emotions. Her eyes were full of tears, and her face was drawn in worry. "I'm sorry, too, Ally; it's just that I've been here watching the clock wondering what could be taking so long. What happened to you?"

Ally walked over to Rene and put her arms around her. She led her mom to the couch and sat down with her. "It's okay, Mom; I'm all right."

"Ally, it's just that I've got this horrible feeling that you're in danger, and it doesn't go away. I haven't wanted to worry you about it. It's probably just this awful situation but please, please be careful."

"To tell you the truth, Mom, I've been worried since this whole thing started, too. You don't have to remind me to watch my step."

After a few minutes, Rene said, "Okay, don't keep me in the dark! Tell me what happened."

Ally sank back into the couch, wrapping a blanket around her shoulders. "The morgue was more modern than I imagined. I thought the morgue would be something that was built in the 1950's; it would be dark and dimly lit. It wasn't like that. It was a new brick building with high ceilings and blue trim. The building even had a family center and counseling offices. It was eerie at night though; isolated, dark."

"What about the child?" Rene pressed.

"I was gearing up to that." Ally took a deep breath, ignoring the burning at the back of her throat.   She rubbed her arms briskly, as if suddenly chilled. "The girl's name was Priscilla McCabe. It appears she disappeared last year. Her body was well preserved. Although I didn't spend much time looking at her, before I nearly fainted. I didn't receive any special visions or impressions."

"What took so much time?" Rene asked, ignoring Ally's emotional state. By nature, Rene felt it was best to be open with your emotions, good or bad. She hated to see Ally so closed off and guarded.

"A woman, Lily Martinez, came into the morgue to identify the child,"   Ally responded. "It's a long sad story. Is seems that Priscilla McCabe and her teen-aged mother, Debbie, lived in foster care with Ms. Martinez several years ago. Now Debbie is in prison. Priscilla was placed with her biological father when Debbie was arrested. The father failed to inform the authorities that his child was missing. It seems as if he was fearful that he might get blamed for her disappearance, because he's a registered sex offender."

"You've got to be kidding! You can't be serious!" Rene said in disbelief.

"I just wish it wasn't the truth. It doesn't sound like Debbie had an intact family; her mother died from alcoholism. There was no family member to sound the alarm when this child came up missing. Ms. Martinez tried, but she was brushed aside because she's not related to the child."

"It's tragic," Rene sighed.

"Afterwards, I was talking to Neal. It's bothered me that the killer seemed to know so much about these children. He seemed to know that the children's disappearance would not be detected right away or amass a huge inquiry. I mentioned this to Neal before, but he just related it to the gossip pool in a relatively small community. Now he believes the killer may have had inside information through a community action program: he's checking into it."

David entered the house, startling both Rene and Ally. He looked from one to the other. "What's up? You look scared to death."

Ally ran over to David and flung her arms around him. David was taken aback. He returned her embrace and rubbed her upper back. "Did I miss something?" he asked.

"David, remember the body, the crime scene technicians were trying to pull out from the shaft at Horseshoe Bend? They finally recovered the body. Due to the arsenic levels and the coolness within the shaft, the body was still recognizable. I met Neal at the morgue tonight, to see if anything would come to me. It didn't: no visions, impressions, nothing. A woman came to the morgue while I was there; she was able to identify the child. Neal has a few more leads to follow up on now."

"Oh Ally, you should have called me," he soothed.

Rene gave Ally a serious look and said, "Yes. See what I mean? I told Ally that very thing. You know what they say about like minds. Well David, I hate to cut it brief, but I'm exhausted so I'll say my goodnights now. I'll let you two talk." She gave David a slight hug and turned to Ally, brushing her bangs away from her face. We can talk some more in the morning." Ally was watching

David, she didn't know why, but there was a strange stillness about him.

There was nothing that Ally would have liked better than to head to bed, too, but she couldn't go to bed, yet.

Turning to David, Ally said, "Would you like a cup of hot chocolate? That sounds wonderful to me right now."

David nodded. "We've finished the Smitty promotional. I'll have to go in for about four hours tomorrow, but the rest of the weekend should be free. We can go to the Christmas Fair with your mom. There will be some children's dance groups performing."

"That sounds wonderful." Ally filled their cups and brought them over to the table.

"It sounds like the investigation is going full throttle." David said briskly, picking up his cup.

"I'm hoping they catch the guy soon," Ally said hesitating. "Honey, how are you coping with all of this? This is not something we planned for; I just walked into the middle of a nightmare."

"I'm not having problems with your involvement in the investigation anymore. But..."

"But what?" Ally asked sincerely.

"Ally, we were so close; we didn't even need words. I think of how we would sit quietly together for hours without needing to say a word. It was comfortable, not lonely. I knew you were present, right there with me. Now, we can be in the middle of a conversation and I think that I've lost you, you are not even there. You're miles away and I can't reach you, you're always so distant. You never talk about what's going on unless I press, or unless you are having an emotional meltdown and then you just cry. I can't even help because I don't even know where you are, at any level."

Ally was silent for several moments. Then she said, "You're right. When I first started receiving the visions, I thought I was going crazy. Deep-down, I knew there must be some logical reason for what was happening; the nightmares, and the hallucinations. My brain kept reminding me that most mentally ill people believe they are sane. Still, when I have doubts or minimize the extent of my experience, then I have to think of

Bree. She was very real. I can't minimize her existence or what has happened since."

"Then you had your perspective about the exclusive scientific origin and order of the universe. When I tried to tell you what was happening, it was met with skepticism. It's not that I blame you, but I held back even more," Ally concluded, pausing to think what she wanted to say.

"But what about now? Why are you holding back?" David said wistfully.

"This whole situation is taking its' toll emotionally. My attitude is turbulent and my ability to cope is shaky, at best. I don't want to bring you down or have my negative attitude affect Breanna. I just want a normal family in abnormal conditions. I try to pretend everything's the same, yet everything in my world has shifted. Sometimes, I feel as if I don't even know myself anymore."

"Honey, everything in life changes, given time. If one of us had been in a car wreck, or had a serious illness, it would have changed our lives or plans. Even when beautiful events happen, such as becoming parents to Breanna, the pattern of our lives changes. You basically are the same person, but different sides are emerging. I just want to join you there. I don't want you to leave me behind because you don't trust me to ride out these changes."

Ally smiled weakly. "I'll work at getting there. I know we need to talk this out. I don't know what will happen once this case is over. In the back of my mind, I always thought that once this investigation was over, everything would return pretty much to normal. But, I know this is not true because I've changed. I just hope you love the new me as well as the old."

"You need to let me get to know you, Ally. I'm sure I'll like what I find.' David leaned his head in towards her, and she did the same. "Ally, I know we've talked a lot tonight, but I want you to think about one more thing. I know you love Breanna with all your heart, but, you are so consumed with ensuring her safety and protecting her. Are you enjoying being with her? Being her mother?"

Ally stared at David; the question struck a nerve. She didn't have an answer. "I've been concerned about her picking up on my tension or sadness about the situation. Under the circumstances, I don't think that I have had a chance to give her my undivided attention. I don't believe that's the way it should be."

"Ally, don't be so hard on yourself. You can rarely orchestrate life to the way it should be; too many variables. Try to enjoy the time you spend with Breanna, without fear. Just enjoy the moments she breaches new milestones. Hold her for enjoyment, and not to ensure yourself of her safety or to ward off evil." He pulled her in his arms to give her a deep hug.

Ally was in bed, sweating profusely. She just had a dream, or was it? She was in the middle of inescapable darkness. She could feel a cold and evil force surrounding her. She was clutching her arms tightly to her chest. Her head folded inward towards her chest as she cringed against the force. She hoped to shut out this evil, but she felt a surrounding force compressing her more tightly. She was collapsing from the pressure.

Ally saw a bright flash of light, as if a flash bulb effused. Neon lights seemed to be pulsating around her, keeping the evil force from destroying her. She could hear a distant chant; it slowly increased in volume as she struggled to make out the sound. It was becoming increasingly loud and pulsating along until she could make out a single word: "Beware." Over and over again in a litany of vibrations: "Beware! Beware! Beware!"

Ally lay there, afraid to go back into her dreams where evil lurked, but also scared to leave the protection of her blankets. Her unease translated into a desperate need to go and check on Breanna. She pulled herself up, slinging her legs over the side of the bed as if each movement had to be thought out and carefully executed. She headed out of her bedroom door and into Breanna's room. She watched the gentle rise and fall of Breanna's chest, her upper lip quivering slightly as she slept. Ally recalled what David had said earlier tonight, and knew he was right.

Whenever she looked at her daughter, she thought that some monster might hurt her. The thoughts were unbearable, making her uncomfortable and uptight in Breanna's company. Ally felt leaden and sat heavily in the rocking chair, holding her little vigil. Ally just hoped to God that she could manage these emotions. She whispered a little prayer.

After this prayer, she felt comforted as warmth spread through her body. She got up, gently caressing Breanna's head before making her way back to bed.

Ally awoke in the morning feeling stronger, at least stronger than she had in the last few days. David was already up. She went straight to Breanna's room. The house was warm and cozy; either David or Mom must have turned up the heat. Ally could hear some distant movement in the kitchen.

Breanna was wide awake. Ally studied her appearance; she had grown so much over the past couple of months. Thick soft tufts of auburn hair surrounded her small face in waves, and her eyes were still slate blue. Breanna did not look like her or David having her own combination of each of their features. She was watching the mobile above the crib. "Hi, Sweetheart. Are you having a good morning?"

Breanna responded to Ally's voice, looking up at her mother. Breanna's eyes followed Ally's movements as she walked over towards the crib. Breanna was waving her hands in excitement, making cooing noises. Ally held out her hand to Breanna who promptly grasped her finger. Ally moved her hand gently up and down. Then, Ally followed with her second finger and watched as Breanna pulled herself up toward her. Breanna had almost made it into a full sitting position.

Ally reached in with both hands to pull Breanna into her arms. She cradled her gently as she kissed her soft hair and then her forehead. Ally breathed in the sweet baby smell of her, and felt Breanna's movements within her arms.

Ally retrieved a diaper from the holder attached to the closet door and a warm outfit from her drawer. Breanna could no longer fit into her 0-3 month clothes. Ally chose a new 6-month outfit: a white ribbed cotton bodysuit imprinted with little red roses, denim jeans with matching roses embroidered on the pockets, and booties as red as the matching cardigan. Ally grabbed a new receiving blanket.

Ally headed into the bathroom with Breanna, setting the clothing, blanket and diaper on the cabinet. She was talking softly to Breanna as she prepared her bath. Breanna loved her bath. She splashed the warm water with her hand, and squealed with delight. Ally shampooed her hair and rinsed it with the warm wash cloth. Ally had dried Breanna with the towel and was rubbing lotion over Breanna's squirming body when her mother entered the bathroom.

Rene placed her hands lightly on Ally's shoulders. "There you two are, I was just about to get worried. Isn't she just an angel? I always loved bath time. She sure loves her bath time."

"Where's David?" Ally asked.

"He said he had an absolute craving for those cinnamon rolls, I love so much. He was going to get some rolls and a newspaper. David really is very thoughtful. He should be back in twenty minutes. I've got some coffee on."

"Hmm, sounds good," Ally said.

"I know it's none of my business, but how are you two getting along?"

Mom always would jump in where angels feared to tread; there was never an off-limit question. Ally thought a moment and responded honestly. "It's been difficult, Mom. At first, neither of us could completely accept my psychic experience. I guess David's feelings probably echoed my own. Was I psychic or psychotic? When the murders began to unfold, David was upset that I was getting involved in matters that didn't concern us, and bringing on trouble.

Now, in trying to keep David and Breanna away from this mess, I've cultivated a gulf between us. We really need to work on the relationship, or I'm afraid we won't make it." Ally was intense and emotional, but her tone very matter of fact.

"You know, I believe in keeping matters simple, Ally. You should open up and talk to David. He is an adult and he's responsible for his own feelings. You can't spend so much time focusing on what has happened or what could happen that you lose all sense of beauty in today. You are blessed, Ally. You and David have each other, your health, a good lifestyle, and a healthy, beautiful daughter. You've got a lot going for you in the present. Don't lose sight of this while you're submerged in this investigation."

"Thanks Mom. I just hope it isn't too late." Ally said softly.

"Hogwash Ally. It's never too late to try. That is just a convenient excuse people use to get out of working on the problems. Anything worth having is worth some struggles."

"I think Breanna is ready for some breakfast," Ally said, changing the subject. She picked up Breanna and headed towards the kitchen. Rene followed, wondering if she had pushed too far.

David returned home while Ally was feeding Breanna. "Hello, I'm back. The lines were terrible." He set the cinnamon rolls and newspaper on the kitchen table and walked over to give Breanna a kiss on the forehead. Then he briefly brushed Ally's lips as if unsure of his reception. Ally returned his kiss.

"Those cinnamon rolls look like they were worth the wait," Rene said. She went to retrieve three dessert plates, forks, and napkins.

David filled his coffee cup and held up the decanter. "Does anyone want a refill?"

Ally said, "I'll have a refill. Thanks."

"How about us going to the Christmas Fair?" David asked. "We could leave about eleven this morning. I have to go into work for about two to three hours this evening. I should be back by six or seven. Tonight, we can drive around and look at the lights. Or depending on the weather, we can walk around the Villa. They really have it decked out. They even have a horse-drawn sled you can ride around the park. It should be a lot of fun."

"I can hardly believe the Christmas Fair has started already." Ally commented.

"Yes, it starts today, November 14th, and ends December 20th."

"That sounds absolutely terrific, David. While you're at work, maybe Mom and I can do some Christmas shopping. I haven't got any shopping done. How does that sound, Mom?"

"Don't worry about me, I'm along for the ride; just lead the way."

Eric arrived at his spot within view of the Sullivan residence at five in the morning. It was cold and windy; the skies were dark and heavy with clouds. It was cold enough to snow. He was hoping it would hold off, in accordance with his plans. Hell, if it snowed, it would be almost impossible to get to the mine. He might have to delay his plans.

There was no movement until he saw David Sullivan leave the residence at 7:05 am. It was Saturday. Would he be working? He hadn't thought about that. He watched the asshole pull away, and debated on whether or not he should follow him. He'd better not, he thought.

At 7:45 am, Eric saw Sullivan return. The interior light of the garage illuminated Sullivan as he got out of his car with a doughnut box and newspaper. Oh, fucking great! He's not going to work. It was beginning to look like he might have to delay his plans, at least for the weekend.

Everything he needed was in his back seat, duct tape to chloroform. Just waiting to be used. He caught sight of Sullivan, eyeing his rental car. He knew Sullivan could not see him from his viewing angle, but it was still unnerving. Nothing was working right today. Sullivan turned back, mounting the short stairwell up to the interior door of the residence. Pushing the button, the garage door slowly descended. Eric didn't want to draw attention, should Sullivan go out again. He would leave and return after dark.

CHAPTER 22

As David held open the door, Ally brought in her purchases, and Rene followed behind with Breanna. Ally had started the beef stew in the crock-pot before they left for the Christmas Fair, and now, the warm tantalizing aroma engulfed the air. Her stomach rumbled hungrily; they had not had any lunch because they were planning for an early dinner. They had, however, snacked on some kettle corn from the 'marching band' booth at the fair. Given that the band was raising money to sponsor their trip to Los Angeles, to perform in the parade.

David went to get their Christmas tree from the back of the Explorer. The plan was to set up a live Christmas tree this year, and plant it in the yard after the holidays. It would be a special memento of Breanna's first Christmas. Ally carefully inspected several gifts she'd purchased from the various craft booths, and the Christmas figurine she'd bought for herself. It was an angel with a lion lying by her side, and a lamb curled up on the other. Carefully unwrapping her figurine, she placed it on the mantel. She envisioned how it would look with pine garland hanging beneath it, surrounded by white Christmas lights, and three large red-velvet bows. She would top it with her brass candleholders and white taper candles. It would look beautiful. Ally placed the gifts on a shelf in the closet, planning to wrap them later. She made a mental note to get wrapping paper, ribbons, and bows when she went out tonight.

"Ally, I think I'm going to opt for a short rest before dinner, unless you need my help. I don't know why I'm so tired." Rene said.

"I'm fine. Most of the dinner is ready, just going to make some breadsticks and a salad." Ally headed towards the kitchen to finish her dinner preparations.

Afterwards, Ally prepared a bottle, taking Breanna out of the swing to feed her. Ally then placed Breanna in the carrier seat while she set the table. She lit the candles and called David in to dinner. Lightly tapping on the door of their guestroom, Ally called softly, "Mom, dinner's ready."

"Okay dear, I'll be out in a minute," Rene muttered.

David was in an exuberant mood as they sat down to dinner. It had been a wonderful day, Ally thought to herself. She had hardly once thought of the investigation or Eric Morrison. She mentally shook herself to stop her train of thoughts for she was going to continue to enjoy this day.

After they had finished eating, David was telling her and Rene a funny story about something that happened at his store. "Then, this little 2-year-old boy managed to elude his mother while she was trying to change his pull-up training pants in the restroom. It seems that as soon as the mother had taken off the old pull-up, another woman entered the restroom. The little guy seized the opportunity and ran out the door and throughout the store, bottomless, with his frantic mother, diaper in hand, chasing after him. You should have seen her jostle her way through the crowd of shoppers and displays. The little boy was giggling the whole time, thinking it was a jolly game! " David was putting dramatic gestures into the storytelling. Rene was laughing so hard that tears were rolling out the corner of her eyes. Ally grinned; then all fell silent.

"David, why don't you call your Dad? He may want to go look at the lights with us tonight, and help us decorate the tree tomorrow. I can pick up a pie for later, tonight."

"Sounds great; I didn't even think about asking him. I'll call him later; I've got to get to the store now." David gave her a kiss, "I shouldn't be too long; it's not a big order. But it's rather complicated, so I want to handle this one personally."

"I thought me and Mom could go to Discount Mart, and then to the downtown shops to look around. Is that okay with you, Mom?"

"It's fine with me," Rene replied.

"See you in a while," he called over his shoulder. Ally heard the garage door close as David left.

Ally started to clear the table, and Rene joined in to help. "Mom, I don't think I'm going to go back to work at my old job. I'd like to find a job, working with troubled kids in some capacity."

"Have you talked to David about it?" Rene said, as she helped load the dishwasher.

"Not yet, I've just started to think about it. This experience has been a real eye-opener. I had no clue about what some children go through and how little the system can do in response," said Ally thoughtfully.

"I made a report to CPS once about a family in our church; it was investigated. I learned later that the parents received some counseling and parenting classes. It seemed to work for them," Rene responded.

"But Mom, from what I've seen, many children fall between the cracks, or for some reason, the system wasn't able to intercede. I even contacted a social worker to try and find out what some of the problems are."

"So, what were you told?" Rene inquired.

"Well ...After a few questions, I got an ear-full. The social worker, Ms. Ferris, told me that the system which protects children is broken. That the system is reactive in nature, and not proactive. There are very few programs that work with children and families to prevent problems from happening in the first place. Also, I didn't realize how little money, resources and manpower are available to agencies that work with troubled families. Many initiatives are started but soon are deferred or cancelled due to bureaucratic stagnation, or lack of available funding. Children in the system, the most vulnerable kids within our society, don't even receive adequate medical or mental health care. These services are very limited, and a vast number are in need of assistance. Ultimately, children don't have a voice or an advocacy group to continually speak up for them. The few children's groups that are out there are just interested in litigating change. This further bankrupts an already financially deficient system. These groups don't advocate programs or help before a child suffers injury. They just sue once there is a problem. They're looking for scapegoats."

Ally continued fervently, "You know I started looking at our priorities in this country. We pay our movie stars and sports heroes millions of dollars a year for entertainment, or think of the massive amount of money that goes into advertisements and political campaigns nationally, yet a foster child gets a little over a hundred dollars per year for clothes. There are no funds available to pay for yearbooks, school rings, team sports, or even orthodontic work for children in foster care. "

"I knew the foster-care situation was not the best, but I didn't realize it was so dismal," Rene replied.

"I sure was oblivious to these problems. As I'm sure that most people in the general public aren't aware of all these difficulties. If it is not part of their reality, it's too depressing to think of a child in pain or living under poor conditions. It is easier to dismiss, and to ignore these issues. However, it is this very denial that allows these abject circumstances to persist and fester. These types of problems are deteriorating our society and exacting their costs in ballooning magnitude. The overall cost to society is too high in terms of human potential, strength of the family, and strength of community. Besides you can't imagine the astronomical fiscal cost to the criminal justice system, child welfare, juvenile probation, mental health services, health care, and educational system."

"It sounds as if you have a future as a crusader. You've found a cause."

"You think so?" Ally asked wryly. "Are you ready to head out now or do you want to wait until later?"

"We should do our shopping now to make sure we have enough time." Rene answered. Ally packed several diapers, bottles, and a change of clothes into Breanna's diaper bag. She laid out a blanket sleeper for Breanna.

"Mom, could you get Breanna bundled up while I go get the car warmed up? The stroller and a blanket are already in the trunk."

After leaving the Sullivan residence, Eric pulled off to the side of the road to make a call on his cell phone. Rummaging through the glove box, he found his receipt from the orange juice he had purchased from the Smart store on Grant Street. The phone number of the store was printed on it. He dialed the number and asked to speak to David Sullivan. He was told that Mr. Sullivan was not there, but would be in later this evening. He was told to try back around five in the evening.

He saw the "lo bat" sign illuminated on his cell phone, and plugged it into his car charger.

Eric was restless as he headed into town in search of a pay phone. He would start this morning with a call to Julie. He located a booth at the far corner of a gas station and dialed Julie at her home number.

"Hello, Julie? It's Eric Morrison. Could I speak to you for a few minutes?"

"Uh yes," Julie hesitated. "It's good to hear from you. How are you doing?" He could hear the uncertainty in her tone, unsure whether or not she should be speaking with him.

"I drove by the office yesterday," he began. "I saw all the police cars around our building. Julie, what was going on?" Eric asked urgently. His anticipation masqueraded as concern, and Julie responded to his distress.

"Eric, the police had a search warrant for our offices, the whole dental office."

"What in the world were they looking for?" he had asked her, as if perplexed.

"They took appointment books and employee records," Julie replied. "Oh, and I don't know why, but they asked if they could borrow the framed pictures in the lobby."

Eric felt his heart, pumping in his ears, deafening in its intensity. His muscles were so taut that it felt like they could jump through his skin.

"Thank you, Julie. I've just been beside myself wondering what is going on. I'm trying to avoid my apartment, because I don't want the press bombarding me with their endless

330

questions. Julie, you have been a wonderful friend. I appreciate the information." He hung up.

After he had disconnected, he picked up the receiver of the pay phone and slammed it down repeatedly. He began kicking the sides of the booth. He noticed a man across the street, watching his outburst. He yelled out, "What the fuck are you looking at?" The man hurried away. It was not good to call from a public phone. He did not want to draw any attention.

Shit was coming down fast; he needed to make a move. He couldn't be frozen in his indecision. He looked through the dilapidated phone book within the booth, searching for a residential number for the Bitch, since he had left her number in his work directory. Eric found a number and called. When she answered, he knew that he had the right number because he recognized her voice. He responded, "Must have gotten the wrong number." He hung the phone up, abruptly.

Maybe he could call, and draw her out of the house tonight. His phone would be charged by then. No, the police might check the phone records, he thought. I can't leave an evidence trail. He would have to wait.

Now, with the approaching darkness of evening, he was headed towards the Sullivan house. He averted his head as he eyed David Sullivan's car approaching his own. Sullivan, he assumed, was commuting to his job at the Smart Store.

Eric might get his opportunity tonight, after all. Hell, he wished he could settle down. The anxiety was killing him as he rocked restlessly back and forth. He needed to be calm and keep his wits about him.

He pulled up just past the hedge bordering the Sullivan residence. The Bitch's car was in the driveway; she must be planning to go out. His luck was getting better by the minute. He was wearing a dark sweater with a lightweight navy-blue hooded jacket. The hood was pulled tightly against his head. He had tight-fitting brown work gloves on with old running shoes. It was very cold; the brisk wind robbed him of breath as he quietly opened the car door.

331

It was painful to inhale the cold air as he rounded the vehicle to open the rear passenger door. He would leave this door open, so he could push the Bitch into the car. He brushed away a missed shard of heavy textured plastic from the interior lamp, which he'd broken out earlier.   He felt around for the Chloroform, rag, and duct tape on the rear, driver-side seat. He quickly located the rag and duct tape, but the Chloroform bottle must have rolled under the front seat as he came to a stop. He couldn't use a flashlight; it might alert someone to his presence. He felt along the seat, then along the rear floorboard. Lying as flat as he could, he reached under the front seat. Losing patience, he swore under his frozen breath.

He went around the car again, opening the driver's door and stooping down to feel underneath the front seat and along the edges of the guider rails. God, he should have placed the chloroform and rag in his glove box or in the front drink holder. Standing up, he bent forward to feel along the rear floorboard again. He could tell he was not his usual meticulous self. He would get his game back, and soon. Ah yes, he found the bottle up against the rear seat. He had to squat low and stretch; his head pressed tightly against the drivers' seat, as his fingertip rolled the bottle into his grasp. Quickly, he shoved the small bottle in his front pocket. The rag and tape were easily obtained from the rear seat.

Still bent over, Eric came up sharply, hitting his head on the doorframe as the front porch light flashed on. He grabbed his throbbing head, dropping the tape and rag on the asphalt below, smothering an audible yelp of pain. He quickly grabbed the tape and rag; the chloroform was still tucked securely in his front pocket. He made a mad dash across the yard towards the rear gate. He barely reached the edge of the house when he heard the front door open. He continued quietly towards the end of the hedge, dropping into the shadows, trying not to heave loudly as he heard the jangle of car keys. He saw her open the car door, setting what appeared to be another book bag behind the seat. She climbed inside the car as he struggled to get the chloroform out of his front pocket. He watched helplessly as she started the engine and fiddled with adjustments on the dash. Fuck, he had lost his opportunity, at least for now. Wait. She was opening the door again. She had only come out to warm up the car. Of course, she didn't have the maggot with her yet! He couldn't believe his luck.

Ally went back inside the house. Rene held a finger up to her lips: Breanna was fast asleep in the baby carrier, which doubled as her car seat. Rene said in a barely audible whisper, "I'll be out in a minute, going to grab my purse. I don't want to disturb her. Could you go and open the car door, and then you can help me secure this contraption?"

"Mom, I can take her out." Rene flipped the top of her fingers to waive Ally away. "I might as well learn how to belt her into the car now, since I know I will baby-sit her a time or two."

"Okay, if you want to," Ally hesitated, protectively wanting to take charge of her daughter. But she reluctantly acceded as she saw the pride in her mother's face. Ally turned the lock on the door. "I'll leave this door slightly ajar. Just pull it tightly behind you. Are you sure you don't..." Ally's question, still in hushed whispers, trailed off as her mother went into the living room to retrieve her purse.

Oh well, Ally thought, she would be able to manage. She quickly rushed out into the dark night. Ally opened the rear passenger door and left it wide open as she made her way to the other side. She then opened the rear driver side door. Eric watched her uncomprehendingly. Why had she left both rear doors, open? Was she loading some packages? He was already out in the open, slumped low in front of her car. He had left his hiding spot once he heard her traverse the porch and front yard; she had made her way so quickly. There was no time to turn back, for she would surely see him. This wasn't going according to plan. What in the hell was she doing? Never mind, he had to move now. He hovered in a bent position towards her back as she watched the front door of the house. "Everything's ready," Ally called out.

Oh God, someone else was with her! Damn it all to hell! He'd better hurry before the newcomer saw him. He braced himself with his back leg, still squatting low. He reached up with his right arm, rag in hand, and slammed it over Ally's face, pulling her back into his shoulder. His face was tight against hers as he struggled to open the folded knife blade with one hand. After several stunned moments, Ally began to struggle as she never had before, twisting her head and body in different directions. Eric shifted his glance from his struggling captive to the knife in his left hand. He did not see Rene exit the house.

He heard a blood-curdling scream followed by the loud wail of a baby's cry. Eric momentarily lost his grip on Ally, and she pulled away. Dropping the rag, Eric re-secured his advantage by grabbing the hair at the back of her head. He pulled her backwards, and she fell heavily against him. They both toppled to the ground.

Ally, free from the constraining pressure on her face, hoarsely barked out commands towards the newcomer, a woman about fifty years of age carrying an infant carrier. "Go inside, lock the door, and call 911."

When the woman continued to stare in stunned silence, Ally cried, "Quick for God's sake Mom, get Breanna in the house!" Her body going lax suddenly, as she ceased to fight. Eric dropped the knife, reached for the rag, and wrapped his left arm under her arm into a shoulder hoist. He twisted her hair against her head with his right hand as he pulled her backwards towards the awaiting car.

He struggled heaving himself into the back seat and pulling her towards him. "You fucking Bitch! You're going to pay for this," he spit out venomously. "You're as good as dead now," he said through labored gasps. He pulled her the rest of the way into the backseat. He pushed up his elbow, lifting her arm, and shoved his hand hard into her face, grinding it back and forth.

Ally tried to keep her reason through the flood of pain. She thought she heard something crack. Ally could taste blood in the back of her throat. She could feel sweat, trickling down her back; that caused her sweater to crease painfully and stick to her skin. Eric scooted himself forward and sat astride on her chest; Ally could barely breath. He pinned her arms to the sides of her body with his legs, his back towards her face, as he stretched forward as far as he could to close and lock the door; the rubber insole of his shoes ground into her arms. She desperately tried to lift her upper body to knock him off balance and out of the door. He was too heavy, and he came down hard on her chest, knocking the air out of her. "Don't try anything like that again; you won't like the consequences," he warned   He pinched the skin of her inner thigh, twisting it as hard as he could, until he could hear her yelp in pain and start to sob.

He pushed his left hand down hard into the side of her stomach, rotating his knees towards the back of the seat and across her chest until he was facing forward, straddling her body. Ally felt him reach down. He was feeling for something on the floorboard of the car. God, was this it? She thought desperately. Maybe he was searching for a hammer or maybe a gun or knife? She winced closing her eyes tightly against the coming blow.

Then he reached in his back pocket. Ally could just barely see a glint of glass. It must be a small bottle; sleeping pills? Ally could feel hot liquid spill onto her sweater, burning the skin beneath it. Eric lifted the end of her sweater towards her face. He was trying to knock her out. How was she going to escape? She wanted David and Breanna to be with her, a million miles away from here. She started crying hard as she thought of her family. Please God, please, help me get back to them.

As Eric brought the soaked end of her sweater towards her face, she turned her head slightly towards the back of the seat and held her breath. She continued to struggle, and then slowly stopped, as she continued to hold her breath. She willed her body to go limp. Ally kept her breathing steady, and her eyes shut as he pulled the sweater away from her face. She continued her pretense despite throbbing pain of her nose and a burning sensation around her nose and mouth.

She struggled not to choke, as she tried to ignore the itchy irritation at the back of her throat. She could hear the tape being stretched out from a roll, and felt it encircling her wrists, then her ankles. Eric was floundering in the darkness, wishing for light to speed his process. He was about to place the tape over her

335

mouth when he heard a distant siren. Suddenly, he remembered that he was in a cul-de-sac with single road access.

He climbed over the center console into the front seat and slammed the driver's door. Lying length-wise across the back seat, Ally figured the keys must have been in the ignition, because they were peeling away within seconds. She was nauseous from whatever drug he used, but she was conscious. She also knew that she would be dead if she didn't escape. Ally hadn't seen the man's face, but she knew it was Eric. He was enjoying her fear and pain. He could have killed her immediately when he grabbed her, but he didn't. That meant he had other plans for her, which probably meant unimaginable suffering. She knew what he was capable of, and the thought burned a shaft of pain through her heart. Her throat was unbearably dry.

Ally's resolve to live gave her a small sense of calm. She could not allow Eric to deprive her of her future with David and Breanna. Eric would not deprive Breanna of her mother; it was that simple. She ran her bottom teeth along the tape back and forth, trying to find an edge to work on. She finally found a corner after what seemed like an eternity. He had turned to his right. The road was rough and bumpy as they turned onto a dirt road. Only a minute had elapsed since he had started driving. He must be on the BLM land. It was the only unpaved road that she could think of within the area. She continued to work at the corner of the tape which sheared off almost immediately. At this rate, it would take all night to shed the tape.

She started over again, pulling tightly against her restraints. She pushed her hands together in a prayer-like fashion, pushing out with her wrists as the tape pulled and stretched on the bottom. She pushed her wrists together and pulled her hands apart, over and over again, as her bonds began to loosen. It hurt like hell, but she tried to ignore the pain. The whole front of her face was throbbing and burning. She thanked her lucky stars that Eric had not had time to do a better job, as she managed to pull her hands free. She freed her feet from the tape as quick as she could, it seemed to take forever. She did not want Eric to know she was conscious.

Now what? She screamed silently, looking at the back of a hooded head. She saw his eyes flash a glance in the rear view mirror. She lay as still as possible as her captor continued driving on the rough road. He had slowed down to maneuver around a large rut in the road. It was now or never, she thought desperately. She grabbed the handle of the rear door; it didn't budge. It must have childproof locks, she thought numbly, she glanced up to see if he had heard her, but his focus seemed to be on the rough road ahead of him.

Darting a glance through the window, she could see snow had started to fall, brushing and melting on the pane of glass. Eric was going around something on the dirt path; she needed to act quickly. She pressed the button to lower the rear window and reached out to open the car door externally. She felt the violent surge of the vehicle as it slammed forward into the weedy terrain. The door swung open as she surged forward.

She heard the shift in gears as the vehicle was thrown into park. Eric reached over the front seat to grab at her legs. Pulling herself forward into a balled position, she kicked wildly at his head. He let out a yelp of pain and then a string of profanities. Determined and intense, he started to reach for her again. She rolled over, swinging her legs wide and out of the door. He made a frantic grab for her hair, but missed it by inches as she fell to the cold hard ground.

Ally scrambled through the weeded terrain, trying to secure her footing. She tripped and lunged forward, falling against her upper arms. Thankfully, she was close to the ground at the time, or she might have broken something. She could hear Eric's heavy breathing and fast-approaching footfalls pursuing her, but could not tell how close he was. She could not spare any time looking over her shoulder as she half ran, half stumbled, over the rough unmaintained thicket. Did he have the knife trained at her back? She expected at any moment to feel the razor-sharp metal tearing into her flesh.

She would have to tread carefully as she stumbled towards a wild blackberry patch. There were blackberry patches all over out here, and she would tear herself to pieces if she ran or fell into one of these thickets. She hysterically thought to herself that this was the least of her worries.

She continued through the darkness with no idea where she was headed, her heart beat and her heavy breathing thundering in her ears, obliterating the sounds of the pursuant predator. She saw a big rock looming ahead of her. Stepping around the far side of the boulder, Ally rested her back against its hard cold surface, momentarily unable to continue running. Her skin was hot and damp, in spite of the bitter cold air. She desperately tried to catch her breath; she was unsure how long she had been running. She listened cautiously for his pursuit, but could hear no one in the dark silent night.

Now what? She tried to formulate a plan through her panic-stricken brain. She was lost in the darkness with the ultra-cold night closing in on her. She didn't have a clue as to where she was. The thought hit home that no one but the predator knew she was out here. It was so dark and cold. She could easily die of exposure when the temperature nose-dived in the early hours of the morning. Anxiety and hopelessness flooded her senses, temporarily leaving her immobile and frozen with indecision. Wiping her tears away with the palms of her hands, Ally muttered a silent prayer, "Please, please Lord, help me survive this night! Please help the police find me; I don't want to die out here."

Ally took several short, abrupt breaths as the cold air painfully pierced her chest. She felt her tremendous sense of forlorn subside as she became increasingly resolute in her determination to escape. Am I just going to lay down now, right here, and die? Ally demanded of herself.

Somehow, she needed to retrace her steps and get back to the main road. Ally fought back the tears and desperation as she tried to remember which way she had run, but it was all a blur. She ran in blind panic, trying to escape him. Relax, she screamed silently at herself. If you panic, you're dead. It's as simple as that, Ally.

Ally hastily fumbled through a stress reduction exercise, which she'd learned in the past. She took another deep breath that burned her lungs. She held it in and counted slowly. She repeated this process several times: listening to herself inhale and exhale, focusing on this process. She felt warmth radiate from the pit of her stomach. I can do this, she told herself forcefully.

Ally rebounded around the boulder, keeping low. She almost fell to the ground on her hands and knees. She was stiff and numb from the cold, but she could not think about it right now. She couldn't give up, but her traitorous mind kept returning to how cold she was. She started to sing the lyrics of songs she remembered in the back of her mind. Ally was determined to keep her mind off Eric and this bitter cold night. It was barely working. If only it wasn't so dark.

She reminded herself to keep low to the ground. Her half formulated reasoning was two-fold: to help her detect her earlier trail, and to keep a low profile so Eric Morrison did not see her. Hopefully, he would never dream that she would backtrack her original path, and he would be looking elsewhere. She made the slow journey, her mind giving away to panic frequently along the way. She paused to do her deep breathing exercise and trudged on.

Ally slammed her chest against the frozen ground as she saw Eric's headlights. Trying to surmise whether or not the driver could see her, Ally remained pressed tightly to the frozen terrain. She hoped that the overgrown weeds adequately hid her. The car continued its slow prowl until it was out of sight.

At least, Ally now knew where a road was. If she headed back to this unpaved roadway, she could use the road to get out. Even at the best of times, Ally had no sense of direction. If she followed the roadway, would she end up deeper into the forest? God, she hoped not. She could barely feel her frozen limbs now. She unsuccessfully tried to determine how much time had elapsed since this nightmare began. She had to keep moving. She decided she would go half a mile to the right, to see if she could see any lights from the neighborhood, or any other signs of civilization. She walked in the opposite direction from the one that Eric had taken.

She heard the car at a distance, and frantically searched for a hiding spot. She jumped down into a dry creek bed where a low hanging tree offered the protection she sought. She shivered uncontrollably as she crouched lower to the ground. She watched the light shift irregularly through the branches of the trees, casting outlines of the few stray leaves against sides of the red clay embankment.

Listening to her own thick heavy gasps, Ally was afraid she might encounter an unwelcome guest like a rattlesnake, but she didn't believe that even a snake would be out on a cold night, like this. She continued to pray that God would deliver her safely home. She also prayed that her daughter and David would manage okay without her if she didn't survive.

The car was almost out of view now. It was time to move. She forced her frozen limbs to obey her command to go forward. How in the world am I going to get out of this place? Don't think about it, just do it, she ordered herself through her exhausted tears. She rubbed her eyes roughly, wincing because her face hurt. She then trudged up the embankment, proceeding in the same direction the car had gone as she reached the roadway. She hoped she was going the right way.

Flakes of snow started their leisurely descent again. She felt the wet flakes brush her eyelashes and co-mingle with her tears as she slowly, but persistently pressed on, through the darkness. Ally continued moving forward like an automaton, now too tired to think about or fear her predicament. Her senses, however, were in a hyper vigilant state, responding to every small sound or shift of shadow. She even caught sight of one of the few remaining colored leaves as it slightly trembled and fell towards the frozen earth below.

Ally heard the distant hum of an engine and scanned her environment for a suitable hiding place. At a distance, maybe a hundred yards off the main trail to the right, she saw some plywood placed strategically into an inclined slope. Her eyes continued to scan the radius, there were many other makeshift ramps within the immediate area of this clearing. The local children must use it for their mountain bikes.

She rushed as fast as her feet would move her to one of the larger ramps. It was roughly three feet by four feet and inclined against a fallen tree trunk. She lowered herself to the ground, her head against her forearms; anchoring and pushing herself with her tiptoes underneath the slope of the plywood. It was a tight fit Ally thought, as she drew her knees into her stomach to hide her legs from view. She was contorted with her chin against her hands in a dog-like pose. Her back was twisted in an unnatural position. She hoped that Eric would pass by quickly, her back already aching.

The headlight moved ahead in a slow, deliberate progression, then came to a complete stop. Morrison got out of his vehicle, walking around the front of the car. Briefly, the headlights illuminated his face, vaguely confirming his identity. He walked slowly into the clearing. Oh God, did he see her? She let out an audible gasp that she prayed he didn't hear. His eyes were scanning the clearing, looking for any signs of her presence. She sucked in air and held her breath to avoid breathing too loudly as he continued to survey the area.

"Fuck! Damn it all to hell!" Eric screamed into the darkness, as he kicked at a rock at his feet. Ally subconsciously winced as this rock landed about two feet from her face. She was trembling violently from cold and fear, and was trying desperately not to disturb the plywood shelter above her. He turned abruptly towards the car and made his way back. Ally didn't dare leave her protective haven for a good five minutes after he left. Roughly dislodging herself from her confinement, she ran as fast as she could in her stiffened fashion down the roadway, pausing to look ahead for any red taillights. Her surroundings now looked vaguely familiar as she surveyed the vicinity. She saw a light. She struggled to make out what this light was as she rushed towards it, gaining several yards. She studied the light again; it came from an exterior lamp attached to a house. Thank God. She released her breath as immeasurable relief coursed like electricity through her numbed body. She made her way towards the light, each step feeling like a traveled mile until she was traversing the driveway of the house. She pounded unceremoniously on the door; the porch light set ablaze. She heard an elderly voice from within, call out, "Who are you? What do you want?"

"Please, please, I need help. Please, would you, please call the police?" Ally struggled to formulate the words. Her exhaustion triumphed over her taxed senses; Ally's legs crumbled underneath her as she sank towards the porch.

CHAPTER 23

A door opened with an acute wave of warm air. The bright light blinded Ally with its sudden intensity.   She slowly raised her head, sighting first slippers, than half socks, an antiquated housedress, and then owl-like eyes behind framed lenses with a crown of white, disheveled curls.

Ally was unaware of her own appearance as she materialized from her heap on the porch, looking like a creature from a low-budget horror film. Her hair was a tangled and matted mess; there were weeds and leaves entwined through her hair and clothing. Her red swollen face was grossly distorted, and her make-up coiled in darkly streaked circles around her eyes. She looked pleadingly at her benefactor as she muttered, "Help, please." She fainted.

The blare of sirens barely penetrated her exhausted senses as she sought consolation within the dark recesses of her mind. She was aware there was danger and evil outside of herself, so she withdrew inward, feeling temporary secure and safe in her retreat. She was vaguely aware of hands lifting her, of questions being posed. Ally could not discern what the questions were, let alone formulate a response. Now, a siren was blaring in her head as she struggled to lift her hands to barricade her ears from the confusing noise. Someone grabbed her arms and said, "Relax; you're safe. Take it easy."

Ally continued to fight weakly, but persistently, against the restraining hands. She was unable to decode the verbal message of the words as she hovered between consciousness and unconsciousness, trying to make sense of what was going on around her. She heard someone call out, "Need to use the restraints before she hurts herself." The words rang loudly in her ears.

Ally was disoriented when she awoke. She couldn't tell

whether it was day or night. Where am I? The monitor, the rails on the bed; she was in the hospital. What happened?

Gradually the prior events began to fall in order. "Oh my God," she groaned. At least she had survived; she couldn't see or feel any bandages, but her whole face hurt. How had she gotten to the hospital? The last clear memory she had of last night was pounding on someone's door; they must have called emergency services.

Ally wondered where David, Mom and Breanna were. Did they know she was alive? David and Mom must be going out of their minds. She desperately needed to hold Breanna. She pulled herself up and started to stand, but she was too woozy to complete the process. She fell back towards the bed. The wall clock read 10:09. Was it really only a few short hours since the attack? She found the bell for the nurse. Ally watched as a stocky nurse with curly red hair entered the room. The pin on her smock identified her as Theresa.

Theresa set a notepad with attached pen on the nightstand, and tried not to let her frustration reflect in her attitude. There had been several crises tonight; it had been a helluva busy night. There was no hospital social worker on duty, tonight; they were so short-staffed due to the recent lay-off. Now she was responsible for gathering information about this unknown patient.

Theresa moved in a crisp, perfunctory manner. "Oh, you're awake now. How are you feeling?" She asked as she took Ally's wrist, timing her pulse rate.

"A little woozy, but I think I'm all right? My face hurts. Did anyone notify my husband that I'm here?" Ally asked haltingly.

"No, we had been trying to figure out who you are since you had no identification on you when you arrived at the hospital. We thought may have been in an accident or been attacked. We contacted the city police. They sent an officer over to take an initial report, but he had to respond to another call. He said he would return in a few hours, when hopefully, you would be coherent."

Ally was trying to keep up with the flow of her conversation through her hazy consciousness.   "Could you contact my husband and my mother? Tell them I'm okay?"

Theresa checked herself and then continued in a gentler manner. "It's all right.   I will call your family, but I need to know what happened first. If you can tell me?" She pulled a rolling chair to the side of the bed, picking up a notepad and pen.

"My nose, is it broken?" Ally questioned identifying the source of her pain.

"We don't believe so, but we haven't x-rayed it yet. The doctor felt for broken bones, checked your breathing. It's swollen and bruised, but it seemed okay. I'm sure he'll want to recheck it now that you're conscious; he may request x-rays. You've been rather delirious and incoherent, but you are responsive now. Are you currently taking any medication, legal or otherwise?"

"No, not at all," Ally then thought of Eric's small bottle. "Wait, I was attacked. He put something over my face. I tried to hold my breath and not inhale, but it might be in my system."

"We got a little off track," Theresa interrupted. "Could you tell me your name and age?" She poised the pen over the spiral notepad, making a few notations.

"I'm Alyssa Sullivan, age 28."

"Alyssa, have you ever been a patient at this hospital before tonight? Do we have any medical records for you?"

"Is this Tri-County Memorial?"

"Yes."

"Then yes, I was here when my daughter was born back in August."

"So you have a baby about three months old? What is her name?"

"Breanna."

"Where is Breanna, currently?"

"She's at home."

"Alone?"

"Heavens, no, she's with my mother. Listen, I managed to tell my mother to go back inside and call the police when I was attacked. My mother saw it happen. She'll be out of her mind with worry!" Ally was agitated and far beyond polite amenities.

345

"It's okay, Alyssa, just relax. Honest, I plan to call your family in about fifteen minutes, but it's always best if we have enough information to make sure you and everyone else is safe. Could you give me your birthdate?"

"February 23, 1970," Ally said impatiently.

"Well Alyssa, could you tell me what happened?"

Ally briefly recounted what had happened between the time she walked out of her house and ended up pounding on the door of that unfamiliar house. Theresa stopped her a few times to get clarification. Once she finished, Theresa asked gently, "I know you didn't indicate it, but I need to ask. Were you sexually assaulted?"

"No, no, that didn't happen," Ally said. A chill descended her spine as she involuntarily shivered.

"Did this person use a weapon?"

"He had a knife! I think he dropped it, but I can't be sure."

"Any other weapons?"

"Not that I'm aware of."

"Did you get a good look at who attacked you?"

"Initially, I could not see his face, because it was so dark outside; but then, I briefly saw his face at a distance when he walked in front of his car headlights. I can't be sure, but I think it was Eric Morrison. He looked different; he had a beard."

Theresa looked down at her notes, trying to cover her shocked reaction. She knew Eric Morrison; they had been in the same grade throughout their years at Sunnyside Elementary. She had had her first childhood crush on him back then. Theresa had been shocked, dismayed, and saddened by the recent reports about Eric, but she knew that most people had their secrets.

"Do you personally know this man, Eric Morrison? Why did you think it was him?"

"I've been working with Deputy Neal Bryant as an intern. I have been assisting the Sheriff's Office with those murder investigations involving children." Ally broke off, unable to continue. After a long pause, she added, "I've had in-person contacts with Mr. Morrison on several occasions."

"Oh, I'll call the Sheriff's Office to let Deputy Bryant know you are here. I'm sure he will want to speak to you." Teresa knew Deputy Bryant and respected the man. "Are you sure you are not in pain anywhere else except for your face?"

Ally shook her head and said, "I feel sick to my stomach and lightheaded."

"The nausea might be an after-effect of the drug your attacker used, or a residue of shock. What's your husband's name and phone number?"

"It's David. David Sullivan, or you can speak to my mother, Rene. Our number is 755-0309. Just let them know I'm okay."

The next few hours passed in a whirlwind of activity. The treating physician wanted to keep her overnight for observation, and to get a set of x-rays of her face.

David and Rene got to the hospital past visiting hours, but David insisted that he, Rene, and the baby visit for a few minutes to ensure themselves of Ally's safety. The charge nurse agreed. She knew Ally was anxious to see her family and might relax once the visit was over.

Ally saw the color leave David's face as he looked at her. Love, grief, and anxiety were all evident in the gray pallor of his face. He rushed over to the bed, but did not know what he should do. Fearful of hurting her, David lifted his hand and gently stroked the side of Ally's face with the backs of his fingers.

"Are you okay?" David asked. He was staring at her swollen face and bruised arms. Ally reached over and held his other hand with her own, grasping his hand firmly, as if to ensure herself that he was there.

Ally almost broke down in tears. "I'm fine now. Just a little worse for wear." There was a long silence between them, but no words were necessary.

"Ally, I thought I'd lost everything. I don't know how I could have continued without you."

Ally whispered softly, 'I felt the same David. I couldn't imagine not making it back to you and Breanna. I love you two with all my heart." She gave him a little half smile, before wincing in pain. Ally had not been aware of her mother and Breanna's' presence in the room until Rene moved forward.

Rene's eyes were red and swollen; her features were nearly as distorted as her daughter's from fear and worry. She held Breanna securely against her shoulder. "Oh Ally, I'm so glad you're safe. I've died a thousand deaths tonight. I never in my life felt so completely useless and helpless. I told you Ally, that I had such a bad feeling."

"It's okay now, Mom. I don't have any serious injuries. Just a little shaken, that's all," Ally said, clasping her mother's hand in her own. Then Ally reached up and gently withdrew Breanna from her mother's shoulder. She nestled her head against Breanna's soft curls and breathed deeply. This reunion is what had sustained her through the hellish night; the desire to hold her daughter again. Ally could see the small quiver of Breanna's bottom lip as she slept through the reunion.

After several minutes, David said, "I promised the nurse that if she let us see you, we wouldn't wear you out too much. I intend to keep my promise. I'll take your mother and the baby back out to the lobby. I want to talk to Deputy Bryant when he gets here. The nurse told me he was in route to the hospital. Meanwhile, will you, please get some rest?"

Ally was groggy when Neal entered her room; she had been struggling to stay awake. Upon seeing Neal, Ally said weakly, "Hello Neal."

"Oh damn, Ally. Are you okay? How are you doing?"

"Just shaken up and worried that he might finish up where he left off."

"Was it Morrison?"

"It was so dark; I only saw his face once briefly, at a distance. The man looked like Morrison, but he had a beard so I couldn't be sure."

"That's not a strong eyewitness statement," Neal said definitively.

"Sorry, it happened so fast; I was grabbed from behind, and he used some sort of chloroform."

"No need to apologize, I will bring Morrison in for questioning. Hopefully, we will find some solid connection. Don't worry, I will take you off this investigation."

"Please Neal, don't do that." He looked surprised at her urgency.

"Neal, I know in my heart that it was Morrison that attacked me. He has a personal grudge; I don't think it will matter to him if I'm still involved or not. He wanted to hurt me. I will not feel safe until I know he's behind bars. I would feel much better if I were in a position to help bring him in. I want to be part of stopping him. You can even use me as bait if you need to," Ally said resolutely. She knew her safety, her family's safety, as well as the safety of some other child would be compromised until Eric was locked up again.

"Everything you said is logical, but I am extremely worried about you and your family."

"I am going to be on the defensive. You'll get a call if anything out of the ordinary happens."

"Okay, if that's the way you want to play it. Tell me exactly what happened."

For the second time this evening, Ally recounted what had happened. After Ally had finished, Neal fell silent for a few minutes. Then he said, "He must have been staking you out. He knew the layout of your house, street, and neighborhood. Have you recently noticed anyone or any unusual vehicles on your street?"

"I haven't, but maybe David has noticed something. Breanna had a fever; I haven't really left the house much for the past few days. Before that, there was nothing out of the ordinary. We all went to the Christmas Fair earlier today."

"I know you didn't get a good look at the guy's face, but what about height, weight, or other information that might identify him?"

"He was tall, at least over six feet, and slender. His clothes hung loosely, and he was wearing a dark, hooded jacket. He wore gloves at all times, and he had on tennis shoes. He had a short beard and moustache. That is all I can remember."

"What about the vehicle he drove?"

"A dark colored, four door sedan. The interior light was out," Ally yawned.

"I'd better let you get some sleep so you can get well," Neal responded. He closed his notepad and left the hospital room. Neal found David and Rene in the lobby.

David was already on the offensive. "Bryant, what in the hell are you going to do about this? Did you see what the asshole did to her? If you don't get this creep, I will kill the bastard!" David was escalating, but checked himself when he saw Rene's pale face.

"I'm sorry, Mom. It's just that this jerk thinks he can waltz in, wreak havoc, and there is nothing anybody can do to stop him."

"I know, David, but I'm sure Deputy Bryant is doing everything that is legally possible to bring this man in."

"Yes, Mr. Sullivan, I will have extra patrols of your neighborhood, but I doubt the suspect will attack your wife or family again. It would be too risky, and I'm sure this individual is smart enough to know it. Meanwhile, if you could answer a couple of questions, it might help me bring this guy in."

"Okay." David was frustrated; his arms folded tightly across his chest, as he paced in an inconsistent manner.

Neal cut straight to the heart of the matter. He didn't think that David Sullivan would appreciate any soft talk at this point. "Mr. Sullivan, I believe your wife's attacker has been staking out your place. Have you noticed any unusual people or vehicles in the area?"

David spoke without pause or reflection, "Yes. There was a dark, new-model Honda Accord parked near the house to the left of ours. I noticed it for the first time on Wednesday, and then I saw it parked there this morning.

"Did anything draw your attention to the car?"

"No, not really. The house next to us has been sold so the car could belong to the new owners. I guess what got my attention is that I've seen this car, but there's been no activity within the house. I've been watching. I was curious about the new owners and wanted to introduce myself."

Rene chimed in, "I've got a license plate for you." This information surprised both men.

"You have a license plate number for the car that your daughter was taken in?" Neal repeated slowly.

"Yes, when I saw someone grab Ally, I went back inside with the baby and called 911 on a cordless phone. I put the baby down and watched out the front window. I could see the license plate as the person pulled away from the curb into the street. I gave the number to the police officer who came out to speak with me."

"What was the officer's name?"

"Officer Carlson."

"Hold on, I will call the city police to see what happened when they ran the plate.

David Sullivan and Rene half listened to Neal Bryant's end of the conversation, unable to track the meaning of the one-sided flow of talk. After the cell phone conversation had ended, they waited for him to speak.

Deputy Bryant turned to speak to David and Rene, "That was Officer Carlson. He has a name and address of the owner of the car you reported. He is following up on the information he received. I will let you know when he has a suspect."

David interrupted, "Was it Morrison?"

"At this time, I'm not at liberty to discuss the investigation with you."

"Thanks a hell of a lot," David snapped. "That son-of-a-bitch better not come near my place again!"

"Mr. Sullivan, I will let you know when I have this matter resolved." Neal turned to Rene. "Thank you for the information and your cooperation. Hopefully, we can resolve this matter as soon as possible." Neal turned to leave.

On the way to his car, Neal stopped to make a few notes on his interviews with Ally, David, and Rene, and Officer Carlson. Ed Carlson had told him that the license plate number had been traced back to a dark green Honda Accord, which belonged to a man named Robert Chavez.

Carlson had located a home address and telephone number for Robert Chavez. Carlson went to the residence, and Robert's wife, Maria, had come to the door. She told Carlson that her husband, who worked in the city planning office, had gone to a symposium in Houston for the week. She gave Carlson the name and number of the Hilton Hotel where her husband was staying. Carlson was on the brink of making contact with Mr. Chavez when Neal called him.

Neal had told Carlson that he would call him back in 45 minutes to give him the scuttlebutt on Alyssa Sullivan and what took place on his end.

It was nearly an hour and a half later when Neal made his follow-up call to Carlson. "Hey Ed, what have you got?"

"I called the Hilton, and the manager confirmed that Robert Chavez is staying at the hotel and that there was a symposium that ended yesterday. I asked to be connected to Chavez's room, and that Chavez guy sounded bewildered. He told me he had been in the symposium all week and stayed an extra day to attend a special workshop. He has a six-thirty flight back to Acacia. He promised to call the department from the airport and talk to me upon his return. I told him that I wanted to check out his vehicle."

"Did you get his driver's license number and run it?"

"Yes, of course. He has no criminal record, at least not in this state."

"What about his identifying information? Height? Weight?"

"He has black hair and brown eyes. He weighs 230 pounds and is five feet, eight inches tall."

Neal paused. "The vic, Ms. Sullivan, told me that her attacker was over six feet tall and had a slender build. Ms. Sullivan has been interning at my office. This attack most probably is related to a case she has been assisting me on."

"You don't mean the Morrison case?"

"Bingo! She cannot positively identify Morrison as her attacker, but she saw the guy briefly and thought it could have been Morrison."

Morrison had heard the roar of sirens as he pulled up to the entrance road of the BLM land. He saw the ambulance fly by him. He drove quickly out the area, fearful that he would see a follow-up police car any moment.

Eric drove straight to his 'headquarters,' which took roughly twenty minutes. He sprinted inside the trailer to turn on his scanner. He had it tuned to the frequency that most of the boys in law enforcement used. There were response calls. "Officer Jewkes had responded to Tri-County Memorial; he didn't recognize the code. It must be the Bitch, he thought wildly. There were some other calls during the evening: a prowler, a domestic violence call, attempted theft from a vehicle, nothing. He left the scanner on as he paced back and forth within the cramped space, chewing on his thumbnail. He heard Officer Carlson responding to a follow-up regarding a vehicle that was suspected to have been used in the commission of a crime. The boys must be trying to track down the misappropriated plate on his rental. He wasn't stupid. He had cased the airport parking lot to find another Honda Accord. He had not been able to find a dark blue one to match his rental, but he had located a similar forest-green Accord. He would switch the stolen plate back to the original rental plate now, while he was thinking about it, and turn in the car tomorrow in Acacia before anyone was the wiser.

CHAPTER 24

On Monday, Ally awoke early to see David off to work. David sat on the edge of the bed, looking at her with a worried, frightened expression on his face.

"Ally, I don't want to leave you here alone."

"David don't worry about it; I'll be fine," She replied.

"Your Mom, told me about your part in Morrison's arrest. Why didn't you tell me what was going on, Ally?"

"I don't know. ...I was afraid, and I didn't want to upset you."

"How can I help protect you and the baby, if you're not honest and upfront with me?"

"I know now that I should've told you. I didn't think he'd try anything like that, when he was a suspect." Ally said miserably.

"Okay, I don't want to argue the point now. You've been through so much. But, I'm afraid Morrison may try to attack you again! He obviously knows where we live, and something about our routines." He paused, and then stated firmly, "I'm going to call in and get John to sub for me today."

"Why David? Mom's here with us, and there is a phone if we have any problems. I don't want Eric Morrison to take control of our lives. I'm not going to live in fear anymore; my life is too precious to wither it away like that!" Ally was emphatic as she felt her anger toward Morrison surge through her again.

"I would call Dad, but I'm afraid I've hurt his feelings or let him down. I didn't call him after you were attacked. He came over yesterday while you were sleeping, only to discover what had taken place. You should have seen the look in his eyes, like I'd sucker punched him." David continued talking, as though he hadn't heard her or was choosing to ignore her protest.

"Why didn't you call him, David? Are you still having a hard time talking to him?" Ally asked sympathetically.

"No. Honestly Ally, I was so worried about you that I didn't think of anyone else. Contacting Dad just slipped my mind; that's all. I guess the fact that we didn't speak for years didn't help put Dad or his feelings in the forefront of my thoughts. I need to find a way to apologize or at least explain this to him."

"David call your Dad, just talk to him. Don't let this situation fester!"

"I will Ally; I just need to think through the conversion, so I don't make the wound any deeper." He picked up the phone, "I'm calling John."

"David, I'm serious; go to work! You're getting me all uptight again. You're climbing the walls; you need to keep yourself busy. I'm going to stay in and rest all day. Neil told me that he would have deputies patrolling the neighborhood. Obviously, Eric Morrison isn't going to try anything at this point."

"Okay, but I'll be home early. Call me if you have any problem whatsoever." David looked at her tentatively. "Promise?"

"I promise," Ally said. David leaned forward to kiss her before he left.

Ally made a bottle for Breanna at eight. At eleven, she made another; she noted that she was low on formula. She checked the cupboard for additional cans; there was none. She hadn't gone shopping this weekend. Oh great, she thought, she wasn't supposed to drive. The doctor had prescribed Tylenol with codeine for her fractured nose. Besides, she thought, I don't want anyone to see me like this.

"Mom," Ally called out to Rene in the front room.

Rene came bounding into the kitchen, and asked in a panic-stricken voice, "Are you okay?"

"Sorry. Yes, Mom, I'm fine. I just realized that I'm low on formula. It won't last the day. Could you, please run to the store and pick up some for me?"

"Yes, of course, but should I leave you two here alone?"

"I'll be fine Mom, but I was hoping you could take Breanna with you. My meds make me feel rather dopey and tired."

Ally helped get Breanna ready for the trip to the store while her mother warmed up the car and put the stroller in the back of the car. After her mother had driven away, Ally curled up on the sofa and started to doze off. She heard the phone ring through her sleep-fogged mind.

Still half-asleep, Ally grabbed the phone and said, "Hello?"

"Is this Alyssa Sullivan?" said the barely audible voice on the phone.

"Yes, this is Alyssa."

The voice broke into hysterical sobs, through the broken gasps, "I think... Eric has got her."

Ally gripped the phone receiver so tightly her knuckles turned white. She wondered if this was a nightmare.

"Breanna?" came out of Ally's tightly knotted throat in a breathless croak.

"No. No, Lizzie's gone. They cannot find her anywhere. She was just playing outside. She had a blanket draped over her head, like Mary, and was pretending her doll was the baby Jesus. They turned away to help a boy who had fallen down, and she was gone. Oh my God, she's gone. Help me get her back." The woman was sobbing uncontrollably. Ally placed the voice with the name: it was Eric's sister, Caitlyn. Ally made the connection: Caitlyn had a daughter named Lizzie.

"Caitlyn, calm down. Please listen to me. Have the police been called?"

"Dee called the police, then she called me. I don't know what to do. Please help me. Please, please, I can't stand to lose her." Caitlyn was operating on panic mode.

"Caitlyn, you need to help Lizzie. To help Lizzie, you need to listen to me. Give me the telephone number where you're at right now."

"842-3443, but..."

"Caitlyn, I'm going to hang up now and call Deputy Bryant. Stay right there, I'll call you right back and let you know what he wants you to do. Please do not leave." Ally hung up the phone and dialed the sheriff's dispatch number. She asked them to page Deputy Bryant; it was an extreme emergency. It seemed to take forever, but in reality it was a matter of minutes. The phone rang.

"Yes Neal, thank heavens, you've called! No, Morrison is not here. Listen Neal, Caitlyn Mathews just called. I told her I would call her back after I spoke to you. Her four-year-old daughter, Lizzie, has come up missing. I don't know.....either preschool or day-care. A woman, Dee, called law enforcement. Caitlyn believes Morrison has taken her daughter. She is half out of her mind with fear. It wouldn't be good to have her drive anywhere. Here is the number where she can be reached: 842-3443. Neal, I'm going to come in. I know Caitlyn, and you're going to need extra hands."

Ally pressed down on the receiver and immediately phoned the store to tell David what was going on. She was just hanging up the phone when Rene walked through the door.

"Mom, I'm going to go get changed. I'm going to need your help to drive me into the Sheriff's station."

"Ally, what in the world is going on?"

"I'll explain everything on the way. I'll be ready in a minute."

"I'll change Breanna's diaper and pack her diaper bag." Rene said compliantly.

Ally ran into her bedroom to change clothes. In the master bathroom, Ally stood in front of the mirror as she ran a brush through her tangled blond hair. Heavens, she was a mess, she hoped she wouldn't frighten anyone. Her swollen face was distorted still; the puffed purple and green bruising which cascaded over the bridge of her nose into the sockets of both eyes stood out in sharp contrast to the pale whiteness of her face. Her lips and cheeks were dry and chapped, due to the exposure to the cold, damp conditions on Saturday evening. No amount of make-up was going to make her look even halfway normal, so she would just have to forego the vanity at this juncture. She quickly gave herself another dismissive glance as she reached for her toothbrush.

That was it; she would see if Larry is at home. Perhaps Mom and Breanna could pay him a visit after they dropped her off at the Sheriff's Station. She did not want either Mom or Breanna alone here at the house. She also felt that both her mother and

Breanna were currently safer if she was not around them. Her mind settled; she went to rejoin her mother in the living room.

Ally leaned across the passenger seat to give Rene a brief hug and whispered against her cheek, "Give me a call when you get to Larry's house, Okay?"

"Ally, how long are you going to be?"

"At this point, I don't know Mom. I'm not even sure how I can help except maybe making phone calls. I keep praying that this is all a silly mistake, just a horrible coincidence, and Eric Morrison does not have that little girl."

"Ally, do you think he has killed her?" Rene asked.

"God, I hope she's safe…. I keep hoping for some earth-shattering information from beyond to bring an end to Morrison's reign of terror, but the messages aren't coming."

"Why don't you just let Deputy Bryant handle this situation from here on out? You are not a trained police officer."

"Mom, I just can't. I won't sit around waiting for something horrific to happen, for more damage to be done, or for the information to come to me. I have to actively pursue Morrison before anyone else is hurt. Hopefully, Lizzie…"

"Ally, try not to make it too long. You still haven't recovered from your experience the other night. I'm worried that you might have an emotional breakdown or something, especially if the news is not good."

"I'm more than aware that there may be a tragic ending," Ally said. "It has been my worst nightmare throughout this entire ordeal that another child would be attacked and killed. That I might have to personally live through another killing, and be unable to prevent it. It's what keeps me awake at night."

"Right now," Rene admitted, I'm being rather selfish. "I'm concerned about you, Breanna, and David, and I cannot see past my personal involvement."

"Mom, the sooner we can shut this guy down and lock him up, the safer we all will be. Just keep saying prayers for all of us, okay?"

"You know I'm doing that. My poor knees are red and raw. I'll let you go. Take care of yourself. Be careful!"

"Love you, Mom." Ally strode quickly through the glass doors and continued through the personnel entrance.

Karen looked up as Ally entered, staring with astonishment at Ally's face. Then, catching herself, she broke away from the stare, stealing furtive glances at Ally.

"Hi, Karen. Like my beaut of a shiner? Right now, I can't make it look any prettier, but at least it's not broken."

"I heard about it this morning when I came into type up some reports. Are you doing okay?"

"Yes, no permanent damage. My nose is fractured, and I'm bruised up."

"It has been truly crazy around here. So much has happened, even over the weekend, but I had better let Neal fill you in. You take care of yourself, you hear?"

"Yes, thank you. Where is Neal?"

"He's in talking with Ms. Mathews, he told me to buzz him when you got here...Yes, Neal, Alyssa Sullivan is here. Yes, I'll send her back.' Karen looked up at Ally and said, 'He said to send you back. He's in room four."

Ally walked briskly down the back hallway and entered the interview room. Caitlyn Mathews looked up at Ally with red, swollen, hollow eyes. She looked nothing like the self-possessed, confident woman that she had met a few days prior. Ally did not know what she could do at this point to alleviate her fears.

"I'm sorry you have to go through this Caitlyn. I'll do anything I can to help."

"Chris is home manning the phones, I had better join him. The TV news station is going to issue an alert." She spoke in a slow, lifeless voice.

Neal said, "I'll have John Bowden take you home, Mrs. Mathews. I'm planning to phone the FBI and request their help in finding your daughter. Could you give John a recent photo, so I can send it out to all the law enforcement agencies, statewide?" Caitlyn was nodding almost imperceptibly to his statements.

"Please Alyssa," Caitlyn pleaded, "call me as soon as you know anything, promise?"

Ally looked at Neal as she responded, to make sure she was saying the correct thing. "Caitlyn, as soon as there is a legitimate or solid lead, I'll let you know. From what I've learned, there is often so much unreliable information that comes in. If you listen to all the unreliable leads, you'll go crazy. You need to stay as emotionally strong as you can under the circumstances for Lizzie and your boys."

Caitlyn was nodding absently again. "I know you don't believe this disappearance is pure coincidence. Anything is possible, but one would have to be an idiot to ignore the likelihood. Eric is responsible, and you have to stop him before...." Caitlyn could not finish her sentence for the cruel image it evoked. She shot Neal a steely glance. "Please don't follow some written procedure at the expense of my child. Please find some way to bring Eric in before he can do anymore damage!"

"We will do everything we can to explore all possibilities as quick as humanly possible." Neal left the room to get Deputy Bowden. Caitlyn started to cry; a shrill, high-pitched wounded cry. Ally rushed over and clasped Caitlyn's hands in her own.

"Caitlyn, please don't give up! There are many people looking out for and praying for Lizzie; just waiting to bring her back to your arms." The words hung heavily between them as Neal re-entered the room with John Bowden.

"John will take you home, now. He will stay with you just in case there are any calls or leads. He is going to record any calls you receive. I'll be in touch with you."

Neal waited several minutes to ensure himself that Caitlyn Mathews was completely out of the building before he spoke to Ally.

"We have every man available looking for that little girl. The FBI is on stand-by, ready to send a couple of agents at my request, for informal assistance at first. We are assuming this is a kidnapping and not a missing child case. After 24 hours, the FBI can assume jurisdiction in a kidnapping case. We will have to wait and see if Lizzie is still missing this time tomorrow. A citizen's group is searching the backcountry.

I didn't want prematurely to crush Caitlyn's hopes for seeing her daughter alive again, but remember those tech- pictures I told you about from Morrison's office? Morrison used a rather simplistic photo-editing program; VICAP was quickly able to descramble the mosaic pieces within the images. The three descrambled pictures were time-lapsed photos of a separate death scene; each picture was based on a different victim.

"I want to see the photos...." Ally started.

"No Ally, you don't!" Neal said resolutely. "The photos are graphically violent, and some of these pictures are very sexually explicit. You don't want those images stuck in your head."

"Oh my God!" No, it wouldn't serve any useful purpose to view those pictures; Ally surmised, feeling gravely ill. ..."Is there anything else?"

"We issued an arrest warrant early this morning; Eric Morrison's name went out over the statewide system."

"We have a DNA sample from the letter to the editor; we just had to compare the sample with Morrison's DNA. It's a match. My guess is that Morrison caught wind of the arrest warrant and responded in desperation, which means that this kidnapping will be much sloppier. He will likely leave evidence all over the place. On the other hand, he doesn't have anything left to lose, which makes him even more dangerous."

The phone rang, startling both Neal and Ally. Neal picked up the receiver. "Yes Karen, who is on the line? Yes, you can transfer the call." Ally had watched Neal tense in response to this call; it couldn't be good.

"Yes, this is Deputy Bryant, how can I help you Mr. Brentwood?" Ally could hear the stiff politeness in Neal's voice. She could tell he was angry from the set of his shoulders and the edge of his tone.

"Oh, so you will have my head if I don't bring in Morrison? I'd advise you not to threaten me in such a manner, or it will be construed as a terrorist threat. I'm more than willing to pursue criminal charges! I would remind you that it was your own maneuverings which brought us to this point. You might want to consider that little truth, butt out, and let me do my job. I have no desire to see another child harmed in any manner." He replaced the receiver, disconnecting the call. "That sanctimonious jerk. Where he gets the gall to speak to me like that, I'll never know."

"I admire your restraint," Ally replied.

"Brentwood mistreated Morrison, as a kid. Then, he gets him released and creates a public spectacle to protect his political interests. Yet, he takes no responsibility for what's happened. Instead, Brentwood places the blame on me and tells me that I'm not doing my job. The nerve of that guy." Ally was barely listening; she flashed back on her vision of the sad, lonely boy, waiting for his mother to pick him up from the group home. The young teen with the cold, indifferent step-father, who wouldn't allow him to return home.

"He called Morrison a 'malicious, spiteful, little punk,' Neal said, "I guess some people never change!"

"Guess not," Ally said. She subconsciously felt the bridge of her swollen nose, and her anger rose again. Nothing excuses what he's done.

Ally hung around for a couple of hours doing some clerical work, but she didn't seem to have much to contribute. Neil was in and out, answering phones and holding telephone conferences. He seemed to be going in forty directions at once. There was not much he could delegate to her without lengthy instructions and explanations, which he currently did not have time to give. She called her mother to pick her up. Ally stopped Neal in the hallway. "Neal, I'm going now. I'll stop in tomorrow to see if I can help."

"Thanks Ally, for all your help."

His life circumstances had come full circle. Eric sat in a stiff, straight back chair staring at his newest conquest through the dim light of his battery-operated lamp. Should he kill her now? The pressure was building, and he knew a quick kill would relieve it. Yet, this discard held distinct merit; the spawn of the little princess -herself, and from Brentwood's own lineage. This discard, this killing... was the culmination, his zenith. The montage from the kill would be his masterpiece. This kill, therefore, deserved a brilliant, unparalleled plan. How would he kill her? Brutal for sure! It would be a bloodbath. Eric crossed his arms, and started rocking back and forth.

Restlessly eyeing her sleeping form, he got up, retrieving another sleeping pill and a bottle of water. He knelt before the sleeping body on the floor and opened the water bottle. He reached across her face, pulling the duct tape towards him. He pinched her cheeks between his thumb and the forefinger of his left hand, and dropped the pill inside her mouth with his right. He picked up the water with his right hand and poured some down her throat. Waiting a few seconds, he secured the duct tape over her mouth once again. He returned to his chair, sat down, and continued to scrutinize the heap on the floor.

The abduction had been too easy. He had cruised around the block of the preschool, noticing a neighboring county building. He pulled into the county parking lot to survey the preschool, when he saw that the preschool staff had been distracted. The staff had left dear Lizzie all alone on the front stoop. He quickly exited the car and walked over to the fence. He called out softly to her. Lizzie came running, stopping about two feet from the fence.

He asked Lizzie if she remembered him: Uncle Eric. She had nodded affirmatively. He had told her that her mother was hurt, and had asked him to pick her up. If Lizzie could climb the fence halfway, he could help her, the rest of the way. Lizzie complied, and he quietly ushered her to the car. He was out of there in less than five minutes.

Now what? He was rocking harder and faster. The body, what should he do with the body? Should he dispose of it quietly, hidden away never to be found, or should it be found ten years down the road? No, it was too late for that. He could dispose of it on Caitlyn's front porch; lay the discard at her feet. The holy rolling FBI or the local pigs would be posted at Caitlyn's house, or, should he say, mausoleum? Would it be better if he dumped the discard in his mother's yard? Yes, flaunt the carcass in Brentwood's face on his own turf! The pigs shouldn't be holding a vigil there. Hell, his mother probably wouldn't even notice. She'd kick the discard to the side in order to get to the beauty parlor! What about the Bitch? Would the Sullivan house still be under surveillance? Maybe he would gift-wrap this discard especially for her? Christmas was coming up soon; it was never too early for a well-thought out gift. His whole body was caught in the rocking motion. He grabbed the sides of his head, increasing the pressure. Think, damn it, think!

Ally laid in bed that night, staring at the ceiling above her. She thought David was asleep until he asked, "You can't sleep?"

"No, I just keep thinking of Caitlyn and Lizzie. I feel I should be doing something, but there is nothing I can do. I just have this knot in the pit of my stomach that won't go away. I keep hoping beyond reason that Lizzie is not with Morrison. I guess this is what they call denial."

"Honey, you're one person. Everyone is trying their best to bring Lizzie home. You can't take the whole burden on your shoulders, or take it as a personal failure if she doesn't make it back. Hopefully, she will. Meanwhile, you can't make yourself sick."

"You're right. I just wish I could get my heart and body to listen to logic." David turned over and kissed her lightly. Ally returned his kiss, holding him tightly as if to brace herself against the storm. "Please David, just hold me."

Ally awoke early the next day. She had been dreaming. She struggled to recall the entire dream. There was a little girl with long brown hair; the sides of her hair were pulled back in a loose ponytail. She was wearing a white lacy dress and tights with shiny black Mary-Jane shoes. She was sitting in a small child's rocking chair with a book called "The Little White Bird" by Sir James Matthew Barrie. There was a beam of light centered overhead. She looked up from her storybook and said, "Once upon a time, a long time ago..." That was all Ally could remember of the dream. Was it the entire dream or just a fragment? Ally wondered if she just had a simple dream or if the child in the dream was another victim of Eric Morrison. Was this child the fifth victim? A young, innocent girl in old-fashioned clothing -Caitlyn?

Ally came into the Sheriffs' station the next morning. When she entered Neal's office, there was another man present. Neal stood up and said, "Ally, this is Charles Stills. Remember, I told you that he was Eric Morrison's Juvenile Probation Officer?"

Charles Stills stood to shake her hand. Charles was a tall black man with wide, caring eyes. Short curly white hair crowned his head. He appeared to be in his mid-sixties. Charles gave Ally a huge disarming smile as he took her hand and said, "I'm Charlie to my friends."

"I'm Alyssa Sullivan, Ally for short." Ally immediately felt comfortable in Charlie's presence. He seemed to emit warmth and humor, with an air of compassion. She didn't know how to explain it, but she felt safe and secure in his company. He seemed perfectly suited for his work as a juvenile probation officer; she could see kids gravitating to him for support and guidance.

"Charlie stopped in to see if he could help. Charlie and I go way back. I was just telling him about your visions and how you have helped spearhead the investigation."

Charlie said, "I have family members' way back that had similar gifts. I always wished I had the gift myself. I've got plenty of intuition, but if I had the gift, maybe I could reach some of these tougher kids."

"Right now I feel like my psychic powers were just a fluke," Ally said. "In the beginning, the images and visions were strong; now, it seems that occasionally I get just a faint impression. I never had psychic experiences before, and I don't know that I will have them in the future."

"Maybe, you were in the right place at the right time to make it happen," Charlie replied. He looked at Ally intently and continued. "Or sometimes, I would guess that it would be hard to get that close to evil and ugliness and not feel tainted by it."

"So you worked with Eric Morrison when he was young?" Ally asked, changing the direction of the conversation. She needed time to consider what he said. Was she closing off this connection because she was afraid that somehow it would unleash an ugliness within herself? "What was Eric like? Please tell me about him."

"It's hard to say. I knew Eric, but I didn't. He had already built up his walls when I came onto the scene. You want to know what made him a murderer. That I cannot give you. I can tell you my assessment of Eric when he was younger. Part of my job is also to assess the family and social history.

Eric seemed to want at least one parent to love him or show they cared, to prove that he could be loved. His father, Randy Morrison, had made a fast exit once he divorced Susan Brentwood. Eric set his sights on his one remaining parent, his mother. Eric placed his mother in the center of his universe. I suspect Susan is still front and center in Eric's world in one way, or another. The relationship is there, a sick, twisted relationship but a relationship all the same. I suspect that Eric would have done anything to get Susan's approval, or at least her attention. And to tell you the truth, I have never in all my years met, such a self-centered and self-involved woman as Susan Brentwood. That woman did not have one maternal bone in her body; it's a shame she ever had children. I don't know what made Susan the way she is. Don't want to know, but she crafted Eric in her own image.

I remember a story Greg Coe told me about Eric and his parents. Greg also worked for the Juvenile Probation Office. Years earlier, he went to a party at Denise Thurman's house. Randy Morrison was seeing Denise, so he was at the party. During this party, Randy's ex, Susan, drives up and blares the car horn. It's 1:30 in the morning, and when she gets no response, Susan comes marching up to the door. She had a five year old Eric in tow. Eric is bare-foot and in pajamas. He looks as if he was just awakened, taken straight from bed. Susan starts banging on the door, telling Randy to get the fuck out there. She was screaming, 'you take him, I don't want him.' Meanwhile, Randy is sneaking out the back door to hide in the trees. Susan opened the door and pushed Eric inside the house. Then she jumped in her car and peeled off. Randy Morrison was nowhere to be found; he left the house, too.

Greg's girlfriend, Theresa, finds a blanket for Eric while the police were notified. Eric told Theresa that his mother said she didn't want him anymore. Then Eric said to Theresa, 'That wasn't a nice thing for her to say. Isn't she being rude?' Greg was taken aback. Eric was talking so maturely, but he was such a frightened little boy. Greg was trying to distract Eric; he asked him to draw a picture of his family. Eric drew himself in a bubble, crying; he had no arms or legs. Eric drew his mother in the same manner in her own bubble. Randy Morrison was drawn a distance, away from the bubbles. He had no bubble around him. Randy had both arms and legs and a big smile on his face. The drawing seemed to indicate that Eric felt helpless, hopeless, and emotionally isolated. He and his mother shared this emotional state, but there was no emotional connection between them. His father was happy to have escaped away from the family"

Ally could not believe how childish both of Eric's parents were. "It's unbelievable that adults could behave so irresponsibly. In my opinion, Randy is even more culpable than Susan. He had to know that Susan wasn't stable enough to raise a child, and he just left Eric in that situation." This unsavory union reminded Ally of Eric's relationship with Tammy; unfortunately, these dysfunctional family patterns did seem to repeat themselves.

"Believe me, it wasn't just a lapse in judgment that night. The two of them never got any better. Randy Morrison fell off the face of the earth as far as his son was concerned, and Susan Brentwood might as well have. Then Alex Brentwood entered the scene and my, what a piece of work he was. The Devil himself has more compassion and generosity then Alex.

According to Alex and Susan, Eric was a very disturbed child who nearly tore his mother apart. Alex insisted that Eric needed rehabilitation; the more punitive, the better. He wanted the county to place Eric in one of those paramilitary survival programs. Of course, he also wanted the county to pay the tab while he called the shots. Alex didn't have a spare dime to help Eric, although he and Susan lived in a mansion and vacationed in Europe.

Alex and Susan almost went through the roof when I recommended family counseling. Alex said that if I didn't know how to deal with a little punk like Eric, the case should be transferred to someone with better credentials. Brentwood was friends with several judges and department heads; I knew I was fighting a losing battle.

I also believed that Eric was physically abused or traumatized by Alex in some way. Eric hinted that he could also have Alex arrested on abduction charges. The boy specifically implied that the situation with Caitlyn was tit for tat, but he would never elaborate, or divulge any specifics. Furthermore, Eric seemed fearful of Alex. When I asked Alex what Eric might be alluding to. Alex said, 'Eric is a pathological liar who loved playing victim, one never knew what he might say next.' I still believe to this day that Alex was covering his butt." Ally remembered that vision she had of a boy, being locked in a cellar. It must have been Eric

"You also told Neal that Eric claimed that he was sexually abused by his mother?" Ally questioned. Now, Ally comprehended the source of Eric's rage and violence.

"Yes. Eric again, would not disclose any specifics, and immediately shut down." Charlie expounded.

"Did you believe him?" Ally didn't believe this was just a manipulative ploy on Eric's part, but she wanted Charlie to confirm her suspicions.

"Hell yes," Charlie shook his head, "but I could never get him to talk about it. Alex and Susan refused to acknowledge any personal involvement in any of Eric's problems. It was always Eric's problems; no other problems existed in their family."

"I continued to work with Eric, who would usually stare me down or share trivial conversation with me. Initially, Susan put in a few appearances for show, but she quickly lost interest. I remember when Eric was fifteen; we were waiting for a court hearing. Eric says to me 'you know my Mom isn't going to show for the hearing. You're stupid if you think she will.' I was watching Eric from the corner of my eye. His eyes never left the corridor leading to the courtroom. He kept hoping his mother would suddenly materialize and show him that she cared, but it never happened. Eric had no one else in the world; besides his mom, and he could care less about the rest of the world."

Ally paused, "I can tell you, I despise Eric Morrison. I would sooner lock him up and throw away the key, but I feel terrible for what he went through. It's a shame that any child has to endure that kind of existence and that there is no punishment for either of those parents. It's a shame that just anyone is allowed to have a child." It's a shame that an innocent can be turned into a monster.

Charlie shook his head, "Remember Ally, you never know what made Eric's parents the way they are. Sometimes, there are generations of either abuse and neglect, or mental illness to combat. Given the circumstances, however, the authorities could not intervene any sooner to help Eric. It seems that parents have a lot of rights, and to hell with any of the responsibilities of being a parent. Just let the chips fall where they may. I can see where Eric's anger comes from, not that I excuse anything that he has done. It doesn't sound like Eric's sister, Caitlyn, had it much better. But she chose to give her children a better life than she had. She also uses her energy to help others as a public health nurse."

"She is a good person," Ally agreed. "Any thoughts about where Morrison would take Lizzie?"

"No. I wish I knew," Charlie sighed. Just sharing my recollections. It's a shame. I think that I'm just getting too old for this work."

Ally looked intently at Neal and Charlie, "What do you think he'll do now?"

Neal said, "We just don't know. The FBI has sent a profiler, they officially assigned Brezo, to take part in this investigation, and we have some state assistance in manning the search. I've decided to keep a low profile, so I won't have to deal with the media hype as much.   The FBI has not decided whether to take jurisdiction, since there is no proof that this was a kidnapping case; they are taking a wait-and-see approach. Morrison has preferred to stay local with his killings and the disposal of the bodies, so I expect he is in the back country in this region.

Ally said, "If you'd like, I can help answer the tip line and take messages at the sub-station."

"I'm sure they are always in need of warm bodies," Neal agreed.

Ally answered the phones for several hours. Many of the calls were just worried parents, troubled because their child had been to see Eric for dental work. They asked if they should have their child examined or seen by a therapist for sexual abuse. Ally had a list of local crisis intervention counselors who could discuss these concerns with the parents. Others callers were just curiosity seekers, who wanted even more information than the media was providing. It was often difficult to get the callers off the line. There were no real, valid leads.

Ally found listening to the blow-by-blow media coverage regarding Lizzie much too nerve-wracking. She would tune in intermittently to catch an update.   Her mind set on a little girl who was last seen playing the mother, Mary, caring for the infant, Jesus. It was pure sacrilege to think of such a sweet, innocent child in the hands of that monster, so Ally unsuccessfully tried not to obsess on this thought. She felt completely helpless and sad. "Please God, protect Lizzie and keep her in your sights, and please help Caitlyn and her family survive this nightmare.

CHAPTER 25

Eric was on top of the world! He had his game on. He had sorted out all the minute details of his plan and he was ready to roll with it. He was so jazzed. This kill was going to be magnificent and spectacular. It was so twisted that it would be talked about for years to come.

He had already set up his photo shoot. He just needed to wait for the heap to awake. Initially, she had to be awake for this to work. He would take down his family and the Bitch in the bargain! Neal, the fucking prick, would win the loser of the year award at the end of this fiasco. Hell yes, life is good!

Ally felt vacant at the core. She sensed a massive black hole sucking everything in her path into darkness. It had been three days, and still, nothing. No news regarding Lizzie, she thought hopelessly. Everything seemed beyond reach, beyond comprehension. She was plagued with horror on the perimeter of every waking thought. Her sleeping state wasn't much better. The nightmares involving Breanna being harmed had resumed. There was absolutely no way to redirect or refocus her thoughts on anything else. She dreaded hearing any horrific news regarding Lizzie. Her agonizing days passed in perpetual slow-motion. Ally was lethargic and full of anguish. She knew she would have to pull herself out of this despair, but how?

Thanksgiving was a week away, but she could not get into the spirit of the holiday with Lizzie still missing. Mom had volunteered to do the preparation and the cooking for their Thanksgiving Dinner; she was trying so desperately to cheer Ally up. She knew her Mom and David were worried about her, but she just didn't know how to alleviate their fears any more than she could her own.

Mom had taken Breanna into town; they were going to grocery shop for Thanksgiving. The doorbell rang, and Ally went to the front peephole. She saw only the retreating, back of the UPS man. She cautiously opened the door and found a narrow rectangular package on the front porch. The package was addressed to her. She recognized the return address as being that of the Sheriff's Department. What in the world would they be sending to her? She eyed the package suspiciously. Leaving the package on the front porch, she made her way back inside towards the telephone. She couldn't help but envision a Unabomber scenario.

She called the answering service and had Neal paged, then impatiently awaited his return call. When the phone finally rang, she picked up the receiver before it could ring a second time. "Neal, is this you? Yes, did you or anyone in the Department send a package to my house? No, the package was just delivered; the return address is the Sheriff's Office. No, I didn't touch it; it's still sitting on the front porch. I'll clear the premises, just in case. I'll leave out the back door and go wait for Mom and Breanna on the corner. Yes, Mom took Breanna out shopping with her. Thanks Neal, I'll give you a call later."

Ally pulled on her shoes and grabbed her coat and purse. She headed out the back door towards the main road to watch for Mom and Breanna. About twenty minutes later, Ally saw a K-9 unit and white van enter her cul-de-sac. Ten minutes after that, Ally saw Rene and waved her down.

Ally opened the passenger door and said, "Mom, let's go for another drive."

"Ally, what is going on? Has that man tried to get you again?" Rene's voice was nearly hysterical.

"It's okay Mom, I just got a package delivered. The return address was the Sheriff's Department. I called Neal, and he said they hadn't sent anything to me. He's going to check out the package at the crime lab."

"Ally, when is this ever going to stop?"

"Hopefully soon, Mom; the police do have a warrant for Morrison's arrest. Let's go back into town and have another walk around."

Ally returned to the house at 2:30 in the afternoon; the menacing package was gone. She entered the house first, and looked around before going back to the car to collect Breanna. Breanna had been crying non-stop for fifteen minutes; she was hungry and wet. Ally held Breanna in one arm as she prepared a bottle. She would just have to be wet for a little while longer. "Mom could you spread out the receiving blanket?' Ally placed Breanna on the receiving blanket, continuing to hold the bottle. 'Now could you hold the bottle while I change her real quick?"

After Breanna was fed, Ally rocked her in the rocking chair.

"Mmm, this feels wonderful," Ally sighed as Breanna slept.

"I'm glad you noticed. I was really starting to get worried about you, Ally."

"Sorry Mom. I just don't know how to separate my emotions right now."

"I don't know what to tell you, but Ally, you still need to be a mother and a wife."

"And a daughter. I know Mom. I do know, Mom, but I have a hard time conquering my emotions."

"You don't need to learn to defeat them, just how to function with them."

"Yeah," said Ally, wearily rubbing her forehead. "I'd better bring in the groceries and put them away." Ally and Rene put away the groceries in heavy silence; each absorbed in their own thoughts. Ally's thoughts were focused on the investigation and the contents of the package found on her doorstep. Rene was trying to hold her tongue, not wanting to be critical of Ally's behavior, given the circumstances. She used to be able to get Ally to open up about any problem or situation, but now she felt she was losing touch with Ally. David did not seem to be doing much better in breaking down her emotional barriers.

"I'd better call Neal and find out what was left on my doorstep," Ally said evenly.

She went into the kitchen to call and returned a short time later. "Mom, I spoke to Karen. She said Neal was due back in the office at four, I think I'll go over and see what's going on. I'm going to be worried until I find out. You're okay looking after Breanna? I'll give you a call if I am going to be past five."

Ally arrived at the Sheriff's Office just as Neal was pulling in. She stood on the curb waiting for him to exit the car. "Hi Neal, just needed to find out what was in that package?"

"Why don't we go inside? I don't want to be overheard by any reporter nosing around."

Ally followed Neal into his office in silence. He motioned for her to sit; he was still standing as he rubbed his palms over his eyes. "Neal, what is it?" she asked anxiously.

"Ally, it was another one of those mosaic-piece prints."

"Oh God, Neal. She's not dead, is she?"

"I don't know yet. I ran the print to the FBI office in Acacia. They have a copy of the descrambler program downloaded into their system. They'll fax me a copy of the initial photos. They promised to make it top priority. I'll go check the fax machine."

Ally stared numbly into space for several minutes. Then she caught sight of several colored Xeroxed copies of a digital print and also, of a Christmas card, on top of Neal's desk. The mosaic print displayed a gingerbread man running, with the caption, "Run, run as fast as you can!" Then, the Christmas card was laid out flat, and Ally could see that the card had been encased in plastic before being copied. It must be evidence.

Ally picked up the colored copies, and saw that the top half of the card was blank except for a small inverted, centralized logo. The other half displayed a snow-covered meadow surrounded by pine trees. The woodland animals were gazing at a bright star that illuminated the sky above. Far back amongst the trees, there was a small glimmer of light, as if the manger was just out of view over the horizon. "SEASON'S GREETINGS" was embossed in red across the top of the winter scene. The next copy displayed

374

the interior of the card, which read: "Wishing you all the simple pleasures of this joyous season." It was signed, "Enjoying my simple pleasure, Wish you were here, Yours Truly." Then Ally saw the faint blood smear on the internal portion of the card.

Ally's stomach felt hollow, except for the rock hard knot right in the center. For a minute, she thought she was going to heave as she moved closer to the trash can. She heard Neal enter the room. She did not turn but asked in a low voice, "These are the copies of the mosaic print and card, which were sent to my house?"

"Yes, we've sent both to be analyzed."

"Did you receive the fax?"

"Yes, it wasn't a death scene photo. The girl was still alive. She was bounded and gagged, but alive."

"That's because he is going to draw out the suffering for Lizzie, for all of us."

"Ally, you don't know that."

"Yes, I do. He wants to prolong the agony for Caitlyn, for his mother, and for me. He wants one-upmanship over Alex Brentwood and you. He will not kill Lizzie until he feels he is cornered. He will just keep toying with the notion of her demise, sending taunts and quite possibly torturing Lizzie along the way. Are they going to send you the photo?"

"Yes, they're going to have a copy of the photo delivered. There was just one photo in this picture. It was not as detailed as the others."

"Will you show me a copy of the photo when it gets here?"

"Yes."

"I'm going to head home now," Ally replied tautly.

Neal called the next day, Thursday. "Ally, I've got the photo. I also, need a favor. I need you to talk Caitlyn and her husband, to prepare them, before they receive any messages. It would be a disaster if they received some contact from Morrison and spoke to the press before talking to the FBI or our Department. Caitlyn trusts you, and the message will come across much better if you deliver it."

"Yes, I'll talk to her."

"I talked to Jennings, the FBI agent involved. He is more than willing to let you talk to Caitlyn. I think Caitlyn is wearing him thin. Jennings will stay in the background. Caitlyn is beyond listening to anyone in law enforcement. He's afraid she'll do something unpredictable or stupid. Can I pick you up in an hour?"

"I'll be ready." Ally returned the receiver and went to talk to her Mom.

"Mom, Neal is coming to pick me up in an hour. I'm going to talk to Caitlyn Mathews about the developments. I promised her that I would keep her posted and she seems to lack faith in the men involved in the case." Ally pulled Breanna up into her arms. She held Breanna closely, enjoying the small movements she made. Ally bent to give her a kiss on her forehead, breathing in her scent, gathering her own strength.

"Thank you, Mom. You're a life-saver. I don't know how I would have coped if you hadn't came into town when you did. I hate to involve you in all this during your visit."

"Nonsense. This is the only place I want to be."

"Well, thanks again, I'm going to get ready."

Neal arrived at the door, and left the sheriff's car in the driveway. Ally introduced him to her mother. "Neal, I'd like you to meet my mother, Rene Michael. Mom, this is Neal Bryant." Rene gave Neal an appraising look.

"We met at the hospital, but we were never properly introduced."

"Hello, Ms. Michael. I wish we could have met under better circumstances."

"So do I," Rene answered wryly.

"Mom, I should be back in less than two hours."

Once in the sheriff's car, Neal handed an envelope to Ally that contained a glossy photo of a small girl tied with ropes securing her hands and boot-clad feet. A piece of silver duct tape was draped over her mouth. Above the tape, the girl's large brown eyes were tear-drenched. The child was propped against a peg-board wall; the ground below her appeared to be cold, barren concrete. Was he hiding her in a garage or shed? The interior of the premises emitted a sickly yellow glow. Ally saw that aged newspapers covered the windows, and light was being filtered through the newsprint. Ally tried to make out any distinctive features of the interior of the structure, but it seemed the photographer had cleared the area in preparation for this shot.

Ally tried to visualize what Lizzie would look like minus that menacing tape. She realized that she had subconsciously avoided looking at any of the photos of Lizzie that had been circulated since the search began. Ally had given these photos just a cursory glance. Had she given up hope of finding Lizzie alive from the very start?

Ally was now seeing Lizzie for the first time. Lizzie had long brown hair with bangs cut straight across. Her face and body retained the chubbiness of latent toddlerhood. It was difficult to know for sure, but Ally guessed she would be approximately three feet tall and weigh thirty-five pounds, if that. A small cherub; she should be home playing with her dolls.

Neal and Ally arrived at the Mathews' residence and were allowed entry onto the sidewalk leading up to the front door by one of the uniformed officers. Ally could see some reporters barricaded behind yellow police tape. She caught sight of a reporter who gave her a brief curious stare as she approached the front of the ranch-style home.

Agent Jennings opened the front door and quickly ushered them inside, closing the door rapidly behind them. Jennings pulled both Neal and Ally into a small foyer, explaining in rushed whispers the details he wanted protected and those that could be discussed with the Mathews.

Ally entered the living room, where Caitlyn Mathews sat stiff-faced with her husband upon a large couch. They sat without touching, as if any physical contact would cause a maelstrom of emotion.

Ally sat down on the edge of the tweed loveseat, diagonally to the left of Caitlyn so she could speak directly to her. She began softly and continued in a slow fashion, allowing the couple to absorb the information as she spoke. "Caitlyn, I told you that I would contact you if there was any solid information. I received a photograph of Lizzie. She looked okay. She didn't seem to be seriously hurt in any way. An unpleasant message in a Christmas card came with the photo. I wanted to warn you that the person who has Lizzie might try to hurt or intimidate you in the same manner. It is important to follow the directives of Agent Jennings here and be careful what you tell the media, so we can bring Lizzie home safe."

Ally met Caitlyn's dull, vacant stare, then continued, "I believe he will keep Lizzie hidden to play some sort of sick game with all of us. But trust me, he is tipping his hand and leading us to Lizzie. We don't want to scare him off. As long as Eric believes he is control, he will keep Lizzie alive. If Eric believes he's cornered, then Lizzie is in extreme danger."

"Thank you for letting me know," Caitlyn said feebly. Tears started flowing down her cheeks again. Her husband had a steel-gray pallor with a green tinge around his mouth and eyes; he looked positively ill.

"Where are your sons?" Ally did not even realize that she had spoken her question out loud.

"The boys are staying with Chris' family. We wanted to protect them from all this publicity and chaos."

"I'll let you know if anything else comes up." Ally stood up; her legs felt like gelatin, she didn't know if they would support her weight. She continued out the front door without stopping until she collapsed into the passenger seat of the sheriff's car.

Neal sat down in the driver's seat, staring straight ahead while he buckled his seat belt. He said, "I just want to let you know, you did great in there. I couldn't have asked for better."

They drove back to Ally's house in silence. Ally opened her door and stood up. "Please let me know if anything happens."

"You can count on it. See you later."

Ally walked in the front door to hear Christmas music playing on the stereo. Rene had pulled out the boxes of Christmas decorations and was carefully unwrapping the nativity figurines. "Are you going to help me?" Rene asked. "I thought we could use a little Christmas around here."

Ally's eyes filled with tears: this was Breanna's first Christmas. She had been missing it. "Sounds good to me, Mom. I could do with a cup of hot chocolate. How about you?"

"That sounds wonderful."

"I just realized we never got to the tree; we were going to decorate it on Sunday. Maybe we could get the ornaments and lights down and have the tree ready to decorate by the time David gets home. We'll surprise him."

It was dark as Ally blindly reached for the phone, feeling her way along the cord. "Hello?" she said hoarsely, still caught between dreaming and wakefulness. "Who is this? Neal?"

Ally tried to shake the sleepiness aside. "Could you tell me again? What? You caught Morrison...You caught Morrison! Where's Lizzie? Is she all right? She's still out there, and he isn't talking? Oh my God, she's still out there." Ally was brought abruptly into full consciousness. "Of course, we both understand why Caitlyn is emotionally devastated and hostile, but I wish she'd at least, cooperate with you and Agent Jennings. Still, I agreed with you, she will respond better to me because she sees me as a mother. I'll go with you to speak to Caitlyn, first thing in the morning. I'll see you at eight then."

It was four in the morning; she knew she wouldn't sleep. Why bother to just lay here? Slipping on her slippers, she grabbed her heavy terry cloth robe. Ally silently made her way towards the kitchen. She stepped out of the sliding glass door and onto the back porch, breathing in the cold crisp air.

The night was overcast. A thin layer of clouds veiled the full luminous moon. It was so light outside; the night took on a surreal quality. The ground retained a few patches of snow, but most of it had already melted away. The air was still, with just a slight rustle of a breeze. The atmosphere should be peaceful and calm, but Ally knew different.

Tension sparked and flickered along her nerve-endings, sending a fierce and dangerous code. Deep, red-hot anger surged rampantly throughout her body. Her muscles were taut, but she had no way to dispel the energy. She could just wait; hold her breath, and hope; even though hope seemed irrelevant at best.

She unwillingly visualized Morrison's smug, arrogant face as he was interrogated. He would feel thrilled and triumphant as he coldly refused to answer their urgent question. The question reverberated in her mind: "Where is Lizzie?" Lord, you brought me into this; what do you want me to do? I'm not here just to stand idly by while another child is destroyed, am I? Ally felt like she had failed some type of test. She had been given a gift, but even with this gift, she'd been unable to prevent this nightmare. What was the use?

She sat down in the rigid white plastic lawn chair, folding her arms across her chest, staring at the morning in front of her. She closed her eyes as if, to shield her mind from the onslaught of her thoughts. She was going to have to face Caitlyn tomorrow: Caitlyn with her hollow, tortured eyes, staring at her, pleading for help and reassurance. How could she give either? Would her reassurances sound as phony as they felt in the silence of these predawn hours? How was she going to pull it off with confidence?

Ally sat out on the porch for hours, her mind drifting in unproductive circles. The sky became hazy with the diffused light of the approaching day. She shivered involuntarily in the cold air and pulled the collar of her robe up against her bare neck. She wondered how poor Lizzie was keeping warm.

Ally heard the sliding glass door open quietly behind her. She did not turn as David walked up behind her and started messaging her shoulders. "What are you doing out here, Ally? It's freezing."

"The police arrested Morrison. Lizzie...she is still missing and he won't tell them where she is. I came out here to clear my head."

"I'm sorry, Honey. You must be going out of your mind. But you'd better come back into the house before you get sick." Ally stood up and David gently steered her toward the door and into the house. 'Sit down, I'll get you a cup of coffee. I've got some brewing."

Ally was already out the door when Neal pulled up. She had given Rene the low-down as she fed Breanna this morning. Now she was just anxious to have her meeting with Caitlyn done and over with before she lost her nerve. She was seriously dreading it.

Ally climbed in the passenger seat without preliminaries. She asked Neal if they had found out where Lizzie was being held, or if they had gotten any other useful information from Morrison. Neal shook his head. "They caught Eric at a 24-hour market picking up some groceries. He denied any knowledge of Lizzie's disappearance; he said he had needed time alone, away from any press or news coverage. He accused the officers of harassing him. After the Miranda warning was given, he clammed up. We have to let Caitlyn and her husband know about Morrison's arrest before it hits the news. They're going to have reporters on their doorstep day and night; whenever they step out their door."

"It will be horrible for Caitlyn and her family! I'm sure the media will be insensitive enough to drill the family about what they think may have happened to Lizzie. That just can't happen!" Ally lamented.

Neal nodded. "Some people in the press act like vultures when they're pursuing a story. Caitlyn sure isn't making it any easier on us in law enforcement; I wish we could get more cooperation. Caitlyn's guard goes up whenever Jennings or I enter the room. Her hostility is palpable!"

"Don't take it personal, Neal. I don't think it has anything to do with you or Jennings. I just don't think she likes authoritarian men; too much like her father. She paints you two with the same brush, and assumes you're hypocritical and dishonest. I believe this whole situation has caused her issues with both Brentwood and Morrison to resurface, and she taking it out on the available men on the scene."

Neal looked bewildered.

381

"I couldn't sleep," Ally explained. "I kept thinking about all aspects of this case."

"Maybe we should hire you to do the psychological profiles," he said half-mockingly.

Ally's eyes fell to the two large files, nestled in the seat between them. The one on the top was new and dark brown with a typed label: MORRISON, ERIC. A start date and several identifying numbers were also typed under the name. The file below was a faded light green and had frayed edges and corners. "Eric Morrison" had been hand-written haphazardly in faded ink on the upper tab. Some numbers were worn away and unreadable.

The green file must be Eric Morrison's juvenile file. Ally looked at the flimsy, tattered case file; several papers seemed to be falling out of their restraining clips. The quality and maintenance of the folders at the credit department was much better than this. She figured that the juvenile system must be lacking support personnel, such as clerical assistance, and other financial resources.

This small factor added to her dismal assessment of the way the children were devalued in society as a whole. If there was no money for supplies or clerical support, then she doubted there were financial resources for quality therapeutic interventions or programs. Ally suspected that children were mostly housed and penalized, rather than given rehabilitation services. It defied logic, since more therapeutic interventions at younger ages would prohibit additional delinquency or even adult recidivism.

I must be tired, Ally thought; I'm making mountains out of molehills. She leaned her head back against the passenger seat and closed her eyes. She turned her head sharply when she heard a small voice whisper in her ear, "In the beginning, there was a boy..." Then, as quickly as the voice was there, it faded away. A sense of déjà-vu rushed over Ally as she tried to remember where she recently heard those words before. "That's it!" she thought. "It was that dream about a little girl reading a story."

In the beginning, in the beginning, Ally rapidly thought. In the beginning, a long time ago ...Eric kidnapped Caitlyn. That was the beginning of his pattern. It wasn't Shilo. Where did Eric take Caitlyn initially? It must have had some kind of significance for him. Eric would find satisfaction at the irony of taking Lizzie to the same place he had taken Caitlyn so many years ago. He was going to keep punishing and condemning Caitlyn for her mere existence, simply for being born. Ultimately, Eric was still just a spiteful little boy seeking retribution against his perceived enemies, and trying to engender the attention of his mother. He never really grew up emotionally past that point. "Neal, where did Eric hide his sister, Caitlyn? Is it in these records somewhere?"

"It was an antique car renovation shop outside the town limits of Alpine."

"Who owns the place now?"

"The Road House," Neal answered. "Last I heard, the county had heavy liens against the property due to back taxes. The owner went bankrupt years ago. After his demise, the county tried to auction off the property, but couldn't. An environmental impact study revealed the place was full of contaminants, such as oil, that had saturated into the ground. I even believe they had used lead based paint around the shop. Who knows what else? The current well is polluted, with unacceptable levels of mercury in the water. The cost of the toxic clean-up surpasses the value of the property. There is regular talk within the county about bulldozing the place. The county finally put a locked chain-link fence around the place last spring, since the local kids used it as a party site. It has been a definite liability. Usually we patrol the place in the summer, but it tends to be quiet during the winter months."

Is the property far from here?" Ally asked.

"It's about twenty-five minutes northeast on Highway 40, and another five minutes down a dirt road. You think Morrison took Lizzie there?"

383

"I'm not sure, it's just a thought. Could we go there and take a look around? You could give Agent Jennings a call to say we've been delayed."

Neal gave Ally a serious look. "If that child is out there, we need to get her as soon as possible, or she may die of exposure. Let's just take a quick look to see if there has been any recent activity out there.

CHAPTER 26

Neil made a U-turn and headed towards Highway 40. He made a radio call to dispatch, asking them to inform Agent Jennings of their pending hour delay. They traveled in silence. Ally was taunt, highly charged with anticipation. Neal was resigned; another lead to follow. Hopefully it's useful, but most likely not. He was putting off the inevitable: telling grieving parents that it was highly probable that they would never see their child again.

Ally felt the hard knot in her stomach expand, making her queasy. I can't be sick right now, she told herself sternly. She tried to ignore the persistent pain in her gut and think of something else, anything else. It was no use, the thoughts of Lizzie came crashing in on her.

Ally pressed her fingers tightly against her forehead, as if to force her mind into clarity. "Neal, how in the world do you ever get used to this?"

"Ally, this is about as bad as it gets. This is the worst investigation that I've personally been involved in. I've had many smaller cases to help condition me for this experience. Don't be so hard on yourself. Sometimes you have to continue going through the motions because there is nothing else you can do."

"If Lizzie's there, do you think we'll find her alive?"

"Ally, I honestly don't know. We both know what Morrison is capable of doing. It's also been very cold; she could have died of exposure. We just have to deal with what we find, and remember, we may find nothing. Don't get your hopes up. You can stay in the car if you'd like."

"No, I have to see this through, whatever the outcome."

Ally stared out the window; she absently noted that the thin veil of cloud cover from the pre-dawn hours had completely dissipated. The unencumbered sun gleamed brightly over a steady band of cedar trees, which graciously gave way to a sprinkling of houses. Many of these homes hosted an attached

385

paddock for grazing horses. A regular cluster of small cottage-style homes came into view; she saw a few children playing off in the distance, heedless of any danger. Off a side street, Ally could see a cluster of businesses among the narrow, tree-lined road: a gas station and auto repair, a mom-and-pop café nestled next to a small post office which announced the fact that they were in Alpine. Up a small grade, Ally saw an isolated church, brilliant white, sporting a very tall steeple. This section must be the entire business district.

The town was picturesque, the stereotypical locale for one of those heart-warming Christmas specials. It was repugnant to think that Morrison might have chosen a beautiful place, such as this, for this monstrosity. It was the type of crime that could forever mar and taint the atmosphere of this township: a disease, spreading fear, erasing the carefree security and splendor of this peaceful community. God, she hated Eric for defiling this innocuous setting! Ally especially resented Eric for all the negativity he represented: the evil, hate, violence, callousness, and ugliness. The corrosive effects of these destructive energies were a malignant scourge that encroached on decent communities, like this one, infecting our society.

Wait, Ally thought to herself, Eric- most likely grew up in this town. He was only twelve when he walked six-year old Caitlyn to the Road House. Alex and Susan Brentwood, with their two beautiful, young children, must have appeared to outsiders as the upstanding, 'perfect' family within an ideal community. The family image disintegrated when Eric hid his sister away and drew attention to their familial dysfunction. Again, perceptions clashed violently with realities.

The houses thinned out again as the tree line thickened. Neal said, "The turn-off is just ahead."

Neal turned onto an unmarked dirt road. The unpaved road was very wide at the mouth and narrowed precipitously into a rutted, muddy trail. Neal made a concerted effort to proceed very slowly and cautiously, to ensure that they did not end up stuck in the mud. Water from the melted snow had pooled and iced over some of the deepest holes. Ally observed some tire tracks in the muddy patches, but she would not venture to guess how old these tracks were.

They drove up to a six-foot chain-link fence and came to a stop. The fence enclosed an authentic cobblestone building; the rectangular stone façade hosted twin oversized heavy wooden doors, painted red. The red paint was flaking away, exposing a yellow undercoat. The cement driveway was cracked and chipped away; weeds were overgrown in the crevices. The brush surrounding the building was over waist-high, crowding the structure, bearing witness to many years of neglect. There were empty beer cans and remnants of broken bottles scattered about, glistening in the direct sunlight, intertwined within multitudes of old cigarette butts and bullet castings.

Ally stared at the antiquated building. "I didn't think this place would be so old."

"I believe the building is most likely a hundred years old or more. It was a mining store for some the smaller mining operations. It even filled some smaller orders for the railroad companies and sold nails, lumber, and some hand-forged specialized tools." Neal pulled sharply on the padlock, which secured the gate. "This isn't a Barrier lock. The county has a contract with Barrier's locks. They won the bid with the entire county, so the company is the primary vendor of all our security systems and locks." Neal unlocked the trunk of the police cruiser and pulled out the bolt cutters, quickly snapping the padlock.

Neal put the bolt cutters back in the trunk, and he pulled on a pair of latex gloves.

Ally asked, "Just in case, did you want me to put on a pair?"

"Yes, just to be on the safe side. Follow close behind me. Stay in single file, so we don't contaminate any evidence. This could be a crime scene. She followed quickly behind him as he made his way to the front of the building. He tried to open the two heavy wood doors, which seemed to be securely fastened. The doors didn't show signs of recent use, due to the large deposit of wind-blown debris piled against them.

Ally followed Neal, treading carefully on the edge of the path, watching her footing on the slippery underbrush as they made their way to the rear of the building. She saw a single door to the right rear side of the building. The door was buckled from being pushed in, and hung haphazardly on loose hinges.

Sidestepping over the raised threshold, Ally stepped into the cold, hazy workshop. Her breath formed a white vapor in front of her. The floor was littered with additional beer cans and some empty hard liquor bottles, more cigarette butts, and empty cigarette boxes, empty chip bags and various wrappers. The litter formed a heaping ground cover over the concrete floor.

The peg-board walls were plastered with various painted and scratched profanities and crude phrases. Ally looked up at the broken out, florescent-lighting fixtures overhead that dangled precariously from above. Articles of clothing, a flaming hot pink lace bra, and several singular shoes remained lobbed over the fixtures where they had been thrown. There was a brown crusted stain several feet from the door they just entered. Ally surmised that one of many teenagers did not quite make it outside before he, or she puked. This must have been a major party house for the local teens.

As they moved further into the building, the light became dimmer, which made the interior hazy. Ally raised her eyes again to the windows, and saw that several had been broken out. She and Neal continued to the left side of the building through a door-less passage into a second smaller room, where the business office must have been located. The larger window within this room was covered in newspaper; the wall was covered in pegboard, which descended from the window. The remaining three walls were sheet rock. Several boxes of papers had been piled unceremoniously in a corner under cheap sheet metal shelving. Metal folding chairs were propped against the far front wall. There was another high, small, square window, also covered with newspaper. Ally froze. Lizzie had been here. The photo had been taken in this very room.

"Neal, Lizzie's picture was taken here in this room; see the peg-board wall and the windows covered in newspaper?" Ally pointed to the backdrop area of the familiar photo.

"I believe you're right. The boxes were shifted over into that corner; you still can see their outline on the floor."

Ally involuntarily screamed out Lizzie's name. "Lizzie! Lizzie! Please answer! We're here to take you home to your mommy." Her scream echoed hollowly in the deserted building.

Ally and Neal scoured the building. Ally irrationally searched several boxes, desperate to find any sign of Lizzie. They combed the building several more times, but there was no sign of Lizzie.

Then an unwelcome thought reverberated through Ally's being. Lizzie was already dead; they were too late. Eric had left last night to dispose of the body. Ally's legs gave way as she sank to her knees on the hard, unyielding floor. She covered her face in her hands and let out a hoarse moan. "She's dead. He's killed her. Her body's been dumped. Oh poor baby, we couldn't save you. I failed you. Oh Caitlyn, she can't take this! How is she going to survive?" Ally sobbed as she roughly got back onto her feet. "Eric will never tell Caitlyn the truth; she will never know what happened to her baby. It will drive her to desperation; Eric damn well knows it! He's won; he's got what he wanted. We lost; we couldn't afford to lose. How could we have lost? It's not right; it wasn't supposed to end this way."

Neal grasped her shoulders, "C'mon, Ally. I'll get you home."

"No. No. I won't be a coward. I've got to be there and face Caitlyn."

"You don't have to be there. I've had to talk with grieving parents before. Delivering bad news is part of the territory."

"I will not be able to live with this if I don't talk to Caitlyn. It will haunt me. I will be alright in a minute."

"Liar,' Neal softly prompted and continued gently. "You're only fooling yourself Ally if you think that you can 'quickly' come to terms with this horrible tragedy. It is going to take much longer than that to get past the trauma. You should get some crisis counseling once this is over. I'm serious. Not because you're hurting right now, or because you're female. You need to talk this through with someone trained to listen. I know an excellent therapist; I've spoken to him once or twice myself. I will give you his name and number."

"I'm ready to go now," Ally stated abruptly, angrily stowing away her tears. What was the use in tears? They wouldn't help Lizzie now. Ally wiped her face with her hand and smoothed down her hair.

"Okay?" Neal sensitively queried in a double entendre manner; briefly responding to her abrupt statement, but subtly inquiring, as to her emotional state. Neal met her eyes; when Ally failed to respond, he decided now wasn't time to press the issue.

They made their way out of the rubble. Stepping over the raised threshold, Ally slipped on the wet weeds, ending up sprawled out over the overgrown terrain. Neal turned to help Ally to her feet. She tried to secure herself with Neal's arm. Still unsteady, she lost her balance and grabbed the doorjamb.

Ally's foot throbbed where she had hit the top of it.   She said irascibly, "Neal could you hold up a minute? My foot hurts."

"Did you sprain it?"

"I don't think so. I just banged it up a bit." Ally took several deep breaths as her eyes absently scanned the area. She wondered if Morrison had dumped Lizzie's body somewhere here on the adjacent property. Ally caught a glance of a thin trail of smoke in the distance.

"Neal are there any houses close by?"

"Are you hurt?" Neal tone was sharp and concerned.

"No, no, I just see some smoke from a chimney over there."

Neal didn't reply; he headed abruptly in the direction of the smoke. Ally, forgetting about her foot, followed in pursuit. "Neal, what is it? Where are you going?"

"I forgot all about it. There is a small one-room cabin, just inside the fence. It has been around as long as the building has."

Ally was struggling to get through the overgrowth as it brushed against her body and tangled around her feet; she continued her labored journey through the unkempt foliage, trying to keep pace with Neal. Upon seeing the small stone cabin, Ally could immediately detect signs of a recent intrusion into the area. The fencing behind the cabin had been cut away to form a flap. This opening was gerry-rigged with plastic ties to secure the fence to the metal poles. The open flap had been secured with wire, allowing the intruder to get in and out of the property at this location, yet be hidden from view of the main road by the weeded surroundings.

Neal approached the front door of the cabin. It opened easily as he called out, "Sheriff's Department," and entered the dwelling.

The smoke had come from a wood stove that graced a large portion of the small interior room. There was a cot against the right wall. An upside-down cardboard box was being utilized as a nightstand. On the make-shift nightstand, there was a battery-operated lamp and an over-the-counter box of sleeping pills. At the foot of the cot, there was an open backpack filled with clothing and toiletry items, a paper sack with some food items, and a five-gallon plastic jug of water. Then, in the left corner, Ally saw a child heaped on the rough wooden floor. She was still bound at the wrist and ankles, with duct tape enclosing her mouth.

Ally ran quickly to the child and gathered her in her arms. Ally had seen her before Neal had. The body was warm; Lizzie was breathing. "Neal, Neal, she's alive!" Neal turned abruptly to find Ally cradling the child. Neal grabbed the radio to call for law enforcement assistance and an ambulance. He also asked Dispatch to call Jennings, with instructions to have Agent Jennings and Lizzie's parents, meet them at Tri-County Hospital.

Neal made his way to Lizzie and gently pulled at the tape around her mouth. He used his pocketknife to cut away the bonds securing her arms and legs. Lizzie still did not respond. Neal suspected that the child had been heavily sedated with the sleeping pills lying next to the lamp. Her color was good. She was breathing steadily and did not appear to be in distress.

Thank heavens, Ally thought. Morrison must have thought he would be back today. He had left the place warm in preparation for his return. It wasn't for Lizzie's benefit. He was most likely not ready to have her die yet.

"Can you carry her?" Neal asked. "I don't think the ambulance will be able to get back here; I'm going to take her to the main road. I just need to get the fence open."

"No problem." Ally stood up with Lizzie still in her arms and walked out the door that Neal held open for her. Neal untwisted the wire and held the gaping fence flap as far down as he could for Ally to traverse. Ally carefully stepped over the fencing and circled away from the opening to protect Lizzie from the rebounding fence. Neal took Lizzie from Ally's arms and set forth on the rugged trail. Finally, they reached the sheriff cruiser. Ally opened the passenger door and quickly sat down in the passenger seat. She reached for Lizzie. The child still had not stirred; Ally was anxious to get her to the hospital. Had she been overdosed with sleeping medication? The car had just made it to the main road when Ally heard the roar of the ambulance siren.

Neal flagged down the ambulance. Two EMT's came around the Sheriff's car to place Lizzie on the gurney. Neal recited the name and dose of the sleeping medication before they left. Neal turned to Ally. "We need to wait for assistance, someone to cover the crime scene before we can leave."

Just as Neal spoke, another sheriff's cruiser pulled up with two deputies inside. "I'll be back in a few minutes." Neal rushed towards the second car and spoke to the men as they were exiting the vehicle. Ally could see Neal gesturing towards the building and then pointing in the direction of the cabin. He continued to speak for several more minutes before returning to the vehicle.

"Okay. Are you going to go to the hospital with me?" Neal asked.

"You better believe it," Ally replied.

Ally entered the emergency room entrance of the hospital. Neal spoke to the charge nurse, who directed him to a small interior waiting room. Ally noticed that there were several, law enforcement officers present, most likely due to the magnitude of this investigation and the publicity involved. Hidden in the opposite corner of the room, she saw Chris and Caitlyn Mathews.

Neal signaled for Agent Jennings, and the two men walked down the corridor, out of earshot of the assembly. Caitlyn caught sight of Ally and headed towards her. She looked healthier, both physically and emotionally, than she had yesterday. Caitlyn placed both hands on Ally's shoulders and leaned her head towards her. "Thank you, Ally. Thank you. I don't know all the details, but I know that you and Deputy Bryant found Lizzie." Caitlyn's voice filled with emotion and she was unable to continue speaking for several minutes. 'The hospital let us see her for about five minutes. The doctor told us that Lizzie appears a little dehydrated. She was still sleepy due to some sedatives, but she is going to be fine. He wanted to do a blood panel and also a physical exam to check for any sexual trauma. The doctor indicated that the initial exams did not show any signs of sexual abuse, but he felt a complete exam would be prudent. He will let us see her afterwards." Caitlyn had almost choked on the words "sexual trauma." However, Ally sensed that Caitlyn could face anything, as long as her daughter was alive.

"Caitlyn, I'm so glad to hear she will be okay. I can't begin to imagine how painful the last several days have been for you." Ally saw Neal was returning from the corner of her eye. "I wish you all the best. Please let me know how Lizzie is doing, okay?"

Neal approached and said, "I hate to rush you, Ally, but are you ready to go now?"

Ally nodded, clasping Caitlyn's hand one more time.

Leaving the hospital, Ally finally felt the sweet rush of relief. She felt like laughing and crying. She felt disbelief mixed with a light-heartedness that had been lacking for too long now. The perpetual sense of doom and despair that hovered over her for many months had magically lifted.

Later that day, Neal called her to tell her that the weaker charges against Morrison had been compiled with the newer charges. A Preliminary Hearing was set for February 24th.

Morrison's attorney, Stephan Connor, had recused himself. He was unable to rearrange his schedule to facilitate a major kidnapping and attempted murder trial. Morrison was shopping for another attorney, this time on his own dime. It seemed that Alex Brentwood had withdrawn his support, and was trying to distance himself from his stepson.

The phone rang at 7:15 am, waking Ally from a sound sleep. Ally blindly reached for the phone, her eyes still closed.

"Hello? Oh, Hello Neal." Ally sat up in bed, rubbing her eyes. Ally looked for David and noticed that he was already out of bed.

"Sorry Ally, I didn't mean to wake you. But I wanted to check and see if you would be willing to meet with Andrew Williams this morning at 9:00. He wants an initial meeting to go over your testimony to prepare for the Preliminary Hearing. You know the Preliminary Hearing is scheduled for February 24th?"

"Neal, it's the day after Thanksgiving! David is off work. We all were going to go Christmas shopping, today," Ally lamented.

"Ally, I know this is last minute, but Andrew Williams is going to be out of town for the next couple of weeks. First he has a conference in Dallas, and then he will be gone for vacation. It won't take the whole day. He only wants to meet with you for about two hours." Ally could hear David in the hallway, approaching the bedroom.

"Listen Neal, I need to talk to David about this. I will give you a call back in fifteen minutes." Ally hung up the phone as David entered the bedroom.

"David that was Neal on the phone. He wants me to meet with the D.A. for about two hours this morning from nine to eleven. The D.A., Mr. Williams, is leaving town for a couple of weeks and he wanted to meet me prior to his departure. What should I tell Neal?"

"I don't see a problem," David reassured. "I can take your Mom and Breanna to breakfast like we'd planned and then we can start shopping at whatever store your Mom has in mind. We could meet you at Timeless Toys at 11:30. You know, they have pictures with Santa scheduled there. Then we could finish our shopping."

"Thanks David, I will give Neal a call back and let him know I can make it."

Forty minutes later, Ally carried Breanna out to the car, leaning over to kiss her mother and David good-bye. She buckled

Breanna into her car seat and bent to kiss her one more time before they left. Closing the car door, Ally waved at her family as they pulled out of the driveway.

Ally still had about forty-five minutes before she had to leave the house to meet with Andrew Williams. She thought about Thanksgiving yesterday. It was a wonderful day; since Mom was here, and Larry had joined them. David told Larry that he was out of his mind with fear and anger, when Ally had been abducted. It had left him unable to think of anything or anyone else. Larry told him that he understood, but wanted to be there for David and his family. Larry believed that they had built a closer relationship over the past weeks. David reassured him that their relationship was stronger than ever; and apologized for hurting his father's feelings. Ally was extremely thankful that Larry and David made amends.

Moreover, Ally again offered a prayer of gratitude that Lizzie was now home safe, and Morrison was behind bars. She felt free to enjoy herself and focus on the family and the festivities. The day had passed so quickly. Ally wished she could have slowed it down to savor the experience.

Ally got up off the couch and switched on the television. The late morning news was on, and Ally caught the tail end of an interview with Susan Brentwood. Ally tried to reconcile the mental picture of Susan Brentwood formed by the stories she had heard with the image of this classically dressed woman.

Susan Brentwood appeared to be in her early fifties, and had a very slim, stature. She had expertly dyed wheat-colored hair with milk-chocolate colored eyes. She was wearing a taffy colored satin blouse with a lace camisole beneath, a cream colored wool skirt, and matching heels. She had a pearl choker with matching earrings. Her make-up was immaculate, as were her nails. She looked very distinguished and high society.

Susan Brentwood spoke in her plaintive manner: "I don't know why Eric chose to behave the way he did. Growing up, he was always my 'little man.' I've always done my best for my son since his father was never around. I have always done the very best I could with everything in my life, and it seems like that just wasn't enough." Susan walked away from the microphone, believing the cameras and mics were off. Ally heard her uncouth comment: "It seems as if life always craps all over me!"

Ally could not believe it. Susan Brentwood appeared so self-righteous and indignant; did she honestly believe her own diatribe? Susan's commentary resonated bitterly in Ally's mind. Susan was a crude and self-absorbed woman in a fancy costume. Ally turned off the television in disgust. She retrieved her purse and house keys, and huffily walked out the door.

Ally took the week of Christmas off; she told Neal that she would come in on Tuesday, December 29th. She turned her focus completely onto her family. The holidays were simple but beautiful. Her father and brother made it into town, and Larry shared Christmas Eve and Christmas Day with them. Ally did not watch the news or read the papers. She did not want Morrison to mar her enjoyment of this holiday.

Ally definitely decided that she wasn't going back to her old job with the credit card company. She talked it over with David, and she submitted her resignation. Ally wanted to work with families, but did not know what job was exactly the right match yet. She kept wondering what would've happened if someone had intervened sooner on Eric's behalf. Would it have made a difference? Could someone have made a substantial impact in the lives of those little girls? While she finished her internship with the Sheriff's Department, she would look into other job opportunities. Neal said he would write a reference letter and help her where he could.

It was difficult to say good-bye to her Mom, when she left on December 27th.

"Ally, you call me if you get into a pinch. I'll find some way to come and help."

"Oh Mom, you have helped me through this mess, more than you'll ever know. I couldn't have managed without you. I really do appreciate it."

"I wish the trial was over. Then, I could feel comfortable."

"Mom, this whole trial process will probably take two years. Then, it is possible that Morrison will appeal. It is going to be a lengthy process, but at least he is behind bars and he didn't get out on bail this time. It's going to be fine."

"I cannot help but worry," her mother said. Ally hugged her mother reassuringly, and then, Ally hugged her father and brother before they boarded the plane. Ally watched them until the plane departed. She hunched down next to the stroller to point out the plane to Breanna. "There goes Grandma, Grandpa, and your uncle in the plane." She didn't think Breanna understood, but who knew?

Ally continued to help Neal get reports from various labs, coordinate and document the evidence against Eric Morrison, which was now very substantial. Neal was running non-stop to make sure he had the investigations in order. Finally, it was February 24th. Andrew Williams had asked Ally to be available for testimony, but he did not think he would call her to the stand.

Ally was sitting on a bench seat in the corridor when she saw Eric Morrison being led in shackles into the courtroom. Ally felt the hair on the back of her neck raise as she quickly crossed the corridor to study some of the flyers on the bulletin board. Ally still felt uneasy around the man, even though he was shackled and handcuffed. She was thankful that she did not have to sit in the courtroom. She would only enter if she were called as a witness.

The hearing lasted for an hour; she was never called to the stand. Neal came out first to tell her that she was free to leave. Morrison had been bound over for trial. Ally knew she would be nervous and anxious until the trial was over, but she would just have to deal with it. She dreaded another encounter with Morrison, and the thought of testifying in his trial made her sick to her stomach. Somehow, she'd have to get through the trial.

CHAPTER 27

It was March 16th, a little more than a year since she and David had driven down that isolated road in Horseshoe Bend. The weather outside was unseasonably cold, as a blistering northern wind blew an icy chill through Ally's thick coat. The hard, crunchy snow clung stubbornly to the frozen ground. Ally hated to take Breanna out in this weather, for she had just recovered from an ear infection. Ally carefully plodded her course with the stroller. She did not want to slip and lose control of the stroller as she maneuvered through the maze of visible ice patches. At least the small set of stairs into the sheriff's office had been cleared and salted.

She wasn't scheduled to come in today, but Neal had told her that something very important had come up in the criminal case against Morrison. He didn't want to discuss the matter with her over the phone. So here she was, braving the cold and ice. It had better be good.

As she entered the interior office of the Sheriff's station, Karen and Maggie each offered to hold Breanna while she spoke to Neal. Breanna was always the center of attention during Ally's case conferences with Neal. Ally relented, and asked if Neal was in his office. He was. Ally left Breanna with the women as she headed in.

She knocked lightly and entered.

"Hi Ally have a seat."

"What's up, Neal?" Ally asked.

Neal looked uncomfortable, "Ally, I have a favor to ask of you. You are always free to say no, and I would understand if you did."

"Neal, what is it?"

"I believe Morrison knows we'll get a conviction, but he is more than willing to go to court and draw out a trial. A trial of this magnitude is mostly funded through the state, but still, it has a huge fiscal impact on this county. Also, the media attention has not served our community well," Neal said.

"Where do I come into this?" Ally inquired.

"Morrison may be willing to plea bargain if certain conditions are met."

"Like what?"

"The death penalty is taken off the table. Also, he wants the opportunity to speak to you alone. I don't know what the guy has up his sleeve. He probably just wants to rattle your cage some more."

"I don't believe it!" Ally gasped. "I don't want to see that sick bastard ever again, let alone be stuck in the same room with him."

"I don't blame you, Ally. I was just hoping you'd consider it, to bring this matter to a close."

Ally was silent for several minutes, "Is Morrison willing to tell us the identity of the final victim, and where her body is at?"

"His lawyer, James Carnes, said Morrison wasn't anxious to plea bargain. It didn't seem to matter to Morrison, which way this goes. Morrison told Carnes that he had plenty of time to wait, and he could make his case last for years with costly delays, appeals, and motions. Morrison knew exactly how to do it and was prepared to hold out for the duration. Carnes said, if we chose not to take his 'generous offer,' things could get really ugly."

"I'll do it," Ally resolved. "I don't want to live for the next ten years with Morrison looming in the shadows of my life. I'm not willing to let him have that control; I need to bring this to a close."

"I'll make the arrangements, and I'll go with you for support."

Ally had arranged for Larry to look after Breanna for the day. It was Thursday, March 19th, and the skies were now clouded over. It looked as if they were going to get some rain or possibly snow again. Ally was quiet on the brief ride to the county jail. She did not want Neal to know just how anxious and stressed she was.

399

Ally wondered what was wrong with her. It wasn't really fear that had her so worked up. The guy was locked up, for Pete's sake! Then exactly what was it? Suddenly she knew! Ally felt full of hate, seething in anger, disgust, and fear; she was callous and mean-spirited, whenever she encountered Morrison. Just hearing Eric's name, made her cringe and set off an upheaval. It was her reaction that scared her; the negative energy was palpable and seemed the personification of pure evil within her. Consequently, it drew her closer to Eric's world. It made Ally think of that quote by Friedrich Nietzsche, - 'He who fights with monsters might take care lest he thereby becomes a monster. And if you gaze for long into an abyss, the abyss gazes also into you.' Ally gave herself a mental shake to escape her dark thoughts.

This unproductive pessimism would just siphon off her energy reserves, leaving her empty. She had to use this horrific experience for good, as a motivation to make positive changes, but the problems are too ingrained, in-depth. "What can I possibly do?"

Think outside the box! One person or even a few individuals could never really change the entire system or society at large. Yet if you could convince thousands of people to make a few small changes that could make all the difference in the world. Convince enough people to commit to taking on a few small undertakings, you could make significant inroads into solving child welfare concerns or any other social problem within society. Ally needed to advance this idea. But how?

Neal and Ally arrived at the jail; it was about a half- block away from the morgue through the maze of county buildings. The jail was an old, yellow, cinderblock building surrounded by high fencing topped with three lines of barbwire.

"Are you ready, Ally? It will be okay. You'll be separated from Morrison by a heavy glass partition."

"I know Neal, I'll be fine. Just not looking forward to the trip."

"Leave all your belongings in the trunk of the car. Just bring in your driver's license," Neal advised her. He went to the trunk and placed his service revolver, handcuffs, and wallet in the trunk; he kept his badge, identification, and keys. Ally felt a few cold drops of rain brush her face as she took her driver's license out of her wallet, and slipped it into the pocket of her jacket. She then returned her wallet to her purse, which she nestled in the corner of the trunk. Neal shut the trunk firmly.

"As you know, we have a couple of holding cells at the station, but they are just for very short-term incarcerations. This jail here has some tight security for a county jail; the juvenile hall almost has the same setup. The county really stepped up security after they had a few problems about five years ago," Neal informed her.

Ally followed Neal's lead. The dark entrance to the jail stood isolated beyond a series of secured gates. Neal identified himself and Ally through the intercom speaker. The correctional officer on the other end pressed a button to open the fence. Neal and Ally were met by another correctional officer at the second gate, which was opened by key. They followed the officer into a security office, and another officer behind a glass partition asked them to sign the visitors' log. They were asked to place all the contents of their pockets into a small bin, and after doing so, to place the bin in the one of the lockers behind them. Ally complied with the request; the officer told her to walk through the metal detector. She was to proceed through the door on her right, go down the corridor, and into the last door on her left.

"I can go into the interview room with you, Ally," Neal started to say.

"Neal, you know that wasn't the deal." Ally's sharp rebuttal was in stark contrast to her personal wishes.

"I'll be here when you get out."

Ally walked over to the heavy metal door. She heard a click and pulled it open. The door shut heavily behind her, locking her into this corridor of white cinderblock. Ally could see portal entries to four rooms, each secured by heavy metal doors. Each door had a small, thick glass window equipped with an internal, reinforced wire-grid. Ally felt her heart pound and a chill shoot through her body. She struggled with the sense of claustrophobia that descended upon her. At the last portal, she glared at the

401

heavy metal door and heard the click. She hesitated again at the door, wanting to leave, but instead entered the small enclave.

The room behind the partition was empty. Beyond the second enclave was another heavy metal door with the same wire-grid window. Ally looked around the tiny, enclosed room. There was a heavy glass panel above a metal base, and there was a steel disk that ascended from an attached metal arm to form a sitting stool. The term, 'stool-pigeon,' flashed into Ally's mind. As she eyed this set-up, she made a mental note to remain standing. An old-fashioned black telephone receiver, equipped with a long silver cord, hung from the base on the right upon the chrome-mesh wall. She approached the window and saw her vague reflection in the glass. This environment was unsettling; she wanted to get out of this place as soon as possible.

Ally saw a correctional officer through the small gridded window on the other side of the partition. Eric Morrison was deposited into the visitation room, and the door locked behind him.

Morrison was dressed in an orange jumpsuit; he was not shaved and had several days' of stubble growth on his face. His hair looked uncombed and dirty; he bore little resemblance to the polished man she had met a few months before. He actually looked younger: his eyes were wide, brown, and guileless. How could someone be so evil and yet look so naive and ingenuous? It was ironic. She could see a jury believing him innocent, despite all the mounting evidence against him. A good reason for making a plea-bargain deal.

Morrison looked at Ally blankly for a few seconds as though he had been expecting someone else. Who had he been expecting? Then, recognition dawned in Eric's eyes, and he gave Ally an ice cold stare. He straddled the stool and lazily, picked up the phone. He cocked his head and gave her a malicious smirk.

Ally moved her hand slow but steadily towards the phone, determined not to let her uneasiness show. She remained standing, deliberately ignoring the stool in front of her. She brought the receiver to her ear, subconsciously crossing her arms across her chest.

"So you've come hunting for missing bodies, have you? Or are you just dying to see me?"

"How could you?" Ally demanded through clenched teeth; quickly losing her temper as her emotions took over. "You snake! What kind of monster are you?"

"You self-righteous bitch," he said with a sneer. "You and your kind didn't give a fuck about those children before I disposed of them. They lived their pathetic, depraved little lives without any outside attention. You didn't even notice they were missing until you tripped over the fucking bodies. Then you start your boo-hoo revelry." He mimicked sardonically.

Morrison's taunts hit her like repeated physical blows, robbing her of breath.

"You're a real bastard!" Ally said venomously."

"Just another by-product of my environment, Madam." He said sarcastically. "Where were all the concerned, child-loving advocates when I was warehoused in that child factory you folks, call a group home? When I was being raised by a so called child-loving society? When I was getting raped and humiliated by fellow inmates in the group home, after being raped and abandoned by my own mother? Did any of those so called concerned professionals give more than a cursory glance to see if I was breathing? I got second hand shoes and clothes, minimal heat, and just enough food to keep the group home in operation while the owners -drove away in their Porches. Good ol' Roy Sommers and his like never came out to see what the tax dollars were used for, let alone to authorize any additional money or oversight to assist. You call me a monster? Well Babe," he kissed the air, "Look in the mirror; you and all the other fuckin hypocrites, out there."

God, she hated him! The pungent grip of blinding rage seized her; ripping away any mental self-command, leaving only visceral reactions in its wake. Eric had spoken in the same, even, sardonic tone throughout, not raising his voice in the heat of his discourse. The anger, pain and resentment were fully ingrained into his persona. Or, she thought cynically, was it possible that he was 'reading' her and manipulating her conflicting emotions? He

403

wanted to incite her, get under her skin, and mess with her mind! He couldn't physically torture her so he would maim her with a psychological ambush.

"Oh you poor, poor baby," Ally snapped. "The world treated you so bad that you were compelled to kill and torture children and their families. What did they ever do to you?"

"What did you and your lot ever do for them? Until I crushed these abysmal roaches, you -Fuck-ups couldn't have cared less! Now, you're hysterically crying about the 'poor, darling children,' from your high and mighty pulpits. How touching," Eric mocked.

Ally ignored his invective, as she jammed her pointed finger in his direction. "You're going down for this! Hard, you hear! Your sob story isn't going to exonerate you!"

"Tut, tut. Oh dear, she still doesn't get it," Eric sneered. "You're so fucking stupid, I'll draw you a map, Honey. I will not get off because I don't choose to. Mama dearest and my dear old step-dad, the Lieutenant Governor, are going to be sweating bullets by the time I'm through. It's going to be impossible for them to bury their dirty little secrets this time because I'm going to be singing my heart out. You know the adoring public can't get enough of this stuff. I will be telling my sad, pathetic story with all the sordid details to any talk-show out there. Telling all the sheep out there how I couldn't control my actions, and how truly grateful I was, to finally get caught." Eric stretched out with his fingers interlaced behind his head, smirking as he first saw the incredulity, and then the hostility etched on her face. Seeing red, Ally would wipe that smirk from his face; if only, she could get her hands on him. She wanted to kill the son-of-a bitch!

"It's all about you," Ally retorted contemptuously, her stiffened muscles jerked uncontrollably, breaking her self-imposed, physical constraints as she shouted at him. "You haven't even given those children a second thought since you murdered them. It's all about your hatreds and settling the score with your family."

"Oh, but you're wrong again. In terms of your first statement, I've relived those blissful moments with those children, 'my discards,' over and over in my mind. You know; it eases my tension. Do you want me to supply each and every, gory and vivid detail? I've got an excellent memory, and an eye for the specifics. How long have you got?"

Eric laughed wickedly at the repulsion he saw in her face.

"No? C'mon I'll tell you everything, you want to know. Have you seen my portfolio? The photos were quite explicit; don't you think? Did you enjoy looking at them too, like I did?" Eric cooed, sardonically leering at Ally.

Eric continued to toy with her, gauging and calculating her reactions to his words. Ally's unconstrained fury had plunged rapidly to ghastly illness as she unwillingly visualized the brutalized girls. The despicable, mental collage remained stuck as a frozen frame in her mind, which she was unable to purge. She was sick to her stomach.

Eric fixed a baleful glare in her direction, silently daring her to speak. "What, you have nothing left say? Too bad! It was sure to be amusing. "Oh, in regards to my family, whoever said this line, said it best, 'revenge is a dish best-served cold.' My only regret was that I didn't reach the end-goal with the spawn of Caitlyn. But, it was an amazing plan; do you want me to elaborate. I can tell you all about it, fill in all the details; if you like."

"Are you finished with your pity-fest? I've got better things to do!" Ally said hoarsely; still trying to expel the vile, mental image which Eric had intentionally and spitefully invoked.

"Oh, like taking care of that baby of yours?" Eric deliberately paused, allowing the question to reverberate. "You'd better run home. You never know who may be waiting around the corner now, or even at some future date. By the way, you heard that they are removing the death penalty? I like to keep my options open. I have big plans; you know." Eric emphasized, and then resumed in a low menacing tone. "Honestly, you actually don't know what pain is, but you will. Hope you have sweet dreams tonight, Bitch. I know I will; I'll be thinking of your daughter."

Ally tried to return the receiver to the base, but missing it. The phone swung wide. She grabbed at the phone while trying, but failing, to hide her fearful reaction to his words. Morrison smirked at her as she stood in front of the metal door (which led to the corridor) pounding on it with her fist, only to find that it was not locked. Ally felt foolish, as she quaked with fear. She ran down the cinderblock corridor, trying to regain her composure before encountering Neal. She grabbed the prisoner log, anxiously signing out, to escape.

Neal stood as she approached, "As bad as all that?"

"You were right. He wanted to gloat and rattle my chains some more. He succeeded. I'm sure I'll have nightmares about this." Ally's voice quavered hysterically.

"Are you going to be okay?" Neal asked in a concerned manner.

"I'll be okay. At least, I will not have to see him on a daily basis as I would if he were going to trial. It's finally over."

"Ally, I want to thank you for your help. We wouldn't even be close to this juncture if it weren't for your involvement. Hell, we probably would not have discovered the murders. It still blows my mind that he got away with it for so long without anyone in law enforcement discovering a pattern."

"Without a body, there is no murder investigation, right?"

"I hate to admit it, but in almost all cases that is true," Neal replied reluctantly. "After the initial attempts to locate a person, it becomes a missing person case, and it doesn't get much attention."

"I hate to think what has become of all the children reported missing each year. Their families never finding out what happened or why."

"Well, I'll take you back now," Neal said, opening the door for her.

Ally and Neal walked back to the car in silence. There was no rain or snow fall evident now, but the overcast lingered on. Neal unlocked her door and headed for the driver's side of the car. Once they were seated, Ally said despondently, "Neal, I let him get to me. Let him control me. I didn't find out a damn thing about the fifth victim."

"Ally, Morrison was using the identity of the fifth child as bait to reel you in. He never planned to give you that information. He will hold on to that information and eventually use it as leverage or as a bargaining chip to secure something he wants." Yes. Ally realized that Eric had baited her, ensuring this final show-down. He had taken control of her every thought and reaction as easily as if she were a puppet. He knew how to poke and prod at her vulnerabilities and make it hurt deep. She ended up running for cover, despite the fact that he was the one behind bars. Ally was now humiliated that she'd easily allowed Eric to manipulate her so effectively. Her emotions had overwhelmed any rational logic and, as a result, she had lost sight of her goal. She never even attempted to get any information about the remaining victim.

"Do you have any idea who that child may be?"Ally asked miserably.

"I wish I could tell you yes. We have located all the children served through the Child Abuse Prevention Counsel. The list of missing children has been scrutinized. The only other missing child in this area, fitting the profile was returned to her father's care. The mother had lost custody and took off with the child; later she was arrested. There is a chance that the child was never reported missing. Morrison either never made a mosaic of this child or we haven't found it. He also, never made a mosaic of Shilo, but I believe her death was an impulsive act. I'm afraid that until we locate a body and can analyze the remains, we're at a dead end. Any remains may have been carted off by animals over time," Neal concluded.

"Neal, while I was at the jail, I scared myself because my hatred and anger were out of control. Given access, I literally could have killed Eric. He sitting there all smug and mocking us, while that child is still out there." Ally started off strong but choked up in the end. Neal gave her a strange look and was slow to reply.

"Ally, Morrison is a man who had a lot going for him. He was good-looking, smart, and he had a good career. Yet he let anger, hatred, and resentment consumed him. It made him into a despicable creature. Don't let your anger get the best of you.

Ally was again reminded of her thoughts on the ride over here. Be careful not to become a monster yourself! If she got caught up in the cynicism, Morrison would win by default, becoming a nefarious influence, tainting her perception. Redirect the energy. Sometimes her intensity was her blessing and her curse. As her mom would say, you don't need to eliminate your intensity; you need to manage it wisely.

Eric Morrison was just one vicious man. How many people will Morrison destroy directly? All those little girls; Lizzie and Caitlyn. Or indirectly damage like Crystal, Lily and Ms. Grimes. Throughout the course of his life, he will have destroyed so many. Individuals, like Morrison, do not concern themselves with the pain and destruction they inflict on others. They externalized their pain, and victimized others more vulnerable than themselves. They utilized their past tribulations as an instrument of warfare, creating the same patterns of havoc over and over again. Each of their corresponding victims was at significant risk of becoming a future aggressor. There had to be a way to break the compounding nature of these destructive patterns if enough concentrated effort was put forth.

Ally's thoughts again centered on 'concentrated effort'; the power of many. If one could increase social awareness of these issues, and engage others to get involved in various ways, such as mentoring programs, assisting a family in their community, or simply researching related legislation. How many catastrophes could be averted in the long run? How could you engage other people in becoming involved or making a commitment? You needed to convince enough people that they needed to become part of the solution in order to strengthen our communities and our society as a whole.

"Ally, I'm not trying to criticize you" Neal misinterpreting her silence, interrupted her thoughts. "I'm just worried about you. I want you to drop it. Quit obsessing about Morrison and the remaining victim, or you are going to make yourself sick."

"Okay, you're right," Ally replied resignedly. She had to accept the fact that Morrison's final victim might never be found or identified. In accepting this fact, she knew she had to accept defeat that perhaps this child was lost forever. Yet Ally's mind was still focused on the fifth victim. Why hadn't Eric completed a mosaic for this victim? It didn't make sense. She could understand reasons why Morrison hadn't taken pictures of Shilo. Wait..... No, it can't be! The fifth victim couldn't be... No! She wasn't going to go there. She needed to leave this matter alone!

"Yes. You're right, Neal, there is nothing I can do at this point except move on." Ally said tensely, in fierce determination.

EPILOGUE

Ally was pulling Breanna away from the television knobs, when she heard the phone ring. Breanna was firmly in the 'terrible twos' stage, and into everything. Picking her toddler up in her arms, Ally answered the phone in the kitchen.

"Hello, could you hold for a minute?" Ally pulled out some Tupperware bowls and cookie cutters from the cupboard, and set them on the floor in front of Breanna.

"Hello?" Ally said, as she picked up the phone again.

"Is this Mrs. Sullivan? Alyssa Sullivan?" Said the hesitant voice on the other end.

"Yes, how can I help you?"

"Mrs. Sullivan you may not remember me but my name is Crystal Jamison."

"Oh yes, you are Bree's mother. Please, call me Ally. How are you doing?"

"I'm doing really good now," Crystal responded.

"That's wonderful to hear."

"The day that we talked, I went into a six-month rehab. I've been clean ever since. I met Tom, my husband while I was in detox. Tom and his ex were arrested on drug charges. He was court-ordered into rehab rather than prison. While he was there, his wife booked, and they divorced. But he was as serious about his recovery, as I was. He wanted to get clean, and get his kids back. His brother and sister-in-law were caring for the three of them. He has two boys and a girl, just great kids. We got married last year, and now we got the kids living with us."

"Oh, that is great, just great to hear. It's good to hear from you."

"Ally, I just wanted to thank you for all you did.' Ally could hear the emotion in her voice. "When Bree's killer was caught, I just couldn't come around for the first hearing. You know the preliminary hearing, if that's what they call it? I was into and working my 12-steps; I was scared that the pressure would start me using again. Maybe it was wrong, but I was glad he plea-bargained when he did. I couldn't deal with it, just then. I was such a coward. I hope I didn't let Bree down?"

"Oh no, you must not think that. You did what Bree wanted you to do; your recovery is what Bree wanted the most. I want you to know that Bree had already continued on her journey, and she was at peace even before the arrest." Ally picked up Breanna, who was headed rapidly in the direction of the dog's food bowl.

"Thanks again, I needed to know that. Hey, guess what? I'm pregnant again. I'm six months along, and my stomach is the size of a watermelon. Just had an ultra-sound, it's going to be another girl. I wanted to ask if I could name the baby after you, Alyssa?" Breanna was squirming wildly in her arms.

"It would be an honor."

"Thank you, well, I'd better get going now; I'm going to pick up the kids from school. Still paranoid about letting them walk alone. I don't know if I'll ever get past that. Bye."

"Thanks for the good news," Ally said and hung up.

Ally held Breanna tighter, tenderly kissing the top of her head. Ally blew lightly at her daughter's hair, ruffling the bangs. Ally stepped out into the sunshine of early April. It had been a little more than three years, since Ally first saw Bree; since then her life and perspective had changed dramatically.

During the first year after Morrison's incarceration, Ally had researched and interviewed many psychics to find out more about paranormal phenomenon. She quickly discovered that some of these 'so-called' psychics were phonies. Other psychics were genuine and extremely insightful. However, none of these psychics had ever come close to her extensive psychic experience with Bree; it had been extraordinary. The only theory Ally had, as to why she had such an expansive psychic interval with Bree, was that she was in the right place at the right time. Her world had overlapped with Bree's world to create a merging of their personal histories, and thus, a very special and unique period of time.

Ally still talked to Neal regularly. Neal and his wife, Ruth, occasionally went out to dinner with her and David. About five months after Eric Morrison had accepted a plea bargain agreement, a fellow inmate in prison had severely injured him. She had never asked Neal for details regarding his injuries or how much he had recovered. She did not want to know; it was over.

Ally worked part-time for the Family Preservation Coalition. She provided mentoring and intensive intervention to struggling families. She was currently working with a teenage mother; Taylor and had helped her get back into high school. Taylor was scheduled to graduate next month. Ally was hopeful that Taylor would complete the enrollment process for the community college.

Ally was also was very active in following child welfare legislation. She tracked the voting records of all the local politicians in regards to child welfare. She researched child welfare bills and wrote letters to the lawmakers regarding these proposed bills. Her latest project; writing a grant to fund a parent resource center in their county. She expected to hear whether or not this grant was awarded to the county this coming week.

In the course of her work, Ally had called Caitlyn Mathews for her opinion on legislation regarding children and medical services. Caitlyn and her family were doing well. Caitlyn said that Lizzie wasn't showing any long-term ill effects from her trauma. Initially, Lizzie was clinging, but this behavior dissipated after a month or two. Lizzie seemed to have forgotten about the kidnapping.

Breanna was squirming again as she said, "Look. Pretty." She was looking at a dandelion in the grass. Ally set her down on the lawn, and she raced towards the dandelion to investigate. She briefly felt the fleeting presence of Bree, and had an impression of her saying "Thank you. You were right. It is a very happy place here. ...Your friend -Jennie says she loves and misses you, as much as ever, 'and beyond.' Then, this presence was gone. Just a whisper in the breeze.

ABOUT THE AUTHOR

This is Casey Jo Jukes' first novel. She has an extensive work history as a social worker and counselor in various social welfare programs. She currently lives in Northern California with her husband and two children.

www.ingramcontent.com/pod-product-compliance
Lightning Source LLC
Chambersburg PA
CBHW071642260626
47170CB00001B/197